W9-BYW-496

BELOW THE SURFACE

Other books by Tim Shoemaker

Code of Silence

Back Before Dark

Reboot Your Brain: Byte-Sized Devotions for Boys

Connect with Tim Shoemaker:

www.Facebook.com/AuthorTimShoemaker
@TimShoemaker1

A Code of Silence Novel

BELOW THE SURFACE

Tim Shoemaker

ZONDERKIDZ

Below the Surface

This title is also available as a Zondervan ebook. Visit www.zondervan.com/ebooks

Requests for information should be addressed to:

Zonderkidz, *3900 Sparks Dr., Grand Rapids, Michigan 49546*

ISBN 978-0-310-73501-4

Published in association with the literary agency of Hartline Literary Agency, 123 Queenston Drive, Pittsburg, PA 15235. www.hartlineliteracy.com

Cover design: Sammy Yuen
Interior design: Ben Fetterley
Illustrations: David Conn

Printed in the United States of America

14 15 16 17 18 19 20 21 22 23 24 25 26 27 28 / DCI / 14 13 12 11 10 9 8 7 6 5 4 3 2 1

DEDICATION

To Dad: Thanks for thousands of hours at the lake—a place of fun and adventure that inspires my writing today. And for putting up with the trouble and pranks along the way! Lots of people claim to have the "best dad in the world" ... but you are the best dad in the world for *me*.

To Mom: Without you, none of the above would have happened. Thanks for not pulling in the reins too tight! I love you both very much!

And to my grandkids: Our adventures at Lake Geneva are just beginning!

Special Thanks

To Frank Ball—for tightening, oiling, and tuning *Below the Surface*. What a mechanic!

Nancy Rue—for sound advice and solid support.

Dr. Dale McElhinney—for expertise and input on reactions to fear.

Kim Childress—for expert editing and trusting my judgment.

Cheryl—for encouraging and supporting my writing from the beginning.

GENEVA LAKE

N
W
E
S

Williams Bay

Lake Geneva

Maytag Point

Big Foot Beach

X

Big Foot Beach State Park

The Geneva Inn

Fontana

Black Point

Mooring Spot for "The Getaway"

2 Miles

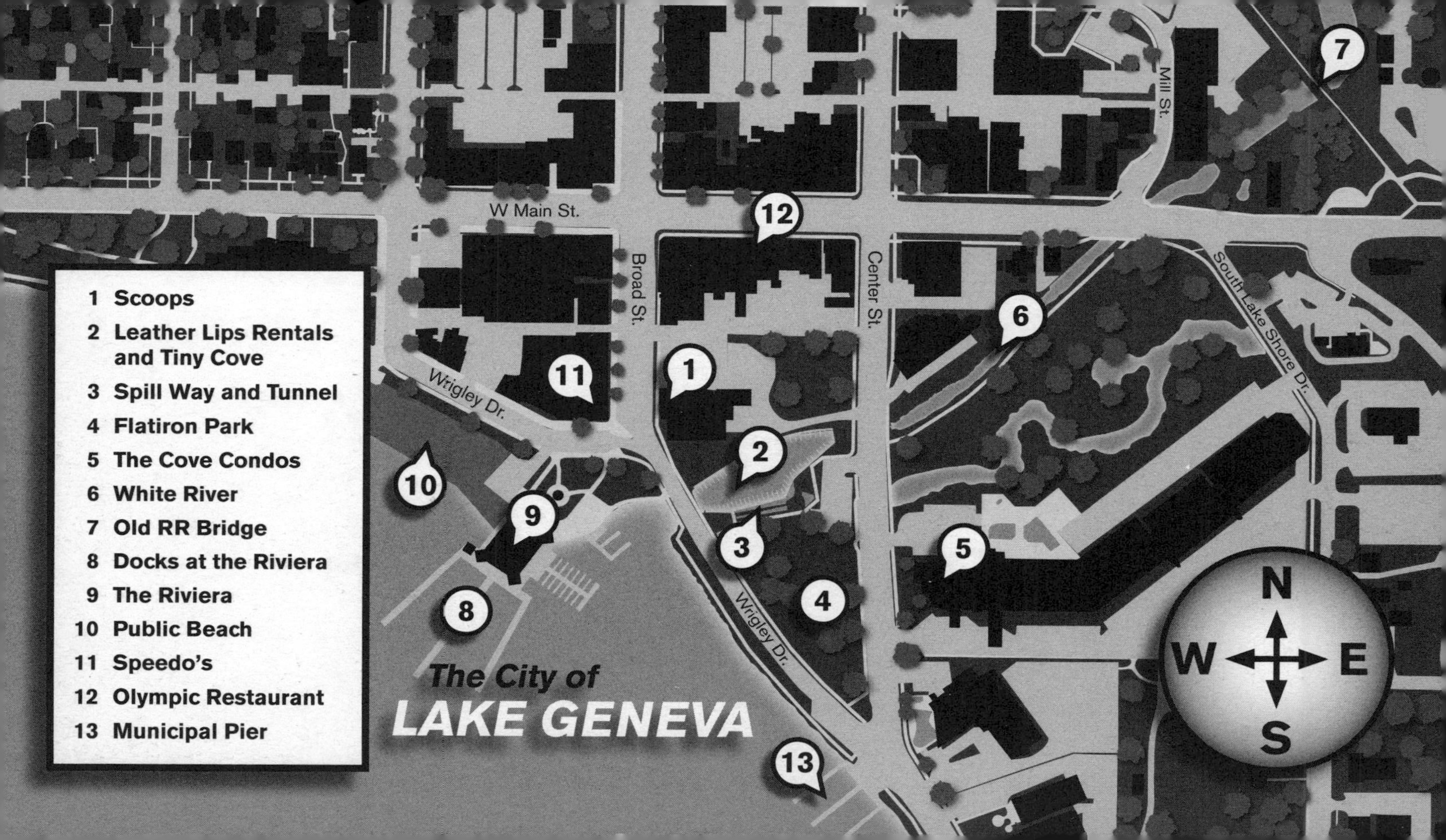
The City of
LAKE GENEVA
1 Scoops
2 Leather Lips Rentals and Tiny Cove
3 Spill Way and Tunnel
4 Flatiron Park
5 The Cove Condos
6 White River
7 Old RR Bridge
8 Docks at the Riviera
9 The Riviera
10 Public Beach
11 Speedo's
12 Olympic Restaurant
13 Municipal Pier
W Main St.
Broad St.
Center St.
Mill St.
South Lake Shore Dr.
Wrigley Dr.
Wrigley Dr.
N
S
E
W

"Fear — like fire — has the power to protect . . . or destroy."

"Courage is not about being fearless, but about doing the right thing . . . even when you're scared."

CHAPTER 1

Vacations were all about having fun—or running from something not so fun. Cooper needed this vacation to be about both. The fact that he was starting high school in a matter of days wasn't what gnawed at him. Not really. It was something way deeper. Buried. And he intended to keep it there.

The more he packed his days with fun, the more effective his escape would be. And thanks to *The Getaway*—rather, thanks to Dad's uncle, who gave them the old cabin cruiser—that's exactly what he planned to do. He stood on the teak deck and looked out over Lake Geneva, or rather Geneva Lake, as it was officially named.

"Hey, Coop." It was his cousin Gordy's voice.

Gordy bobbed in the two-man inflatable raft by the back of the boat, his white-blond hair blowing back from his forehead. He grinned and pointed at the bucket of dead fish propped between his knees. "We doing this or not?"

Cooper eyeballed the target of their prank—the Malibu wakeboard boat tied to a buoy about halfway between them and the beach. "Absolutely."

Hiro gave him a questioning look, as if she wasn't sure this was a good idea. Predictable.

Cooper smiled and hustled to the stern of the boat. He peeled off his T-shirt, swung over the transom rail, and dropped onto the attached swim platform below. The buoy his dad had rented was among a dozen others anchoring pontoon, sail, and speedboats in a corner pocket of Lake Geneva bordering Big Foot Beach State Park. Like the heel of a giant sock, the lakeshore curved in two directions away from where the boats were anchored.

The south shoreline ran nearly straight west from this elbow of the lake. And in the other direction, the beach jutted north along Lake Shore Drive and the park. Eventually this shoreline wound around Maytag Point and on toward town.

The swim to either the beach or to the south shore looked to be about a hundred yards, give or take ten strokes. *The Getaway* was tied to the farthest buoy from either shore, which meant nothing but water between them and the horizon. The spot — and the lake — was absolutely perfect.

"Lunk's gonna wish we'd waited for him," Gordy said. "But we'd be crazy to miss this chance."

"You're both crazy to *take* this chance," Hiro said.

Whether Hiro was worried that something would go wrong or that her dream of being a cop someday conflicted with pulling a prank like this, Cooper couldn't be sure. And he wasn't about to ask.

Cooper glanced at the Malibu wakeboard boat again. The extreme green fiberglass hull with yellow accents practically glowed in the setting sun. Only a navy blue sailboat sat buoyed between them and their target.

Hiro rested her forearms on the rail above him. "Let's go for a walk on the beach instead. You guys can skip stones or something." She smiled and nodded.

Gordy laughed. "Nice try."

Hiro's black braid hung over one shoulder as if it were pointing at them. Accusing. "This is a bad idea, guys."

She was probably right. The Malibu was empty, but not for long. If they were going to do this, now was the time.

"We're on vacation, remember?" Hiro said. "No trouble. No worries. Just fun."

Cooper nodded. "That's exactly what we're doing. Having fun."

Hiro raised her eyebrows. "Is that what you call it?"

Gordy grinned. "Your problem is that you don't know *how* to have fun."

"I can think of a lot more enjoyable things to be doing than planting stinky fish in some innocent stranger's boat." She smiled and shook her head. "What is it with guys?"

She used the word *enjoyable* like that was the goal all along. Which only proved she didn't understand guys at all. This was about taking chances. Risks. And living to laugh about it later. "It gets the adrenaline pumping," Cooper said. It wasn't much of an answer, but it was the best he could do. She wasn't going to get it anyway.

"That's it? That's your explanation?" Hiro looked incredulous. "Five minutes ago a guy built like Superman tied that boat to the buoy and rowed his trophy date to shore."

"He doesn't look anything like the real Superman," Gordy said.

Hiro tilted her head to one side. "The *real* Superman? And here I thought he was a fictional character."

Gordy looked at her like she was weird. "You've never watched the old black-and-white TV show? It's like from back in the fifties or something."

"You might find this hard to believe," Hiro said, "but I find better things to do than watch old TV shows or pull pranks."

"You're right." Gordy didn't even look up. "That *is* hard to believe."

His jab didn't even faze her. "Did you notice the guy and his date — what was really going on there?"

"Yeah," Gordy said. "They crossed the street and went into the pizza place. Blah, blah, blah. We all saw that. What's the problem?"

Hiro sighed that way she did when she was about to make a point. *Here it comes.*

Cooper smiled and climbed into the inflatable.

"When guys are around girls, they like to show off," Hiro said slowly. "Impress them. Prove how tough they are."

Okay. Maybe Hiro understood guys better than Cooper thought.

"And while Superman is chowing down on pizza and romancing his babe, we're going to leave a little surprise in his boat." Gordy grinned. "We'll see how impressed his date is then."

"Exactly." Hiro looked up at the darkening sky like she was hoping for a little help. "You aren't seeing the red flag here?"

Ah. The red-flag approach. One of Hiro's favorites.

Cooper shrugged. "Looks like a green flag to me."

Gordy laughed. "Or a checkered one." He shielded his eyes with one hand and scanned the beach. "I'm not seeing a red one anywhere."

Cooper loved Hiro's exasperated expression. Yeah, this vacation was going to be exactly what he needed.

Hiro sighed. "I hate to sound like the mom here, but you two are running with scissors. You know that, right?"

Gordy shook his head like he was trying to make sense out of what Hiro had just said. "What?"

"You're living dangerously. Run with scissors and eventually you'll get cut."

Gordy waved her off. "It's a harmless prank."

"Hmmm." Hiro didn't look convinced. Or impressed. "We'll see how harmless it is once Superman comes out and catches you two messing with his boat."

Hiro was always seeing the danger in things. Trouble was, Cooper knew she was usually right.

"He's not going to catch us," Gordy said, "unless you keep delaying us. C'mon, Coop."

Gordy scooted to make room in the inflatable. "Sure you won't join us, Hiro?"

"You two have your *fun*," she said. "I'll watch from here. Excuse me if I don't see the point in all this."

"Point?" Gordy looked confused. "We're not trying to make a point. There *is* no point to it."

Hiro smirked. "So it's pointless. Thanks for clearing that up for me."

Gordy reached into the bucket, grabbed a bloated sunfish by the tailfin, and tossed it at Hiro. She ducked and screamed. The dead fish nearly hit her in the face, then slapped the water on the other side of the boat.

Cooper and Gordy laughed.

Hiro glared at them, but the smile was still there. Sometimes she worried about them more than she needed to. Cooper understood that.

"We'll be right back." Cooper pushed off from the swim platform and paddled with his arms toward the speedboat. How long had the couple been inside the pizza place? If they were dining in, there was still plenty of time. But if it turned out to be a carryout order—he'd be wishing they'd listened to Hiro.

He paddled harder. Getting caught doing a prank took all the fun out of it—the mark of an amateur. Not to mention the fact that he *really* didn't want Hiro to have the satisfaction of being right.

They paddled past the sailboat. Probably a twenty-eight-footer. Small cabin for sleeping. *Ra Ra Avis* was painted on the stern. Now the Malibu was in plain view.

Gordy scooped with both hands. "Surgical strike or buckshot?"

Cooper eyed the boat. Buckshot was the quickest—which made it safer. Just get within throwing range and lob the fish into the boat. There'd be no control over where the fish landed—and the boaters would spot them immediately when they got back.

Where was the fun in that?

But a surgical strike meant pulling up alongside the boat and at least one of them going inside to strategically hide the fish. He looked back at the restaurant. No sign of the boaters. "Surgical."

"Agreed." Gordy grinned.

A light breeze out of the northwest kept the green wakeboard boat in a perfect position to block the view of anyone watching from shore. Hiro, on the other hand, would have a perfect view—if she decided to watch.

They quickly closed the distance between them and the Malibu. Cooper grabbed the corner of the swim platform and pulled the inflatable close.

Gordy nodded in the direction of the name painted on the transom. "What's that all about?"

"*Krypto Night.*" Cooper read the name aloud. Immediately he thought of Hiro's nickname for the driver: Superman. The boat's name was obviously a play off the fictional kryptonite that drained Superman of his strength. Was the boat's owner being clever? "Maybe he thinks he's Superman, and this boat is his one weakness." It made sense, in a way. The boat *was* kryptonite green. And what guy wouldn't love a sweet boat like this?

"Well, I hope Superman has a strong stomach." Gordy tapped the bucket. "Some of these fish are getting really ripe."

The boat looked brand-new, and the dead fish weren't going to make Superman happy. Cooper hesitated. Did he really want to do this? He pushed the thought out of his head. He was on vacation. "One of us needs to stay with the inflatable."

"I'm on it," Gordy said. "You can have the honor of planting the fish."

Cooper glanced toward the pizza place. There was still no sign of the boat's owner.

"Okay." Cooper crawled onto the swim platform. "Here we go." He climbed over the motor hatch and crouched on the deck. Staying low, he made his way to the side of the boat. "Ready when you are."

Gordy poured out most of the water, then handed the bucket up to him. "Have fun."

With the water gone, the fish reeked. He lifted a white seat cushion and hesitated. The guy might never get the smell out of the boat. The boat was too nice—or maybe Cooper was. Besides, if he dropped a fish into the storage compartment underneath, the guy would smell it immediately. Figuring out who did it would be easy.

An ice chest sat on the floor just behind the driver's seat. Cooper lifted the lid. *Jackpot.* Ice and drinks. He scooped three dead fish into the cooler. When somebody reached inside for a cold drink, they'd get a real surprise. Cooper stared at the bottles and suddenly knew that Superman wasn't planning to eat in the restaurant. He was going to bring the pizza to the boat. *Time to move.*

An air horn blasted nearby—from *The Getaway*, to be exact. Cooper raised his head just enough to see over the side of the boat. Hiro was motioning wildly as if she were waving a flag—and it definitely wasn't a green one.

"Coop," Gordy said, "Superman just left the pizza place. Let's fly."

The guy and his date walked lazily across Lake Shore Drive. Pizza box. Carryout. *Terrific.*

The thing about pranking was keeping your head if something didn't go according to plan. And this was one of those times.

"You coming?"

Cooper kept his eyes on Superman. "He'll see me crawling over the side. Start paddling. I'll catch up."

Once Gordy started paddling, *Krypto Night* would block any chance of the inflatable being spotted from the beach.

Gordy looked up at Cooper one more time as if to be sure, then laid back and paddled for *Ra Ra Avis*. The sailboat was half the distance to *The Getaway*, and all Gordy had to do was get the inflatable behind it. Cooper turned his attention back to the beach.

Superman hauled a small rowboat off the sand. His date was

already inside, holding the pizza box on her lap. Superman boarded, took a seat with his back to Cooper, and pulled on the oars.

Go. Cooper tossed the bucket over the side. The thing would sink, and they could find it later. Right now it would only slow him down. Staying on all fours, he crawled to the open bow seating area. He glanced toward shore. The guy's back was still to him. Hopefully the girl wouldn't spot him. But if he stayed in the boat much longer, they both would. Cooper slid over the side and into the water without a splash. His head never dipped below the surface.

Gordy had a huge lead, his long arms reaching and pulling. He skimmed around the nose of the sailboat and disappeared from view almost completely.

Now all Cooper had to do was join him without being spotted.

Cooper struck out for the sailboat with strong, fast strokes. *Krypto Night* wouldn't screen his escape for long. He knifed through the water, turning his head to the side to gulp fresh air on every third stroke.

His mental clock was spinning. He didn't dare look back. Superman would be pulling up to *Krypto Night* any second. They'd see him for sure.

Fifteen yards. So close, yet so far.

Ten yards. He'd have to go under. It would be slower, but it was the only way to reach the other side of the sailboat without being seen.

Cooper took a deep breath, jackknifed, and dove. Instantly his heart pounded in panic. Something was down here. Waiting for him. He opened his eyes to a blur of dark greens and black—and let out a gurgling scream. He was going to die. He sucked in a mouthful of water, triggering a violent spasm of coughing and choking and gulping for air. More water went down his windpipe. Was he dying? Surrounded by suffocating blackness, he kicked and spun and clawed his way toward daylight.

After breaking the surface, Cooper thrashed at the water,

choking, gasping, and choking some more. *Get out of here! Get out of here!* Everything was a blur. Grabbing something, he frantically pulled himself up on it.

"What are you *doing*?" The voice sounded far away. "Coop, you're going to sink us."

Everything was still spinning. Cooper grabbed and held on.

"Let go of me, Coop. What's wrong with you?" It was Gordy's voice. Closer now. "Coop! You're safe. Easy now. Easy."

Cooper didn't let go, but his coughing eased up and his vision started to clear. He was inside the inflatable—curled up on the bottom like a half-drowned puppy and clutching Gordy's ankle. How did he get here?

"Tell me this is all an act," Gordy said.

Cooper tried to steady his breathing. His whole body was shaking, and his heart was still doing the mambo.

"Okay. I get it," Gordy whispered. "What did you see down there?"

What did he see? Blackness. But that didn't mean there was nothing there. Whatever it was, it was something that reached right through his skin and wouldn't let go. The invisible hand of death. Cooper let go of Gordy's ankle and looked up at him.

Gordy jerked his hand from the water and scanned the surface of the lake. "Tell me you didn't see an alligator." Gordy looked terrified.

Cooper didn't want to move. He didn't want to talk. He just wanted to get back on dry ground, hop on his bike, and ride and ride and ride. What had just happened to him?

Yet somehow he knew—or had a sense, anyway—that something he'd buried months ago wasn't really dead. And now it was rising from its grave.

CHAPTER 2

Hiro stared at the inflatable. What was Cooper up to? He should have made it to the other side of the sailboat easily—but he surfaced just seconds after going under. He loved the water. Was more likely to swim underwater than on the surface. But he'd thrashed around like someone who couldn't swim at all. And he'd practically pulled Gordy into the water with him while trying to climb into the inflatable raft.

She smiled to herself. It must have been part of his strategy. Act like you're a total novice in the water, and they'll never suspect that you swam to their boat to prank it. Coop definitely looked convincing—a little ammo to tease him about.

Hiro watched the girl holding the pizza box. She was wearing a plain white T-shirt and tight jean shorts. Pretty. Trim. Probably eighteen or nineteen years old, if Hiro had to guess. There was something fluid and purposeful about the way the girl moved—like she'd gone through high school swinging pom-poms.

Superman tied the rowboat to the buoy, unhooked the wakeboard boat, and climbed aboard to join Pom-Pom Girl.

From the instant she saw him, Hiro had a creepy feeling about Superman. She couldn't pinpoint why. Something about him, though, gave her a bad vibe. He couldn't have been more than nineteen or twenty. And the boat couldn't possibly be his—unless he came from some serious money.

He bent down, picked up a camera with a bright green lanyard, and took a picture of Pom-Pom. She struck a flirty pose and he took another shot.

Then the girl grabbed the camera, leaned in close to Superman, and took a picture of the two of them together.

All right, all right. The pizza's going to get cold. Hiro grabbed a dock line and coiled it. She didn't want the couple to think she was spying on them—even though she was.

Superman started the engine and steered out of the bay, heading straight toward *The Getaway.*

Hiro hoped Coop had hidden the fish well. If Superman found them anytime soon, it wouldn't be hard to guess who'd done it. Coop had definitely been spotted—by Pom-Pom anyway.

Hiro watched as Superman's boat approached. She'd had nothing to do with the boys' prank, and she didn't have anything to hide. She waved—and Pom-Pom waved right back. It was one of those princess waves—the type that celebs and beauty queens do on top of parade floats. Superman made eye contact with Hiro, pointed at his heart, and then pointed at her. *He loves me?*

He bent down, picked up his camera, and aimed it at Hiro. The flash went off.

Okay. First you love me and then you're taking a picture of me? This is getting weird, Superman.

Superman handed the camera to Pom-Pom. "Your boat!" he shouted to Hiro. "It's gorgeous!"

Ah, of course. Hiro nodded and waved. *You love the boat—and you weren't taking a picture of me.* She felt her face warm. How could she have thought that anybody—much less a handsome college guy—would notice her? No, Hiro wasn't going to go there.

Superman eased the boat out of the mooring area. He looked over at Hiro and flexed a little. Like he figured she'd get all gaga over a guy with muscles. *Creep.*

Pom-Pom chose a seat in the bow of the boat, not at all close to Superman. She probably didn't want to get any closer to him than Hiro would. Smart girl. But then if she were *really* smart, she wouldn't have accepted a date with him in the first place.

"*Krypto Night.*" Hiro read the name aloud as the boat passed into open water. "Whatever that means."

Some people chose the strangest names for their boats. The navy blue sailboat that Coop and Gordy were hiding behind? *Ra Ra Avis*. The one anchored just beyond it? *Geegers*. And she'd seen plenty of other "interesting" names on the backs of boats since they'd arrived. *Succotash*, *Slingshot*, *Big Boy*, and *Bingo*. Obviously, naming boats was a man thing—and they could have it. Better they pick the names for boats than for their children. *Krypto*, *Geegers*, *Ra Ra*, *Bingo*. Yeah, those names would go over real big with the kids in school.

Hiro eyed the navy blue sailboat. The guys would stay hidden until *Krypto Night* was farther from shore. *This* is how they wanted to spend their vacation? Gee, what fun. She scanned the narrow beach. Still no sign of Lunk.

The beach crowds were gone, and the few people who were left were packing up their stuff. No lifeguard was stationed at this beach, and the water had turned black now that the sun was down.

She checked for *Krypto Night* again. It was still moving toward deeper water. More flashes. Probably more pictures that Pom-Pom would post and tag online tomorrow—complete with some lame comment: "We had a wonderfully romantic date on Geneva Lake."

They were outside the no-wake buoys now, and Superman nudged up the speed a bit.

"Hiro!" Gordy waved at her from the inflatable as he paddled toward her. "You missed it."

Cooper was inside the raft too, but he wasn't paddling. He was hugging his knees and staring at the water. *What's that all about?* The boys ducked under the sailboat anchor line, and Gordy closed the distance between them with long, steady strokes.

"We put fish in their ice chest," Gordy said.

Hiro leaned against the rail and watched their approach. "We? I only saw Coop in the boat."

Gordy waved her off. "I was in charge of the getaway boat."

Hiro laughed. "And you left without Coop."

"Had to," Gordy said. "So we wouldn't get caught."

"And that was ... what did you call it—*fun*?"

Gordy nodded. "Absolutely. The fact is, you totally missed it, and you know it. Now you wish you'd gone with us, and the only way to cope with your deep sense of regret is to tear apart the fun we had." He looked proud of himself. "Am I right?"

"Rarely," Hiro said. "And this isn't one of those times." She looked at Coop. It was like his mind was someplace else. Her comment brought zero response.

Gordy maneuvered the inflatable alongside the teak swim platform. "Wish we could see their faces when they find the fish."

"You're lucky you won't." Hiro looked out toward deeper water. *Krypto Night* had to be two hundred yards from shore. The engine was turned off, and by the angle of the boat she could tell it was adrift. A perfect way to picnic. "The girl was looking right at Coop. She'd have figured it out."

Coop didn't answer. Both boys climbed onto the swim platform. Coop stood on shaky legs.

"Which reminds me. What was with the fake panic attack, Coop?" Hiro smiled. "Or was it *real*?"

He glanced up at her but didn't say anything. His eyes did the talking—and instantly she knew. He *hadn't* been faking. She felt her smile slip away. *Dear God. He really did panic.*

Gordy glanced up at her and drew his forefinger across his throat. *Drop it.* That was clear enough, which only made her more concerned.

Coop busied himself with pulling the inflatable onto the platform—his way of avoiding her eyes. He stood the raft up on end and leaned it against the railing while trying to act like everything was okay. But Hiro had known him too long for that to work. Something clearly wasn't right. She just needed to figure out what it was.

CHAPTER 3

Cooper felt Hiro watching him — even though he didn't catch her doing it. Whenever he looked her way, she turned or was already staring into the darkness. Just as well. How could he explain something he didn't understand himself?

He'd finally had a growth spurt. In the last three months, he'd outgrown all of his clothes. But after what just happened under the water, he felt shorter than ever.

"Wonder what happened to Lunk?" Gordy scanned the beach.

Cooper made his way from the cockpit to the bow and sat at the very nose of *The Getaway*. He slung his arms over the low stainless steel rail and let his legs dangle over the edge.

Hiro joined him.

Was there actually something under the water — something he sensed even though he couldn't see it? Something evil? Even deadly? Was that what triggered his reaction?

Or was it something worse? Something lurking inside his head? One moment he felt fine. The next — like he was going to die.

"I love the way the lake calms after sunset," Hiro said. "All day, the wind can whip the water into a frenzy of white-capped waves. But after dark, everything changes. It's like the lake is alive and knows it needs to rest."

Alive. Cooper looked at the black water. It was still. Almost syrupy. It reflected the moon in a bright pathway that stretched across the lake. Something about the look of it creeped him out. In the daylight, it was different. He couldn't get enough of the water. But now he couldn't get past the blackness of it, even though it had never bothered him before.

"You're awfully quiet," Hiro said. "Want to talk about it?"

Cooper wanted to forget it had ever happened. Bury it. So deep that it could never resurface.

Gordy shimmied along the narrow deck alongside the front windshield and plopped down beside them. "I found the M&M's." He popped a handful into his mouth and handed the bag to Cooper. "You up for a night swim?"

Cooper hesitated, but not because he needed time to think about it. He just didn't want to look spooked. He wanted to make it look like he was really considering the idea. But right now the thought of jumping into that black water made his stomach flip. "Not tonight. I'm feeling pretty waterlogged."

He sensed Hiro looking at him again. She didn't miss *anything.* He knew he needed a diversion. "I'm thinking ice cream run. I'm starving."

"Even better," Gordy said, "how about we bike to town and hit Scoops?"

Cooper nodded. "As soon as Lunk gets here."

Gordy popped another handful of M&M's into his mouth. "Hope he gets here soon."

"*Shhhh!*" Hiro said. "Do you hear that?"

Cooper held his breath. Somebody was yelling. No. Two people were arguing. He leaned forward, trying to get a fix on where the sounds were coming from.

Hiro pointed. "There."

He could barely see a boat sitting far out on the lake. The green and red running lights were glowing at the bow, and a white running light was set higher, clearly mounted on the tower of a wakeboard boat.

"*Krypto Night?*" Gordy whispered.

No doubt about it. It was amazing how sound traveled across the water. The lake seemed to magnify it somehow. The tone of the argument was obvious—and escalating. Cooper tried to make out what they were saying, but he only caught a word here and there. *Jerk. Idiot.* That was easy enough to pick up.

Gordy tried to hold back a laugh—but it turned into a snort. "I guess they found the sushi."

Hiro glared at him. "And it ruined a perfect date. Nice."

"Stop it," the girl's voice said. "Stop. I said *no*!"

Gordy grinned. "Bet he's dangling a dead fish in front of her."

Hiro put her finger to her lips. "I'm trying to listen."

The tower light outlined the boat—but whatever was going on inside was hidden in shadows.

"Take me home." It was the girl again. Her voice sounded shrill. Clear. And something else. Scared? "Take me back. Now."

Superman had some choice words to say to her, but nothing Cooper could repeat. He strained to see better in the darkness. Suddenly there was a flash of light.

"What was that?" Gordy said.

Again, a brilliant burst of light appeared—and then it was gone.

"The camera's flash," Cooper said. Superman was yelling now. Actually, it was more of a roar. Why would someone take pictures in the middle of a really nasty argument?

The girl screamed, and the camera flashed again.

"What's going on out there?" Hiro whispered, as if talking to herself.

Whatever was happening, it wasn't good. Cooper bolted for the cockpit.

Hiro stood. "Coop?"

Cooper grabbed the wheel and laid on the air horns: a long,

hard blast and then two short ones. It sounded more like a train had just pulled into the bay.

Gordy was sitting right in front of the twin horns—cringing with his hands clamped over his ears. "Are you *insane*?"

Hiro stepped up beside Cooper with a questioning look. "What was that all about?"

Cooper strained again to see the drifting boat. He wasn't sure how much he wanted to say. The argument sounded—dangerous. Like the girl needed help. "I was sending Superman a message."

Hiro tilted her head just a bit. "A message?"

"I wanted to warn him that he isn't alone out there. Somebody is watching."

"I like how you think," she said. "But I doubt he appreciated that." She got up on tiptoe to look through the windshield.

Cooper debated sounding the horns again, just to be sure. He listened for a moment ... but heard nothing.

"I think your little warning worked," Hiro whispered.

Cooper slid out from behind the wheel and made his way back to his spot on the bow. He squatted, gripping the rail in front of him with both hands.

Krypto Night's engine roared to life, and the docking lights flicked on like high beams on a car. The boat turned in a fast circle—maybe the distance of a ski rope. The driving looked erratic at best. Seconds later, the boat banked in a tight turn, circling back. What was the guy *doing*?

"I don't like this," Hiro said, crouching beside Cooper. "I have a really bad feeling about this."

In the moonlight, Gordy's face looked deathly pale. "It was just a few dead fish. Why would they get so worked up over *that*?"

Should Cooper hit the horn again? "This isn't about the fish, Gordy."

Another flash—but this time it came from the water directly in front of the boat. Unless the camera's self-timer was turned on, somebody had to be in the water with it.

The girl screamed. Cooper's stomach flipped.

"I'm calling 9–1–1." Hiro was on her feet and punching in the numbers on her phone. She pressed the phone against her ear and hurried back to the cockpit.

The boat crisscrossed the area a couple times at high speed and then slowed to almost a crawl as it approached the spot where they'd seen that last flash. The boat stayed in place, idling.

Hiro hurried back as she pocketed the phone.

"What's he doing?" Gordy said.

Hiro clamped her hand over his mouth. "*Shhhh.*"

Gordy raised his hands in mock surrender.

Krypto Night was moving again. Circling slowly, so slowly, as though it were looking for something. Or *someone.*

Cooper stood. "Are the police coming?"

Hiro nodded. "The way that guy was driving ..."

She stood so close to him that Cooper felt a tremor zip through Hiro's body.

"That was unreal," Cooper said. "He could have hit her."

"I don't see—"—Hiro's body shook again—"—how he could have *missed.*"

CHAPTER 4

Krypto Night stopped. It's docking lights were now trained directly on *The Getaway*—and on the three of them.

"I don't like this," Gordy said. "Think Superman can see us?"

The wakeboard boat was still a distance away from them, but the lights were bright. "Oh yeah," Cooper said. "He's got his X-ray vision on us right now."

"Act natural, guys," Hiro said. "Like we're just out here talking."

Waves rocked *The Getaway*. Aftershocks from Superman's tantrum.

"We should have gone for ice cream—without Lunk." Gordy turned his back to Superman's boat. "I don't know what we saw out there—but whatever it was, I wish we hadn't seen it."

"A little late for that," Hiro said. "What's he trying to do?"

Cooper steadied himself as another set of waves rolled past. "He's answering my message with one of his own."

Hiro sucked in her breath. "He's watching *us* too."

The boat stayed in that position for what seemed like forever. Cooper had no idea how much time actually passed. He could barely hear the low rumble of the engine idling. Superman's boat slowly turned back and combed the waters it had just churned up. Finally it stopped—and the docking lights pointed to deeper water.

Cooper could now make out Superman in the glow of the tower light, standing at the port side and looking into the water.

"C'mon. Get back in the boat." Superman wasn't exactly yelling anymore, but his voice was still loud.

The boat blocked the girl from view—and made it difficult to hear her voice.

"Can you hear her?" Hiro whispered.

Cooper shook his head.

The guy put both palms on the side of the boat and leaned out a bit. "I'm sorry. I'm sorry. I'm *sorry*. How many times do you want me to say it?"

Hiro answered for Pom-Pom. "'Til your face is as green as your boat, you jerk."

"C'mon. *Please*," Superman said. "Don't be an idiot about this."

Hiro looked like she wanted to deck the guy. "She jumps in the water to get away from him, and he uses his boat to whip the waves into a frenzy around her—probably just to make it harder for her to swim to safety. Who's the idiot?"

Cooper agreed. "She'd be an idiot to climb back into the boat with him."

"She wasn't exactly smart to go out with him in the first place," Hiro said.

Gordy was back into the M&M's as if the show was over. "How was she supposed to know he was a total moron?"

Hiro shook her head. "She knew what he was like. Anger problems aren't that easy to hide—and that guy has a big one."

"Maybe she didn't know him that well," Gordy said.

"Then she shouldn't have gone on a date with him. Certainly not alone—and not out in a boat." Hiro said it matter-of-factly, like the answer was obvious.

Superman put his hands on his hips. "Then I'll follow you in." They heard him loud and clear. Either the boat was drifting closer, or he was talking louder. Too bad Pom-Pom didn't have Superman's loud voice. Cooper couldn't hear a word from her end of the conversation, but based on Superman's response, it wasn't hard to figure out what she was saying.

"Okay. Fine!" he shouted. "Thanks for a great time!"

Superman disappeared under the shadows of the tower. A moment later, the boat lurched forward and made a wide, arcing turn toward the beach, which meant he'd have to pass directly by them. *Terrific.*

Gordy hustled toward the stern. "I say we all head to the cabin, douse the light, and pray Superman doesn't fly in for a visit."

Cooper hesitated, straining to see the girl treading water, but it was too dark. He'd need a searchlight. From this corner of the lake, she was about equal distance from the beach and the south shore. Since Superman chose to head for the beach, it was a pretty safe guess she'd swim for the south shore.

"Coop!" Gordy motioned from the rear deck. "Let's move!"

Hiro was already moving to join him. Gordy was probably right. Standing on the bow would be stupid. He hustled to catch up with Hiro. They didn't go into the cabin but stayed on the back deck.

"Get down." Gordy crouched low and peered over the side of the boat.

Cooper sat beside him, his back against the side of the boat. The cabin light was on, glowing out the oval portholes. But there was no point to going dark. The guy knew they were there.

"He's coming our way," Gordy said. "Think we should swim for shore?"

Hiro shook her head. "The way that guy drives?"

"What are we hiding for?" Cooper said. "We didn't do anything wrong."

Gordy kept looking over the side. "Number one, you ruined his date by planting those fish. And two, you blasted those insanely loud horns at him." Gordy rubbed his ears. "My ears are still ringing."

"Sorry, Gordy," Cooper said. "But it looked like the guy was losing it out there—like road rage or something."

Gordy ducked out of sight. "Yeah, well I'd hate to meet *him* on the road."

"The way he treated that girl?" Hiro sat next to Cooper. "I'd hate to meet him anywhere."

Cooper heard the rumbling inboard motor. He chanced a peek over the side and his stomach tightened. Superman was stopping for a visit.

CHAPTER 5

Gordy pressed his back up against the side of *The Getaway*. "Let's just lay low. Let him pass." What if the guy questioned them about the dead fish?

"Ahoy."

Superman's voice. *Great*. Gordy put a finger to his lips motioning Hiro and Coop to stay quiet.

"Who says 'ahoy' anymore?" Cooper whispered.

"Hell-ooo!" Superman sang out. "I know you're there."

Gordy stared at Cooper and whispered. "Maybe he *does* have X-ray vision."

Cooper sighed. "He's not going away—and if we hide, that looks really bad." He stood up.

Just like that.

"Hi," Cooper said.

Okay, how lame did that sound?

"Got some extra pizza here," Superman said. "Anybody hungry?"

"Don't do it, Coop," Gordy whispered from the deck. He just wanted the guy to leave. Of course, if he left the pizza behind, that would be even better.

"No thanks." Cooper waved, obviously trying to look casual.

"Where's the rest of your crew?" Superman said, as if nothing weird had happened out on the lake at all.

"The jig's up, Gordy," Hiro whispered. She stood and prodded Gordy with her toe.

Even though his mind was telling him to stay right where he was, Gordy got on his feet and stood on the other side of Hiro.

Krypto Night idled with its nose no more than three feet from the side of the cabin cruiser. Superman stood behind the wheel, turning it, adjusting the speed so the boats wouldn't bump.

"I'm Tommy." He smiled one of those perfect-teeth smiles. He was definitely younger than Gordy had figured. Probably a college student. "Tommy Kryptoski."

That explained the name of his boat. But if the guy was expecting Gordy to give his name, he'd be disappointed. Coop must have been thinking the same thing, because he just nodded.

"My girlfriend and I just had a little fight."

"Girlfriend?" Hiro stepped up to the rail.

Kryptoski flashed a smile. The guy was a charmer. Gordy knew the type. "My date. Lynn. We've gone out a couple times. But I'm hoping she'll be my girlfriend."

Gordy figured Krypto was going to be in for a big disappointment.

Kryptoski nudged the gearshift into reverse for a moment to keep the nose away from *The Getaway*. "Tonight didn't exactly go according to my plans."

"Poor baby," Hiro said, but so quietly that there was no way Kryptoski could have heard her.

Hopefully. Now it was Gordy's turn to give her a little prod with his foot. *Down, girl. Easy, Hiro. Let's not ask for trouble.*

"For now, it looks like I have *no* girlfriend." Kryptoski shook his head like that was a ridiculous concept. "Women. Can't live with 'em, can't live without 'em, am I right?"

"I can live without 'em," Gordy said.

Hiro glared at him. Kryptoski laughed.

"So where is she now?" Cooper said. The surface had calmed again, but it was impossible to make out a swimmer at this distance.

Kryptoski shrugged. "I'd say she's nearly reached one of the docks on the south shore by now. Probably The Geneva Inn."

"You're not worried about her?" Hiro folded her arms across her chest like she was daring him to come up with an explanation.

"Former captain of the high school swim team? She can handle herself."

"And if a boat drives by—like you did?"

Hiro let the question just hang there. She had a way of doing that. And right now, Gordy wished she'd just leave it alone. He stepped on her toe. Hard.

Kryptoski's smile faded. "I had the same thought. Which is why I'm going to hang around a bit." He pointed to the beach. "If you see her walking to town, would you give a blast on that monster horn of yours? I just want to make sure she's safe."

Which sounded reasonable to Gordy.

"Sure," Coop said.

"Appreciate it."

Krypto threw the gearshift into reverse, spun the wheel, and eased *Krypto Night* past *The Getaway*.

Gordy watched the boat creep out to deeper water.

"Wants to make sure she's safe." Hiro spit the words out. "Right."

A blue flashing light approached from the far side of the lake. Police boat. "Krypto is going to have company."

"Maybe you jumped the gun a little calling 9–1–1 like that," Gordy said.

Hiro pulled her braid over her shoulder and played with it. "It's better to call early and end up with a false alarm than wait until you're sure—"

"And it be too late." Cooper finished her thought.

Hiro nodded.

"I'm glad you feel that way." Gordy pointed to the shoreline. "Because now they're coming by land and by sea."

A police car raced down the hill and roared down Lake Shore Drive with its lights flashing. The car screeched to a stop opposite *The Getaway*. A policeman stepped out and walked around the front of the car, scanning the lake.

"Now what?" Gordy said.

Hiro climbed over the stern railing onto the swim platform. "Hand me that raft."

Of course. The girl who dreamt of being a cop someday wouldn't miss a chance to talk to one. Gordy grabbed the inflatable and handed it to Hiro.

She dropped it into the water and scampered in.

"I'm going with you," Coop said.

Which was a good thing. The distance to shore was a longer paddle than Hiro probably figured. But three people in that raft might swamp it.

"I'll stay here and keep an eye on the M&M's." Gordy needed something to ease the uneasiness in his stomach.

Cooper smiled. "Make sure the boat doesn't sink, okay?"

"Aye, aye, Captain!" Gordy saluted. But it wasn't the boat that was in danger of going down. This was their first night out, and already the police were visiting. The only thing at risk of sinking was his plan for a carefree vacation.

CHAPTER 6

Cooper swung his leg over the transom rail and dropped onto the platform. The boat rocked in slow motion, the dark waters burping up between the teak slats. He stared at the surface of the lake. Black as oil—and just as thick.

For an instant he felt lightheaded and gripped the rail to steady himself. He had the sick feeling that if he went over the side, he'd turn to concrete and drop straight to the bottom. Dead weight. Unable to move. How deep was it here? *Deep enough.*

"You coming?"

Hiro's voice shook him from his thoughts. Their eyes locked for an instant, but it was long enough. Cooper knew that look. She was trying to figure out what he was thinking. Cooper avoided her eyes and climbed into the front end of the inflatable.

"Hold on." Cooper leaned back and used his arms like oars. He did a backstroke for the beach, hoping she wouldn't ask any questions.

Hiro sat in the back, apparently lost in her own thoughts.

That was okay with him. He had some things on his mind too. Like, what had happened to him in the water? The raw fear. The panic. He didn't exactly know what to call it, but whatever it was, it had been intense. Like the dreams he'd been having lately, only this was way worse. This was real.

Even now as he paddled, he had a strange sense that something was below the surface—tracking him, ready to pull him under. He stroked faster.

When he risked a glance at Hiro, she was staring at him again. Analyzing him was more like it. *Great.*

"Coop?"

He ignored her, which was ridiculous. She was impossible to avoid when she had something to say.

"Is there anything you want to talk about?"

Honestly? Did she really think that was going to work on him? *Yeah, Hiro. I'm glad you asked. A while ago, I got totally freaked out in the water. And if I fall out of this boat, I'm afraid I won't be able to swim any better than a rock.* Maybe he could stall her off a little.

She tilted her head and smiled slightly. "Tell me what you're not telling me."

Cooper kept paddling.

"You can talk to me," Hiro said. "You know you can."

Absolutely true. But why would he want to talk about something he didn't even want to *think* about? Besides, more immediate problems were looming. Like police expecting an explanation for the 9–1–1 call.

He leaned his elbows on the edge of the raft and let it drift. "Did you believe that Kryptoski guy?"

Hiro's shoulders drooped like she was disappointed in his change of topic. She sighed and shook her head. "Not at all. You?"

"No. And yes. I mean, when he was whipping around with the boat out there, it didn't look so good." The scene did an instant replay in his mind. "But he had an explanation for everything, didn't he?"

Hiro seemed to think about that for a moment. "Remember Detective Hammer's claim he has a built-in baloney detector?"

Cooper smiled at the thought of the tough Rolling Meadows

cop. He'd become a trusted friend during their eighth-grade year at Plum Grove Junior High. "How could I forget?"

"Well, I think I've got a baloney detector too." Hiro pointed at her arms. "The hair stood up when he talked. Like it was warning me or something. He was lying. I'm sure of it."

Hiro had an almost spooky sense of intuition. And now she also had a baloney detector? Good thing he had no plans to lie to her.

He checked the distance to the beach. Still more than halfway to go.

The police officer leaned against his cruiser and watched them, arms folded across his chest.

Cooper leaned back and resumed paddling.

"So," Hiro said. "We were talking about you. About something you wanted to tell me."

"You were talking," Cooper said. "I was listening."

Hiro scooped a handful of water and threw it at him, dousing his T-shirt.

Cooper ignored the chill and kept paddling.

"I think you need to talk about something," Hiro said.

Obviously, she wasn't going to let this go. "Actually, I don't need to talk," Cooper said. "I enjoy listening to you."

"Coop, I'm serious. I know what you're doing."

Reach and pull. Reach and pull. Cooper kept the rhythm going. Every stroke brought them closer to the cop waiting on the beach. He couldn't get there fast enough.

"You're stalling. Trying to change the subject. Hoping to distract me. Yeah, I'm onto you."

Cooper propped his elbows on the sides of the inflatable. "And I know what *you're* doing. You want to know what happened back there in the water."

Hiro blinked in surprise. Hey, he'd just surprised himself too. But she was his friend. He knew he could talk to her. And a part of him wanted to. Maybe she could make some sense of what was going on. She had a way of seeing things that others missed.

He jerked a thumb toward the beach. "I can't get into it now. Duty calls." And he just wanted to stand on firm ground again.

She looked disappointed but nodded. "Later?"

"Sure, I guess." Maybe it would make him feel better. Maybe.

"Right now," Cooper said, "we need to figure out what we're going to tell the police." He started pulling for the beach again. Faster now.

"Exactly what we saw," Hiro said. "We're eyewitnesses."

"But we didn't actually *see* anything. We only heard."

Now it was Hiro's turn to be quiet. She kept her eyes on the beach. "We tell them what we heard. What we saw. What we think we saw."

"And then we're done," Cooper said. "We'll let the police sort everything out. Right?"

Hiro nodded. "Right."

But her expression said something different. Her mind was already in cop mode. He'd have to be delusional to believe she'd let go of this thing that easily

CHAPTER 7

Cooper gave a few fast paddles to work up some speed before the inflatable grounded itself on the sandy bottom. He hopped out and dragged the boat out of the water as soon as Hiro climbed over the side.

The officer met them on the beach. He looked big. Solid. He had broad shoulders and easily stood over six feet tall.

"Miss Yakimoto?" He had an easy smile about him. "Do you pronounce your first name 'hi-row' or 'hero'?"

"Hero," she said. "It's short for 'Hiroko.'"

The cop held out his hand. "Officer Ryan Tarpy."

Hiro shook his hand, introduced Cooper, and started right into her story. She summed up the situation in sixty seconds.

Cooper stood alongside her, ready to fill in the blanks if she left any.

"He's out there now." Hiro pointed at the lights from *Krypto Night*, two hundred yards offshore. The police boat was closing in fast, heading directly for the beach.

"I know the boy," Officer Tarpy said. "And I know the boat." He turned his head to the side and spit.

The way he said it made Cooper wonder what he wasn't saying.

"So ..." Officer Tarpy let the word hang a while. "When you

called 9 – 1 – 1, the girl was in the water. And the way he was driving that boat, you were afraid— "

"She'd get hit," Hiro said. "He didn't stop his little tantrum until after I'd made the call."

Tarpy nodded. "You didn't actually *see* Lynn after the erratic driving stopped?"

Cooper studied him. He'd asked the question in a casual way, but his look was more . . . deliberate. Was he just checking to make sure Hiro didn't change her story, or was he searching for something more?

"It was too dark. And she was in the water on the other side of the boat," Hiro said. "Still arguing with him."

Officer Tarpy paused. "But you heard her side of the argument. You actually heard her voice. Is that right?"

Hiro's face clouded over. "Well, not *exactly*."

Tarpy raised his eyebrows.

"I mean," she said, "I could only hear his end of the conversation."

"So, you never *heard* her voice."

Hiro shook her head.

The cop looked right at him. "Cooper?"

Cooper shrugged. "Not once she was out of the boat."

Tarpy stared at the dark water like he was replaying the whole thing in his mind. He nodded slowly, like the pieces of the puzzle were fitting together. He turned and walked a few steps, then spoke into his shoulder mic.

Cooper couldn't catch everything the officer said, but the guy talked with his hands—which helped Cooper fill in the blanks. Cooper tapped Hiro's shoulder. "Do you think— "

She cut him off with a finger to her lips. She wanted to listen too.

Tarpy pointed at Kryptoski's boat, then paced toward them. "Yeah. Bring him in. Right here."

Immediately, the flashing blue lights changed course and headed right toward *Krypto Night.*

This could get really awkward. Cooper didn't want to be around when they brought Kryptoski to the beach for questioning.

The cop stopped pacing and faced Hiro. "One more time." Tarpy held up a finger. "They argued. It sounded really heated. Cooper hit the air horns, and things got quiet for a few moments. Right?"

Hiro nodded.

Officer Tarpy held up a second finger. "Then the guy drove like a maniac, criss-crossing the area. You're certain Lynn ended up in the water somehow because you saw a camera flash directly in front of the boat." He raised his eyebrows.

Hiro nodded again.

Third finger. "You heard a female scream, you called 9–1–1, and the arguing stopped. Kryptoski slowed the boat down and circled again, at which time you speculated that he was looking for her in the water. Then he shined the boat's docking lights right on you guys—so he knew you were aware of what had been going on. He sat there for several minutes, maybe more." He glanced at Cooper.

"Right," Cooper said.

Fourth finger. "Then he started talking to the girl again—loud enough for you to pick up what he was saying, but you never actually saw or heard the female in the water."

Hiro sucked in her breath and glanced at Cooper.

The cop held up a fifth finger. "Then he cruised over to your boat, alone, and told you the girl had decided to swim to shore. After that he went back out on the lake to make sure she was safe."

Hiro didn't say a word.

"That's how I saw it," Cooper said.

Tarpy turned to Hiro. "Is that how you remember it? In that *exact* order?"

Hiro nodded, eyes wide.

Cooper looked at the still water in the bay. What if Kryptoski wanted them to *think* the girl was there? That she was angry but absolutely fine. *How do we know Kryptoski was talking to anybody at all?*

CHAPTER 8

Lunk sat in the passenger seat as his mom drove. He angled himself against the door so he could watch her face as she chattered endlessly. He was pretty sure she'd been smiling all the way from Rolling Meadows. He ran his hand over his head—where his hair used to be.

"You getting used to it?" She shot him an apologetic look. "I still feel terrible about it."

All he'd asked for was a summer cut. Something short. Mom had the wrong attachment or something. Got distracted. She'd clipped a path nearly down to the scalp before she realized her mistake. After that happened, he was doomed. She had to do his whole head that way or else he would have looked weird. But he looked weird anway. He felt his scalp. It *felt* weird too. "It's okay. It'll grow back." But not in two weeks. He'd start high school looking like he got scalped.

"If you'd told me in February that we'd be taking a vacation in six months, I would have said you were dreaming." Mom flashed him a smile. "I still can't believe it."

There was a whole list of things that Lunk couldn't believe. Like the fact they were closing on a house in less than three weeks. Just after Labor Day weekend.

She drove up Main Street toward the town of Lake Geneva, then turned onto South Lake Shore Drive. "You excited?"

Lunk smiled. Oh yeah, he was excited. No more moving around. They were going to stay in Rolling Meadows. Permanently.

"And you're still okay with the fact that I'll be staying in the condo rental with the women while you're bunking with the guys on the boat, right?"

The idea of being on the boat in Cooper's backyard was fine. But on the water? "It'll be perfect, Mom. We're both going to have a great time."

She nodded. "I'm especially happy for you, getting along so well with Cooper, Gordy, and Hiro.

"Definitely." Which was one of the biggest surprises of all. Something he never would have guessed a year ago.

They left the lights of town behind them and headed down the twisting Lake Shore Drive toward Big Foot Beach and the state park. As they drove down the hill toward the water, Lunk saw the flashing blue lights of the police car.

Mom braked around the curve and eased off the gas. "Must be a speed trap."

Lunk didn't see a car pulled over in front of the cop car. In fact, the cop was standing on the narrow beach, talking to two people.

"Isn't that Cooper?" Mom said. "And Hiro?"

Lunk's stomach lurched. An inflatable raft sat beached nearby. It was clearly Cooper and Hiro. They looked okay. Lunk scanned the deeper water. *The Getaway* was anchored a good football field offshore. Gordy must still be in the boat. *Hopefully.* He unbuckled his seat belt.

Mom put her blinker on and pulled onto the shoulder several car lengths behind the police car.

Lunk opened the door before she came to a complete stop. "I'll see what's going on."

She nodded. "I hope there isn't trouble."

Lunk patted her arm. "I'm sure everything is okay." But it definitely looked like trouble. He just hoped it wasn't serious.

CHAPTER 9

A car stopped on the shoulder of Lake Shore Drive, and its headlights practically blinded Cooper. But he could see just enough to notice the passenger door open. Somebody got out and headed Cooper's way. *Now what?*

The guy stepped in front of the headlights giving Cooper a perfect silhouette. The big build. The height. His walk was unmistakable. Lunk had arrived.

Lunk hustled over to them. "Where's Gordy?"

Cooper pointed to *The Getaway*. "He's okay."

Lunk nodded. His shoulders relaxed. "No mysteries. No danger. Just a vacation?" He smiled. "I know you want to be a cop, Hiro, but this is ridiculous."

Hiro turned to him. "This is serious."

Officer Tarpy paced the beach as if working something out in his mind. The police boat approached—a tough-looking thing with a massive 300 horsepower outboard on the stern. *Krypto Night* was following close behind. Using both arms, Tarpy flagged the boats like he was guiding planes up to the terminal gate.

"Somebody going to tell me what's going on?" Lunk jammed his hands into his back pockets.

"I think we witnessed a *murder*," Hiro whispered.

Lunk shook his head. "Impossible." He looked at Cooper. "Is this a joke?"

Cooper watched the police boat nose onto the beach. *Krypto Night* did the same. "No joke. It was unreal."

Lunk blew out a loud breath. "What happened?"

The emergency flashers were blinking on Mrs. Lunquist's car, adding their own rhythm to the police lights reflecting off the dark water.

Cooper silently willed her to leave. But the driver's door opened instead. "Lunk, if your mom stays, and she tells the rest of our moms about this at the condo, then they won't let us sleep in *The Getaway*." Then again, if this really was a murder, the idea of staying on the boat and being so close to the crime scene could be really creepy.

Lunk's mom hurried over. "Everybody okay?"

Hiro started explaining the situation, which allowed Cooper to let his mind drift. A perfectly good vacation wrecked before it even started. Terrific. Sleeping on *The Getaway* with the guys was half the fun. Staying in the condo would change everything.

Kryptoski was standing on the beach now, answering questions from Officer Tarpy and the cop from the police boat. He wasn't nearly as loud as he'd been before. He did a lot of pointing toward the deeper water.

Hiro finally stopped to catch her breath or swallow—or maybe she was done telling her story.

Mrs. Lunquist clutched Lunk's arm. *Great. Here we go. She's going to pull in the reins.*

"So this girl—" Lunk said.

"Dead girl," Hiro said, correcting him.

"Okay," Lunk nodded, "this *dead* girl. Did she have a body like a model?"

Hiro gave him a look. "Yeah."

"Pretty face?"

Her eyes narrowed. "If you like the blonde cheerleader type."

"White T-shirt and short jean shorts?"

Hiro looked surprised. "How could you guess that?"

"Either I'm seeing a zombie, or she isn't dead." He pointed up the road toward the state park entrance.

The girl from *Krypto Night* was walking toward them, squinting and shielding her eyes from the police car's headlights. She was barefoot and her clothes were sopping wet.

"I don't believe it," Hiro whispered.

"Is that her—the dead girl?" Mrs. Lunquist said.

Cooper stared at the girl. "Apparently."

Lunk snickered.

"Lynn!" Kryptoski shouted out to her. "Thank God you're okay." He excused himself from the cops and ran toward her. "I'm so sorry. You have to know that."

Lynn marched up, her jaw set. "Arrest him, officer." She poked her finger at Kryptoski. "He's rude. Arrogant. And definitely not a gentleman."

Lunk nudged Cooper. "And a murderer. Don't forget that, lady."

It looked like the argument between Kryptoski and his ex-date was going to start all over again.

Hiro glared at Lunk. "It was an honest mistake."

"Right." Lunk laughed. "Your imagination is a lot bigger than you are."

Hiro waved him off and moved closer to the officers. She stood there listening, rubbing her Chicago Police star necklace.

"What's Hiro doing?" Lunk said. "Looks like she's in another world."

"She is." Cooper shrugged. "Cop stuff draws her into its orbit."

Mrs. Lunquist kissed Lunk on the forehead. "I'll leave now. Are you sure you don't want me to give Hiro a ride to the condo?"

"We'll get her there," Coop said. "By ten o'clock. Something tells me she wants to watch this."

Lunk's mom smiled. "I think you're right."

"I'll get my bike out of the trunk." Lunk walked his mom to the car.

The argument behind Cooper was heating up again. He turned to make sure Hiro wasn't getting too close.

The blonde was in Kryptoski's face, jabbing him in the chest.

"Okay, lovebirds." Officer Tarpy raised both hands to put a stop to the fight. "Settle your differences another time." He whispered something to the boat cop. Then Officer Tarpy looked at Lynn. "Do you have any ID?"

Lynn worked her hand into a wet pocket and pulled out a card. Probably her driver's license.

Tarpy checked it with his flashlight, then shined his light in Lynn's face.

She squinted and covered her eyes.

"Okay," he said. "We're good." He handed the ID back. "Unless you really do want to press charges."

Kryptoski stepped forward and puffed up his chest just a bit. "On what grounds?"

"Being a total jerk," Lynn shouted. "You're rude, obnoxious, a lousy boat driver, and the worst date."

Cooper looked at Hiro. He half expected her to smile—or join in with the insults. But she didn't. She stepped closer to the couple.

Officer Tarpy walked a few paces toward the other cop.

"You want to talk about being a jerk?" The veins bulged on the side of Kryptoski's neck. "Jumping out of the boat and insisting on swimming to shore—at night? That wasn't exactly an Einstein move."

Lynn stepped toward Kryptoski, her fists clenched. "That's because *you* were being a jerk."

"If that dead girl starts swinging, Hiro's going to get herself hurt," Lunk said. "She's way too close."

Cooper was already moving toward her. Lunk leaned his new bike against a speed limit signpost and kept pace with him. They stepped on either side of Hiro, and each grabbed one of Hiro's arms.

"Easy, tiger," Lunk said. "It's not your fight."

Hiro resisted. "Let me go. I just want to—"

"From a safe distance, Hiro," Cooper said. "Back off a little."

Hiro took a step back, but it looked like the argument was over anyway.

"Okay." Kryptoski's shoulders slumped. "I'm sorry. You're right. I was a jerk." He raised both hands and backed up. "It's been a really bad day. Can I get a 'do over' on this date?"

"I don't think so." Her voice didn't sound nearly as angry now.

"You don't have to answer right away," Kryptoski said. "How about I give you a ride home?"

She crossed her arms over her chest.

He stepped back. "Can I call you tomorrow?"

"Maybe." She smiled just a bit. "After you send me flowers."

Kryptoski grinned.

Officer Tarpy stepped between them and faced the girl. "Do you intend to walk home barefoot, or would you like a ride?"

"I'd appreciate a lift, officer." She headed toward the squad car.

"Hop in. I'll be right back." Tarpy walked over to the police boat.

Kryptoski walked with the girl to the car, speaking quietly to her. Whatever their argument had been about, she seemed to have forgotten. Cooper had seen the type before. Kryptoski was a charmer. And to calm her down like he did? This guy was a miracle worker too.

"Coop," Hiro whispered. "Something's not right."

"Yeah, the fact that you're standing too close again. Let's go." Cooper and Lunk backed her away from the scene.

She pulled away. "I need to talk to Officer Tarpy."

The two cops were still talking. Cooper refused to let go of Hiro's arm. Lunk locked elbows with her other arm.

"Let it go, Hiro," Lunk said. "The show is over."

"Let go of me or I'll—"

"Call 9–1–1 again?" Lunk said in a teasing tone. "Hi, it's me again. Sorry that murder was bogus, but I'd like to report a kidnapping this time. I'm being abducted."

Hiro tensed as though she planned to break free.

Cooper and Lunk both laughed.

A dark pickup truck drove past slowly. It pulled into the state park entrance, turned around, and stopped.

Kryptoski left the girl at the police car and hustled across the street. He walked right over to the pickup truck, talked with the driver for a minute or two, and then walked back to *Krypto Night*. A moment later, he was in the boat and powering away from the beach.

Hiro said, "That was weird, don't you think?"

"Hi, 9–1–1," Lunk tried to make his voice sound girly. "I'm back. And I want to report something *weird*. I saw two men talking."

Cooper forced himself to hold back his laughter. Hiro was in no mood for it.

Officer Tarpy helped push the nose of the police boat off the beach, and the cop at the wheel kicked the outboard into reverse. The beast had power.

And so did Hiro. She swung her elbows, and Cooper caught one in the ribs. Then she stomped her foot down hard on Lunk's foot.

"Let me go." Hiro squirmed free.

Officer Tarpy got inside the cruiser and slammed the driver's side door shut. His window zoomed down and he gave Hiro a nod.

"Officer Tarpy!" Hiro said. "Can I talk to you?"

Hiro stepped up to his door and then hesitated. She looked at the girl sitting in the passenger seat. "I-I'm glad you're okay."

She'd needed to get to the car to say *that*? Cooper shook his head. Sometimes she made no sense.

Tarpy smiled. "Thanks for calling 9–1–1. It was the right thing to do."

Hiro nodded, but she didn't look happy.

"I don't get it," Lunk mumbled. "This is a no-brainer. What could possibly be bothering her?"

Did she sense something? *No, no, no . . . this was not happening again.* She was wrong. She had to be.

Cooper stepped up beside her, and together they watched the police car pull away. "Okay, what was that all about?"

Hiro looked pale. She didn't answer, but just fidgeted with her braid.

"What is it?"

She watched the police car cruise down Lake Shore Drive. "I'm not sure it was her."

Lunk made an exasperated face. "The cop checked her ID."

Hiro nodded. "I know. But I don't think she was the same girl that I saw in the boat."

CHAPTER 10

Gordy lowered the binoculars and watched the police boat prowl through the black waters along Big Foot Beach, ready for the next false alarm. Meanwhile *Krypto Night* was headed out to deeper water. Apparently, Superman was going to finish his picnic alone.

The girl Hiro had called Pom-Pom obviously made it to shore safely. The guy didn't get arrested. And Lunk had finally arrived. So everybody was happy.

Except Hiro.

It was obvious by the way she stood — arms folded across her chest, her weight shifted onto one leg. He didn't need to hear a word she was saying to see she was plenty worked up.

Which is exactly what he was going to be if they didn't get to town for a snack before Scoops closed. He hustled to the driver's seat and tapped the air horn. Cooper reacted immediately.

"I'm dying out here!" Gordy shouted. "Are we going to town or what?" Swimming to shore wouldn't be a big deal, even when it was dark. But doing it alone with *Krypto Night* out on the lake? He pointed to the inflatable. "I need a ride to shore!"

Coop grabbed the inflatable and paddled out to pick him up.

By the time they got back to the beach, Coop had him up to speed on Hiro's suspicions.

Minutes later, all four of them crossed Lake Shore Drive. Lunk stood by his bike and waited while the rest of them unlocked their bikes from the trees. Bringing them had been Coop's idea—and a good one. Wheels were as good as wings. They were freedom—and right now that meant food.

The road was quiet all the way into town, and so was Hiro. Gordy wanted to ask about the girl, but Hiro would talk when she was ready—and then there'd be no stopping her. Besides, this was supposed to be a vacation. No sense encouraging her to slip into cop mode. He raised his face into the full force of the warm wind.

Gordy coasted onto Baker Street and down the hill into the town of Lake Geneva, waiting for the others to catch up. Hiro trailed Lunk and Coop by thirty yards—lost in thought. And lost is exactly what she'd be if she didn't put a little more effort into the pedaling.

The road curved onto Wrigley Drive, running parallel to the shore. He crossed the bridge, turned onto Broad Street, and skidded to a stop in front of Scoops. He leaned his bike against a table and checked the sign outside the door. "You want nutrition? Eat carrots." *Nice slogan*. He pulled open the door and stepped inside.

In ice cream places, the AC was always cranked up. It felt good. He stepped closer to the glass coolers housing five-gallon tubs of joy—the most delicious ice cream he'd ever seen.

Zanzibar Chocolate. Snickers and Fudge. Yippee Skippee. Halley's Comet. Superman. Blue Moon. Fat Elvis. And tubs more. Ice cream as different as the names on the labels. It was his second time in the shop, and he already loved this place.

A girl stepped up. *Katie* was engraved on her nametag. She was in her mid-twenties, maybe. Dark hair. Friendly smile. "Back again?" she said.

Gordy nodded. He didn't even need to do the sample spoon thing this time. "Yippee Skippee," he said. "Pile it high."

Katie took a scooper out of the rinse water and leaned into the task.

Coop and Lunk stepped inside the shop. Hiro followed a minute later.

Katie set Gordy's bowl on the counter and started working on Coop's order.

Gordy cruised along the freezer cases looking at the ice cream tubs. "This must be a dream job," he said.

Katie smiled. "Actually I'm a teacher. *That's* my dream job. But this is fun for the summer. I also work the mailboat most mornings." She placed Coop's heaping bowl on the counter.

Lunk leaned against the counter. "Do you make root beer floats?"

Katie smiled. "Not if I can convince you to try something else." She wrinkled her nose. "I *don't* like root beer."

"Don't like root beer?" Lunk looked at her like she couldn't possibly be serious. "Try a root beer float. Something magical happens when you mix vanilla ice cream with root beer."

Katie set the scooper down. "There's nothing magical about ruining perfectly good ice cream."

Lunk snickered and checked the ice cream flavors while Katie took Hiro's order.

Gordy grabbed a table in the back.

Coop was already digging into his Halley's Comet before he sat down.

"How is it?" Gordy said.

Coop closed his eyes and smiled—which pretty much said it all.

Hiro joined them a minute later. She seemed more like herself. Maybe the bike ride had helped. She looked like she was on vacation again.

"What did you get, Hiro?" Gordy said.

She sat with a single scoop. "Chocolate Raspberry Truffle. Rich chocolate ice cream with chunks of brownies, chocolate-covered raspberry cups, and a sweet raspberry ripple. Who thinks of this stuff?"

"A genius," Gordy said.

She took a bite. "Mmmmmm. Oh yes! We're definitely coming back here."

Lunk stood at the counter while Katie dug into one of the ice cream containers.

"So, Lunk," Hiro said. "Nice haircut."

Lunk shrugged. "What hair?"

Hiro laughed. "I kinda like the new look. It's cute."

"Oh, that helps." Lunk shuffled over and sat down with a heaping bowl of ice cream in his hands.

Hiro shook her head. "Vanilla? It took you longer than any of us to make your choice, and you picked *vanilla*?"

"Nothing wrong with that," Lunk said. "Pure. No frills. None of that foo-foo stuff like what you picked."

"Foo-foo?" Hiro shook her head. "You're ridiculous."

"*I'm* ridiculous?" Lunk snorted. "You can't admit that the woman at the beach was the same one you insisted was dead." He took a bite of his ice cream. "You reported a murder before somebody actually got killed."

Excellent. Gordy wanted everyone to forget about the bogus crime. They needed to focus on the vacation.

Hiro put down her spoon. "I don't think it was the same girl."

"White top. Jean shorts. Blonde. Cheerleader type," Lunk said. "Everything fits."

"Seriously? That's like saying she's a Caucasian and all Caucasians look the same. Or all Asians look the same."

"Don't they?" Lunk put on an innocent face. "Asians, I mean."

Hiro balled her hand into a fist and slugged his arm.

Lunk laughed. Seemed like just the reaction he was looking for.

"So what are we doing tomorrow?" Gordy said.

Hiro worked the spoon in her ice cream until the chocolate and raspberry blended into a dark, creamy swirl. "I saw her when the boat pulled out. She looked at me. Smiled." She lifted the spoon and sampled the mix. "But when I saw her on the beach ... she was different somehow."

"Her hair was wet," Gordy said. "That'll change how anybody looks. Except Lunk—because his hair is gone."

Hiro stared off at nothing. "It was more than that."

Lunk waved his hand in front of her eyes. "Why didn't you tell the cop when you had the chance?"

"The girl was right there looking at me," Hiro said. "It creeped me out."

"Baloney," Lunk said. "You're not afraid to tell anybody anything. Not when you're sure you're right."

"I totally agree." Cooper leaned forward. "Deep down you can't even convince *yourself* it was a different girl."

Hiro set her spoon down. "Did it look like the same girl to you?"

She didn't sound sure of herself. It was all about one of her *feelings*. Not facts.

Cooper shrugged. "I barely saw her. I was a little busy thinking about dead fish and wondering if Kryptoski was going to find them before he pulled out of the bay."

Gordy looked at him. Cooper had probably been thinking about that panic attack he'd had too.

Lunk held up both hands. "Hold on. The girl gave the cop an ID. I saw him check it. Her name was Lynn."

"And what does that prove?" Hiro rubbed her necklace again. "Her name was Lynn. Her ID matched. So what? I don't think she was the same girl I saw in the boat."

"Okay," Coop said. "Then let's call the police." He fished his phone out of his pocket and held it out to her. "If you're that sure, make the call."

Was Coop calling her bluff—or was he serious?

Hiro crossed her arms over her chest and eyed Coop's phone. "I'm sure ... but maybe I'm not *sure* sure. Does that make sense?"

Gordy wanted to comment, but held his toungue. Maybe Hiro

needed to take another bike ride and clear her head. Gordy glanced out the window to check on their bikes. A man was standing on the sidewalk like he couldn't decide whether he wanted to come in or not. He obviously hadn't tasted Scoops' ice cream or else he'd be standing in front of the counter by now. But he just stood there with shadows covering his face. This guy didn't know what he was missing.

Coop pocketed his phone. "When you're *sure* sure, we'll make the call. And just out of curiosity, if it wasn't Lynn, who do you think was in the boat?"

Hiro glanced at the man outside and then lowered her voice. "That's what we need to find out."

CHAPTER 11

Hiro had a creepy feeling. She'd felt fine when they walked into Scoops. But something had changed. She looked around to figure out the source of her uneasiness. Not the girl behind the counter. Katie was swaying to the rhythm of some song that must be playing in her head. She held the scoop like a microphone and silently mouthed the words. No, it wasn't Katie.

Hiro looked out the window. The man was still there. Her stomach tightened. Was he watching them? He appeared to be intensely interested in their bikes.

She eyed him, trying not to look obvious. There were too many shadows, and she could only get a side view. He was wearing a baseball cap pulled low over longish blond hair—and the color didn't look natural. Average height. Maybe a couple inches under six feet. He was also wearing a loose jacket—so she couldn't even guess at his weight. And he had a beard. A full one that started just below the cheekbones. Something about him unnerved her. She rubbed the goosebumps on her arms.

Hiro needed a closer look. She wasn't sure why, but she just knew it. Then again, another part of her wanted to get as far away from the man as possible. Why would he be watching them? She stood and moved toward the window.

The man jammed his hands into his pockets and headed up Broad Street—as if he knew she was onto him.

"Let's go," she said. "I'm freezing."

She caught Coop's eye. He gave her a curious look but obviously knew her well enough not to question her. Not out loud, anyway.

"Let's take it outside," Coop said, standing.

Lunk joined him.

"Are you serious?" Gordy said. "We just got here. What if we want more ice cream?"

Hiro made a beeline for the door. "We'll be back tomorrow."

The man in the baseball cap was already two stores away and walking fast. By the way he carried himself, he looked strong. Solid. The idea of running after him seemed beyond ridiculous. Hiro stopped and watched him, hoping he'd glance back. She wanted him to see that she was onto him.

He jaywalked across Broad Street, never once looking behind him. He reached in his pocket for something. *Keys.* The parking lights of a black pickup parked near Main Street clicked on and off. Could it be the same truck she'd seen at the beach?

Gordy was still whining when he walked out of Scoops. They couldn't ride their bikes while holding ice cream, so they locked their bikes and walked toward the waterfront.

Hiro found a bench where she could keep an eye on the pickup.

"Okay, Hiro," Coop said. "Wanna tell us what that was all about?"

"Did you see that man outside Scoops?" Hiro said. "I have a really weird feeling about the guy."

Lunk took a bite. "He wanted ice cream, just like us."

"Then why not go inside?" Hiro put down her ice cream cup and hugged herself. "I felt like he was ... watching us."

"Maybe you're paranoid," Lunk said. "First, you think you see a murder. Then you don't. And then you think that girl isn't who she claims to be, so the murder theory is back. Now you think a window shopper at Scoops is watching you. Don't you think that's a little . . ." Lunk circled his ear with his forefinger.

Hiro took a deep breath. If she let herself get all frustrated, she wouldn't be able to think clearly. "There's something weird about that guy." She pointed at the pickup. "And why is he just sitting there in his truck?"

"Maybe he's texting someone."

Hiro shook her head. "He's watching."

"He's like a block away," Lunk said.

"Close enough to keep an eye on us."

"Okay, Sherlock," Lunk said. "Or should I call you *Shirley* Holmes?" Taking Hiro's wrists in his hands, he stood and pulled her to her feet. She almost dropped her cup of Chocolate Raspberry Truffle. He backed toward the waterfront, pulling Hiro along with him. "I think you've done enough detective work for one night."

Hiro struggled to break free.

"Look at her thrashing around," Lunk said. "It's like she's addicted to cop work. I think we're getting her away from this just in time."

"Let me go, Lunk!" She pulled against Lunk's grip. "Kryptoski talked to someone in a pickup at the beach. It could be him."

"Half the drivers in Wisconsin drive pickups," Lunk said. "It doesn't mean there's a connection."

The truck rumbled to life. A deep sound. Hiro strained to see. "Let me get his plate number."

Gordy stepped in, blocking her vision. "Oh no you don't. We're on vacation."

Coop was still sitting on the bench, watching the scene unfold with a half-smile on his face.

Hiro growled her frustration. "I'm warning you, boys."

Lunk didn't ease up, but pulled her toward the Riviera's shops and excursion boat docks.

"You will not pull me one more inch." Hiro jerked back hard, hoping her act looked convincing.

Lunk took the bait. He took a wide stance and leaned back.

It was exactly what she'd hoped for. She suddenly rushed toward him. Without her pulling against him, Lunk staggered backward, momentarily off balance. Hiro plowed into him with her whole body.

He let go of her wrist, and his arms flailed in the air for an instant.

Hiro hooked his leg with hers and did her best to give him another push.

Lunk went down hard.

Standing over him, Hiro dug out a spoonful of ice cream and tried to look casual. "Don't mess with me, Lunk. I'm tougher than you are."

Lunk blinked in disbelief—and a grin spread across his face.

"Whoa, Hiro!" Gordy said. "Nice move!"

Hiro spun around. "Out of my way, or you're next."

Gordy raised both hands in surrender. "I'm not stopping you."

Hiro pushed past him and looked for the pickup. It was gone. "Thanks, guys. Real smart. We may have just lost our one lead in this case."

"Case?" Lunk brushed off his camo shorts and walked toward her. "There *is* no case."

Hiro took another bite and smiled. "Not yet."

CHAPTER 12

He backed Black Beauty into a parking stall at The Cove and cut the engine. He was a firm believer that every pickup should have a name. Not just Ford or Chevy, but something that made a statement. Black Beauty was a good fit. Dark as night itself. Able to take him wherever he needed to go—fast. And the thing was gorgeous.

But it wasn't his truck the girl was interested in. She must have suspected something. It was sloppy of him. He'd gotten too close. But he had to be sure. And the boss did want him to send a message, didn't he?

Actually, he was glad he'd been spotted. Because the smallest seed of a scare could grow a whole forest of fear. And fear was his most effective weapon.

He slid out of the pickup and made his way on foot. It was better this way. Besides, he did his best thinking when he was moving. Or driving. Sitting in the truck to wait didn't work for him.

He wouldn't be working for Kryptoski forever. And he was good with that. He was good at cleaning up Kryptoski's dirty diapers too. And this one was a doozy. He didn't hate his work, although his feelings for the boss were an entirely different story. There would be a day of reckoning, though. That thought always made his work easier.

It had been a boring job, for the most part. But his employment might end a lot quicker than he'd expected. Not that he wasn't prepared. He chuckled to himself. They had no idea how ready he was. He had his bugout bag packed and in the bed of the pickup so he could disappear off the grid whenever he sensed the time was right. But the kids had changed things. Now there were more plans to make.

He crossed Center Street and walked through the shadows of Flatiron Park. He leaned against a tree and watched the kids. It was amazing how one small turn of events could suddenly make his job so interesting.

CHAPTER 13

Cooper finished off his ice cream and tossed the cup into the trash can. They still had time before Hiro had to be at the condo. He wandered toward the docks and the others followed.

His parents had taken him to Lake Geneva every summer. He'd grown to love the place.

The weather-worn boards thumped and echoed over the still water as the four of them walked toward the end of the pier.

Gordy threw a stick into the water, shattering the glassy surface. "Are we just going to leave our bikes outside Scoops?"

"They're locked," Cooper said. "And that may give us a chance to test Hiro's theory."

"Oh, come on," Gordy said. "Not you too."

Hiro was all ears. "What are you saying?"

"He's saying," Gordy said, "that he's only kidding. He's messing with you, Hiro."

"Coop?" She gave him a skeptical look.

"Okay, I don't believe some guy was stalking us. It makes no sense. Why would he do that?"

"Agreed," Lunk said.

"But," Coop said, "if someone *were* watching us, he'd be watching our bikes. If we see the guy still hanging around when we come back, Hiro may be onto something."

Gordy leaned against one of the posts. "No matter how stupid it sounds?"

Cooper shrugged.

But Hiro looked satisfied. "At least one of you is willing to take this seriously."

They took their time walking to the end of the pier. Cooper sat on the edge and dangled his feet over the side. Everyone followed his lead except Lunk, who sat cross-legged behind them, right in the middle of the dock.

Hiro scooted closer to Cooper. "There's room here, Lunk."

Lunk shook his head. "I'm okay."

She moved a couple inches more. "C'mon."

Lunk's face looked pale. "I'd rather stay here."

Cooper nudged Hiro, hoping she'd get the message to drop it. Cooper was pretty sure Lunk didn't even want to be on the dock. Either Lunk didn't know how to swim, or he couldn't swim well.

"Beautiful, isn't it?" Hiro pointed at the still water. "The reflections of the lights from town are so inviting. I'd love to go for a swim."

At one time, Cooper would've agreed. But not now. Not tonight. The lights on the surface were fine. The darkness below the surface was what bothered him.

Cooper looked down. The water was black here—like there was no bottom. Suddenly he felt like there was some kind of magnetic pull ... drawing him to it.

"Coop, you okay?" Hiro touched his arm. "You're shaking."

"Am I?" What was it with his nightmarish thoughts? Cooper kept his eyes off the water and scooted away from the edge of the dock.

"It's the ice cream," Gordy said. "Does that to me sometimes. The chill zips right through me."

Hiro didn't take her focus off Cooper. "Coop?"

Cooper stood. "We'd better get you back to the condo, Hiro."

Hiro didn't look happy, but Lunk was already on his feet and walking down the center of the pier toward shore.

Gordy jogged ahead. "Maybe I'll get a refill." He held up his empty ice cream cup.

"They aren't refillable," Hiro said. "You do know that, right?"

Gordy grinned. "So I'll order another one."

Cooper could have guessed that. "What flavor are you getting this time?"

"Yippee Skippee."

Hiro shook her head. "Isn't that what you got the last time?"

Gordy nodded. "You should try it. Sure beats Chocolate Raspberry Duffle."

"It's Chocolate Raspberry Truffle, Gordy," Hiro said. "*Truffle*."

Gordy turned around and continued walking in front of them backward. "Trouble?"

Hiro held up a fist. "That's what you'll get if you keep this up."

Gordy laughed as he turned and jogged toward Scoops. Lunk joined him. Hiro fell in alongside Cooper.

"So, Coop, you were going to talk to me, remember?"

Cooper wasn't so sure he wanted to talk. Not anymore. He wanted to forget it. "No time now." He shrugged. "They'll be back in a couple minutes."

Hiro was silent for a few steps. "Tomorrow," she said firmly, like the whole thing was settled.

But it was far from settled in Cooper's mind. Talking about it would make it official, wouldn't it? She'd think there was something wrong with him. He imagined the way her face would look if he told her. Maybe she'd think he needed a shrink. She'd look at him different for sure. Was he running from reality? Maybe. He just wanted the feeling to go away—wanted to get it out of his mind. Bury it.

The fiasco with the police and Tommy Kryptoski turned out to be a nice distraction. It had kept his mind busy thinking about something other than what was wrong with him. He glanced up and down Broad Street as he crossed, looking for any sign of the pickup. Part of him wished he would see it. That might stop Hiro from thinking about his problem too.

"There." Cooper pointed to a dark blue pickup parked at an angle across the street, just past Main. If someone were sitting inside it, he'd have a perfect view of their bikes. "Is that it?"

Hiro shook her head. "It was black. And it was a Ford, not a Chevy."

Obviously she was checking it out too. She stood at the corner and looked both ways, as if she expected the Ford to materialize.

Hiro had gotten herself spooked with the incident at the beach, and that was messing with her head. Not that Cooper planned to mention it to her. And he couldn't blame her. Not really. He'd been pretty creeped out himself—until the girl showed up at the beach.

The guy outside the ice cream shop hadn't been keeping an eye on them. And he certainly wasn't watching them now. He probably wasn't within two miles. Obviously Lunk and Gordy felt the same way.

"He's close," Hiro said. "Really close." She raised her chin in the air as if she were sniffing him out.

Cooper checked up and down the street. No Ford pickup. He looked at the shop doorways for a bearded guy. Nothing. Hiro had to face the facts.

Gordy was exiting Scoops just as Hiro and Cooper reached the bikes. He had another cup of ice cream in his hand. Lunk was still inside, standing at the counter.

"Yippee Skippee," Gordy said. He took a bite. "Great stuff."

Cooper bent over to unlock the bikes. "What's Lunk getting?"

Hiro peered through the window. "His heart broken."

"What?" Cooper followed her gaze.

"Look at the way he's talking to Katie," she said.

Katie was chatting about something, smiling, waving the scooper around as she talked.

Lunk stood there, mesmerized.

"You're totally wrong." Gordy snickered. "She's way older than him."

Hiro kept watching. "Doesn't mean he can't like her."

"Lunk?" Cooper said. "Maybe he wishes he had a big sister."

"What about me?" Hiro said. "I'm like a sister to him."

Gordy laughed. "Coop said *big* sister."

Lunk looked over his shoulder at them. His face turned red, and he backed away from the counter. Cooper turned away from the shop window and had Lunk's bike ready for him when he came through the door.

The bike was used—but new to Lunk. And sized just right for him. It was a nice change from the one he'd been riding for who knows how many years. But Lunk still had the concrete-filled bat strapped to his bike—just like it had been on his old bike. It had come in pretty handy last May when Gordy was taken. Cooper shuddered. He hoped Lunk would never have to use it again.

Lunk took the bike without a word, his face still glowing.

"Couldn't find anything you liked, Lunk?" Hiro's eyes danced.

He didn't answer.

"Or was she too old?"

Great, Coop thought. Hiro just couldn't let it be.

Lunk glared at her. "Your problem is, you think you're right about everything—even when you're dead wrong."

Hiro shrugged. "We'll see."

Coop smiled. No matter what they threw at Hiro, she had a way of catching it and zinging something right back.

Lunk rolled his eyes at Coop in frustration. He turned back to Hiro. "Aren't you supposed to be at the condo?"

Hiro laughed. "Something tells me we'll be coming to Scoops a lot during this vacation." She waved to Katie through the window. "Yippee Skippee."

Lunk swung a leg over his bike. "I have no idea what you're talking about."

"Nobody does," Gordy said. "Ninety percent of the time, Hiro makes no sense. The other half of the time isn't much better."

Hiro gave him a sideways glance. "That's one hundred and forty percent, Gordy."

Gordy took a bite. "There she goes again."

Hiro slapped her thighs. "I give up."

"Finally." Lunk pushed off and pedaled hard for the condo. Gordy's comment had taken the spotlight off Lunk, and Lunk probably wanted to get moving before Hiro could bring up the topic again. Cooper gave him a little space.

They crossed the bridge by LeatherLips watercraft rentals. Cooper glanced over the railing and down at the jet skis docked in the tiny cove below. They looked like fun.

Hiro was quiet during the short ride to the condo. Was she thinking about the bearded guy in the pickup truck or the murdered girl who turned out to be alive? Or maybe it had something to do with the talk she wanted to have with him. He didn't want to ask.

Lunk cut through Flatiron Park and zoomed up the drive to The Cove. Leaving Hiro at the condo wasn't as easy as Cooper had expected. There were last-minute instructions from his mom, Gordy's mom, and Lunk's mom. *Be careful biking back to the boat. Don't leave the boat once you get out there. Keep your phone on.* Only Hiro's mom didn't add to the advice.

Cooper was afraid the list would keep growing. He looked for his little sister. "Where's Mattie?"

"Already asleep." Mom pointed at the bedroom door. "And remember, if this doesn't work out tonight, we'll have to make some kind of change."

They'd be doing that anyway when Cooper and Gordy's dads joined them for the weekend. Dad was bringing the tent, and they'd camp in the state park. There wouldn't be room on *The Getaway* for all of them.

"We'll be fine," Cooper said. It was time to get out of there before the moms thought up some more warnings. "G'night, everybody." Cooper kissed his mom on the cheek.

Hiro mouthed the words: *Text me.*

Cooper nodded and waved. Minutes later, the three guys were back outside unlocking their bikes.

"Coop!" It was Hiro's voice.

He spotted her standing at the railing of a second-floor balcony.

"You three be careful," she said.

And exactly *what* were they supposed to be careful about? Cooper waved and started pedaling with Lunk and Gordy beside him.

"Don't worry, Hiro!" Gordy called back to her. "We're on vacation!"

Hiro cupped her hands on either side of her mouth. "Just don't take a vacation from your brains!"

But that's exactly what Cooper wanted to do.

CHAPTER 14

Hiro watched the boys pedal out of the parking lot and onto Center Street, where they headed for Wrigley Drive. She wanted to be with them. Really wanted it. Oh, sure, she complained about the guys. It was all part of the game. But there was nobody else she'd rather be with. She couldn't imagine how much fun they were going to have on the boat together. Just the idea of sitting on the bow and looking up at the stars sounded wonderful.

And she'd have a chance to talk to Coop. Get him to open up and tell her what was going on. She'd never seen Coop act the way he had when he surfaced.

If she was on the boat, they'd likely talk about Tommy Kryptoski too. And then there was the whole topic of Pom-Pom. Maybe Hiro was taking things a bit far and letting her imagination — or her desire to be a cop — influence her thinking too much.

She leaned against the railing and heard her mom laughing inside the condo. It was time to join the group. She knew that. But she wanted to stay on the balcony a little longer. But why? It's not like the boys would be coming back for her.

She heard an engine start up somewhere in the parking lot. Deep. Rumbling. A pickup pulled out of a spot and headed for the exit. It was black. It was a Ford. And the driver hadn't turned on his lights yet. Hiro strained to see the license plate. No luck. And from this angle, the truck's roof blocked the driver's face from view.

Was it a coincidence? Or was this the same guy who'd met Kryptoski by the beach? And the same guy outside Scoops?

The truck paused at the parking lot exit.

She worked her phone from her pocket. Should she call Coop? They already thought she was acting paranoid. If she called him now and it turned out to be nothing—she'd never hear the end of it.

But what if the guy really was following the boys? She needed to warn them. Then again, why would anyone be following *them*? They hadn't done anything wrong.

The truck sat there. No blinker. *Make a decision, Hiro.* She bounced her phone in her palm and let her mind spin through her options. If the driver turned away from the lake, she wouldn't make the call. But if he turned toward the lake...

The brake lights blinked off. The truck rolled forward and started its turn. The headlights flicked on, and a switch turned on inside her gut. The driver *was* following the guys. Hands shaking, she dialed Coop.

CHAPTER 15

Cooper hugged the shoulder along Lake Shore Drive as they rode out of town. It was too dark for the lakeshore path now. Occasional streetlights marked the way on what was otherwise a dark stretch. Massive estates lined the road, all with tall hedges, stone walls, and iron fences. The owners were sending a message that they wanted their privacy.

Gordy lagged behind, still working on his ice cream. Lunk rode halfway between them. Keeping up was no longer an issue since Lunk had bought a bigger bike.

"Hiro can get under a guy's skin sometimes," Lunk said. "You know that?"

"Firsthand," Cooper said. When she got something into her head, she couldn't seem to let it go. "She's like a tick that burrows in deep."

Lunk laughed. "Got that right."

Cooper's phone rang, and he checked the number on the screen. "And here she is."

"Probably checking to see if we went back to Scoops," Lunk said. "I was just talking to the girl. I don't know why Hiro made such a big deal of it."

"Because she's Hiro." Cooper connected and swung the phone up to his ear.

"Coop." Hiro's voice sounded rushed. "A black pickup just left the condo parking lot and is headed your way."

The girl was truly taking this too far. Cooper glanced behind him. Gordy was done with his ice cream and finally catching up. No headlights followed them. "The guy from Scoops?"

"It could be. But I couldn't see the driver."

"Hiro ..." How could he tell her how ridiculous she sounded without hurting her feelings?

"I know you think this is really stupid; but if he drives by, just get his license plate number. Would you do that?"

Cooper's mind jumped back to May when he'd tried to remember the minivan plate number after Gordy was kidnapped. Trusting his memory might not be the smartest thing to do.

"Coop?"

He tucked the phone between his shoulder and ear and reached into his pocket. "Just looking for a pen," he said. "I'll write it on my hand."

"Thanks," she said. "That way if he shows up again, we'll know it. I'll prove to you guys that the bearded man is tailing us."

Cooper laughed. "Okay."

"Anything yet?"

Cooper did another shoulder check right as a set of headlights swung around the bend from Baker Street—headed their way.

"Okay, there's a vehicle coming."

The lights crossed the double-striped center line before jerking back into the right lane. Was the driver tired? Texting? The passenger tire dropped off the pavement and rumbled on the gravel for a moment before the driver corrected himself and got the vehicle back where it belonged.

"Coop? What's going on?" Hiro said.

"I think he's drunk," Cooper said. "Call you back."

"Coop, be care— "

Cooper disconnected and checked once more over his shoulder. "Gordy, get off the road! We've got a drunk behind us!"

They all had lights on their bikes, but they wouldn't be much help if the driver was plastered. The vehicle passed under a streetlight. A pickup. Black. And it had the extended mounts on the side mirrors—the type guys use for towing stuff behind the truck.

The truck's right tires dropped onto the gravel shoulder—heading directly for Gordy. "Hit the ditch!"

The driver hit the gas.

"Gordy, move!" Lunk shouted.

Eyes wide, Gordy cut sharply off the road, into the ditch, and up the other side. The pickup barreled past them, swung onto the pavement, and then veered back onto the shoulder again, closing the gap on Lunk.

Standing on the pedals of his bike and pumping hard, Lunk tore through the ditch and plowed into a hedge just as the pickup skinned by him.

Cooper rode through the shallow ditch, but a stone wall blocked him from getting farther out of the truck's way.

The engine roared.

He was trapped.

"Coop!" Lunk shouted. "He's gonna hit you!"

Cooper hugged the stone wall and just missed the rock at every turn of the pedals. The world reeled into slow motion. He saw everything. Heard everything. The gravel churning under the pickup's tires. Close. So very close. Coop's body tensed for the impact that would surely slam him into the ground or crush him against the stone wall.

"Cooooooop!" Lunk's voice sounded distant.

The truck was there—close enough for Coop to touch and moving fast.

An explosion of pain erupted in his left shoulder. Must have been the side view mirror. The impact rocketed him against the stone wall. His bike hit at a sharp angle. Going down...

His mind raced at the speed of light, yet his body still moved in slow-mo. The truck was passing fast, and the ground was coming up to meet Cooper while the wall tore at him along the way.

Cooper saw the truck's tire roll by, mere inches from his head. He hit the ground hard and couldn't breathe. He bounced. Rolled. The truck roared past. He saw the back end for only an instant. The license plate was covered with something. Mud?

As the world returned to warp speed, Cooper rolled over and over before ending up on his side. He saw the taillights of the pickup. Everything was spinning.

"Stupid idiot!" Lunk yelled. He sprinted past Cooper with his concrete-filled Wiffle ball bat in hand and flung the bat at the retreating pickup. It flew end-over-end at a speed that seemed absolutely superhuman. Still, the bat fell short, pitchpoling down the pavement. The driver must have sobered up fast, because he was driving straight as a lance now.

Lunk ran back to Cooper, sliding to his knees in front of him. "You okay?" He leaned in close. "Your head is bleeding. Talk to me, Coop."

Cooper's head felt heavy.

Gordy dropped down beside Lunk. "Coop!"

Cooper closed his eyes. He had to stop the world from spinning.

"Should we call an ambulance?" Gordy said.

No—he was okay. He was okay. Why couldn't he speak?

"Definitely," Lunk said.

I don't need an ambulance, Cooper said. But did he say it out loud?

"Stay with me, amigo," Gordy said.

Cooper struggled to sit up.

Lunk held him in place. "Gordy ... his helmet is split. Make the call."

I'm fine. Coop tried to open his eyes, but they wouldn't open. Almost like they were glued shut.

"Hi, my name is Gordon Digby, and my cousin just got clipped by a drunk driver."

Gordy must be pacing along the road. His voice grew more distant.

"Coop, it's Lunk. Squeeze my hand or something."

The ground stopped rocking. Coop felt a hand holding his. He squeezed it.

"Okay," Lunk said. "Thank God."

It was funny to hear Lunk thank God. He wasn't a believer. Not by any stretch. But he respected Cooper's beliefs. Kind of strange that Cooper was even thinking about that now.

Cooper was lying on his left side with his arm pinned underneath him. It felt prickly. Was it asleep? He could smell the grass, and his head cleared a bit. His shoulder ached, and his head was pounding. He tried to shift his weight ... but he felt so weak.

"We're getting help. Hang in there," Lunk said.

"I'm okay." Cooper opened his eyes. "Just dazed for a second." He tried once more to sit up.

Lunk held him down. "Not until you get checked out. Relax."

Cooper didn't want to be checked out. He wanted to get back on the boat. "No, let's get out of here. If the paramedics come, they'll have to call my mom. Then we'll all be sleeping on the floor of the condo."

"Too late, Coop." Lunk was studying him. "You hit hard. You need to see a doctor."

"They're on their way," Gordy said, squatting down beside him. He pocketed his phone and held up two fingers. "How many fingers am I holding up?"

This was ridiculous. Cooper tried to sit up again, but Lunk didn't let that happen.

"How many fingers?" Gordy said again.

Well, if they weren't going to let him leave, at least he could have some fun with this. Cooper stared at Gordy's hand. "Four."

Gordy glanced at Lunk, and held up four fingers. "How many fingers am I holding up now?"

Cooper made an effort to squint as though he were concentrating. "Eight?"

Gordy froze and his mouth opened slightly, but he didn't say anything.

It's time to finish them off. Cooper looked up at Gordy's face, then over to Lunk, and back to Gordy again. "Who are you guys?"

Gordy's eyes widened. "He's got amnesia!"

CHAPTER 16

Completely out of sight of the kids now, he eased off the accelerator. "Whoa, Beauty. Easy, big fella." He didn't need to speed—and he certainly wasn't about to risk it. The Illinois state line was an easy ten-minute drive from here. But that was too obvious.

He took a quick left on South Street and then another on Wells. He'd double back into town and head to the casino.

He checked his passenger side mirror. It looked okay. He didn't mean to clip the kid—but he wasn't sorry he'd done it either. "Put a little scare into them. Give them something else to think about." Those were his boss's exact words, and that's exactly what he'd done.

The kid would be fine. He was shaken up, no doubt, but no permanent damage. He chuckled as he rolled down the window, stuck his left arm out, and let the warm breeze dry his sweaty palm. He wished he could drive back to the scene and see what was going on. But he could imagine it. Was the kid feeling a cold fear creeping over him yet? Hopefully. And there'd be more to come.

"Watch your back, kid. I'm just getting warmed up."

CHAPTER 17

Hiro sat on the couch with her phone in hand. Her mom was laughing, talking, and joking with the other three moms. They were all having the time of their lives, but Hiro felt miserable.

She couldn't track their conversation and didn't want to. She wanted to be with the boys. Why hadn't Coop texted her yet?

They should have been on the boat by now.

A siren wailed in the distance, and a sick feeling gripped her. She went out on the balcony to text Coop again. The night air was cool. Typical for late August in Wisconsin.

The siren rode the airwaves easily as the sound circled Hiro's head. Echoing. She tried to get a fix on its position.

Just then a police car raced down Center Street—its lights flashing but no siren—and it was headed toward Lake Shore Drive.

"God, no," Hiro whispered.

She dialed Coop's phone this time, but it went right to voicemail. Hiro disconnected and stared over the balcony. Should she say something to her mom? To Coop's mom?

But what did Hiro know? Nothing. Yet her heart told her something different.

The siren stopped wailing, but another one started up

somewhere in the distance. And it sounded like it was headed in the same direction. Not good. Pacing the balcony, Hiro worked her Chicago Police star necklace between her thumb and forefinger and checked her phone again.

Thumbs flying, Hiro tapped in Gordy's number. She heard the phone ring. "C'mon, Gordy. Pick up."

When Gordy's phone went to voicemail, she disconnected and growled in frustration. Something had happened, and Hiro knew that black pickup was involved.

She couldn't call Lunk because he still didn't have a phone, and she'd given up on trying to sell him on the idea.

Suddenly her phone rang and Cooper's picture smiled at her from the display screen. "Coop!" She pressed the phone against her ear. "What took you so long? I heard the sirens." She stopped. No sense telling him how worried she really was.

"Ah, no, Hiro. It's not Coop. It's Lunk."

Hiro froze. "What happened?"

"There's been an accident," Lunk said.

"No!" It came out more like a wail. "Is Coop okay?"

Lunk paused.

"Lunk!"

"Yeah, I think so."

"You *think* so?"

"The paramedics are checking him out right now."

CHAPTER 18

Lunk sat in the waiting room of the ER and watched the others from a distance. The initial frenzy had calmed. The doctor had been out to assure Coop's mom and the rest of them that Coop was going to be fine. No signs of a concussion, thanks to the helmet. His right shoulder was bruised, and so was his right leg, thanks to the fall after the truck clipped him. But there were no broken bones. Scrapes and shallow cuts—nothing more serious.

Coop's amnesia act had Lunk going for a minute. Lunk smiled to himself. Coop was going to be okay. But Lunk didn't deserve any thanks for that. His smile faded.

He was Coop's bodyguard—not that Coop knew it. But it was a commitment he'd made a year ago after Coop saved his hide at Frank 'n Stein's Diner. The restaurant's co-owner, Joseph Stein, had trapped them inside the restaurant, but Coop's quick thinking saved their lives. Somehow Lunk would find a way to return the favor.

Yet it seemed like Coop kept saving Lunk's life instead. First of all, he'd pulled Lunk into his little group of friends. And for a guy like Lunk, who'd never really had friends before, this was huge.

Lunk tried to be there for Coop. He really tried. But he hadn't exactly been successful. Three months ago, he'd almost lost Coop when his friend pulled a "Lone Ranger" after Gordy's abduction.

And now he'd failed to protect Coop again. *Why did that truck miss me and not Coop? Why did I escape while Coop crashed into that lousy stone wall?*

Coop could have been killed, and Lunk wouldn't have been able to stop it. Some bodyguard he was.

Hiro walked over. "Hey."

Lunk nodded. He didn't feel like talking.

She studied his face. "You're bleeding. You should get looked at too."

"It's just a few scratches. I plowed into some nasty bushes. I'm okay."

"Hmmm." She walked toward the women's restroom.

A minute later, Hiro was back with some wet paper towels. She folded up one of them and dabbed at his face.

"Forget it, Hiro. I'm o ... kay." He overemphasized the word hoping she'd get the message.

Hiro pressed her finger on one of the scratches.

He jerked away from her. "Ouch! What are you doing?"

"Proving that you're not *o . . . kay*." She smiled slightly. "Now sit still and let me help, or else I'll do that again."

Hiro had a way of making him want to tear his hair out.

She wiped his cheek some more. "What's on your mind, Lunk? What are you thinking about?"

Like he was going to tell *her*. He was feeling closer to Gordy and Hiro, thanks to Cooper. But opening up wasn't exactly his style. Not about this, anyway.

"Going to make me guess?" Hiro held the paper towel in front of him so he could see the blood. "You're thinking about that pretty girl in Scoops. Wishing you were a little older."

Lunk smiled. "You're losing your touch, Hiro. I thought you could read minds."

"I can," she said. "When I want to."

"Well, you're not doing such a great job right now."

Hiro pressed on one of his scrapes.

He winced. "Hey, watch it."

"It's not smart to insult a girl when she's helping you." She moved to the other side of his face. "I saw you brooding over here. What is it?"

"You tell me, mind reader."

Hiro looked at him.

He looked at the floor.

"You're thinking I was right. That you should have listened to me when I thought that guy in the pickup was watching us." She ducked her head a little lower so she could look into his eyes. "And you want to tell me that you'll listen to me next time. Am I getting warm?" She dabbed at a scratch on his chin and raised his head at the same time.

Lunk smiled. She was really laying it on thick. "Stone cold."

She nodded like she knew that. "I'm giving you a chance to tell me yourself."

"Right." He laughed slightly. She was fishing.

Hiro tilted her head to the side. "Okay. How's this? You were beating yourself up about what happened to Coop. You feel like you failed him somehow."

He stared at her for a moment.

One corner of her mouth turned up. "Am I getting warmer?"

He shrugged. If she expected him to admit it that she was right, then she was truly delusional.

"You didn't let anybody down. You're a good friend to him, Lunk. To all of us."

Lunk stared at the floor again.

She tapped his forehead. "I know what's going on in there, big guy."

Tough. Stubborn. Maddening. A tongue that could cut like a razor—or heal, depending on her mood. Hiro was all of that and more. And he had the feeling she'd known all along what he'd been thinking. Her first two guesses were just her way of playing with him, getting him to lower his guard. Which meant there was another word he could use to describe her.

Spooky.

CHAPTER 19

Cooper sat on the bow of *The Getaway*. It had to be way past midnight. He didn't want to know what time it was. It had been the longest day—but he still felt wired.

There would be no more riding into town or back after dark. At least not on the road. Mom had laid down the law on that one.

He could understand that rule, really, even though he didn't like it. He was lucky his mom was letting them stay on the boat tonight. Of course, there weren't any other great options with the size of the condo.

Still, Mom could have figured out *some* way to keep the boys closer. But to her, this was all about a drunk driver. So she probably thought the safest place in the world was on the boat.

And that's all it had been, right? A drunk who just happened to almost kill Cooper. It wasn't his first brush with death. There'd been that narrow escape with Gordy and Hiro after they'd witnessed a robbery at Frank 'n Stein's Diner. That almost got him killed.

Joseph Stein—now *ex*-partner of Frank Mustacci—had borrowed money from the wrong people to pay off his gambling debts. Did he realize that loan shark was up to his gills in organized crime? Maybe not at first. But when he was late with his payment—he found out in a hurry. So to save his own hide, Stein worked out a little payment plan with the loan collectors. The plan was simple: He set up Frank 'n Stein's to be robbed by some mob muscle on a night when Frank was closing up the restaurant. The robbery was supposed to wipe the slate clean, but Stein never expected Frank to fight back. And he definitely didn't expect the incident to escalate into attempted murder—or for there to be witnesses.

Stein got a chance to clean up his mess when he trapped Cooper and Lunk with the intention of silencing them for good. But Stein messed up again, a fact for which Cooper would be forever grateful. God bailed out Cooper that night, and Lunk too. And that experience had forged a loyalty and friendship between Lunk and him that had been getting stronger ever since.

Cooper wasn't the only one who escaped that night. Stein made a clean getaway and hadn't resurfaced since. Probably because he was wearing concrete cowboy boots at the bottom of some pond. While the police still hadn't found Stein, Cooper suspected that the guy Stein owed money to had, and he'd probably made sure that Stein would stay quiet—permanently.

Cooper's mind went back to the bizarre fact that he'd had so many close calls. His third brush with death—this time in a flooding basement—had happened after Gordy was abducted back in May. If Cooper was like a cat with nine lives, then he was going through them way too fast. He'd used up at least three of them. Maybe four now, thanks to this drunk driver incident.

And what about that feeling of death he'd experienced after pulling off the stinking-fish prank on Tommy Kryptoski? But that was just a feeling, right? He wasn't in any real danger ... was he?

Cooper shuddered and looked out over the lake. The water appeared as black as it had been inside that flooding basement, and just as deadly. All he wanted was a chance to escape all of that. Forget about his fears. Forget about his recent scrapes with death. But then tonight he'd had *another* scare. Not as bad as the others—not nearly as bad. Still, it wasn't the best way to start a vacation that he'd hoped would help him forget.

"Coop?"

Gordy's voice almost made Cooper jump over the bow.

"Do you think you should be out here—all alone, I mean?"

Did Gordy's concern have to do with whatever had happened to Cooper under the water earlier? Or maybe he thought the hit from the pickup might still be affecting him.

"I'm just thinking," Cooper said.

"Well, why don't you think inside the cabin instead?" Gordy said. "What if you get dizzy and fall over the rail?"

Now there was a comforting thought.

"I'm working on a plan for a new prank. I'll tell you about it inside."

Cooper shook his head. "That last one had some flaws." The argument aboard *Krypto Night* hadn't been a part of the plan. But something unexpected always seemed to happen. And truthfully, the idea of pulling more pranks wasn't really doing it for Cooper. Not like it once had.

"This plan still has a few kinks in it," Gordy said. "But I'll get 'em all worked out. This one's a total knockout. A good prank will get you feeling better—pronto."

Cooper stood and winced at the sudden pain in his shoulder. He skirted the windshield and followed Gordy below. He wasn't in the mood to talk about pranks. But joining the others inside might be a good idea. Maybe the bright cabin would get his mind off his dark thoughts.

Lunk was sitting at the table in the cabin—and he was wearing a lifejacket. All four nylon straps were buckled tight. Okay, so Lunk didn't like the water. But obviously his fear went deeper than that.

Cooper's camping lantern sat in the center of the table, giving them all the light they needed.

"I still feel this thing rocking," Lunk said. "And it's calm outside. Doesn't the boat ever settle down?"

Gordy laughed. "There's always waves. Currents. Even when it's calm. This is nothing. Wait 'til we get a storm."

Lunk shot Cooper a concerned look. "We'd stay in the boat during a storm?"

Cooper shrugged. "The boat can handle it."

Lunk didn't look so sure.

"So, picture this," Gordy said. "We prank the mailboat—aka the *Walworth II*." He grinned like he expected Cooper to get all excited.

"Picture this," Cooper said. "The three of us handcuffed and standing in front of a judge. You're talking about messing with government business."

"We won't touch the mail. But the mail jumper—the girl who jumps off the boat to drop the mail in the box—we delay her just a bit so she can't get back on board." He patted the table. "This is the pier at The Geneva Inn. If we slow her down just right"—he used two fingers to simulate the mail jumper and his other hand to represent the boat cruising by the pier—"she'll miss the boat and go for a swim." He ran his fingers to the end of the table, made them jump—and miss.

Cooper imagined a mail jumper leaping for the boat and falling short. Another girl in the water—just like earlier tonight. No way he wanted to see that happen. "She could get hurt."

"It'll be safe," Gordy said. "I want to scout out the *Walworth II* and work out some details. You interested?"

"Not a bit."

"I'll take that as a maybe," Gordy said. "How about you, Lunk? You in?"

Lunk sat there for a moment as if picturing the whole thing in his head. "If Coop's out, I'm out."

Gordy laughed. "I'll work out some details. You'll both love this."

"Don't count on it." There was no way Gordy was going to change Cooper's mind on this.

The cabin got quiet.

Cooper's mind was on the pickup again. It had been a close call. Really close. If the truck had veered just a little more, he would have been plastered against that stone wall, his body turned into some kind of mortal mortar, filling in the cracks and crevices between the stones.

"Anybody up for a creepy story?" Gordy said.

Cooper was trying to get his mind off of one.

"They say that years ago—like out West—people got buried when they weren't even dead."

Cooper smiled. This was one of Gordy's favorites.

"Right," Lunk said.

"Seriously! They didn't embalm people like they do now, so lots of times they'd bury someone in a pine box the same day he died. Only some of the people weren't dead. They were in a coma or something."

Lunk snorted. "And how on earth would they know that?"

Cooper shook his head. Lunk was walking right into this.

"Because," Gordy paused, "decades later—maybe when a new road was being built or something—the workers would dig up these old graves and find claw marks on the *inside* of the coffins."

"Like the guy woke up and was trying to get out?" Lunk said. "That's sick. It's always a good idea to be sure that whatever you bury is really dead—or else it might come back."

Gordy nodded. "Exactly. Unless we're talking about zombies. I mean, if you bury a zombie, you'd better bury it deep because you know it's going to claw its way out eventually."

"Zombies," Lunk said. "Ridiculous."

"Are they?" Gordy said, his eyes wide as if he'd seen one. "*Are* they?"

Here we go. Cooper had heard Gordy's zombie stories before on campouts and overnights. Gordy *loved* telling stories, and he always managed to scare himself somehow. But right now the thought of zombies, or bodies somehow rising, was kind of creeping Cooper out too.

A set of rogue waves made the boat dip and rock as they passed.

Lunk gripped the table with both hands. "What is *that* all about?"

"A boat probably passed by," Cooper said.

Lunk didn't let go of the table. "I didn't hear a motor."

"Zombies," Gordy whispered. "Bodies of the undead rising from the bottom of the lake."

Cooper didn't want to hear any more. It was too real. Too fresh. He'd felt something so evil, so dark, under the water. He did *not* want to think about it. "The other boat could be out in the middle of the lake, so we'd never hear it," Cooper said. "It takes time for the waves to travel to shore."

Lunk nodded.

Coop wondered if Lunk was going to wear that lifejacket while he slept tonight—if he'd even be able to sleep. And with the pain in his shoulder and the thought of zombies lurking under the boat, Cooper wasn't so sure he'd be sleeping either.

CHAPTER 20

Gordy woke early Monday morning and dragged himself out of the cramped cabin bed. Actually, *berth* was the correct term for a bed on a boat. While Gordy had scraped and painted the boat with Coop and Uncle Carson, he'd learned all kinds of funny names for things on boats. Bathrooms were *heads*. The right side of the boat was *starboard*; the left was *port*. The front of the boat was the bow, and the back was the *stern*. The back wall was the *transom*. The floor was the *deck*, but the boat itself was the *hull*. And that was only the beginning. If you tied a boat to a buoy and anchor, the spot was now called a *mooring*. It was like a whole new language.

Outside on the deck, Gordy stretched and rummaged through the ice chest for something to eat.

Widgets. Deep-fried biscuit dough covered with sugar or cinnamon sugar, widgets were like donut holes, only bigger—and better. Coop's mom had picked up two bags of them yesterday afternoon from the Dari-Ripple in Walworth at the far end of the lake.

Gordy grabbed the remaining bag and stuffed a widget in his mouth. Not quite as amazing as when it was fresh out of the deep fryer, but it was still really good.

Only a few fishing boats dotted the horizon. No sign of the

mailboat yet. It was probably way too early. A rough plan had taken shape in his mind, but he wanted to see the boat in action before telling Coop and Lunk about it. And he hoped to do it before Hiro joined them. She'd try to squelch the whole idea. Especially after what happened with *Krypto Night*.

The green wakeboard boat was still out there, tied to its buoy like it had been last night. But a canvas tarp covered the boat now, and the only ones aboard were a half-dozen seagulls. Flying rats, really. They'd already turned the boat into their personal outhouse. Gordy smiled. Another mess for Tommy Kryptoski to clean up.

Gordy wanted to go for a swim, but he didn't feel like getting wet. He eyed the inflatable raft. Grabbing a water-ski towrope, he tied one end to the raft and wrapped the other end through a metal loop-thingy bolted near the stern. Minutes later, he was lying on his back inside the inflatable, floating seventy-five feet behind *The Getaway*.

This was living. Especially since he'd thought ahead and brought the widgets with him. Dark clouds glided overhead as though they were looking for picnics to rain on or freshly washed cars. As Gordy drifted on the lake, he noodled through more details of his mailboat prank.

Simplicity was the key. Fewer chances for errors that way. And it all came down to timing. If he could delay the mail jumper long enough, she'd miss the boat. But for how long and how would he do it? The balance would be tricky. Too short a delay, and she'd hop back on the boat without a problem. Too long, and she wouldn't jump at all. She'd wait until the boat circled around to pick her up. Where was the fun in that?

He could tie the door of the mailbox shut. But that would take her too long to open. Tape might be smarter. Not too much. Just enough to delay her. Make her tug at the door a couple times. Yeah, taping it shut would be better. And maybe he'd leave a dead fish for her inside the box too.

He popped the last widget into his mouth and brushed the

sugar off his hands and into the water. His plan would work. He was sure of it.

What he needed was a pair of binoculars so he could get a little intel on the mailboat—how much of a delay he'd need to put the mail jumper into the water. He rolled onto his stomach and used the towrope to pull himself back to *The Getaway*. He climbed onto the swim platform and let the inflatable drift. It couldn't go far. The towrope bunched up around the stern of the boat. There was no point cluttering up the back deck with it anyway.

Still no sign of Coop or Lunk. Gordy pulled out a large toolbox Coop's dad had loaded on board. The lid had a waterproof seal, and he flipped open the latches to get the binoculars.

Uncle Carson's dive knife was right on top of the bundled nylon dock lines. Gordy slid the knife from its sheath. Black rubber grip. Six-inch stainless steel blade with a wicked-looking edge, slightly curved tip, and a serrated edge for sawing. Part of him wanted to strap that baby on his leg and go for a swim. Instead he sheathed it, laid it on the deck, and pulled the dock lines out of the box.

Gordy pulled the binoculars out of the leather case, looked through them, and adjusted the focus. He slung them around his neck.

Below the binoculars sat a bundle of light sticks. They could come in handy during a night swim. Next to them, a molded plastic case. Gordy opened it and stared. A flare gun with six rounds of ammo.

"My kind of toolbox," Gordy said. He carefully removed the orange gun and made sure the chamber was empty. Some night, they definitely had to shoot that thing over the lake—though the chances of that happening were pretty remote if Hiro had anything to say about it. And she would. They'd have to do it after she was back at the condo.

He put the flare gun back into its case. At the bottom of the toolbox, he found a single key attached to a nylon string holding a jumbo red-and-white fishing bobber. "Jackpot." Gordy smiled.

So that's where Uncle Carson kept the spare ignition key for *The Getaway*. Good to know. But there was only one way to be sure.

He grabbed the key and tiptoed to the console. He checked the door to the cabin below. Still no sign of Coop or Lunk. He slid the spare key into the slot on the dashboard. It fit perfectly. He looked at the vintage instrument panel—at the chrome stick levers for forward, reverse, and speed for each of the twin engines.

He stared at the key hanging from the ignition slot. The bobber swung with a teasing rhythm, like it was daring him to turn the key and start the engines just to hear how they sounded.

Gordy backed away from the instrument panel and ducked inside the cabin. Coop was still zonked out. And with the pain meds he was on, he'd be sleeping deep. Maybe he wouldn't even notice. Besides, Gordy would do this really quick.

Gordy reached for the dash—and a moment later the engines rumbled to life. The vibration under his feet felt good. He resisted the urge to rev the motors. He sat in the captain's chair and eased the control lever into reverse. The transmission whined as the boat crept backward, slowly, like an elephant backing up in a circus ring. Gordy was the trainer. The boat pulled against the buoy line in front. *Easy, Dumbo. Good elephant.* Gordy shifted into neutral—then inched the gearshift forward until the buoy line went slack.

A total rush. He couldn't imagine how good it would feel to actually drive *The Getaway*. He turned the engines off and pulled the key from the slot just as Cooper climbed out from the cabin, rotating his bad shoulder.

"Is my dad here?"

Gordy laughed. "That was me, you idiot." He dropped the bobber into the toolbox. "I found the spare key."

Cooper looked fully awake now. "Are you out of your mind?" He latched the toolbox and stowed it. "I can't believe you just did that."

Lunk stepped out on deck, squinting. He was still wearing his camo shorts, black T-shirt, and the lifejacket.

Gordy raised his hands in mock surrender. "It won't happen again. I was just checking it out. No harm done."

Cooper smiled. "It sure sounded good, didn't it?" He looked around. "Where's the inflatable?"

Gordy pointed. "I've got everything under control." He grabbed the towrope and started pulling the inflatable in. But the rope seemed to be snagged on something under the boat.

Cooper must have seen it too. He climbed over the stern to the swim platform and traced the line to the water. He pulled. It didn't move.

"Tell me you didn't put the boat in gear," Cooper said. "Tell me you didn't run over the rope and get it wrapped around the prop."

Gordy got a sick feeling in his stomach. He shrugged. "Oops."

CHAPTER 21

Cooper tugged on the line. It didn't budge. "I'll need a mask," he said.

"On it," Gordy said.

The moment Cooper raised his arms to pull off his T-shirt, pain shot through his left shoulder. He lowered his arms and worked his shoulders in small circles, trying to loosen them up.

A moment later, Gordy was back with two masks. "I'll go with you." He climbed over the rail and joined Cooper on the platform.

"Help me get this T-shirt off, would you?"

Gordy gave him a hand and let out a low whistle. "That's one ugly bruise."

"Gee, thanks, Gordy." Cooper really wanted to forget the whole thing. The bruised shoulder wasn't going to make that easy.

Lunk watched from the rail. "How bad does it hurt?"

"Probably not as bad as it looks," Cooper said. "It's just sore. And stiff."

Lunk nodded, but he didn't look at all relieved.

Gordy had his mask in place and stepped off the edge of the platform, disappearing into a splash of water and bubbles.

Cooper adjusted his mask, took it off, rinsed it, and put it back on again.

Gordy surfaced. "You gonna do this?"

The truth was, Cooper didn't know *what* he was doing. Thoughts of yesterday's episode under the water were still messing with his head.

Gordy ducked below and swam under the boat.

Cooper wanted to do that. He wanted to snorkel and swim underwater like he'd always done before. Instead, he squatted down and peered over the lip of the swim platform.

Gordy was back again, treading water. "Coop—what's wrong with you?"

"Nothing." Cooper sat on the edge of the platform and eased himself into the water without getting his head wet. He took a fresh grip on the platform, took a couple of deep breaths, and put his face into the water. He could see the bottom and felt no signs of panic. Okay, this was good. Really good. He let go of the platform, treaded water on the surface for a moment, then went totally under, feet first. He was fine. He could do this. Whatever was wrong with him before didn't seem to be a problem now. He surfaced for a fresh breath of air, nodded to Gordy, and went under.

Gordy dove under at the same time, and together they inspected the propellers and rudder. A warning went off in Cooper's head. Just being so close to the props was a little creepy, even though they weren't moving. If the engine were suddenly turned on, they'd be sliced to ribbons.

The towrope was twisted around one of the propellers and shaft. Cooper reached over and pulled. It felt like steel cable—stretched tight. Without any slack in the line, there was no way to untangle it. He motioned to Gordy and surfaced.

"We'll have to cut it."

Gordy lifted his mask to his forehead. "Sorry about that, Coop. Think your dad will be mad?"

Cooper shook his head. "He'll be fine." He looked up at Lunk. "My dad's dive knife is in the toolbox. Can you grab that?"

A minute later Cooper and Gordy were back under the hull,

sawing away at the ropes. It was slow going. Cooper held on to the propeller shaft, the knife in his other hand. Gordy kept pulling the rope away as Cooper cut to expose the next layer. The exertion burned his oxygen supply fast. He signaled to Gordy, and they kicked back to the surface for another breath.

"Got it?" Lunk looked over the rail.

"Getting there," Cooper said.

Cooper and Gordy went under again. Cut and clear. Cut and clear. Then back to the surface. "One more time," Cooper said.

Gordy nodded. "Let's do it."

Cooper cut the last few strands of rope from the propeller and shaft. Gordy swished them away and flashed a thumbs-up sign.

Cooper gave it one more look, making sure the strands were far enough away not to get tangled again. He nodded at Gordy, and the two of them swam under the platform and surfaced on the other side.

"All clear." Cooper hiked himself onto the swim platform and handed the knife to Lunk. He felt energized somehow.

Gordy coiled up what was left of the rope and retied the inflatable to a metal, oblong cleat. "What do we have to eat around here? I'm starving."

"Me too," Cooper said. "We still have a bag of widgets."

"Oops." Gordy shrugged. "I think they're gone. What else do we have?"

Cooper had a feeling Gordy knew exactly where the widgets went. "Check the ice chest in the cabin for milk and juice. We've got boxes of cereal in the cupboard, with bowls and stuff." Three guys could live for a couple of weeks on all the food Mom had stocked on the boat. Which meant that with Gordy aboard, they had enough to make it to the weekend. Maybe.

Cooper toweled off and climbed over the stern rail. He felt like celebrating. He'd gone underwater without a single twinge of fear. Whatever it was that had been bothering him was now history. He wanted to believe that—but deep down he knew better. Maybe the impact that had busted his bike helmet had also reset some kind of default setting in his head. If that's what it took to get rid of his fear, the trip to the ER was totally worth it.

Gordy was banging around inside the cabin.

Cooper glanced at Lunk. "How 'bout some breakfast?"

Lunk was staring toward the beach. He didn't seem to be focused on any one thing. "Go ahead. I'll be there in a minute."

Something was definitely weighing on Lunk's mind. What guy would delay breakfast, even for a minute, if he didn't have to? Had Cooper done the right thing in inviting Lunk along? Their friendship had grown in the last few months. And Lunk was fitting in really well with Gordy and Hiro. But maybe this vacation was too far out of Lunk's comfort zone. While Gordy loved the water as much as Cooper did, Lunk was a different story. Did he actually sleep in that lifejacket? Sure he did. Lunk would rather be on the beach than on the boat. He'd probably do better camping this weekend. But even that might be a problem, because Gordy's and Cooper's dads would be there. Would that be one more painful reminder of what Lunk was missing?

Cooper ducked through the hatch and joined Gordy in the cabin. He wanted Lunk to be here on this vacation. He really did. But he wasn't so sure Lunk felt the same way.

CHAPTER 22

Lunk looked out over the water. More boats were on the lake now. A couple of jet skis were pounding toward the north shore. The houses along the water looked like palaces. The beach was empty, but it was still early in the day. No matter where he looked, this was a different world.

People here were all about luxury. Fancy boats. Jet skis.

Lunk was about being practical and careful with his money. His mom had basically forced him to buy the new bike. New to him, anyway.

But he had to be careful, didn't he? Mom was happier now than he'd seen her in years. They both loved the fact that they were buying a house. Settling in someplace, in a town where they both had real friends. Lunk just had to do his part to make sure they didn't lose what they had.

Maybe the question that was bothering him was a little closer to home. Yeah, he had friends—for the first time in his life. Coop. Hiro. Gordy. And he needed them. More than they knew. More than he'd ever admit. Maybe he needed them more than they needed him—a possibility that gnawed at him.

What did he really bring to the group, anyway? Coop was the leader. That was easy. Hiro was the heart. The conscience. She kept all of them in line. Gordy was the court jester, maybe. But he was also a peacemaker. He always wanted to keep them together.

But where was Lunk's place? What was his contribution? If a person doesn't bring some sort of value to the table, pretty soon he won't be invited to eat there anymore. Was he just a guest? Somebody they were reaching out to? Like some kind of Christian service project? *Hey, let's be nice to the kid whose dad walked out on him.*

So was Lunk just a charity case to the others? Did they need him—really need him—for anything? He wanted to be a protector here too, just like he was at home. And the truth was, they needed some protection. But he hadn't done so well last night. Coop could have been killed, and Lunk was powerless to stop it. Instead, he'd run for cover and plowed his bike right into that hedge. *Nice contribution to the team, Lunk.*

Did Lunk bring anything to the group? No. The answer was just as obvious, just as overwhelming as the water that surrounded him. It was only a matter of time until the others figured it out.

CHAPTER 23

He'd parked Beauty a couple of blocks away from the library. It was still early, but there was no sense in taking any chances. A public library was a wonderful place where a guy could find just about any information he needed. And the little Google search he'd been doing had proven to be even more successful than he'd hoped.

He drummed his fingers on the desk and looked at the diagrams on the computer screen. All the specs he needed on *The Getaway* were right here. And it looked like he wouldn't have to spend a dime for tools or supplies. He already had everything he'd need to do the job.

He studied the line drawings of the stern of the boat. At the bottom of the transom, just below the waterline, there was a threaded plug. It was designed to drain all the water from under the floorboards when the boat was up on a hoist. But it would be just as effective for letting water in. It would be silent. Quick. Clean.

He scrolled and looked at more detailed drawings. The hatch going into the cabin interested him—and one more component of his plan clicked into place.

Just to be safe, he'd need to get on board. He had to be absolutely certain Plan A would work before he launched it. When the big moment came, he wouldn't have time to figure out a Plan B.

And checking the boat would provide another opportunity to spread a little fear. He could kill two birds with one stone. But he'd need to get on board today—without cover of darkness. He had to be ready to put his master plan into action if this whole thing with Kryptoski imploded. And the way he saw it ... that could happen sooner than anyone thought.

CHAPTER 24

Hiro stood on the balcony and looked at the lake sparkling in the sunlight. What were the guys doing? She resisted the urge to text them; she didn't want to be annoying. What she really wanted was for Cooper to text her. Start things rolling. She checked her phone again. Nothing.

She loved being with the women. She really did. It was a nice change of pace to have a mature conversation. But she wanted to be back with the guys even more. Coop's mom had talked to him earlier and relayed a good report. Coop had slept okay. He was sore but not as bad as he figured he'd be.

But Coop also had a way of hiding what was really bothering him. Or he'd downplay it so others wouldn't feel bad. Well, Hiro would feel better when she saw him for herself.

The women were going to the outlet malls in Kenosha. Any other morning, that might have sounded fun. But not when the guys would be having adventures at the lake.

Would the incident last night change the vacation for them? Would the guys do everything they really wanted to do—or would Coop be in too much pain? Then again, what did Coop really want from this vacation?

Gordy was easy to figure out—he was all about the fun. And

Coop almost seemed to be riding the same rails. He acted like he wanted to have fun just like Gordy. Or was the fun just a way of keeping himself distracted?

And then there was Lunk. He was a complete mystery. What did he really want? She'd have to think on that one a bit. It would be a challenge.

And what do you *want, Hiro?* She hated it when she asked herself tough questions. Before this vacation, the answer would have been easy. She wanted to hang out with her best friends. Have fun. Slip her mind into neutral and coast for two weeks before school started.

And there were deeper things, weren't there? Like the fear that high school was going to change things between them. What if they drifted apart? They'd be in different classes. Meet new friends. Coop had reached out to her when they'd moved to Rolling Meadows after her dad died. He and Gordy had been the best friends she could ever hope for. Then Coop pulled Lunk into their circle. Even though Hiro hadn't liked the idea at first, now she couldn't imagine the group without him.

But what if Coop got sucked into a different world of friends—one that made Hiro feel like an outsider? Ridiculous. It made no sense to worry about the future. The important thing was to just enjoy her friends now, like she'd intended to do all along.

But after last night, something had changed. If she had witnessed a murder, she might be the only one who could stop the killer. How could she have a good time and ignore the fact that something awful might have happened to that girl? Wasn't finding the truth more important than any vacation plans? The boys seemed content with Lynn's story. Hiro wasn't ready to buy into it. Not yet.

Hiro's mom joined her on the balcony. "Are you sure you want to hang out with the guys today?"

Hiro nodded. "You won't feel like I'm ditching you, will you?"

Mom put her hands on Hiro's shoulders. "Not at all. I want you to have a good time." She handed Hiro some money. "For lunch."

Hiro gave her a hug.

She kissed Hiro on the forehead. "I'll give you a ride to the beach after I finish getting ready."

It seemed to take her mom forever. At least the delay would give her time to process yesterday's events. Day one of their vacation had started with a bang. There was Coop's bizarre behavior in the water. And then the whole thing with Tommy Kryptoski and Pom-Pom Girl.

Did they simply witness an argument—or was it a murder? Was the guy outside the ice cream shop the same guy who talked to Kryptoski at the park entrance? And if there was a connection there, what did it all mean? What about Cooper's accident? Was it a drunk driver or someone trying to scare them? And why would somebody want to do that?

Every time Hiro reviewed what she knew, she felt a nagging doubt that there were any connections at all. She was playing a dangerous game, at least when it came to being a good investigator. She was trying to connect too many dots when there wasn't nearly enough evidence. She was trying to take unrelated pieces of fabric and make something out of them. A prison uniform, to be exact. And she wanted to see Tommy Kryptoski wearing it.

CHAPTER 25

Cooper hadn't gotten a moment's rest since Hiro got on the boat. She kept watching him like she thought he was hiding something. He deliberately took the binoculars up to the bow of the boat, just to see if she'd follow him.

He focused on a dark blue-and-white wakeboard boat cruising along the shoreline. A man stood smiling in the open bow, coiling a rope. The boat had nice lines. The name *Axis* was written on the side. Cooper wasn't sure if that was the name of the boat or a brand name. Two young families were inside. He spotted two toddlers wearing lifejackets and one set of happy-looking grandparents. A little girl was helping grandpa drive the boat. Nice. Safe.

Hiro sat beside him. "Feel like talking?"

"Aha," he said. "I was right."

Hiro looked confused. "About what?"

Cooper shook his head and smiled. "It doesn't matter. What do you want to talk about?"

"Actually, you wanted to talk to *me*. Last night on the way to the beach, remember?"

How could he forget? "I'm doing better now. I'm okay."

"Coop." She paused like she was trying to pick her words carefully. "Something happened to you in the water after you planted those fish on *Krypto Night*. Something terrified you when you went underwater."

There was no denying it.

"What did you see?"

Did she think he'd seen the creature from the Black Lagoon or something? Cooper took a deep breath and let out a sigh. "Nothing. Just darkness. I couldn't see the bottom."

She stared at the water. "So you sensed something? Maybe something in the water?"

Cooper shrugged. "I thought I was going to die. I can't explain it—but I've never felt anything like it before. I don't even know how I got back into the inflatable boat."

Hiro picked at her braid. Processing, no doubt.

"But whatever it was, it's gone now," Cooper said. "A towrope got caught under the boat this morning. Gordy and I had to free it from the prop."

She just looked at him.

"I went underwater and I was okay. Just like normal."

"No feeling like you were going to die?"

Cooper shook his head. "Not a hint."

"I still think you should talk it out more," Hiro said slowly, "Something triggered that ... attack."

That was a good word for it. It had been a *surprise* attack—hard and sudden. No warning. "Maybe there was a full moon last night or something." Cooper tried to laugh, but it sounded hollow, even to him.

"You bring up an excellent point," she said. "It was nearly night then—at least, the water was dark. Maybe that's why it didn't happen again today."

"Because I could see?"

Hiro shrugged.

That wasn't exactly what he'd wanted to hear. Whatever the problem was, he wanted it to be gone. History. He didn't want it affecting him day *or* night. But Hiro's words struck a chord. He knew he hadn't seen the end of it.

"Hey, guys," Gordy stepped around the narrow walkway to the bow. "Krypto and his girlfriend are back." He pointed toward the shore.

Cooper welcomed the interruption. He didn't want to talk about his water phobias anymore. He followed Gordy to the stern of the boat. Tommy Kryptoski was walking along the beach hand-in-hand with Lynn, the girl he'd argued with. "Looks like they're back together."

Hiro joined the boys, her arms folded across her chest. "I'm still not sure she's the same girl."

"Give it up, Hiro," Lunk said. "She fits the description—perfectly."

"Not to me. Something was off."

Lunk snickered. "Now you've got a photographic memory?"

Hiro gave a single nod. "Maybe I do. Which can be annoying at times." She gave Lunk a sideways glance. "I keep seeing your face in my head."

Cooper smiled. He loved to see the two of them spar with each other. It kept her off his case.

"This is their second time down the beach," Gordy said. "What are they doing?"

"Communicating," Lunk said. "Probably talking it out."

Hiro reached for the binoculars in Coop's hand and trained them toward the beach. "They're not talking at all. They're searching for something." She kept the binoculars up to her eyes. "Kryptoski hasn't turned her way once. He's looking down at the beach."

Cooper lost interest. He scanned the lake behind him. "What would they be looking for?"

Hiro didn't answer. "He just kicked a clump of seaweed. What does that tell you?"

"That maybe he doesn't like seaweed on the beach," Lunk said.

Hiro sighed. "Maybe he lost something last night while he was talking to Officer Tarpy."

"A set of keys. His wallet. Driver's license." Lunk shrugged. "What difference does it make? I'm thinking we should go to town and get some ice cream or something."

Hiro lowered the binoculars. "You mean we should go to Scoops and see Katie."

Lunk's face grew red. "I just feel like having some ice cream."

"Yippee Skippee." Hiro smiled.

"Don't start, Hiro." Lunk picked up a docking line and coiled it.

"Hey, Hiro," Gordy said.

She turned toward him, but Gordy looked like he had no idea what he wanted to say. Maybe he was just trying to keep the peace again.

"Many years ago," Gordy said, "two high school kids were walking along that very beach at midnight. They saw this *thing* step out of the shadows and run right for them."

"Puh-lease," Hiro said. "You're not going to tell us another ghost story."

"Not ghost," Gordy said. "Sasquatch."

"What?" Hiro laughed. "The big hairy ape-thing? Ridiculous. There's never been a sasquatch sighting in this area."

"Really?" Gordy said. "How do you think Big Foot Beach got its name?"

"This area used to be inhabited by Native Americans." Hiro laughed. "And Big Foot was the name of a Potawatomi chief."

Gordy pasted on a look of mock confusion. "Was he really tall—and hairy?"

"Ridiculous," Hiro said.

Gordy shrugged. "They never did find that couple."

Hiro shook her head. "Save your stories for bedtime."

Cooper stood at the rail and watched the beachcombers climb into a rowboat.

"Hey," Gordy said. "They must have found it."

Hiro raised the binoculars again. "Did you see them pick up something?"

"Not exactly. Or maybe they're giving up."

The two were already seated in the rowboat. Kryptoski was pulling on the oars, heading for *Krypto Night*.

"You couldn't pay me to get into a boat with that man," Hiro said. "That girl is a fool." Hiro lowered the binoculars.

"Done spying on them so soon, Hiro?" Lunk said.

"No, Mr. Lunquist, I am not. But I'm not going to be obvious about it either."

Kryptoski removed the tarp from the green boat, tied the rowboat to the buoy, and fired up the engine. They idled toward the south shore. He kept his eyes on the water as they crept closer and closer to the shoreline.

Hiro raised the binoculars again. "They're still looking for something." She sounded excited.

"Which means they didn't find whatever they were looking for on the beach," Cooper said.

"Exactly. It also means the missing object can't be something that was dropped on the beach when he was talking to the police. It might be something he lost from the boat."

Which made sense, really.

Hiro scanned the shoreline with the binoculars. "I wish we knew what it was."

Gordy hiked himself up and sat on the rail. "Why don't we do a little beachcombing ourselves? Maybe we'll find it."

Hiro smiled. "Gordy ... that's a brilliant idea. I am truly impressed."

Gordy looked proud of himself. "We'll have no idea what we're looking for though."

Hiro kept her eyes on the beach. "I have a feeling we'll know it when we see it."

CHAPTER 26

With *Krypto Night* still prowling the bay area, Cooper didn't want their little scouting expedition to look obvious. They'd already stuck their noses a little too far into Tommy Kryptoski's business.

They split up. Lunk and Gordy threw a Frisbee back and forth while they worked their way down the beach. Hiro and Cooper walked the beach, but tried to keep it looking casual. Hiro kept her eyes focused on the waterline, while Cooper picked up flat rocks from the shallow water and skipped them across the surface. The throwing motion seemed to loosen up his shoulder, and he kept his eyes peeled for anything unusual.

A flip-flop. An empty sunscreen bottle. A few dead fish and plenty of seaweed. But there was nothing that looked like it held any value to Kryptoski and his girlfriend.

A man and his chocolate Lab were playing on the far end of the beach. He threw a tennis ball into the water for the dog to retrieve.

"That dog is sure having fun," Hiro said. "Do you miss Fudge?"

Cooper nodded. From this distance the dog looked a lot like Fudge. Dad would bring her up with him this weekend. "She'll love the water."

"A lot more than Lunk does," Hiro said. "Poor guy. But he puts up a good front."

Cooper agreed.

Hiro poked his shoulder lightly. "Does it hurt?"

Cooper pulled away and laughed. "When you do that, it does."

"Do you think the driver of that pickup was drunk?"

Cooper had asked himself the same question a dozen times. "Seemed like it. Up until he took off afterward."

They walked in silence for a while.

"What if it was the same guy Kryptoski was talking to in the pickup? What if he's the guy who was watching us at Scoops?" It didn't seem like she was looking to him for the answer. More like she was trying to come up with one of her own. "What if the driver wasn't drunk, but this was some kind of warning?"

Cooper glanced at her. "Like a shot over the bow?"

"A what?"

"When the Coast Guard is trying to get a suspicious boat to stop, they shoot a warning shot over the bow of the boat—just to let them know they're serious."

Hiro nodded. "That's exactly what I think it was. A shot over the bow."

"But it makes no sense. Except for that stupid prank with the dead fish, we haven't done anything wrong."

"We meddled," Hiro said. "We got involved. You blew the air horn when things went berserk on *Krypto Night*. I called 9–1–1."

Cooper thought about that for a moment. "And you're saying the pickup that ran me into the wall was warning me to back off before something worse happens?"

"Exactly," Hiro said.

Cooper scanned the water. *Krypto Night* was still creeping along the south shoreline. He had no problem leaving this mystery alone. He never wanted to be involved in the first place.

The chocolate Lab bounded through a wave and ran up the beach toward them, the tennis ball clamped firmly in its jaws. The dog stopped directly in front of Cooper and Hiro and shook himself happily. Water droplets sprayed over both of them.

Hiro ducked behind Cooper. "Bad puppy," she laughed.

"Sorry!" the man down the beach shouted. He whistled, and the dog tore through the shallow water to get to him.

Cooper's phone vibrated. He checked the screen. "It's a text from Gordy." Lunk and Gordy were maybe forty yards away. Both of them were squatting on the beach, looking at something.

Hiro tried reading the screen over his shoulder.

Cooper read the message out loud. "Tell Hiro I think we have something."

Hiro's eyes widened—and she bolted over to Gordy and Lunk. Cooper hustled to keep up.

"What is it?" Hiro rested her hands on her knees, trying to catch her breath. "What did you find?"

Gordy pointed—at a child's plastic yellow sand pail and shovel. "What do you think?"

Lunk snickered.

Hiro glared at them. "Very funny. You made me run over here for this?"

"We have no idea what we're looking for," Lunk said. "We didn't want to take a chance. This might be important."

She put her hands on her hips. "Ridiculous. I'm going to keep looking. Maybe you two can start."

"Actually," Lunk said, "you've got the best chance of finding whatever it is that we're looking for."

Hiro tilted her head. "Because I'm going to be a cop someday?"

A smirk betrayed Lunk's sincerity—or lack of it. "No. Because you're so short. You're closer to the ground, so you've got a better chance of spotting something."

Hiro slugged him in the arm. "I'm out of here." She did a one-eighty and headed down the beach.

Cooper thought about joining her but decided she might need

some space to cool off. And she'd only want to talk more about how the pickup was connected to Kryptoski. Cooper wasn't so sure.

"There she is." Gordy pointed toward the *Walworth II* cruising along the south shore. "I wish I had the binoculars." He whipped out his phone and tapped on the stopwatch app.

The mailboat slowed as it approached the white dock in front of The Geneva Inn. The boat skimmed along the front of the pier, but didn't stop. By the time it passed, the tourists inside the mailboat were cheering.

Gordy moaned. "From this angle, I couldn't even see what happened."

Cooper had missed it too. But obviously someone had delivered the mail successfully.

Gordy checked his phone. "The mail jumper has just eight seconds to hop off the boat, open the mailbox, stuff the letters inside, and get back on board. All we have to do is delay her for a few seconds."

Honestly, pranks weren't even on Cooper's radar right now. Pranks could be a nice distraction—like from the more serious issues that Hiro wanted to talk about. But this one had all the signs of turning into a disaster.

"I think we should do it," Gordy said.

Lunk looked at Cooper.

"Coop?" Gordy's eyes were on fire.

Cooper laughed. "I haven't changed my mind on this. Why would I want to mess with the mailboat?"

"Don't ask yourself *why*," Gordy said. "Ask yourself why *not*?"

But there were at least two really good reasons why not. He'd definitely learned some pranks didn't rank so high on the ol' smart-o-meter—like hiding dead fish on board *Krypto Night*. And messing with the mail jumper didn't rank at all. What if the person got hurt?

"I'm not looking for a commitment this minute," Gordy said. "Think about it. We're talking about a harmless prank here. What could go wrong?"

CHAPTER 27

Hiro kept searching. But for what? The boys had clearly given up. She stopped to watch the three of them romping around on the narrow strip of beach with the Frisbee.

The chocolate Lab joined them, and now they were playing keep away with the tennis ball in the shallow water. The dog ran from one boy to the other, trying to get her chompers on the ball. The boys were driving her crazy.

They were driving Hiro crazy too. None of them were taking this as seriously as they should. Not even Coop. He was on vacation; and when it came to common sense, he'd obviously packed a little light.

"Hi."

The girl's voice startled Hiro. She whirled around to see Kryptoski's girlfriend approaching. Apparently he dropped her off on shore.

"Sorry, did I scare you?"

Hiro shook her head. The girl didn't scare her. It was her boyfriend. Kryptoski was still in his boat, watching them. The way he just stood there with his arms folded across his chest was really creepy.

"Lynn Tutek." The blonde held out her hand and flashed

an expensive-looking smile. Perfect teeth. "We met last night. Remember?"

Like Hiro could forget. She shook Lynn's hand. "Hiroko." Hiro didn't trust the girl enough to give her more info than that.

"That's an unusual name. Is it Asian?"

Hiro stared at her. Did she really just ask such a stupid question? "Norwegian."

"Really!" The girl look surprised.

Not as surprised as Hiro felt for even saying it. She wanted to take it back and tell the girl she was just kidding. But it was a little late for that.

"So, I noticed you've been walking up and down the beach," Lynn said. "Find anything interesting?"

Hiro's pulse spiked. She was right. They had lost something. Hiro couldn't let her excitement show. "Just doing a little beachcombing."

Lynn nodded in a casual way, but her eyes darted to Hiro's hands. *She's looking to see if I found it. But what?*

Hiro had to know. "Did you lose something?"

Lynn hesitated. Clearly, she hadn't planned on Hiro asking any follow-up questions.

"I could help you look for it," Hiro said. "Or if I find it, I could make sure you get it."

Maybe Lynn was weighing it out and wondering what her boyfriend would say. She glanced toward his boat. "Well, actually, yes." She flashed her perfect teeth again. "My boyfriend's camera is missing. It was pretty expensive—totally waterproof."

Of course. That made complete sense.

"It has an extra-long lanyard on it." Lynn held her hands two feet apart.

"I remember it," Hiro said. "I noticed it when your boat passed by ours last night."

Lynn's smile remained in place, but the blank look in her eyes said she didn't remember. Maybe that's because it was a different girl in the boat last night.

"Your boyfriend took a picture of our boat, remember?" Hiro pointed at *The Getaway* bobbing from the buoy.

"Oh, that's right," Lynn said quickly. "How could I forget?"

Easy. You weren't there. Hiro needed something more. Something to help prove this wasn't the same girl on board the *Krypto Night*. "So how many pictures did he take of our boat anyway?" Hiro tried to make it sound casual. Like she was just making conversation, not building a case.

Lynn met her eyes for an instant—but long enough for Hiro to see that the girl was calculating. Determining how to answer in a way that wouldn't appear suspicious.

"Who knows?" Lynn waved her hand in a dismissive way. "But the camera floats. So we're hoping it will drift onto the beach. If you find it, I'd really appreciate it if you returned it to me."

"I'll definitely be looking for it." The girl had no idea just how badly Hiro wanted to find that camera.

Lynn angled her head to one side. Suddenly Hiro was sure this girl was a lot smarter than the blonde act she was putting on, and she knew exactly what Hiro was doing.

"If I'm not around," Lynn said, "I suppose you could just put it in my boyfriend's boat." She pointed at the green *Krypto Night*.

"Okay," Hiro said. *Or I could take it to the police. Right after I scroll through the pictures.*

CHAPTER 28

Cooper kept an eye on Hiro from a distance. Her body language looked okay, like she was just having a casual conversation with the girl. But if Kryptoski stepped one foot on shore, Cooper would hustle over there.

"Think we should join her?" Lunk waded over beside him.

Lynn walked away from Hiro and headed toward the docks across from the park entrance.

Hiro looked toward the boys and made the slightest movement with her hand, motioning them over.

"I think she just answered our question," Cooper said.

Lunk and Gordy joined Cooper, wading through the shallow water. Hiro started walking toward them.

"She definitely looks happy," Lunk said. "I wonder what improved her mood."

Hiro looked like she couldn't wait to tell them. She walked faster.

"They *are* looking for something," she said the moment she got close. "The camera. They lost the camera."

That made sense. The way Kryptoski was whipping around in the boat last night, Lynn probably dropped it just to get out of his way.

"And there's more," Hiro said. "I'm positive she isn't the same girl who went out in the boat with that moron."

Cooper tried to concentrate as Hiro detailed her theory—which all seemed to come back to her feelings, not any real facts. His mind kept going back to the way Kryptoski whipped the boat around in such a reckless way.

"So she's telling me she can't remember how many pictures Kryptoski took of our boat."

Lunk shrugged. "What's the problem with that?"

Cooper agreed. If this is what she was building her case on, it was a really weak foundation.

"I noticed him take one picture. Just one!" Hiro paused to swallow. "How could she possibly forget that?"

"She's blonde?" Lunk said.

Gordy and Cooper both laughed.

Hiro glared at them.

"I'm not saying *you're* ditzy," Lunk said. "Your hair is black."

"Any time a guy makes a joke about a blonde, he's making a joke about *all* women," she said.

"Oh, here we go," Lunk said.

"Don't worry," Hiro said. "I won't go there. *This* time. But you guys are totally discounting what I'm telling you."

Maybe she was right. But Cooper didn't want to believe that Kryptoski had pulled off some kind of a switch. Because that would mean they'd witnessed something truly horrible. "Look, Hiro, let's imagine for a moment that you're right."

"Imagine?"

Lunk and Gordy laughed.

"All right. Let's *say* you're right. Let's say this Lynn has a stunt double out there somewhere."

"Pom-Pom," Hiro said.

"Okay," Cooper said. "Pom-Pom. And let's say Kryptoski got angry with her, she jumped out of the boat, and he tried to scare her."

"Hit her," Hiro said. "He was trying to hit her with the boat."

Cooper waved her off. "Doesn't this whole thing sound a little farfetched?"

"Yes," Hiro said. "It does. But only because you're thinking like you."

"What is that supposed to mean?"

Hiro folded her arms across her chest. "We live in a dark world, Coop. People do very bad things."

"Like murder."

Hiro nodded.

"But the guy pulled up to our boat afterward," Gordy said. "Don't you think he would have looked—I don't know—shaken up or something?"

"I thought about that," Hiro said. "He's a sociopath."

"You've watched too many detective shows, Hiro." Gordy shook his head. "You're unbelievable."

That didn't faze Hiro. "Sociopaths can be outgoing, friendly, charming even. But they lack one important thing." Hiro paused to be sure they were all listening. "A conscience. They can do awful things without feeling one ounce of guilt. They're totally selfish. Totally self-absorbed. They don't think about the needs or rights of others. Oh, they pretend to—and they put on a good act. But deep down, it's all about them. It's all about getting what they want. They use people. The way they see it, others exist only to serve their needs. Beyond that, other people are irrelevant."

"Whoa, Hiro," Lunk said. "Stop to take a breath."

She folded her arms across her chest. "I'm serious. Sociopaths are dangerous. And they're tough to live with, at best. And at worst..." She let her statement hang there.

"What?" Gordy said.

She leaned close. "They're *impossible* to live with."

"Meaning?"

"They're dangerous. If you cross a sociopath, you may not live to do it again."

"Hiro," Lunk said. "Really? Get a sociopath upset and he may kill you? C'mon."

Hiro raised her eyebrows. It was that look Cooper had seen so many times before whenever Hiro wanted to drill home a point. "Road rage. School shootings. Nasty things people say and do on social media. There are all kinds of degrees—but it's real."

Okay, even Cooper had to admit she had a point. But to say Kryptoski was a sociopath was a bold step.

Lunk looked at her like he thought she was funny.

Hiro looked like she was getting frustrated. "Look, who knows how many people in our society have sociopathic tendencies. But I bet you rub shoulders with sociopaths every day."

"I had a teacher who was a sociopath," Gordy said. "She gave pop quizzes with no warning at all. No conscience. No regrets."

"I'm not joking, Gordy," Hiro said. "Sociopaths are dangerous. And they're everywhere."

Lunk snorted. "How come I've never met one?"

Hiro's face turned red. "Really? You've never met one? You're blind."

"Blind?" And you're going to help me see, is that it?" He shook his head. "More like the blind leading the blind."

Hiro didn't seem to hear Lunk—or she chose to ignore him. "All I'm saying is, if you think you've never met a sociopath, then you're overlooking someone."

Cooper's mind went to Joseph Stein.

Lunk shook his head. "Can't think of one. So tell me, who is the sociopath that I supposedly know?"

"Forget it," Hiro said.

Lunk laughed. "Oh, that's convenient. You can't name one, can you?"

"I'd rather not."

Lunk looked a little annoyed. "C'mon, Hiro. Who?"

Hiro's eyes flashed with frustration. "Your dad."

Lunk's mouth opened slightly and his face paled. He took a step back.

Cooper stared at Hiro.

She clamped her hand over her mouth.

"Hey, I'm starving!" Gordy's voice sounded higher than usual, like it did whenever he got nervous. "Let's get some lunch!"

Lunk's jaw muscles twitched, and he clenched his hands into fists.

"Lunk," Cooper said. "Gordy's right. Let's go get some lunch."

Lunk stared at the sand and nodded. Without another word, he headed up the beach and across the street where the bikes where chained to a tree. Gordy hustled to walk alongside him.

"Hiro," Cooper whispered. "Why?"

He could see she was torturing herself already.

Hiro started to cross the street. "I know I blew it." She looked at Cooper. "I hurt him bad, didn't I?"

Cooper watched Lunk walking ahead of them. He had his old swagger back, covering up the hurt like he used to do behind a tough-guy façade. "Yeah, I think that one cut him pretty deep."

She sighed. "I feel awful."

"Good," Cooper said.

She gave him a questioning look.

"At least I know *you* aren't a sociopath."

CHAPTER 29

Lunk pedaled toward town without waiting for the others. Hiro's comment had proved something, hadn't it? What he'd feared all along. He'd been wondering what he brought to the table, and he hadn't come up with much. So maybe he wasn't as much a part of this group as he thought. As he wanted to be.

But what Hiro just said about his old man gave him a whole new perspective. Lunk was different from them. Really different. All three of them had decent dads. Coop's dad was everything Lunk could want in a father, and Gordy's dad was nothing short of heroic. When Gordy had been kidnapped, his dad searched for days with little or no rest. He nearly ripped Michael VanHorton apart when he suspected the man had taken his son.

Lunk had never met Hiro's dad, but the guy had been killed in the line of duty. He was a bona fide hero. But Lunk's old man was a different story. He was a biological dad—but not a real dad. He was a lying, scheming cheat who beat his wife and took all her money. A guy who took advantage of anyone who was weaker than himself. A user. A boozer. A certified loser.

Lunk kept a fast pace. By the time he crested the hill on the far side of Big Foot Beach, he felt sweat pouring down the middle of his back.

"Lunk, wait up!" Gordy's voice. That figured.

Lunk kept pedaling. He didn't need a peacemaker right now. He just wanted a little peace and quiet. He heard Gordy tearing through the gravel behind him.

Lunk had never been in the lead before. Not when it came to biking. But now that he had a bigger bike, he easily kept up with Gordy and Coop. But that's where the lead ended. When it came to life, he'd always been behind, hadn't he? Would that ever change? Would he ever measure up?

Lunk's mom was an angel straight out of heaven. But his old man? He was no angel. And he definitely didn't come from heaven. More likely from that place straight south of there.

"She didn't mean it, you know." Gordy pulled up alongside Lunk. "Sometimes she says things she doesn't mean."

Lunk gave him a sideways glance. "She meant it. And you know it."

His old man believed he was always right. Lunk couldn't remember a time when his dad had ever admitted that he was wrong. Even after he'd hit Mom. Lunk had never heard his dad say he was sorry, either.

Lunk always figured it was his old man's pride. His monster ego wouldn't allow him to apologize. But what if it was more than that?

A scene replayed in his mind. One Lunk hated. Lunk was sitting on the edge of his bed in his room. His old man was shouting—no, *screaming*—at Lunk's mom. He wished the abuse would stop. He'd known the day was coming when he'd be big enough, man enough, to stand up to his dad. Yet he didn't want to do it. Because he knew that once he did, everything would change.

His mom shrieked, and before Lunk could think, he was in the kitchen, plowing into his old man and knocking him to the floor. All of Lunk's pent-up rage broke free. He hammered his fists into his dad like the man was some sicko who'd broken into the house.

Lunk won the fight, yet he lost at the same time. His old man left for good that night, and he only came back every now and then to hit them up for money. But he never hit Lunk's mom again. And he never would.

But his bio-dad had never said he was sorry. He never showed any remorse. It was more than just a pride thing, wasn't it?

"I'm sure your dad isn't a psychopath," Gordy said.

Lunk almost smiled. "Agreed. I think a psychopath is the type of guy who ends up killing lots of people on cop shows. But Hiro is right. My dad is definitely a sociopath."

CHAPTER 30

Cooper waited for Hiro, and that gave Gordy and Lunk a big lead. Unless the other two stopped, they'd never catch up to them before they reached town.

"I've got to apologize," Hiro said.

Cooper agreed. The question was *when*. Gordy dropped back from keeping pace with Lunk. Gordy looked back at them and gave a little shrug.

"Looks like Lunk needs some space." Hiro sounded defeated.

"Talk to him at lunch," Cooper said. "He'll be okay."

Hiro nodded. "I hope you're right."

So did Cooper. He pushed harder on the pedals to close the gap between them.

They were approaching the spot where he'd been run off the road.

"Where did it happen?" Hiro glanced at him. "Last night with the pickup."

Cooper wondered at her timing. He pointed.

She slowed a bit, probably imagining the whole scene.

Cooper wanted to forget it. Still, he found himself checking over his shoulder just to be sure the truck wasn't tailing them.

"Lunk!" he shouted. "Speedo's?"

Lunk didn't turn around but lifted one arm and waved.

Minutes later, they coasted down the hill into town and rode along the waterfront to Speedo's. They ordered at the walk-up window, took their food to a grassy spot near the water, and dumped their bikes onto the ground.

Lunk sat with his back to the town, looking out over the harbor of docks, rental boats, and a string of buoys stretching across the bay to the municipal pier on the other side.

Hiro stood for a moment with her carryout bag in hand, as if deciding where to sit. She finally sat next to Lunk. Neither of them said a word.

Like Lunk, Gordy had two hamburgers in front of him. "How 'bout these burgers, huh, Lunk?"

Lunk nodded.

"What did you get, Hiro?" It seemed like Gordy's strategy was to get them talking to him, and then maybe they'd start talking to each other.

"Chicken strips."

Hiro's voice sounded as small as she was. She picked at one of the strips and glanced up at Lunk ... then back at Cooper.

Cooper mouthed the words, *Just say it*. He motioned toward Lunk.

She took a deep breath and let it out slowly. "Lunk?"

He turned her way.

"I am soooo sorry," she said. "I never should have said that. It was wrong, I—"

"Forget it." Lunk cut her off. "You spoke your heart."

She hesitated. But she needed to finish. Get it all out there. Unless she did, there'd always be a wall between her and Lunk.

Cooper caught her eye and nodded toward Lunk—silently urging her on.

"I guess I did speak my heart," she said. "But my heart wasn't in the right place. I was totally unkind, and I never want to be like that."

Lunk stared at his hamburger. "Because you don't want to break your personal code of conduct?"

She shook her head. "It's more than that. A lot more. You're my good friend—and I hurt you. That was so wrong of me."

Good, Hiro. Cooper held his breath, hoping Lunk's reaction would be as solid.

Lunk sat there for a moment. "Actually, I think you were right about my dad. I think he is a . . ."—he hesitated—" . . . a sociopath. I just never thought of it that way."

"It was wrong how I said it, though. Will you forgive me?"

"For telling the truth?"

"For not doing it in a kind way."

Lunk looked at her. "You're serious?"

Hiro nodded. "Forgive me?"

He looked unsteady, like this was new territory for him. "Sure. Yes. Of course."

Hiro reached over and gave him a hug.

Lunk hesitated and then hugged her back. "You really are a softy under that tough cop exterior."

Hiro laughed and wiped her eyes.

Cooper let out a sigh of relief.

"All right," Gordy said, "I'm glad that's settled."

"Me too." Hiro reached over and snatched one of Lunk's fries. "I'm famished."

Lunk smiled and shook his head. He took a massive bite of his burger and placed the bag of fries between them within easy reach for Hiro.

She smiled back and took another handful.

"Okay," Gordy said. "We need some adventure. After we're done here, let's show Lunk and Hiro the spillway. And the tunnel. Maybe White River."

It sounded like a good idea to Cooper.

"Then we'll get a little snack at Scoops," Gordy said.

That sounded even better.

"A tunnel?" Hiro said. "And you figure I'll think it's fun?"

Gordy shook his head. "You'll hate it. But we'll have fun watching you."

"Oh," Hiro said. "Real nice."

A police car cruised along the waterfront and parked in one of the angle spaces near Scoops. Officer Tarpy stepped out and stretched.

"I think I'm going to tell him about the lost camera," Hiro said.

Gordy didn't look too happy. "Really? C'mon, Hiro. We're on vacation. You're supposed to relax. Do fun stuff."

"This *is* fun for her," Lunk said.

It didn't sound like he was teasing her this time. More like he was defending her.

Hiro took a few more of Lunk's fries and headed toward the policeman. "Be right back."

CHAPTER 31

Gordy watched Hiro cross the street and flag down the cop. "Ay-yi-yi. That girl just can't leave things alone." He took a bite of his second burger. "And she's gonna drag us into it too."

Lunk laughed. "We're already in it."

"That's what I'm afraid of." Gordy pointed at her with a fry. "Now we need to back off. Have fun. Leave the investigating to the cops."

"I'm definitely okay with that," Lunk said. "But good luck selling Hiro on that plan."

Gordy looked at Coop. His cousin just shrugged and nodded.

"Aw, c'mon, guys. Let's take charge here," Gordy said.

Coop balled up his carryout bag and tossed it into a trash barrel. "Sounds like you have ideas."

"I do," Gordy said. "We can't drive *The Getaway* until this weekend when your dad gets here, right?"

Coop nodded. "Although you did kind of jump the gun on that this morning."

Gordy waved him off. "So this afternoon, let's do a little exploring around town."

Coop was obviously tracking with him. "Okay. You mentioned the spillway. The tunnel."

"Exactly. And the pipeline under the old railway bridge. Then we can hit Scoops or something."

Lunk definitely looked interested, but Hiro would be a different story. He checked across the street. She was still talking to the cop, making hand motions like she was taking a picture.

Lunk seemed to be watching Hiro too. "Think she told the cop her theory? That the girl on the beach wasn't the one in the boat?"

"Oh yeah," Cooper said. "And how the camera is missing."

Lunk kept watching. "I'm no expert on body language, but Officer Tarpy doesn't look convinced."

Gordy agreed. The cop's body language was all wrong.

"You have to give her credit," Cooper said. "She's really trying to sell it."

Lunk turned away. "I can't watch. This is pitiful. The cop isn't buying it."

Good. Maybe Hiro would drop the whole thing. Get out of cop mode and back into vacation mode. "Before Hiro gets back," Gordy said, "let's get one more thing on the vacation schedule." He looked from Coop to Lunk and back again.

Lunk leaned forward. "Well? Are you going to tell us?"

"The mailboat plans are shaping into a really sweet prank. I think we should do it."

Coop shrugged. "Let's just stick to exploring town."

"This one is foolproof." Gordy grinned. "And Hiro will hate it. Imagine the mail carrier jumping for the boat, falling in the water, and the tourists on board rushing to the rail to snap a picture."

"You're right about one thing," Lunk said. "Hiro will hate it."

"Hate what?" Hiro said from behind them.

Gordy froze. He didn't know what to say. She'd try to put the kibosh on his plans for sure.

"Gordy's plans to prank the mailboat," Lunk said.

"Right." Hiro sat down. "The truth."

Cooper laughed. "That *is* the truth. But don't worry, he hasn't even convinced *us* yet. And right now Gordy wants to show you some of the lesser-known tourist sites of Lake Geneva."

Gordy took a bow.

"Will I hate that too?"

Coop shrugged. "Probably."

Lunk stood and stretched. "Let's go then."

"Maybe I should stay right here," she said.

Gordy debated that for a moment. If she didn't come, she couldn't stop them. But it would be way more fun if she came along.

"You've got to come," Gordy said.

"And the reason why would be . . . ?" She let the question hang in the air.

"Because we're friends," Gordy said. "And friends stick together."

She groaned. "That's not fair."

Gordy reached for her hands and pulled her to her feet. "We'll lock the bikes to a tree. You're about to get a tour of Lake Geneva's underground. We're taking you to the tunnel."

"Okay, okay." Hiro tugged her hands free from Gordy's grip. "I'm coming. How bad could it be?"

Gordy snickered. "Obviously you haven't been there before."

CHAPTER 32

Cooper had been through the tunnel a handful of times — and no two times had been alike.

He headed for the road alongside Hiro. "So you told Officer Tarpy that you think Pom-Pom and Lynn are two different people?"

Hiro nodded. "And about the missing camera."

She was quiet.

"So what did he say?"

She shrugged. "He was polite — but he wasn't interested."

"He said that?"

"Didn't have to. I read it all over him."

Like Cooper could read the disappointment all over her now. It was hard enough when her friends discounted her police work. But when a cop did it? Her mouth formed a tight, straight line. Obviously, she was done talking about it for now. Cooper let it go and hoped she'd let this whole investigation thing go too.

They hustled to the other side of Wrigley Drive. Gordy led the way across the bridge, which spanned the narrow inlet to the miniature lagoon below. Only small boats and jet skis parked in the bay. Nothing larger could make it under the bridge. Everything about the place was small. Even the docks between the boats were made with a single two-by-ten strung between posts. Walking one of those docks would be like walking a plank.

Boats and Waverunners belonging to LeatherLips Watersports took up most of the slips on the north end of the cove, while the boats on the south side were privately owned. The boats were covered and tied—waiting for adventure. *Ruby Slippers. Pretty Girl. Svenska Flicka. The Boys' Bomb.* And over a dozen more on this side of the lagoon.

"This bay is tiny," Gordy said, "but it controls the level of the entire lake—thanks to the spillway."

Hiro scanned the water below them. "Spillway?"

Gordy pointed to a low concrete wall running along the south side of the bay. Water rushed over the top into a moss-covered chute. "When the lake is high, water goes over the wall and into the spillway—which is pretty much like a long, steep driveway. It funnels down into a tunnel."

Hiro stepped off the bridge and followed the sidewalk ramp toward the docks. "A tunnel?"

"Yeah," Gordy said. "Dark. Creepy. Seems like it goes forever before it dumps into the White River."

"Lovely," Hiro said. "And you expect me to go in there?"

"We'll all go," Gordy said. "Together."

"Because if you go in there alone . . ." Lunk made a creepy face, " . . . you may never come out."

Hiro folded her arms across her chest. "And that's supposed to encourage me to join you?"

Gordy shook his head. "No, to stay close. Some say the tunnel is haunted."

Lunk snickered. "Ghosts?"

"Hiro doesn't believe in ghosts," Cooper said. "It'd have to be demons."

"That's it." Hiro covered her ears. "I am not going in that 'demon' tunnel."

"C'mon, Hiro," Gordy said. "We're messin' with you. The tunnel will be . . . fun."

"I hope you enjoy it," Hiro said. "I'll meet you on the other side — wherever that is."

One look at her face, and Cooper knew that trying to convince her would be useless. And in a way, he was relieved. She'd be scared in the tunnel. Really scared. He didn't want to see her pressured into it. He pointed. "See that parking lot?"

Hiro nodded.

"Now, the road just beyond it?"

"Center Street," Gordy said.

Cooper motioned. "And that section of trees on the other side?"

"Got it," Hiro said.

"That's where the tunnel dumps into the White River," Cooper said. "We'll meet you there."

Hiro's mouth opened slightly. "The tunnel goes *all* that way?"

"Yeah, and I guarantee you it'll seem a lot longer when you're in the tunnel," Cooper said.

Hiro looked at Cooper like she knew he was trying to protect her.

Gordy grinned. "Amazing, right?"

"I'd call it ridiculous."

She shook her head. "I will never — ever — go into that demon tunnel. Is this even legal?"

Gordy made a broad sweeping gesture. "No signs saying we can't do it."

Hiro looked disgusted. "They probably don't see the need for a sign because they figure nobody would be this stupid."

The concrete walls on both sides loomed higher as the spillway dropped lower into the ground. The tunnel was a black hole, sucking up every bit of water that the lake sent its way.

"C'mon, Hiro!" Gordy said. "Be daring."

"You're insane," Hiro said.

"For going into the tunnel?"

Hiro shook her head. "For thinking you could convince *me* to."

"You're going to miss out," Gordy said. "You'll never see this on some tourist map."

"Good."

"Okay." Gordy shrugged. "I give up. See you on the other side."

"If you make it," Hiro said.

"I'll make it, all right," Gordy said.

Hiro shrugged. "Lord willing."

Cooper, Lunk, and Gordy practically doubled over, laughing.

Hiro walked along the railing that overlooked the tunnel entrance. "Have a good time."

Gordy saluted and led the way. He ran back to the docks, hopped into the shallow water, and stepped over the spillway wall. Their shoes were soaked anyway.

Cooper and Lunk were right behind him. The water was shallow but still moved fast. Lunk lost his footing on the moss, slid onto his side, and never got back on his feet.

"Nice, Lunk!" Gordy shouted. "Wait for us at the bottom." He took a wide stance like he was surfing, and slid halfway down the chute before falling.

Cooper slipped once, regained his balance, and then lost it again. The concrete wall had absolutely nothing to grab on to. He felt a sharp stab in his shoulder and didn't want to chance smacking it again. He sat down feet-first and let the force of the water and the law of gravity do their work.

Like an entrance ramp to a highway, the spillway dropped steeply with high concrete walls on both sides. The tunnel was dead ahead—round at the top but flat on the floor. At its highest point it stood nearly five feet tall. Gordy and Lunk were standing in the knee-high water as it rushed into the gaping mouth of the tunnel.

Hiro stood at the rail nearly fifteen feet above them and shook her head.

"Last chance, Hiro!" Gordy pointed at the tunnel. "I bet you wouldn't even need to duck."

"Go have your fun!" Hiro said.

She seemed fine now. Maybe because she knew she wasn't going into the tunnel.

Cooper waved. "See you on the other side."

She smiled just a bit.

Cooper focused on the blackness of the "demon tunnel," as Hiro called it. He'd forgotten how long it was. The opening at the far end seemed small. Really small.

"I'll lead." Gordy ducked inside the tunnel without hesitation.

Lunk followed.

Cooper glanced up at Hiro one more time and then stepped inside the concrete tube. Cool. Damp. And echoing. The tunnel darkened quickly, and with Lunk and Gordy walking ahead of him, there was little view of the light at the other end.

Water rushed past their legs, and the tube magnified the gurgling, sucking sound.

"Watch the wires," Gordy said.

Wires ran the entire length of the tunnel. They were loosely attached to the wall every ten feet or so, and they sagged dangerously. Cooper wondered if anybody ever checked them. Rats could have gnawed through the insulation, exposing the wire underneath. Grabbing the wire while walking in the water? Potentially deadly. Cooper kept his distance from them.

"You doing okay, Lunk?" Gordy's voice echoed around them.

"Wonderful."

Gordy laughed. "Imagine doing this at night."

"No thanks," Lunk said. "I can hardly see as it is.

Spider webs clung to Cooper's face, stretched, and broke free. And that was after Gordy and Lunk had burst through webs ahead of him. Apparently the tunnel didn't get visitors often—and least not ones walking on two legs. He looked back. If Hiro had been along, she would have turned around by now.

"Whoa—whoa—whoa!" Lunk sloshed around. "What is that—a snake?"

"Fish," Gordy said. "Sometimes they get inside the tunnel. In the spring I've felt humongous carp in here. Slimy. Totally creepy. I really wish Hiro had come along."

Gordy and Lunk laughed and kept moving forward. They took it slow. Rocks, sticks, and other debris littered the tunnel and made little dams along the way that caught on their shoes, snagged their laces, and tore at their legs. By the time they were halfway through, Cooper remembered exactly why they hadn't done this more often.

The water felt higher now. Deeper. Was it rising? Impossible. It had to be his imagination. The darkness was playing tricks on his mind, conjuring up memories of being chained in a flooding basement.

The air in the tunnel was really stale. Musty. As if the webs stretching across the tunnel had never let the air get a fresh exchange. He'd be glad to get out of here. "Is the water getting deeper?"

"Seems like it, doesn't it?" Gordy said.

The tunnel must have a slight downhill pitch—which meant the water naturally rode higher in the tunnel the closer they got to the end. Terrific.

The tunnel was different than when they'd explored it last summer. Fear lived in this tunnel now. Cooper couldn't see it—but he felt it. Fear thrived in the dark. Its clammy hand reached out from the black waters and groped for his heart. Goose bumps rose on his arms. Something hooked his foot.

This is a tunnel. I've been in it before. I'm not chained. I'm not alone. I've almost reached the other end. Just keep moving.

Lunk and Gordy had a solid lead on him now. Cooper looked over his shoulder at the darkness behind him and sloshed faster to catch up.

"I heard they found a body in here once." Lunk's voice echoed back.

So Gordy wasn't the only one with stories. But Cooper wasn't in the mood for a creepy story. Not here. Then again, the tunnel was exactly the kind of place you'd expect to find a body.

The concrete walls changed to stone and mortar. Ancient-looking. This had to be the stretch under Center Street. Almost there.

"Any bats in here?" Lunk said.

Bats were certainly in this area of Wisconsin. This would make a perfect lair for them. Did any of them cluster on the ceiling? Cooper hoped not.

He wished he had brought a flashlight along. But maybe he wouldn't want to see the kinds of creatures that made a place like this their home. He kept his head a little lower, just in case.

"I still wish Hiro were here," Gordy said. "Hey, Hiro!" he said as if she was walking behind him, "Did I ever tell you the story about the convicts who were found hiding out in here? Even the police wouldn't go in after them. And the convicts were never caught. Some people say one of them still lives in the tunnel—and comes out at night to feed."

But it was always night in a place like this. Cooper pictured a Gollum-like creature crawling on all fours and feeding on the crayfish and whatever else crept around in this slimy underground tube.

"If you told her a story like that in here," Lunk said, "you'd have to be sure she didn't catch you once she got out. She'd give you a Hiro-schmeero lesson."

Gordy's laugh echoed. His laugh had a calming effect, though. The walls changed again as the stone gave way to corrugated metal, like a colossal drainage pipe.

"End of the line," Gordy said.

The light appeared as Gordy and Lunk stepped out of the tunnel.

Finally.

The tunnel opened into White River, which wasn't much more than a creek at this point.

Cooper straightened as soon as he stepped into the river. He glanced back to see the opening at the other end. The tunnel had never seemed this long before. Trees growing along the river blocked the direct sunlight, but Cooper still squinted at the brightness.

Hiro was sitting on a rock, waiting for them. "How was the coal mine?" She picked her way down toward them.

Gordy shook his head. "You missed it, Hiro. Totally missed it."

She pulled a cobweb from Cooper's hair. "And I'm very happy I did." She peered inside the tunnel. "This would make a perfect place to film a horror movie."

Cooper agreed with her on that point.

She wrinkled her nose. "Smells like something died in there."

It was true. Cooper hadn't noticed it smelling that bad inside the tunnel, but the air coming out definitely smelled rotten. "You were smart not to go into the tunnel."

She looked at him to see if he was kidding. "That bad?"

Cooper nodded. "You would have hated it."

Hiro didn't say anything. Maybe she was imagining how bad it was. But even she couldn't imagine the worst of it. Cooper was sure of that.

Gordy and Lunk headed down the middle of the shallow river. Cooper followed at a distance, with Hiro walking along the bank.

She pointed to Lunk and Gordy. "So how far are they taking us?"

"Eventually the river winds along a golf course," Cooper said. "And on the way, there are old iron pipelines bridging the river—bigger around than a telephone pole." He made a circle with his arms. "We walk along the top to cross the river, and then go under an old railroad bridge."

"Lovely." Hiro said. "Suddenly the outlet mall is sounding better and better."

Lunk and Gordy were waiting when Cooper and Hiro approached.

Gordy was beaming. "Isn't this great?"

"If you're into playing Lewis and Clark," Hiro said.

Gordy laughed. "It beats playing Sherlock Holmes."

Hiro was trying to be a good sport, but Cooper could see right through her. He suspected Officer Tarpy's lack of interest in her theories was still bothering her—and their little expedition wasn't doing much to get her mind off it.

"Okay." Lunk held up his hands. "Let's go someplace we can all get into."

Maybe Lunk had picked up on Hiro's mood too. Cooper looked at him. "Where?"

Lunk shrugged. "Scoops."

CHAPTER 33

Hiro stepped inside with Coop. The brightness of Scoops and the smell of ice cream was a welcome change from the river.

Katie was already scooping Gordy's Yippee Skippee when they walked in. They had the place to themselves. Apparently there wasn't much demand for ice cream on Monday afternoons. Katie nodded at her and smiled. "Where have *you* guys been?"

The boys really did look like a mess. Scrapes from the spillway and tunnel. Mud from the river bank.

"Exploring," Gordy said.

"Is that what you call it?" Katie asked. "Looks like you got lost."

Lunk stood at the counter watching her and looking a little lost himself.

"I like her," Hiro said.

Coop smiled. "So does Lunk."

There was something about her. Hiro couldn't put her finger on it, but she knew Katie could be trusted.

"Let me guess," Katie said to Lunk. "Vanilla."

Lunk nodded.

"C'mon, Lunk," Gordy said. "How 'bout Halley's Comet?"

Lunk shook his head.

"You need to pick a flavor that says something about you."

"He already did," Katie said. "Vanilla is strong. Dependable. A classic — all by itself. It doesn't need anything added to it and will always be in demand." She piled the vanilla high and slid the cup across the glass countertop. "Good choice."

"As long as I don't add root beer," Lunk said.

She gave him a disapproving look. "Don't even go there."

Oh yeah. Hiro liked Katie a lot.

Katie started wiping down tables. "The guys look like they've gone through the shredder. How'd you come out without a scratch?"

"I didn't follow the boys," Hiro said.

"Oooh," Katie said. "Smart girl."

At least someone thought she was smart. Hiro's mind drifted to the man with the pickup. She was sure the man had been watching them last night. And whether or not Coop wanted to admit it, the bearded man could have been the guy who ran him off the road.

"Hey, Katie," Hiro said. "Last night there was a man hanging around outside while we were here, but he never came in. Beard. Baseball cap. Did you happen to see him?" She tried to make the question sound casual.

Gordy gave Hiro a suspicious look. She was veering off his vacation agenda again, and apparently he was onto her.

"Fat Elvis," Katie said.

Gordy laughed. "He was big, but I wouldn't call him fat."

"His name isn't Elvis, either," Katie said. "That's the flavor of ice cream he orders." She finished wiping a table and glanced at Hiro. "Why do you ask?"

Hiro suddenly felt unsure about how far she should take this. How weird would it sound?

Katie angled her head and studied Hiro for a moment. She looked around the shop. "He isn't here now. Talk to me."

Hiro shrugged. "I had a bad feeling about him."

Katie raised her eyebrows. "You should."

Hiro's heart picked up the pace. "What do you mean?"

"I see a lot of guys in a place like this," Katie said. "Cheaps. Peeps. Creeps. And once in a while, I spot one that I'd like to keep." She smiled.

"That's it," Coop said. "This is turning into girl talk." He grabbed his cup of ice cream. "I'm eating outside."

"I'm with you," Gordy said. "Let's go, Lunk. We don't want to hear this."

Lunk looked like he did want to hear it. But he got up and followed the other two anyway.

Hiro waited until the door closed. "So back to the cheapers, peepers, keepers, and creepers. Which kind is he?"

"Fat Elvis?" Katie winced as though she'd just tasted something sour. "He's a total creep."

Hiro knew it.

Katie took a seat. "He works for a big casino in the area. Spends a lot of time around town."

"Doing what?"

"Babysitting, if you ask me."

"Babysitting?"

Katie smiled. "The casino is managed by a guy named Kryptoski."

Hiro sucked in her breath. "Tommy Kryptoski?"

Katie shook her head. "Jerry. Tommy is his son. He's the one who needs babysitting."

"I met him," Hiro said. "His boat is moored right by ours."

"The green one?"

Hiro nodded.

"One of his many expensive toys."

"So," Hiro said, "he's a spoiled rich kid."

"And a real charmer with the ladies," Katie said. "I think Fat Elvis was hired to keep Tommy out of trouble."

Hiro's mind flashed back to the black pickup. "And maybe Fat Elvis is supposed to clean up Tommy Kryptoski's messes too."

Katie shrugged. "That's my take on it."

Is that why Fat Elvis was snooping around Scoops last night? Assessing whether or not Hiro and the guys might be a threat to Kryptoski? Was he cleaning up Kryptoski's mess? Hiro's excitement rose.

"I have to charge you for the ice cream, but the advice is free," Katie said. "Want a scoop of that?"

Hiro nodded.

"Stay away from them." Katie glanced toward the front window like she was afraid they might hear her somehow. "Far away."

A chill tingled down Hiro's spine. It sounded like good advice. It really did. But if she stayed far away, how would she find out if she'd witnessed a murder?

CHAPTER 34

Cooper noticed something different about Hiro when she walked out of Scoops. She was excited. Distracted. Processing. Something was on her mind. And he was pretty sure he didn't want to know what.

All he knew was that he wanted to go for a swim.

Hiro peered up and down the street like she was looking for someone. Or checking to see if someone was watching her.

"Let's head back to the boat," Cooper said.

Everyone seemed to like that idea. Minutes later they were riding their bikes along the shore. The path dipped and wound its way past huge estates. Pedaling on the path wasn't as smooth as taking the road, but no drunks would be driving their pickups here.

"I learned some things about our mysterious friends," Hiro said. For the next few minutes she talked about Kryptoski and a casino and the man in the pickup, a guy she was now calling "Fat Elvis."

Lunk didn't look like he was buying it. Gordy clearly wasn't listening. And Cooper just wasn't sure.

"I don't think you're grasping this," Hiro said. "The pickup at the beach had to belong to Fat Elvis," she said.

Lunk glanced at her. "Because?"

"Because it makes sense."

"You mean because it works in your little theory," Lunk said.

"My theory is logical," Hiro said. "Suppose Kryptoski actually murdered that girl last night."

"Lynn?' Lunk said.

"No, Lynn is obviously alive." Hiro sounded annoyed. "I'm talking about the *first* girl. Pom-Pom."

"But that's who Lynn claims to be," Lunk said. "The first girl. The only girl."

Hiro shook her head. "There were two different girls."

"Two girls who look so similar that you can't be *sure* there were actually two girls."

"I'm sure of it," Hiro said.

"You'd swear to it on a witness stand?" Lunk said.

Hiro hesitated.

"So you're not absolutely sure," Lunk said, "but it fits nicely into your theory."

Hiro waved him off. "And that same pickup nearly killed Coop last night."

"We have no proof it was the same pickup," Lunk said. "It could have been exactly what it appeared to be. A drunk driver."

Hiro clenched her jaw. "Fat Elvis was not drunk when I saw him at Scoops."

"That's not helping your case any," Lunk said. "The guy who almost ran over Coop was drunk."

Cooper played back the scene in his mind—the glimpse he got of the pickup fleeing the scene. He'd been driving pretty well at that moment.

"All we really know for sure," Lunk said, "is that Kryptoski and Fat Elvis are connected."

"Oh, and how do we know that, Mr. Lunquist?" Hiro said. "We can't prove that we've seen them together."

"Katie said so."

"So when Katie says something, it's truth," Hiro said. "But when I say something, it's just a theory?"

Lunk didn't answer that one. Smart move.

The path opened onto the front lawn of the massive Stone Manor.

Hiro turned to Cooper. "*You* see what I'm saying, right?"

Cooper had to handle this one just right. He didn't want Hiro to feel like they were ganging up on her; but honestly, she seemed to be making a pile of assumptions. Then again, this was Hiro. She wasn't always right, but she was never completely wrong.

"Okay, we know Kryptoski had an argument with his date last night. We know his date ended up in the water, and Krypto drove his boat around like a madman," Cooper said.

"Right," Hiro said. "We know he could have hit her."

"Could have," Lunk said. "*Could* have."

Hiro held up a hand. "Let Coop finish."

Lunk smiled and nodded to Coop. "My apologies. You've got the floor."

"We know Krypto went back to the shore without her. And we know a girl fitting her description and claiming to be that same girl showed up dripping wet." Coop pedaled for a moment. "These are the things we know. But if it *wasn't* the same girl, then Krypto somehow phoned some woman he knows who looks close enough to double for her. And then she agreed to cover for him and was able to get down to the beach pretty quickly."

Cooper paused for a breath. "If the pickup driver who was talking to Krypto at the beach was Fat Elvis, and if Fat Elvis followed us to Scoops to see what we knew and then ran me off the road—then yeah, you've really got something, Hiro."

Hiro slumped. "So you don't agree with me either."

"Actually, I think your logic makes sense," Coop said. "I'm just saying a lot of 'if's' have to be proven true for your theory to work."

Hiro nodded. "Circumstantial evidence."

Her theory seemed to fit a little too perfectly. Which probably meant they were trying too hard to make it work.

They rode in silence past the bright white docks surrounded by boats tied in slips or hoisted onto canopied lifts.

"The camera is the key," Hiro said. "We need to find it. The photos will prove there's been foul play."

"Careful what you wish for." Lunk wasn't smiling.

Hiro gave him a questioning look.

"If you're right, then that lanyard might be hung around the neck of Pom-Pom's dead body."

CHAPTER 35

Cooper noticed something was different within seconds of boarding *The Getaway*. The cabin door was hanging open, swinging back and forth with the rhthym of the waves. He hadn't locked it when they'd left that morning—but he knew he'd shut it tight and thrown the latch.

"Somebody has been here," Cooper said quietly, pointing at the door.

"Think that somebody's still inside the cabin?" Gordy whispered.

Cooper had no idea. He stepped over to the toolbox, grabbed his dad's dive knife, and pulled it from the sheath. His mind went spinning back to that night in May when he'd strapped it to his leg after Gordy was abducted. It had been a big help to him at the time. He hoped it would prove as useful now.

"Coop?" Hiro stared at him.

Cooper held the cabin door open with the knife blade and hesitated, letting his eyes adjust to the shadows. The way looked clear. "Stay outside, Hiro."

Cooper entered with the knife extended. If anyone charged him, the guy would end up like a hot dog on a roasting stick. The moment Coop stepped inside the kitchen, Lunk was standing beside him.

The blinds were open in the sleeping area. He knew they'd been closed tight. He hadn't wanted to look at the mess they'd have to clean up before his dad arrived. But if somebody had come looking for something, he would have needed more light to see.

Hiro gasped from behind him. "Somebody totally ransacked the place!"

"Actually," Cooper said, "this is pretty much how I remember us leaving it."

Hiro picked a T-shirt from the floor and tossed it onto the berth. "Disgusting."

"I thought you were going to wait outside," Lunk said.

Coop finished checking the entire cabin before he sheathed the knife. He opened drawers, inspecting every storage spot. Nothing appeared to be missing. If it weren't for the cabin door and blinds being open, he wouldn't have known someone had been there.

Gordy put the knife back in the toolbox. "Do we call the police?"

"And tell them what?" Hiro said. "Nothing is missing. They already think we've got too much imagination."

Lunk cleared his throat. "*We've* got too much imagination? You've got enough for all of us."

"Sorry, Mr. Lunquist," Hiro said. "I meant *me*. You'd do well to feed your malnourished imagination a bit more."

Cooper couldn't clear his mind. Somebody had been on the boat. "Why would someone be in here? Looking for money?" Deep down he knew that wasn't the answer—and he didn't like what his heart was telling him.

Hiro shook her head. "Not money. Something else." She walked around the cabin as if hoping to find a clue. "So who would do this — and what was he looking for?" She looked at the others as though she were their teacher, and they were her students.

"Something tells me that the one with all the imagination thinks she has all the answers too," Lunk said.

Ignoring his comment, Hiro turned to Gordy. "What might someone come here to steal?"

Gordy's eyes opened wide. "Oh no."

Hiro nodded. "Oh yes."

Gordy lunged for the food chest and lifted the cover. He rummaged through it frantically, then turned and smiled. "It's all here. You had me worried for a second."

Hiro looked up at the ceiling in exasperation and closed her eyes. "You are absolutely ridiculous sometimes, Gordy." She turned to Cooper. "You know, don't you, Coop?"

Cooper nodded. "But I hope I'm wrong."

Her eyes lit up. "Tell me what you're thinking."

Apparently she didn't want to share her theory just yet, which made sense. Every time she brought up something, the rest of them seemed to discount it. She wanted Cooper to say it first.

"Okay," Cooper said. "Sometimes you have to look at the obvious. We know Krypto and his girlfriend are looking for that camera."

Hiro nodded and smiled.

"They saw us nosing around on the beach, so they were checking to see if we found it and kept it for ourselves."

"Bingo," Hiro said.

The others were quiet for a moment.

"Just because they're looking for the camera," Lunk said, "doesn't mean Lynn wasn't the girl on the boat. She said it was a waterproof camera. It was probably expensive. They don't want to lose it, that's all."

"Right," Gordy said. "It doesn't prove there was a murder."

Hiro shrugged. "No, it doesn't. But it also fits my theory."

She was getting excited. "If there *was* a murder, that camera could contain the proof. They would do anything to get it."

Lunk's face clouded over. "That means things could get dangerous."

Gordy moaned. "No! We're on vacation. Va-ca-shun."

Hiro put her hands on his shoulders. "You're right, Gordy. We need to have some fun too. Let's forget the mysteries for a while."

Gordy felt her forehead.

"I'm feeling fine," she said. "And I'm up for a bit of exploring—just not inside a creepy tunnel. You want to join me?"

Gordy gave her a suspicious look. "Maybe."

"It would be fun to explore the shoreline in the inflatable boat. Around the docks. Around the rocks. Stuff like that. But I'm not sure I can paddle that far."

Gordy's face brightened. "You really want to do this?"

She nodded.

"If you're serious about exploring, we could even scoot under the docks," Gordy said. "We'll lie on our backs and use our hands to grab the posts and push ourselves along."

"We won't get stuck?"

Gordy laughed. "I'll get the inflatable and meet you on the swim platform in thirty seconds." Gordy ducked out of the cabin.

Lunk wagged his finger at her. "You're a sly one, Hiro. I know what you're doing."

"Me?" Hiro plastered a naive look on her face. "I'm making sure Gordy enjoys his vacation."

"While you look for the camera," Lunk said.

"The camera?" Hiro looked innocent. "That thing is probably long gone. Or else they'd have found it by now."

"If they had," Cooper said, "they wouldn't have come here looking for it."

Hiro broke into a mischievous smile and put her finger to her lips. "What Gordy doesn't know won't hurt him." She laid her phone on the counter.

If Hiro's theory was right and Kryptoski was a murderer, then they knew too much already. Enough to get them all hurt.

CHAPTER 36

The rest of the afternoon passed quickly for Cooper. The fact that somebody had been on the boat unnerved him. And the intruder had been sloppy too. Leaving the door open? The blinds up? It was almost as if they wanted Cooper to know. He kept an eye on Gordy and Hiro with the binoculars every once in a while. After an hour, they came back. Gordy was stoked. Hiro, not so much.

They rode their bikes into town and met their moms at the public beach to swim and hang out for a while.

After two hours, Cooper and Hiro pedaled back to *The Getaway* to grab her phone while Gordy and Lunk stayed behind.

Hiro biked alongside him on the lakeshore path. "You didn't tell your mom that somebody was on the boat."

"No need to worry her," Cooper said. "Nothing was taken." What if she got spooked and didn't let them stay overnight on *The Getaway* anymore? "Maybe it was kids messing around." They didn't really know anything for sure. That was the truth. Still, he felt funny about not mentioning the incident to her.

Hiro glanced over at him. "You honestly think some kids got on *The Getaway*?" It almost seemed like she was testing him.

Cooper thought for a minute. "I wish it were true. But no."

"Then who?"

Hiro had her own ideas, Cooper was sure of that.

"Lynn knew you were looking for the camera. She could have done it."

"Maybe," Hiro said.

"You think it was Krypto?"

"He's got the nerve to do it."

"And don't forget that he's a sociopath." Cooper looked her way and smiled.

"Tease me all you want, Cooper MacKinnon. You'll see I'm right."

That's what he was afraid of. If she was right — if a murder had taken place — then all of them were witnesses. Sort of. They slid into single-file formation to scoot through a hedge.

"But there could have been a third person on the boat."

Cooper looked over his shoulder. "Fat Elvis?"

She nodded. "You can't rule out any possibility."

"Why do you think — " Cooper hesitated.

"Think what?"

Did he really want to go there? He'd be encouraging her to keep investigating.

"Coop?"

"Whoever was there didn't bother to hide it. Why?" Deep down, he knew the answer.

"What do *you* think?"

"I think we need to be careful," Cooper said. "This was another shot over the bow," Cooper said.

Hiro nodded. "Another warning: Back off. Or else."

Or else what? Cooper honestly didn't want anything to do with the whole investigation. They weren't involved anyway. Not really. He had no problem backing off. Hiro would be another story.

The sun smacked Cooper in the eyes until the path curved south just after Maytag Point. They passed the Lake Geneva Youth

Camp docks and cruised on the gravel shoulder along Big Foot Beach.

Hiro fell behind, and after a quick check over his shoulder, Cooper knew why. She was scanning the waterline for the camera.

"You go ahead," Hiro said. "I'll catch up."

"Good luck." Cooper zoomed ahead, but kept one eye on the beach. Finding the camera would answer a lot of questions. He looked ahead to *The Getaway* moored in the bay and saw the police boat tied alongside it.

Cooper stood on the pedals and pumped hard. "Hiro!" he shouted over his shoulder. "*The Getaway*!"

He had no idea if she'd heard him, but he couldn't wait to find out. He swung onto the pavement for better speed. Did this have something to do with Kryptoski and what they'd heard last night? Or had somebody reported that a person had been snooping around on their boat?

He skidded to a stop by the inflatable and dumped his bike. Hiro was twenty yards behind him, closing fast. By the time she locked up her bike, he had the boat in the water.

Hiro jumped into the inflatable, and Cooper leaned backward over the front, backstroking toward *The Getaway*.

"What do you think they want?" Hiro's face was flushed, and she was breathing hard.

"I'm afraid to guess."

They passed *Krypto Night*. The boat was empty, which suited Cooper just fine. He wished he'd never seen the boat in the first place. And he never wanted to see it again.

Cooper's T-shirt was soaked, but he tried hard not to splash Hiro. She sat in the back, one hand holding the side of the raft, the other one rubbing her Chicago Police star necklace. Her lips were moving but no words came out. Praying again. Actually, that wasn't a bad idea.

"It's Officer Tarpy," she said.

Cooper turned to look. He coasted a few feet with the forward momentum, then paddled the rest of the way. He steadied the inflatable as Hiro climbed out. He followed right behind her.

"Permission to board?" Tarpy held on to the side of *The Getaway*. He was smiling, like he wanted to set them at ease. But this was no social call.

Cooper nodded, and Officer Tarpy climbed over the side rail. "I'd like to talk to you a little more about your theory."

Her theory. The one Coop, Lunk, and Gordy had ripped apart.

Cooper expected Hiro to look honored or something. She didn't. She folded her arms across her chest. "Really? You weren't that interested this afternoon."

"I never said that," Tarpy said.

Hiro barely concealed a smile. "You didn't take any notes."

Tarpy whistled softly and looked at Cooper. "She's good."

Cooper nodded. "Oh yeah. And FYI, she's got a double dose of woman's intuition."

"Well, what do you say you run everything by me one more time?" Tarpy said. "This time I'll take notes."

"Something's changed," Hiro said. "Something big. Am I right?"

Tarpy cleared his throat. "I'm not really— "

"At liberty to say," Hiro finished for him. "I know."

Tarpy shook his head. "But yes, something has changed. I'd like you to come with me."

"Where?" Cooper said.

"The police station."

CHAPTER 37

Hiro stood next to Officer Tarpy as the police boat roared toward town. The lake had calmed, and the boat gobbled up the water and spit out foam-crested wakes. If the boat hadn't been moving, he'd definitely see her trembling. Fear? Maybe. Excitement? Definitely. This wasn't just about hearing her story. Something big was happening—and somehow Hiro had a part in it.

"I don't suppose you'll tell me what this is all about," Hiro said loudly.

Officer Tarpy kept his eyes on the water. "At the station."

Coop sat in the back with his eyes closed and his face turned toward the wind. His hair was whipping every which way. Sort of like what Coop himself had been doing since last night. One minute he seemed to be tracking right with Hiro. The next minute, he was back siding with Gordy and Lunk and acting like she had a hyperactive imagination. He opened his eyes and they met hers.

He said something to her. Not verbally, of course, but with his eyes. He did that sometimes—just to test her, to see if she could figure out what he'd said. And right now she had no idea.

Coop just smiled and shrugged. "You're losing your touch!" he shouted above the roar of the engine.

She stuck out her tongue and faced forward again.

They were coming up fast on the Riviera docks. "When we stop," Officer Tarpy said, "give your mom a call. Maybe she can meet us at the station."

"Coop comes too."

He gave her a sideways glance and nodded.

Whatever was going on, it was enough to make him agree to her request. She rubbed the goose bumps down on her arms.

As they passed the no-wake buoys, the boat slowed. Coop was texting someone—probably telling Gordy what was happening.

Minutes later they followed Officer Tarpy down the pier and entered the pass-through beneath the Riviera ballroom. Gift shops lined both sides of the tunnel.

Coop caught up with Hiro and walked alongside her. "Is your mom coming?"

Hiro nodded.

"Did she sound worried?"

She nodded again. "Did you text Gordy?"

Coop smiled. "I did indeed."

"Why are you smiling?"

"I told him the police were taking us to the station, and he texted back immediately—asked if I knew what it was all about."

"What did you say?"

"I told him I was sure it had nothing to do with the dead fish prank. Pretty sure, anyway."

Hiro giggled. "You're mean."

Even before they exited the tunnel, Hiro saw the police car parked at the curb. Their ride to the station, no doubt. They walked past the fountain without another word. She scanned the area for Gordy and Lunk, and it didn't take long to find them. They were kitty-corner from the police car, standing outside Scoops. Each boy held a cup of ice cream in his hands. Vanilla and Yippee Skippee, no doubt.

Clearly they hadn't seen her or Coop yet. Hiro put her hands behind her back. "Coop," she said. "Make like you're cuffed."

Coop laughed and followed her lead. "You're bad."

"Just finishing what you started with that text."

"Serious face," he said. "They're looking for us."

Hiro saw Gordy's expression change when he spotted her and Cooper. She hiked up one shoulder like she wanted to wave at him but couldn't. Even from across the street she could see his eyes grow wide. He pointed and said something to Lunk.

Officer Tarpy looked over his shoulder, probably to make sure they were still following. He gave them a double take. "What's with the charade?"

"Our friends are across the street," Hiro said. "We thought we'd give them a scare."

"I'll do what I can to help." He pointed to the police car, opened the back door, and motioned them inside. He played along with their little act, even to the point of putting his hand on her head to help her duck into the vehicle.

Gordy and Lunk were staring—and looking shell-shocked.

Officer Tarpy sat on the passenger side and pointed toward Scoops. "Is that them?"

"Yep," Hiro said.

"Light 'em up," Officer Tarpy said to the young cop behind the wheel.

The cop snickered and flipped on the lights and siren. Traffic stopped, and he tore out of there like they'd just collared Bonnie and Clyde. Hiro glimpsed Lunk as they passed. He was on his bike, frantically pedaling in pursuit.

"Well, that was fun," Officer Tarpy said. But his smile faded and his expression grew serious. Obviously he was back in cop mode.

Hiro had a sickening feeling that the fun and games were over.

CHAPTER 38

An hour later, Hiro felt more confused than ever. The police were being nice. Really nice. But if her mom hadn't been there with her, she might have ended up in tears.

It was all the questions. The repetition of them.

"Tell me about the girl with the pizza box."

"What did she look like?"

"What color was her hair?"

"What was she wearing?"

"Can you describe her T-shirt?"

"How long was her hair?"

"Was she wearing it pulled back or hanging down?"

"Did you notice any distinguishing marks on her?"

"Did she have any tattoos?"

"Did she have braces?"

"What color were her eyes?"

Over and over again. Officer Tarpy asked questions. Made notes. Asked more questions. The more he asked, the less Hiro felt she knew. She hadn't seen any tattoos. She didn't notice if the girl had braces. Pom-Pom was too far away for Hiro to notice her eye color.

"White T-shirt. Shoulder-length blonde hair parted in the middle. Jean shorts. Great figure." Hiro sighed. "That much I know."

Officer Tarpy looked up from his notes. "Are you describing the girl you call 'Pom-Pom,' or Lynn Tutek?"

"Pom-Pom." Hiro shrugged. "But I guess I'm describing both of them. I can't think of one thing that would prove they're two different people."

The only details she was absolutely sure of could have been used to describe Lynn just as easily as Pom-Pom.

"Did you notice any jewelry? A ring? Bracelet? Earrings? Necklace?"

Except for the necklace hanging around her own neck, Hiro had never been a fan of jewelry. Even if Pom-Pom had been wearing some, Hiro wouldn't have paid much attention to it. "She didn't have a Chicago Police star necklace." Hiro would have noticed *that*. "That's all I know."

Officer Tarpy's eyes dropped to the necklace, then back to her eyes. "Friend or relative?"

Hiro fingered the necklace. He got it. She didn't need to explain that somebody she loved had died in the line of duty. "My dad," she said.

Officer Tarpy closed his eyes. "I'm sorry." He turned to look at Hiro's mom. "I'm sorry, ma'am. I really am."

He paused, as if unsure whether he should continue the questioning. And really, Hiro hadn't given him anything more than what she'd already told him outside of Scoops.

"Did you notice if she was right- or left-handed?"

Hiro pictured the scene in the boat. "She waved at me with her left hand and held the pizza box in her right." She remembered that perfectly.

Officer Tarpy pursed his lips. Obviously her answer was inconclusive. Again. The girl could have been either right or left-handed. "Okay, tell me about that camera."

Hiro tried to visualize it. "It had a long lanyard."

"How long?"

Hiro held her hands two feet apart. "She had it around her neck—and it hung below her belly button."

Officer Tarpy didn't make a note.

"The lanyard was bright green. Nylon-looking. And the camera looked like it was some kind of underwater model."

"What made you think that?"

Good question. And one Hiro couldn't answer. Not well anyway. "Not sure. It's just a gut feeling. Or maybe it was something Lynn told me on the beach. She said it was totally waterproof."

Officer Tarpy tapped a pencil on his notebook. She obviously wasn't giving him what he needed. Her stomach tightened. Twisted. She was going to be a cop someday. Why hadn't she paid enough attention so she could remember some detail that would actually be helpful?

But helpful for what? Why was she even here? Because of the questions she'd raised outside Scoops?

Officer Tarpy pulled out a file folder, slid a half-dozen photos from it, and arranged them in a row on his desk facing her. "Does anyone here look like the first girl you saw?"

Hiro studied the pictures. They looked like they'd been taken from a high school yearbook. Actually it looked like a cheerleading tryouts lineup. All the girls were blonde. Beautiful. If Pom-Pom was one of them, Hiro couldn't be sure.

"Take your time," Officer Tarpy said.

Maybe it was a test. Maybe he didn't even put Pom-Pom in this group to see if Hiro really saw a difference. If she picked the wrong one, she'd lose all credibility—if she even had any. The fact was, none of them looked like the girl—and they all did. "None of them are jumping out at me," she said.

"Okay," he said. "Earlier today you were positive that Lynn wasn't the same girl you'd seen in the boat when they pulled away from their mooring. Correct?"

Hiro nodded.

"Would you testify in court that you saw two different women that night?"

After how miserably she'd done when trying to pinpoint even

one definitive difference between Pom-Pom and Lynn? She'd look ridiculous. "No," she said. "Not unless my feelings are admissible as evidence."

Officer Tarpy sighed. "Thanks for your honesty."

Great. That was a really polite way of saying, *Thanks for wasting my time. You've been absolutely no help to me.*

He closed his notebook and smiled. Interview over, apparently. Good. This hadn't been nearly as much fun as she'd hoped.

"I'm sorry I wasn't more helpful."

"Nonsense," Officer Tarpy said. "I was out to find the truth, and you were kind enough to give it to me."

But she had the feeling her answers had disappointed him. "Can I ask you a question, Officer Tarpy?"

"Shoot."

"Why all the sudden interest in this?"

Officer Tarpy drew a deep breath and exhaled loudly. "Nothing really. Just a shot in the dark."

So there *was* something more to this. Hiro looked at him and held his eyes with her steady gaze. It was a little technique that she'd perfected on Coop. It made it really hard for someone to hide the truth from her. "Meaning?"

Officer Tarpy chuckled. "I'm doing my duty to follow up with a concerned citizen."

"You mean me?" Hiro said. "There were too many questions for that answer to wash—if you'll excuse my forwardness."

"Hiroko," Mom said.

It was all Mom needed to say. It was her way of letting Hiro know she'd crossed the line. But Hiro had to.

Officer Tarpy waved at Hiro's mom. "No, she's fine." He leaned back in his chair. "This afternoon, after you talked to me outside Scoops, I got a missing persons report."

Hiro's heart double-timed.

"The girl roughly matched the description you gave me."

CHAPTER 39

Cooper tried to read Hiro's face when she walked out of Officer Tarpy's cubicle with her mom. Her eyes were blazing. And the way she was rubbing her necklace, she could start a fire.

Hiro's mom gave Cooper a hug. "I just talked to your mom. We'll all meet for dinner at Culver's. Lunk and Gordy are already there."

Dinner sounded great. But what he really wanted to do was talk to Hiro and find out what had happened in there. When Tarpy agreed to bring him along, Cooper didn't figure he'd be stuck in the waiting room the whole time.

"Sooo," Cooper said. "Everything okay?"

Hiro's mom nodded. "I think everyone will be relieved to hear there's no connection between what you saw—or heard, rather—and the missing girl."

Cooper eyed Hiro. "Missing girl?"

She drew a finger across her throat.

Okay. Cooper got the message. She didn't want her mom to be any more concerned about things than she already was. But Hiro would talk later. Cooper would make sure of that.

Dinner took forever. The four moms sat at the next table with Lunk, while Hiro and Gordy joined Cooper and his six-year-old sister Mattie at their own table. Cooper tried to stay engaged and seem interested in Mattie's endless stories about the outlet mall. But his mind kept reeling him back to the thought of a missing girl. Had Hiro been right?

Hiro smiled. Chatted. Nodded. She gasped with excitement when Mattie showed her the T-shirt she'd bought. But Hiro also kept rubbing that necklace of hers.

Lunk was sitting next to his mom. She smiled a lot and used her hands when she talked. By the way her hands were flying now, it seemed she'd had a wonderful day. And Cooper saw a side of Lunk that he'd not seen before. Lunk leaned forward as she talked. He listened. Smiled. Nodded. Lunk acted like she was the only person in the room.

Gordy sat back and looked at the ceiling, lost in thought. Cooper followed his gaze to where the train was running around the perimeter of the ceiling. One of the flat freight cars carried the Oscar Meyer Weinermobile. A classic.

"You know," Gordy said, "a guy could throw a fry up there and derail the train."

Cooper pictured the train veering off the tracks and crashing onto a table below.

Hiro looked up like it was the first time she'd noticed the rails. "You will do no such thing, Gordon Digby."

Gordy laughed. "I didn't say I wanted to do it. But if someone did, there'd be a real train wreck. Which is how our vacation is going to turn out if it keeps going like this."

Hiro looked confused. "Aren't you having a good time?"

"I'm trying to." Gordy looked dead serious. "We came to Lake Geneva to have fun. No mysteries — remember?"

Hiro leaned forward. "This one found us."

"But now you're going after it." Gordy looked like he wanted to say more but didn't dare. Not with the moms sitting so close.

"How am I doing that?"

Hiro asked the question, but she didn't need to. The answer was obvious, and Gordy was right. She was the one who kept looking for the camera. She sought out Officer Tarpy with her theories. She was watching for black pickups around every corner.

"I think you know exactly what I'm talking about," Gordy said. "Please don't turn this vacation into a train wreck."

"Not to worry," she said. "I don't think there's anything else I can do anyway."

Gordy nodded but looked skeptical.

Mattie trotted over to the counter to get some frozen custard. Hiro went with her.

"Why can't she leave it alone?" Gordy asked as soon as Hiro was out of earshot.

Cooper shrugged. "Cop blood."

"Don't cops ever take vacations?"

Cooper laughed.

Mattie took her treat to the other table. When Hiro sat down across from Cooper, she placed a flier on the table between them. It was a color photograph of a smiling blonde. The word MISSING was written in bold caps across the top. Cooper's stomach turned. For an instant he saw Gordy's picture in the girl's place. A few months earlier, that's exactly where it had been.

"Where did you get that?" Gordy said.

She pointed to the counter. "Somebody just asked the manager if he would post one on the glass door. I asked if I could have a copy of it."

Cooper studied the picture. He'd barely seen the girl in the boat—and definitely not well enough to identify her as anybody other than the girl he'd seen walking down the road after the cops got there.

"Officer Tarpy showed me the original photograph," Hiro said.

Coop read the caption below the photo. "Last seen Sunday, four p.m." It listed her height, weight, hair color. It was all there. "Braces." Cooper read out loud. "Tattoo on left ankle—a pair of dice."

Cooper read the girl's name. "Wendy Besecker." He looked at Hiro. "Is this the girl you saw?"

She shrugged. "I'm just not sure." She tilted her head as if seeing the picture from another angle might help. "This is a studio picture or something," Hiro said.

Cooper knew what she was saying. Her hair was up. That would make anybody look different. But still, the girl in the photo could have passed for Lynn's sister. Maybe Lunk was right about how much people resembled each other.

"Did you see her braces — or the tattoo?"

Hiro shook her head. "Officer Tarpy asked me the same questions."

"Does she have any connection to Kryptoski at all — did you ask Tarpy that?"

"I did. And if the girl had a connection, he wasn't aware of it. I think he was hoping *I'd* be the connection."

"You?" Gordy's voice sounded flat.

"If I had identified her by the picture, or the tattoo, or the braces — he'd have the connection he needed to bring in Kryptoski for questioning."

Cooper looked at her. "He told you that?"

"He didn't have to. It was obvious."

"So that's it, then," Gordy said. "End of the road. If you can't positively ID her, there's no reason to be involved anymore."

Hiro didn't say anything. But she didn't let go of her necklace either.

"But what if he did do it?" she whispered. "And he gets away with it? Where's the justice in that?"

Gordy didn't answer.

"And if there's no justice, no payday for that creep, then he could do it again," Hiro said.

"Well, I guess you'll just have to pray that God exposes the guy — if he's really guilty," Gordy said. "There are no other witnesses."

"The camera is the silent witness to the whole thing. I bet it has a story to tell," Hiro said. "Find that camera, and we'll be able to prove whether Pom-Pom and Lynn are the same person."

"*We?*" Gordy looked at her. "This is police business, not ours."

Hiro looked down.

"You're going to do it anyway, aren't you? No matter what anybody says."

"Do what?"

Gordy shook his head and looked up at the train. "Throw fries on the tracks."

CHAPTER 40

Lunk got the lowdown from Coop after the moms went back to the condo. The tension between Gordy and Hiro was obvious. Actually, it was kind of funny seeing Hiro so steamed at somebody else.

Cooper walked ahead with Gordy. Probably trying to cool him down. Lunk kept pace with Hiro. He'd do what he could to help them patch things up.

"Do you really think you're going to find the camera?"

Hiro looked up at him. "I wish."

"Realistically," Lunk said.

"If the wind was blowing toward the opposite side of the lake? Sure. It would drift to the north shore."

"But the wind was coming from the northwest," Lunk said.

Hiro looked miserable. "Exactly. It would have reached shore within hours. And I searched the area really well."

"You couldn't have missed it?"

"With a two-foot bright green lanyard attached to it?" she said. "Not hardly."

Lunk agreed. "And we know Kryptoski and his blonde didn't find it."

Hiro nodded. "Either it doesn't float, or somebody else picked it up."

"So it's gone," Lunk said.

Hiro jammed her hands into her pockets. "You could try giving a girl a little hope."

"You've got to *face* the facts, Hiro. That camera is g-o-n-e."

She kicked a pebble off the sidewalk. "Krypto is a creep. I can feel it. And I hate the thought that he might get away with this."

"If he did anything wrong."

Hiro gave him a half-smile and slugged him in the arm. "You are absolutely no help. Do you know that?"

Lunk laughed. "Thank you very much."

They walked in silence for a while. Lunk looked at her. "Why not let this thing go—at least for now—and make up with Gordy."

"Hummph."

Lunk wasn't sure if it was the thought of letting go or the idea of patching things up that irritated her more.

"How would I do that? I'm not going to promise him that I'll stop working on this."

"We still have an hour of daylight," Lunk said. "Why not suggest that he show you the other part of the river he was talking about? He'll forget all about being upset."

Hiro appeared to be thinking and her shoulders relaxed a little. That had to be a good sign, Lunk thought. Maybe he could help Coop bring the group together again. "Then we could go to Scoops afterward. He'd love it."

"*He'd* love it?" Hiro was smiling now. "I bet you would too."

Lunk felt his face getting warm. "I'm just saying—"

"I like your idea," Hiro said. "Watch how fast I change his mood. Hey, Gordy!"

Gordy turned. "Yeah?"

"We're really close to the river. Think there's time to show me that pipeline you were talking about?"

Gordy stopped. "Are you serious?" He definitely looked skeptical.

"Absolutely! I feel like doing something—fun."

Gordy's face brightened. "Well, yeah. Why not?"

"Lead the way," Hiro said.

Gordy clapped his hands and started jogging.

Coop pointed at her. *Thanks*. He mouthed the word, but Lunk was sure Hiro caught the message by the way she smiled back.

Hiro and Lunk jogged after them. "That *was* fast," Lunk said.

"He's no match for me," Hiro said.

"Who *is*?"

"Exactly," Hiro said. "Don't forget it."

Cooper and Gordy kept a good lead. They crossed the street and passed an old brick building. As much as Lunk didn't want to think about the camera, he couldn't keep his mind off it. Why? Maybe the challenge of finding it. Or maybe he wanted to make Hiro as happy as Gordy looked right now. Maybe both.

"Hiro?"

She kept jogging, but glanced up.

"You said the camera floated."

She nodded.

"What if the boat clipped it good? Maybe the prop or something—and the housing cracked. What if it sunk?"

She stopped dead—her eyes wide. "Oh my goodness. Lunk, that's it!" She stared at the sidewalk. "Everybody's been looking on shore. It could have dropped straight to the bottom." She paced a few steps. "Coop has masks and fins on board. We could do a little snorkeling if it's not too deep." She held out her hand. "Please accept my apologies."

He reached out and shook it. "What's that for?"

"I think I was wrong." She smiled.

"Hiro? Wrong?" Lunk cupped his hand around his ear. "Run that by me again. I don't think I heard you right."

She slugged his arm. "You heard me. I was wrong."

"About what?"

"Maybe you're a big help after all."

CHAPTER 41

Gordy led the way down the steep, wooded path to the river. The water was high—which was perfect. They'd get a little whitewater. The muffled roar of the water drowned out all sounds from town. They could have been miles from civilization. It felt like they were.

The iron pipeline angled across the river and under the old concrete railroad bridge. Even from here Gordy could make out the graffiti-covered walls beneath the bridge.

Gordy hopped onto the pipeline. He could lie flat on his stomach and wrap his arms around the pipe and grab his wrists. He'd tried it the last time he was there. Years of people using the pipeline as a footbridge had polished the top surface smooth as a cannon. He trotted halfway across and waited for the others. Lunk followed, then Coop.

"Isn't there another way across?" Hiro looked totally unsure of herself.

"Not unless you want to get wet," Gordy said. "You can do it. Just like that guy who did the tightrope walk across Niagara Falls."

"Nik Wallenda," Hiro said. "And he had a safety line."

"But he never needed it," Gordy said. "And he walked on a wet steel cable in gusty winds. You've got a nice big, dry pipeline to walk on—and it isn't exactly high off the ground." But for a girl with a fear of heights, it was high enough. She couldn't climb a six-foot fence without getting dizzy. No sense in reminding her of that now, though.

Cooper held out his arm. "You'll be fine."

She grabbed his hand. Coop started slowly walking backward. Hiro took a step onto the pipe. "I do not like this. I. Do. Not."

Gordy snickered and jogged in place. "What's the matter, Hiro? Just pretend you're one of those Flying Wallendas."

Hiro shuffled a few steps. "If I fall, Gordon Digby, *you're* going to go flying."

Gordy waved her off and hustled down the pipeline all the way to the railroad bridge. He moved fast—just to show off.

Lunk took the pipeline at an easy pace with his hands in his pockets like he didn't need them for balance. Cooper walked backward, holding both of Hiro's hands in his.

Hiro was bent over at the waist with her arms straight out in front of her. "I. Do. Not. Like. Heights."

Gordy watched her cross the pipeline. It was nice to see her so far outside of her comfort zone for once. "Think this is worse than the tunnel?"

She shook her head. "Nothing's worse than the tunnel."

By the time she got close, even Gordy could see that she was shaking. Now he felt kind of weird about showing off.

"The pipeline gets a little trickier under the bridge," Gordy said. "Just keep your back against the concrete wall and you'll be fine."

Hiro watched Gordy demonstrate. "No. Not a chance. I'm staying right here." She let go of Cooper's hands and sat on the pipe where it angled under the bridge.

"Okay, you can skip the pipeline," Gordy said. "From here we can walk in the river."

"Not me," Hiro said. "I'm good."

She was going to spoil everything. "But we've hardly seen any of it. You'll like it downriver a lot better."

She shook her head. “You guys go ahead without me. I’ll be right here when you come back.” She smiled and used her hands to brush them away. “Go.”

Gordy didn’t like it. Cooper didn’t look too wild about the idea either. Lunk was already standing in the river, picking his way around some larger rocks.

“If I need you, I can call.” Hiro held up her phone. “I’m a big girl.”

Big girl. That made Gordy smile just a bit. He let her comment go. “Okay. If you need us, we’ll come running.” He hopped off the pipe and landed on the riverbed with both feet. The water rushed past his legs like it was trying to take him down at the knees. He loved it.

Lunk was already fifty feet downstream. “What’s the plan?”

“Explore!” Gordy said. The water was a little higher than the last time he’d been here. The trees on both banks met overhead, making a dense canopy over the river. If Hiro had come with them, he’d have hidden his phone somewhere along the bank and picked it up on their way back so it wouldn’t get wet. Then he could have picked up his feet and ridden the river on his back. But with Hiro staying behind, he’d have to keep his phone on him, just in case.

Walking with the current was easy—and fast. He glanced back at Hiro one last time before they reached the bend in the river, where the thick trees and brush on the banks would hide her from view.

She waved at them, looking happy. Okay. Good.

Coop hung back a little, like he was still unsure about leaving Hiro. But her smile seemed to set him at ease. He picked up his pace and caught up to Gordy.

“It’s nice to be back here,” he said.

Gordy agreed. They’d had good times on the river. It was always different—yet always the same.

They finally caught up to Lunk where a tree had fallen across the river and worked like a dam, snagging sticks, branches, and small trees. All kinds of debris swirled around tiny whirlpools and made strange sucking noises.

"Don't get too close, Lunk," Coop said. "Sometimes the bottom hollows out and gets deep. With all those branches, you could get hung up on something."

Lunk took a step backward.

There wasn't a clear way to climb over, so they walked to the bank and worked their way around it.

In the next fifteen minutes, they passed three more blockades. Gordy noticed Coop checking his phone each time. He'd texted Hiro at least once.

The current helped them get farther than Gordy had even hoped to get.

Lunk looked around. "Kinda getting dark out here, don't you think?"

Maybe Gordy's eyes had gotten used to the light, because he hadn't noticed the darkness before now. But Lunk was right. It was no longer the familiar White River that he'd tromped through so many times before. The trees formed dark shadows over them, but there was something more. He felt out of place. Like the three of them didn't belong here. "Maybe we should head back."

Coop nodded. "And we'll be fighting against the current all the way. It'll take us longer." He checked his phone again. "Let's go."

Gordy didn't argue. They all turned and headed upstream. The water seemed higher—and faster now. Making headway was a lot slower than Gordy had anticipated. His shoes turned to lead. Every time he lifted a foot, the river tried to drive him back downstream. He swung his shoulders, trying to get some momentum.

Coop checked his phone again. "I haven't heard back from Hiro yet. That's not like her." He was moving faster now, and even Gordy had a tough time keeping up.

The shadowed river looked like a giant black snake hissing past them. It was definitely taking longer to get back. Way longer.

Lunk plodded along beside him, breathing heavily.

Coop steered wide of the fallen tree and log blockades, taking to the banks. But Gordy wasn't sure Coop was making any better time that way. The brush was dense and tangled, and the muddy banks were slick.

Lunk must have thought anything would be better than fighting the current. He joined Coop on the riverbank but went down hard within seconds. He was back on his feet again without a word. Normally there would have been some friendly teasing. But nobody said anything. They were too focused on the same thing—getting out of there.

The fun of the river had faded with the daylight. Now the place had an eerie feeling. Like they'd gone too far. Stayed too long. Like they needed to get back. There was a sense of urgency that Gordy couldn't explain, but he wondered if Coop felt it too.

"She must be getting worried," Coop said. "Why hasn't she answered me?"

As if on cue, his phone chirped. Coop smiled and swung the phone to his ear. "Hiro?" His smile disappeared.

"Where are you?" Eyes wide, Cooper started running. "Stay there! We're coming!" He pocketed the phone and splashed back into the stream.

Gordy plowed through the current to catch up. "What happened?"

"Some guy is stalking her."

Lunk jumped back into the river too. All three of them charged upstream, kicking their knees higher, trying to get some speed. Which wasn't working.

"I'm gonna try running on shore," Lunk said.

Coop didn't answer but ran along the shallow edge of the river. He ducked under some branches and plowed through others. Gordy kept up, his legs churning the water into a frenzy.

He glimpsed Lunk thundering through the brush, his arms swinging. He was having as hard a time with the branches as Gordy was with the stream.

Gordy tried to make his legs go faster, but he couldn't. He hooked his foot on a rock and stumbled, windmilling his arms to keep from going down. His knee sunk into the mud bank. The river was their enemy now, bent on holding them back.

Cooper's route gave him a nice lead. He rounded the last bend. "Hiro!"

The concrete bridge stood like a giant graveyard monument. The space underneath looked as dark as the river itself.

"Hiro!" Cooper didn't slow his pace but gave an extra burst of speed where the river ran a bit shallower. He disappeared into the shadows under the bridge.

Lunk was nowhere in sight. Gordy raced under the bridge and found Coop standing in the middle of the river—staring at the empty spot on the pipe where they'd last seen Hiro.

CHAPTER 42

Coop shook off his dark thoughts and ran to the pipeline. "Hiro!" He paused to listen. Nothing. Just the sound of rushing water.

"Hiro!" Gordy joined him, turning in a slow circle midstream and scanning the shoreline and the woods beyond. He held up his hand. "Listen!"

Cooper heard it too. Somebody, or something, was crashing through the brush and obviously not concerned about stealth. He looked around for something, anything, to defend himself with. He groped along the bottom of the river, pulled up a rock the size of a Burger King Whopper, and advanced to the shoreline.

Whatever it was, it was coming fast — and right toward him. Cooper braced himself and raised the rock, ready to use it.

Suddenly, Lunk crashed out from under the cover of thick brush. "Find her?"

Cooper let out his breath. He didn't even know he'd been holding it. "Split up," he said. "Gordy, take the path back up to the road. Lunk, search the woods on this side of the river." He looked up. "I'll climb to the top of the railroad bridge."

The guys scattered. Cooper sloshed through the river, ducked under the pipeline, and scrambled up the embankment on the other side. *God, please protect Hiro. I shouldn't have left her behind.* The soft ground gave way under his feet. He climbed up on all fours, using saplings and roots for handholds.

"Hiro!" Lunk's voice came from somewhere below him, across the river.

Cooper hesitated, listening for Hiro's voice to respond. Nothing. He clawed his way up the final ten feet and stepped onto what was once the bed of the railroad tracks. Now it was a hiking path. No railroad ties. No rails. And no Hiro.

He dashed halfway across the bridge and looked over the crumbling concrete wall to the river fifty feet below. "Hiro!" Nothing but whitewater—and dark fears.

Cooper's phone chirped. He whipped it from his pocket and read Gordy's text. "Got her. She's fine. By the street." *Thank God.*

He scanned the woods beyond the shoreline. "Lunk—we got her!"

Some brush moved and Lunk stepped into view. He spotted Cooper and waved.

Cooper pointed to his own chest and then back to the river.

Lunk nodded as if he understood.

Cooper headed down the embankment, which felt like plodding down a steep sand dune. The soil collapsed under his feet and started mini avalanches. Twice he lost his footing and slid on his seat for a yard or two. When he got to the river, all the mud on his shoes made crossing on the pipeline too dangerous. He needed to clean off a bit anyway. He slipped back into the river and worked on getting the mud and dirt off his legs, hands, and swim shorts.

Lunk splashed across the river to meet him. "So where is she?"

"With Gordy." Cooper pointed up the path. "By the street."

"Did he say what happened?"

Cooper shook his head. "We're sure going to find out, though."

They quickly cleaned up and ran up the path.

Cooper was happy to leave. The river, bridge, pipeline—all of it had changed. He looked back to be sure they weren't being followed. Their old secret place had secrets of its own. By the time they got to the road, Cooper had imagined all kinds of scenarios. None of them good.

Hiro stood next to Gordy, hugging herself. She was facing their direction, watching for Cooper and Lunk to appear. She gave Cooper a half-smile as he hustled over to her.

"Are you okay?" Cooper said.

She nodded. "Just scared."

"What happened?"

Hiro shrugged. "I was just trying to explain it to Gordy." She pulled her braid in front of her shoulder and fidgeted with it. "It seemed like you guys had been gone a long time. And it was getting dark."

Cooper felt a twinge of guilt. She was right. They'd left her alone too long.

She looked toward the path heading to the river. "I was getting a bad feeling."

Cooper studied her eyes, which still looked haunted. "Like you thought something had happened to us?"

She shook her head. "No, nothing like that."

Cooper stayed quiet, which took some effort. He wanted her to get to it. But if he let her tell it in her own way and at her own speed, he'd probably learn more.

"There was something bad about the place. Dark." She hesitated, like she expected one of them to make a joke about it.

Nobody said a word.

Hiro shrugged. "Like something awful had happened there before. And would again."

"Like what?" Gordy's eyes got wide.

"I don't want to know. But the feeling grew worse. I kept watching for you guys to come back." She paused like she was reliving the whole thing. "I couldn't stand it anymore. I had to get out of there."

A chill crept over Cooper. He'd sensed something about the

area just as they were leaving, hadn't he? Hiro had obviously experienced something too. Only worse.

Lunk stood next to Cooper. "What was that about a stalker?"

"I heard someone—in the woods."

Cooper waited.

"It was coming toward me. At first I thought it was you guys. That you'd given up on the river. But it was coming from the wrong direction. And slowly. Like he didn't want me to hear him."

Lunk eyed the path back to the river, like he expected somebody to appear.

Cooper scanned the street in both directions.

"That's when I called you, Coop."

Cooper nodded. He hated to think of her being scared and him not being there.

"I know you told me to stay there, but the sound was coming closer. I was afraid to move. But I was *more* afraid to stay. I could feel someone watching me," she whispered. "He was coming for me. If I'd stayed there, I ..." Hiro stared past Cooper like she was a zombie—or imagining one.

"Hokey smokies," Gordy said. "Why didn't you call 9–1–1?"

Hiro stared at the ground. "I didn't even think of it. I was clutching my phone in my hand. I wanted to call Coop again—but I never thought of calling the police."

Lunk shook his head. "Hiro didn't think to call the cops? You really *were* scared."

Cooper checked over his shoulder toward the river. "So then what?" She was giving details way too slowly.

"I crawled back across the river on the pipeline."

"But what about the guy?" Cooper asked. "Did you get a good look at him?"

Hiro shook her head. "Once I got over the pipeline, I hit the path running. I didn't look back until I got to the street. Then I just stayed here until Gordy found me."

"You *never* saw him?" Cooper said.

Hiro shook her head. "I *felt* him. Close."

"What did he feel like?" Gordy said.

She turned pale. "Evil."

Gordy swallowed hard and looked back toward the river.

So much for Gordy's plans for fun at the river. Would his cousin ever want to go back there? "You wanna get out of here, Hiro?" Cooper said.

She nodded.

"Me too." Cooper hooked her arm through his and headed toward town. Gordy did the same with her other arm—like she was Dorothy in *The Wizard of Oz.* Lunk walked directly behind them. The rear guard.

The farther from the river they walked, the more she seemed to relax. She looked up at Cooper. "Where are we going?"

"Scoops."

CHAPTER 43

He watched them from the cover of the trees along the river. He'd shaken her up pretty good, hadn't he? She never saw him—but he made sure she heard him. And he couldn't have asked for a better reaction. She'd taken off like a scared rabbit.

And she was still spooked. He noticed her body language. The way she moved her hands when she talked. Oh yeah. He'd scared her good. It was as obvious as the black braid hanging down her back.

Fear was the ultimate weapon. No license required. No state registration needed. He was an expert shot—and he'd hit his target.

And the beautiful thing about fear was that it was contagious. Even now the boys kept looking back toward the river as they walked toward town.

"Afraid somebody's going to sneak up on you, fellas?"

He chuckled. "You should be."

CHAPTER 44

The more distance they put between them and the river, the better. Hiro's oppressive feelings were gone. And so was her hope of enjoying a "normal" vacation. This mystery—if she could call it that—seemed to follow her everywhere, no matter whether she was playing or investigating. She'd rather be working the investigation.

A flier about Wendy Besecker was taped to Scoops' door.

Hiro imagined the tattoo on the girl's ankle. Why would she pick a pair of dice for a tattoo? Obviously she was a girl who liked to gamble—or live dangerously. Was she the one Hiro had seen on the boat yesterday? If so, she'd gambled with the wrong guy, hadn't she?

Katie was working behind the counter again. Everybody ordered their usual. But along with his Yippee Skippee, Katie handed Gordy a taster spoon of Halley's Comet. Maybe she wanted him to broaden his tastes.

The boys sat at one of the tables, but Hiro stayed at the counter.

"You have a picture of a missing girl posted on your door," Hiro said. "Do you know her?"

"Wendy?" Katie nodded. "I do."

Hiro waited, hoping Katie would say more. Nothing. Time for a little prodding. "Is she a nice girl? Good?"

"Nice," Katie said. "But not necessarily good."

"There's a difference?"

Katie nodded. "A lot of people are decent to others. They're nice. But they hang out with bad influences and end up making lousy choices. When you mix it all together like that, it just turns out bad."

Hiro processed that for a moment. Katie used few words, but she was actually saying a lot. "Who did Wendy hang out with?"

"She had time for anybody," Katie said. "Always smiled and talked when she came in here."

Not exactly the kind of specifics Hiro was looking for. "Did she ever hang with Tommy Kryptoski?"

Katie eyed her. "I see you didn't care for the scoop of advice I gave you this afternoon."

"I'm staying away from him," Hiro said. "Believe me. It's just that ..." She stopped, wishing she could fill Katie in on everything. Krypto's date. The argument. Whether Wendy had been the girl on the boat instead of Lynn. Fat Elvis conveniently showing up at Scoops. The supposed drunk driver who clipped Coop. Somebody snooping around on *The Getaway*. The stalker by the river.

Katie was still watching her. "It's just what?"

Gordy stepped up beside Hiro. "It's just that this Halley's Comet is out of this world." He waved the sample spoon and grinned. "Get it? *Comet? Out of this world?*"

"We get it, Gordy," Hiro said.

"It's not as good as Yippee Skippee," Gordy said, "but it almost put me into *orbit*."

Hiro held her hands over her ears. "Please, no more."

Gordy grinned. "Halley's Comet," he shouted, "is the *brightest star* in my day!"

Katie laughed. "I hope it filled the *space* in your stomach."

Gordy nodded and moved his hand in an arc high above his

head. "If not, I'll be like a meteor *streaking* on over here for more." He shuffled back to the table.

"You can thank your *lucky stars* we've got plenty." Katie smiled and shook her head and refocused on Hiro, "Now, you were saying?"

Hiro looked over at the guys. Coop had his eye on her. He was warming up to her way of thinking, but none of them were ready for her theories. They still saw them as coincidences. What Hiro needed to do was to prove the connections.

No, this wouldn't be the best time to talk to Katie, not where the skeptics could overhear. "Maybe after the boys go back to the boat, I'll come back here so we can talk."

Katie raised one eyebrow as if she understood. "Sounds ominous."

Hiro glanced at the boys. "I believe it is."

CHAPTER 45

The way Cooper saw it, Hiro was back to being her normal self. She'd been having girl time with Katie at the counter. Talking in whispers. Laughing. Glancing at the boys' table.

"Look at her," Cooper said. "It's like nothing ever happened."

Lunk seemed to be weighing that out. "Technically, nothing did. She got spooked, that's all."

Gordy leaned in. "What about the guy stalking her?"

"What guy?" Lunk took a spoonful of vanilla. "It could have been a deer. A squirrel. Or her overactive cop imagination. She didn't actually *see* anyone."

"Thank you for not pointing that out to her," Cooper said. "That wouldn't have gone over real big."

Lunk shrugged. "It was the boogeyman."

Gordy reloaded his spoon. "There's no such thing as a boogeyman."

"Exactly," Lunk said. "Hiro didn't see anyone. None of us did. I say nobody was there."

Cooper watched Hiro talking at the counter. Could that whole thing have been her imagination? He wasn't sure the explanation was that simple. "But I felt like something dark was at the river too."

Lunk waved it off. "The power of suggestion. One person feels it, and pretty soon everybody does. Now she sees someone behind every shadow. She's got herself all worked up."

"I don't know," Cooper said. "When she gets those feelings, I've learned to pay attention."

Gordy wiped a drip of Yippee Skippee off his chin. "She sure seemed happy on the way to the river."

"She was fine until we left her," Lunk said. "Like a kid home alone, every sound seems scary. It was all in her head."

Cooper thought back to her phone call. "The fear in her voice was real enough."

"True." Lunk said. "I'm not saying she wasn't scared. But there was nothing to be afraid of."

The bell above the door jingled, and Hiro's smile faltered for a moment.

Cooper followed her gaze. Lynn Tutek walked through the door and strolled right over to the counter.

"Hey!" Lynn smiled, snapped her fingers, and pointed at Hiro. "My friend from the beach."

Hiro smiled back. "Any luck finding your camera?"

"Actually," Lynn said, "I was about to ask you the same thing."

That pretty well answered Hiro's question.

Hiro shrugged. "I haven't seen it. You're sure it floats?"

What was she doing? Cooper glanced at Lunk, who seemed to be wondering the same thing.

"Like a beach ball. That's what Tommy said."

Hiro rubbed her police star necklace. "I hope this doesn't sound bad, but if Tommy can afford that sweet boat, why all the effort to find the camera? Why not just buy a new one?"

Was Hiro trying to get the girl to mess up?

Lynn smiled. "The memories. All the pictures. You can't replace those."

"That's true," Hiro said. "But I bet he'd like to replace at least some of them."

Cooper couldn't believe he'd just heard that. Was Hiro baiting her?

Lunk leaned closer and circled his ear with his finger. "The cherry just slipped off Hiro's sundae, if you know what I mean."

Lynn's smile faded.

"I mean, hey," Hiro said, "the way you two were snapping pictures during your argument, I can see why your boyfriend would like to make those disappear. Probably not the type of photos he'd want posted online."

Cooper walked to the counter.

"I was angry," Lynn said. "So was he. Nothing unusual about that."

Hiro shook her head like she'd just heard something insane. "Seriously? There was nothing normal about the way he thrashed around in that boat of his."

Cooper took Hiro's arm and squeezed it lightly.

Lynn took a step toward Hiro. "What are you suggesting?"

"Nothing," Cooper said. "She wasn't suggesting anything. In fact, we were just leaving." He prodded Hiro forward. "Let's go, Hiro."

She squirmed to get free. "I'm suggesting you weren't the one in the water."

Lunk grabbed her other arm. She jerked and pulled, but couldn't break their grip.

Lynn stood there with her jaw hanging open. "I was soaking wet. You saw that."

Hiro twisted back to face her. "But I didn't buy it. Because if you were the one in the water, you wouldn't go near him now—no matter how much he sweet-talked you. You'd be too afraid that he'd hurt you if he got angry again."

Lynn glared at her. "He would never hurt me. He loves me."

"Better hope so," Hiro said. "And pray it never changes. Because if you weren't the girl in his boat Sunday night and you just covered for him—that means you're the only one besides him that knows the truth. And if something were to happen to you—his secret would be safe."

Lynn sucked in her breath.

"Hiro," Cooper said. "Stop it." He helped Lunk muscle Hiro to the exit.

Gordy held the door open.

Lynn took a step closer. "You don't actually believe that Tommy is capable of hurting someone."

"And how could you possibly know that?"

Lynn smiled. "Because if you did"—her voice was as cold as ice cream now—"you'd be afraid to say something that might make him angry at *you*."

CHAPTER 46

Cooper and Lunk got Hiro out the door and away before she could answer Lynn. But the damage was done. They walked her across the street and sat on a bench.

"Are you completely loose?" Cooper said. "I mean, you totally must have something loose up here." He tapped her head. "That was insane."

Hiro raised her chin like she was proud of what she'd done.

Lunk snickered. "I was impressed. Wow, Hiro, you really gave it to her."

"But it made no sense," Cooper said. "You always fly under the radar. Get the opposition to relax their guard. That's your style. If Lynn isn't the girl Kryptoski took on the boat—and I'm not saying she isn't—then the last thing you want to do is let them know you suspect them."

Hiro was quiet, but she didn't look like she regretted what she'd done. Not one bit. And yet her outburst had destroyed any chance of proving her theory. If she was right and Lynn *was* covering for Kryptoski, wouldn't they be more careful than ever?

"I didn't give them anything they didn't already have," Hiro said. "They already knew I suspected something. You think it was a coincidence that Lynn walked into Scoops while we there? She'd been sent."

"By who?"

"Fat Elvis. Kryptoski. Maybe even his dad. Take your pick."

"For what reason? To see if we found the camera?"

Hiro shook her head. "I think we're being watched. The boat is being watched. And if that's true — they know we haven't found the camera."

"Being watched?" Lunk said. "You are soooo paranoid."

"I'm serious," Hiro said.

"Yeah," Lunk said. "Seriously paranoid."

Hiro acted like she didn't hear him. "Maybe there's a snitch in the police department who told them we suspect them. Maybe that's why somebody was following me by the river."

"Now you're really stretching it," Lunk said.

"Stretching?" Hiro said. "How can you think all of this is stretching it? We have a missing person. A missing camera."

Lunk tapped his head. "And I think you're missing a few screws up here."

Hiro sighed and shook her head. "Did you hear what Lynn said? If she had nothing to hide, why threaten me about staying quiet?"

Cooper studied her face. "You didn't lose control in there at all. That was an act." Cooper felt his face getting warm. "You made sure they know that you suspect Lynn is covering for Kryptoski."

"Why would Hiro do that?" Gordy said.

"So they send us another warning," Hiro said. "Something to scare us into dropping this whole thing. Something so clear that even you guys won't miss it."

"You did it so we'll buy into your theory," Lunk said.

Hiro nodded. She was almost smiling. "Yes. And then we'll have something new to take to Officer Tarpy."

"But if you're right about all of these things being connected," Cooper said, "we've already been given some warnings."

Hiro stared at him.

"Kryptoski blasted his horns right back at us last night," Cooper said. "He was sending a message. He wanted us to butt out of his business, right? Even when he drove past our boat and asked us to let him know if we saw the girl—he was warning us that he knew where to find us."

"And if your theory is right," Lunk said, "and the guy in the pickup was Fat Elvis and not some random drunk, then that was a warning too."

"Okay, good." Hiro said. "Maybe you guys are finally starting to believe me. Something bad happened last night. Every one of these things has been a warning for us to stay away—including what just happened at the river."

"So after your little outburst in Scoops," Cooper said, "you figure they'll warn us again—proving that they're guilty."

Hiro nodded. "Exactly."

"But if we haven't backed off after all of these warnings," Cooper said, "what makes you think these guys will warn us again?"

Hiro didn't say anything.

"They'll think warnings don't work on us," Lunk said. "Why keep doing something that doesn't work?"

Gordy's eyes got wide. "If they don't think the warnings will shut us up, then maybe they'll try something else. Something more permanent."

CHAPTER 47

Cooper kept looking over his shoulder—probably as much as Hiro did. But nothing even slightly sinister happened on Monday night. There was no sign of Lynn or Kryptoski. No Fat Elvis or black pickups prowling around. Even Cooper's shoulder didn't bruise as badly as they'd expected it to. It was stiff, sure. But it loosened up pretty quickly. He didn't even need any more of the pain meds.

When they got back to the boat, *The Getaway* was just the way they'd left it. Hiro's little plan was supposed to prove Kryptoski's guilt. But no warning had come yet. *Krypto Night* bobbed at its anchor like every other boat in the bay.

Hiro had been dead certain that her little outburst at Scoops would prove Kryptoski was guilty and Lynn was helping him cover up the crime. But when no warning came, it looked more and more like maybe Lunk and Gordy were right. There was no connection between Kryptoski and the missing girl. Hiro's fears had overshadowed her intuition and logic.

Nothing unusual happened on Tuesday morning either—until Cooper's dad showed up right after lunch with a new bike helmet for Cooper. His photo shoot had been delayed, so he'd hotfooted it to Wisconsin to spend the afternoon with his family. Actually, he spent the whole day on *The Getaway* with the guys.

Cooper water-skied for about ten minutes before his arm felt like it was going to fall off, and his shoulder throbbed for an hour afterward. Gordy acted like he could ski forever. No surprise there.

The real surprise was Lunk. Cooper's dad convinced him to give it a try, and after a handful of attempts, he actually stayed up on his water skis. Cooper had never seen Lunk grin so big—until the moment when Dad invited Lunk to drive the boat. At first Lunk hesitated like he wasn't sure if Cooper's dad was serious. But Dad clearly was. Lunk glanced at Cooper to make sure Cooper was okay with it.

Cooper grinned. "Go for it."

Lunk hustled over to the wheel.

Cooper's dad went over some of the operations of the controls and pointed toward the northwest.

Lunk squared his shoulders and took the wheel.

After a minute Cooper's dad threw his arm around Lunk's shoulders. "You've got it. Have fun."

Lunk glanced up and grinned. Somehow he looked both younger and older at the same time. Like a kid who wanted to please his dad but who also wanted to be seen as a man. Cooper's dad could bring that out in a guy. Maybe that's why Lunk kept trying until he finally got up on the skis. It wasn't like he was trying to prove anything, but more like he was looking for approval. If that was what he'd been looking for, he definitely got it.

Dad stepped up beside Cooper.

"Thanks for that," Cooper said.

Dad nodded. "He needs it." He walked to the stern and stared at the water shooting from underneath the boat. "So tell me about what's happening with my boy."

"Did Mom talk to you?"

He nodded. "I want to hear it from you."

Where to start? Cooper took a deep breath. He told Dad about Kryptoski—and Hiro's suspicions.

Dad listened. He asked questions to be sure he understood. Nodded. Concern showed on his face but not in his words.

Cooper told him about Fat Elvis, the drunk driver, and slamming into the stone wall. He also told how someone had supposedly been watching Hiro by the river.

Dad glanced at him. "You think she was right—that somebody was watching her?"

"I don't know." Cooper shrugged. "Sometimes I think so. But right now it seems pretty out-there." Maybe it was because he was with his dad now, but the darkness of the river, the danger of it all, seemed to fade. Maybe they'd just gotten spooked.

"I wish I could stay here the rest of the week," Dad said. "But I'll be back Saturday and all next week. You guys be careful, okay?"

Be careful. Dad's way of reminding him to stay on guard. Be alert. And Cooper wanted to. He really did. But how was he supposed to do that?

"If anything weird happens . . ."—Dad held up his phone—"call me."

If the week kept going the way it had started, he'd be on the phone with his dad a lot.

"I'll bring Fudge up on Saturday."

Cooper nodded. The chocolate Lab loved camping and loved the water. This place would be like heaven for her.

Dad slung his arm around Cooper's shoulders and gave him a light squeeze, being extra careful of his sore shoulder. "I think I'll check on Lunk."

Dad walked toward Lunk with the swagger of a sailor as *The Getaway* rolled with the swells. "How's it going, Skipper?"

Lunk grinned.

"You're cutting a nice straight course." Cooper's dad pointed at the wake behind them. "Nice job."

Lunk followed Dad's gaze and then focused on the lake in front of him. He stood tall. Straight. He drove the boat the rest of the time until they stopped in Williams Bay for a mid-afternoon snack.

An hour later, they'd had their fill at Skip's and were headed back to their buoy. Just off Black Point, Gordy convinced Cooper to take another turn skiing with him. Lunk was at the wheel again, and he'd never looked happier.

Black Point. Even the water looked black. Not that there was anything different about the water in this spot. It was the deepest part of the lake. It was a hundred and fifty-two feet deep here, according to Dad's old dive chart. Cooper tried not to imagine what the bottom would look like that far down. It would be barren. Dead. Weeds don't even grow at that depth. Cooper eased into the water. The chill felt good on his sore shoulder.

He thought about Hiro's theory. What if there really were two different girls? What if Kryptoski clipped Pom-Pom with the boat? Is this where a body in the lake would eventually settle? He slid his feet into the skis and kept his legs hiked up, wanting to stay as close to the surface as possible.

Cooper and Gordy got up on the first try, which was good. Cooper wanted to get away from this part of the lake.

Gordy was in fine form. "Tomorrow we're pranking the mailboat!" He sounded like it was a done deal.

"Count me out."

Gordy angled his skis and sprayed him.

Cooper wiped the water from his eyes and shot over the wake. Gordy followed. Cooper leaned and gave Gordy a face full of his own medicine.

Laughing, Gordy cut back, jumped the wake, and landed with a clean splash.

Cooper swung out a little wider. Lunk was driving again. Dad stood beside him, but he faced the back of the boat to work as spotter. He motioned to Cooper to jump the wake.

Cooper nodded, angled for the wake, and pulled hard—just as Gordy changed direction and crossed to meet him.

Cooper tried to veer away, but it all happened too fast. They collided—not so bad for either of them to get hurt, but way too hard for either of them to stay up on their skis.

Cooper hit the water headfirst and went deep. Dark. Black. He couldn't breathe. Something was there. Evil. Grabbing for him. Cooper kicked. Clawed. Screamed.

CHAPTER 48

Lunk held the wheel steady.

"He's down," Mr. MacKinnon said.

Lunk throttled back and spun the wheel to make a U-turn.

"Perfect," Mr. MacKinnon said. "You learn fast."

Lunk felt bigger. Stronger. Better about himself. Somehow that simple comment did all of that for him. And he wanted to hear it again.

Gordy bobbed on the surface, his skis floating away in different directions. Coop broke the surface like he'd seen a shark. His arms were swinging; he elbowed Gordy in the face and kept thrashing.

Lunk gripped the wheel.

Mr. MacKinnon sprung into action. "Drop her into neutral and cut the engines." Without hesitation, he dove over the rail and swam toward Coop.

Lunk killed the motors. The boat drifted closer to his friends. Lunk rushed to the stern.

Coop's dad was lifting Cooper higher in the water than the lifejacket was already doing. "It's okay, Cooper. I've got you."

Cooper swung and hit.

What was wrong with him?

His dad didn't let go. "You're safe. Dad's got you."

One arm around Coop's chest, Mr. MacKinnon used his free arm to stroke his way to the boat.

Gordy looked scared. Confused. Blood trickled from his nose. He kept his distance from Coop and swam after the drifting skis.

Lunk vaulted over the rail and landed on the swim platform. Cooper wasn't swinging his arms anymore. He looked limp, like all the fight was gone from him, and let his dad tow him in.

Once they'd pulled him onto the platform, Coop looked dazed. Spent. Scared. It spooked Lunk a little bit.

"Help me get him into the boat," Mr. MacKinnon said.

"I'm okay," Coop said. "I got it." He reached for the rail to pull himself over. His hands were trembling.

What happened to you down there? Lunk wanted to ask—but didn't dare. He glanced at the water, half expecting to see a shark's dorsal fin cut the surface.

Coop climbed into the boat, and his dad was right there beside him.

By the time Gordy handed Lunk the skis and joined them at the stern, the color was back in Coop's cheeks.

"I-I got dizzy. I couldn't figure up from down. I felt like ..." Coop's voice trailed off.

His dad checked Coop's ears. "Could be a ruptured eardrum from the fall. That would make your equilibrium go berserk. Did you smack hard?"

Cooper shrugged. "I'm not sure."

His dad frowned. "There's no blood. If your eardrum ruptured, I'd see a trace."

"Gordy," Coop said, "your nose is bleeding."

Gordy touched it lightly. "Yeah, maybe I ruptured it."

He didn't look happy.

Cooper looked confused. "What?"

"You hit me."

"When I fell?"

He really didn't know what he'd done. It was like he'd blacked out or something. But it was worse than that, wasn't it? Instead of being unconscious, he just wasn't conscious of what he was doing. He'd *blanked* out.

Coop's dad took a look at Gordy's nose. "Doesn't appear to be broken."

"When did I hit you?" Coop asked.

Gordy stared at him in disbelief. "It was just like before—except this time you swung your elbows. What are you going to do next—bite me?"

Coop's dad looked from Cooper to Gordy. "This has happened before?"

Gordy went through the whole story. Lunk listened but could hardly believe what he was hearing. Coop was like a fish in the water. He absolutely loved it.

"It's like sometimes when Coop goes underwater, he hits a ten on the ol' panic meter," Gordy said.

"Sometimes?" Coop's dad said. "But not every time?"

Gordy shrugged. "When the towrope got caught under the boat, Coop had no problems being underwater. Oh, and I'm sorry about that rope, Uncle Carson."

Cooper's dad waved him off. "If your eardrum was ruptured from an earlier fall, you'd feel that disorientation whenever you went underwater. Every time. No exceptions."

Which meant a ruptured eardrum wasn't the issue.

"If it's really light—the water, I mean—and I can see the bottom, then I'm okay," Coop said.

"But if the water is dark or you can't see the bottom?" Coop's dad let the question hang there.

Coop swallowed. "I don't know. I-I feel like I'm going to die."

Gordy touched his nose again. "You almost killed *me*."

"Sorry, Gordy," Coop said. "I don't remember doing it."

"Is that supposed to make me feel better?"

It was a scary thought—that Coop had no idea what he was doing. Lunk looked at his friend and reviewed the water scene in his mind. *Panic* wasn't a strong enough word. *Terror* was more like it.

"Sooo," Lunk said, "this doesn't always happen—but it isn't exactly random either."

Mr. MacKinnon nodded. "And it never happened before this summer—right?"

Coop nodded.

Mr. MacKinnon looked out over the water. "How's this for a theory?" He crossed his arms in front of his chest. "This has something to do with being in that flooded basement last May. You're okay underwater when you can see, but if it's dark, it triggers something in your mind. You're suddenly back in that basement, trying to get out."

A chill flashed down Lunk's back and arms. That made total sense.

Cooper seemed to be processing that theory. "Gordy has no problem underwater. Why wouldn't it affect him the same way?"

"No idea," Mr. MacKinnon said. "Everybody's different. But Gordy was fighting hypothermia, and he was only half there mentally."

Lunk studied his friend. Coop wasn't denying the possibility that his dad was right.

"So what do we do?" Coop said.

Lunk liked the way he said that. What do *we* do? They were all in this together. Lunk had always had to work things out for himself. He had his mom, sure. But sometimes he didn't want to worry her.

Coop's dad put his arm around his son. "We'll figure it out. In the meantime, let's head back to the mooring. We'll be meeting the girls for dinner soon." He fired up the engines and eased them into gear. But it didn't look like his mind was on dinner at all.

Lunk didn't have Hiro's gift for reading people, but he could guess what Coop's dad was thinking about—how to help his son.

What would it be like to have a father who cared like that? He pushed the thought away.

Minutes later, the boat was up to cruising speed. Lunk squinted into the wind. He liked the feel of the wind rushing against him but not moving him.

"It really drags the lake, doesn't it?" Coop's dad jerked his thumb toward the stern.

The wake was huge, and the boat appeared to be digging into the lake, ripping it open, dragging some of it along. Lunk glanced at Mr. MacKinnon. Coop's dad seemed to have been ripped open too. That's the way a real dad was supposed to be. If one of his kids was hurting, a real dad felt his child's pain.

Coop was standing at the stern rail, holding on and staring into the water. Was he thinking about the basement? Sure he was. It was like an invisible chain was still holding him there.

Lunk wanted to free him. He wished he could. But how?

CHAPTER 49

The Getaway slowed down. Cooper glanced forward. They were still several hundred yards away from the mooring.

"I have an idea." Dad slid the throttle into neutral and cut the power. "The ordeal in the basement was totally traumatic. So horrifying that every time you get underwater, when it's too dark to see, it works like a trigger. It shoots you back to the near-death experience in the basement." He shrugged. "So naturally, you panic. But the good news is that it's all in your mind."

Oh, great. So now he was a nutcase. "Dad, I felt something down there. Really. Like something evil was trying to get me. Like it was trying to keep me from reaching the surface."

Dad tapped his head. "But it was in here. Not in the water."

That didn't make Cooper feel any better.

"We'll retrain your brain."

Cooper stared at him. "How?"

"He's going to flood a basement," Gordy said. "You know, the whole thing about climbing back on the horse or bike—or whatever."

Cooper shot Gordy a look. "There's no way he's doing that."

Dad climbed over the stern rail and dropped onto the swim platform. "We'll do it together. C'mon down here."

Cooper hesitated. Whatever happened to him in the water was too fresh to experience again.

"Cooper." Dad sat on the edge of the platform, his legs dangling in the water. "I'll go in with you. We'll go slow."

With Gordy and Lunk watching? Was he kidding? He glanced at Gordy. He actually looked a little scared himself. Lunk stood next to him, still wearing his lifejacket. Lunk's face said something different, but Cooper couldn't quite read it.

"Do it," Lunk said. "Your dad is right."

Cooper climbed over the rail and glanced toward shore. They were way out. The water was too deep. He couldn't see the bottom. Not out here.

"Okay," Dad said. "Sit on the platform."

Cooper did.

Dad slipped into the water. "Okay, nice and easy. C'mon in."

Cooper glanced west. The sun was nearing the horizon—so the water would be dark. "I don't know, I—"

"I'll be with you, Cooper," Dad said. "I won't leave you."

Cooper didn't want to be here. He wanted to be in the boat with the others. He looked up. Both Gordy and Lunk were watching from the rail. Gordy swallowed hard.

Lunk looked like he was in awe of what was happening.

Dad held out his hand. "Just slip into the water. You don't have to put your head under until you're ready."

Cooper nodded and dried his sweaty hands on his swim shorts. Which was stupid because his shorts were still wet, and he was going back in the water. He scooted off the edge, careful not to go completely underwater. He held onto the swim platform with one hand and pedaled hard with his legs like he was on his bike. He had to keep his chin above the water. Something was in the deep below him. He felt it. It was just waiting for him to put his head under. Planning to drag him down. He kept his knees high, trying not to let his feet go deep.

"Coop," Dad said. "There's nothing to be afraid of here."

Of course he was right. In a perfectly logical world. But fear was not logical. After the horrors of being chained in the black, flooding basement, Coop had had his share of nightmares. But Fudge had always been there. Sometimes in the middle of the night, Cooper curled up on the rug next to her.

Dad gripped his free arm. "Put your face in the water. But keep your ears above so you can hear me, okay?"

Cooper nodded.

"You better back away, Uncle Carson," Gordy said. "If he starts swinging, he'll clock you good. Give you a bloody nose."

"Shut up, Gordy," Lunk said. "His dad knows what he's doing."

The thought of hitting his dad seemed unreal to Cooper. But he'd hit Gordy, hadn't he? What if he did hit Dad—and knocked him out? Then they'd both need rescuing.

"I'll be right here. I won't leave you," Dad said.

Cooper took several slow, deep breaths and put his face in the water. His heart settled into a rhythm of heavy thumps—like his blood had turned to sludge.

"Your eyes open?" Dad said.

Cooper shook his head.

Dad gripped his arm. "Open them."

Cooper wanted to. Sort of. But if he looked down into the blurry depths, he would see the blackness. Terrifying blackness.

"They open?"

Cooper lifted his head out of the water. "I can't do it."

"Okay," Dad said. "You're doing fine." He looked up at Lunk and Gordy. "Would one of you give us a hand?"

Gordy stepped back from the rail and reached for his nose, as if he thought Cooper would hit him again.

Lunk vaulted over the rail and landed on the platform. "What can I do?"

"Get in with us. One on each side. We'll go under with him."

Lunk nodded. He hesitated for just a second, then unbuckled his lifejacket and threw it to Gordy. He glanced at Cooper's dad and then eased himself into the water. He gripped Cooper's arm, just above the elbow.

"We're going to bob once," Dad said. "Down and up. You just relax. Lunk and I will take you down a foot—and we'll lift you right back up. We'll all keep our eyes open."

"I don't know, I—"

"Nothing's going to happen. We're with you. Right, Lunk?"

"Absolutely."

"Down and up," Dad said. "Ready? On three."

Relax. Relax. Trust them. Nothing's going to happen. Cooper took a breath and nodded.

"One ... two ... three."

The three of them went down together. Dad's face was blurred, but Coop saw him. With a tug on his arms from Lunk and Dad, Coop was on the surface again. He wiped the water from his eyes.

"You okay?" Dad said.

Cooper nodded. "I felt ... fine."

"Excellent," Dad said. "Let's do it again."

Cooper took a deep breath. They bobbed again. He opened his eyes and was okay—but he didn't look down. Twice more they did it. Now Cooper was beginning to feel stupid. This bobbing thing was probably something Dad had done with him when Cooper was two years old.

"Still okay?" Dad searched Cooper's eyes. He must have found his answer there. "This time don't look at me. Look down. Lunk and I will still be on either side of you.

Do it. You can do it. You have to do it. Cooper went under again. He opened his eyes—tensed—and looked down. The water faded to black. Nothingness. What was down there? Dad and Lunk still held his arms. He stared into the depths, looking for something to rush up at him from the darkness.

But the panic didn't come. No pain or dizziness, so the idea of a ruptured eardrum wasn't likely. That meant only one thing: Dad was right. At least on some level. Cooper's heart was still thumping, but he felt no straightjacket of fear. They lifted him to the surface, and he wiped his eyes.

"Okay?" Dad looked at him.

"I'm good," Cooper said. What was going on here? Were the panic attacks just a fluke? Was he over whatever had been bothering him?

No. But obviously he had more control than he had thought. Somehow the fact that he wasn't alone — that Lunk and Dad were there with a firm grip on him — made all the difference.

Dad looked relieved. "Again?"

Cooper nodded. They went down again. And two more times. With each dive, Cooper felt more relaxed.

"Okay," Dad said. "This proves you're going to beat this thing." He hoisted himself onto the swim platform.

Cooper and Lunk followed.

Dad stared into the water. "Ready to take it one more step?"

Cooper nodded, hoping he looked more confident than he felt.

"Wait here." Dad climbed over the transom rail and returned with his scuba tank.

Cooper's stomach sank. Did Dad expect him to go down there alone?

Dad handed the gear to Lunk and stepped down onto the platform.

Normally the thought of using his dad's tank would totally fuel Cooper. Now all he felt was a sickening dread. "I don't know, Dad." He stared at the water.

Dad looked Cooper in the eyes. "Trust me. We'll do this together. I won't leave you."

Cooper nodded and glanced at Lunk, who gave a single nod back.

Dad opened the chrome valve for an instant, letting off a blast of air. He screwed the regulator in place. Four black hoses split off. Two for the mouthpieces. One for the gauges and compass. One for the missing buoyancy compensator vest.

"Gordy," Dad said. "Grab me a dock line, would you?"

Dad handed Cooper a mask. "Slip it on. I'll wear the tank. But we'll each have our own mouthpiece. We're going to put our heads underwater. Get used to that for a minute. We're in twenty feet of water here. Maybe we'll drop to the bottom. Together."

Cooper felt himself breathing harder. Faster. But he nodded.

Gordy was back with the rope, and Lunk tied it to the swim platform. Dad swung the tank over his head, adjusted the shoulder straps, and buckled the waist belt. He added the weight belt and handed one to Cooper.

Cooper wrapped the belt around himself. Clamped the buckle. Swallowed hard.

"Uncle Carson," Gordy said. "Do you think you ought to strap this on?" He held up the dive knife.

Dad shook his head. "We won't need a knife to protect ourselves. There's nothing but weeds down there."

Cooper wasn't so sure about that. Gordy didn't look convinced, either.

Dad held up the gauge cluster. "Depth. Compass. Air pressure. It's a full tank." He ran through some basics on each and slid his mask in place. "Ready?" Without waiting for an answer, he slipped off the platform and into the water.

Cooper joined him — in body anyway. His mind wanted to stay topside. With Gordy. Maybe even in the cabin. He held onto the swim platform and adjusted his mask to be sure it sealed well around the edges.

Dad handed him a mouthpiece, forcing air through it with the purge valve to clear all the water out of it.

Cooper clamped down with his teeth. He breathed in. And out.

"Okay," Dad said, "here we go. You won't be alone." Dad inserted his own mouthpiece, grabbed the rope with one hand, and locked onto Cooper's wrist with the other. He gave a single nod, then slid under the darkening waters.

Bubbles mushroomed to the surface. Cooper took two short breaths and stopped kicking. Gravity—and the weight belt—did their work. He was sinking.

He saw Dad's face immediately. Saw the strength there. The love. Cooper started kicking again, to hold this depth. And Cooper breathed. Ragged and unsteady at first. But after a minute, it evened out.

Dad must have sensed it. Or else he was watching the rhythm of Cooper's bubbles. Dad pointed at Cooper's eyes, then back at his own. *Keep your eyes on me.* Okay. He could do that. Dad pointed at Cooper's legs and shook his head. *Don't kick.* Cooper swallowed. Relaxed his legs.

The water was getting colder. Darker. They were dropping again. Cooper kicked. He looked up and couldn't see the surface. He pulled against Dad's grip, but Dad's squeeze grew tighter.

Cooper looked at his dad and moved in closer to see his eyes in the dim light. Then his feet touched bottom. He sucked hard and fast on the air. The metallic hiss of the air and the bubbles rippling over his face were the only sounds he could hear. And an engine. Distant.

The last time he'd actually breathed underwater was when he'd been rescued from the flooded basement. His stomach knotted instantly. The panic attacks were related. They had to be. He'd thought he was out of danger when he got freed from the chains—when he got out of the basement. There was no reason to be afraid now. He believed he'd beaten his fear. Killed it months ago. But he'd only buried it. Fear had a way of resurrecting itself, and right now it was crawling up his throat.

Dad pointed at his own bubbles. Then at Cooper's. Then back at his own. Dad took one breath for every two of Cooper's. *Okay. Relax. Even out that breathing. You are not alone.* It seemed to be working. Dad gave him a thumbs-up sign.

The water around them was a deep green, and it faded to black in every direction except up. Cooper didn't see any sign of evil creatures bent on devouring him. But he wished Dad had the dive knife—just in case.

Dad pointed up. *Surface?*

Cooper nodded, and a couple minutes later, Lunk was helping them with the gear. And he still wasn't wearing his lifejacket.

Gordy leaned over the rail. "No psycho-panic thing?"

Psycho-panic thing? He wanted to argue that choice of words, but Gordy was Gordy. That's the way he saw it—and in a way, he was right. "Nothing intense."

Cooper wanted to believe the whole thing was over. But he knew better. He hoisted himself onto the swim platform. This *was* about the basement. It made sense. And maybe he'd always known—but didn't want to admit it.

If there was nothing hiding underwater, what had caused his fear? Something worse. Something lurking in his head.

"When I'm back this weekend, we'll do this again," Dad said.

"What if that doesn't work?" Gordy said.

Lunk cleared his throat. "Gordy!"

There was no mistaking the glare that Lunk fired Gordy's way.

"I'm just sayin'," Gordy said.

Dad climbed onto the swim platform. "It's a fair question. If it doesn't work, then we'll get professional help."

Gordy nodded like he'd had it figured out from the beginning. "A shrink?"

Dad eyed Cooper. "The psychologist who came to the school might help."

"Dr. McElhinney." That would be okay with Coop. He liked the guy. But he hoped it didn't come to that.

"Baby steps," Dad said.

Cooper felt a little bit like a baby. But if Dad or Lunk shared that opinion, it didn't show on their faces.

"I think we made good progress," Dad said.

Cooper nodded, wanting to believe it was true. He'd won this round with fear, but the fight wasn't over. Not nearly. He stared into the dark water. Something was still down there. Watching. Just below the surface. Cooper pulled his feet onto the swim platform. Whatever it was, it wasn't finished with him yet. Cooper knew that in his heart. It was waiting for him. Just waiting to catch him alone.

CHAPTER 50

Hiro didn't see Cooper's dad and the guys all day until they met at the Upper Crust, a short drive from town, for dinner. The pizza place looked like an antique store. Odd memorabilia hung from the ceiling and was mounted on the walls. She sat with Lunk, Gordy, and Coop at their own table. Mattie sat with the adults nearby. With the noise level in this place, the other table wouldn't be joining in their conversation.

"I love this place already," Gordy said. "Wouldn't you like to have some of this vintage stuff hanging in your room?"

Hiro raised her eyebrows. "Like the shark suspended from the ceiling?"

"Especially the shark." Gordy pointed to the stuffed monster overhead. "This place is amazing."

"The only thing amazing about this place is that it hasn't been condemned as a fire hazard."

Lunk snickered. "Guns. Neon signs. Mounted fish and animals. Not your decorating style?"

"Do *not* call this decorating," Hiro said. "Call this a disaster. Men with screw guns gone berserk."

"It's like a museum," Gordy said.

Hiro shook her head. "It's a man cave."

Lunk and Gordy laughed. But Coop was strangely distracted. Was he still upset about what she'd done at Scoops? If that was it, she needed to get things aired out. She didn't want it to spoil their vacation. Actually, she didn't want any kind of a wedge between her and Coop — vacation or not.

Gordy started in about their time on *The Getaway*. Skiing. Widgets. Coop's panic attack — and the theory behind it. And Gordy talked about his nose. Every bloody detail.

Hiro watched Coop. Was that what was bothering him? He still seemed distant. By the time the pizza arrived, she'd built up enough nerve to bring up the topic.

"I went back to Scoops last night," she said, "after you guys dropped me off at The Cove."

Now she had Coop's full attention.

"You went there *alone*?" Coop said.

Ooops. Hiro shrugged.

Coop's face turned red. "First, you mess up by tipping your hand and letting them know you suspect them — "

"It wasn't a mistake. It was calculated. I was *baiting* them."

Coop waved her off. "Which was a *big* mistake. And after all that, you went back there alone?"

She hated the way he made that sound.

"What happened to 'play-it-safe Hiro'?" Lunk said.

"I knew what I was doing," Hiro said.

"Yeah, but did anybody else know?" Coop said.

All eyes were on her. Coop was right. Sort of. She should have let someone know about her plan. But if she had, she never could have talked to Katie.

"Did you just keep *us* in the dark — or did you fail to tell your mom too?"

Now she wished she'd never brought it up. She needed to get them past this. "Katie had some very interesting things to say. Do you want to hear them or not?"

Lunk cleared his throat. "I'd like to know."

"She said you were cute, Lunk."

Lunk's face got red. Good. That should keep him quiet for a few minutes. "I told her what we heard and saw. And our theory."

Gordy laughed. "*Our* theory?"

Hiro gave him a don't-go-there look that she hoped would keep him quiet. "Do you want to know what she said or not?"

None of them wanted to admit it, but Hiro knew she had them. "Four words. That's all."

"Let me guess," Gordy said. "Want more ice cream?"

Hiro made a face to show how little she appreciated his humor. "She said, 'Better watch your back.' What does that tell you?"

"That maybe we should take her advice," Coop said.

"So we sit around and do nothing?" Hiro said.

"Now that you mention it," Coop said, "yeah." He took another slice of pizza.

"I'm with Coop," Gordy said. "Let's not look for trouble."

"I didn't look for it," Hiro said. "It found us."

"That's a stretch," Lunk said.

"So what do we do?" Hiro wasn't about to let it go. But she'd feel a lot better about it if the guys bought into it. Even just a little.

Cooper sighed. "Aren't you always reminding me to leave the investigation to the police?"

"This is different," Hiro said. "I've got a feeling about this."

"Ah ..." Lunk raised his eyebrows and nodded slowly. "The feeling."

Gordy laughed. "You're pulling that women's *intermission* thing on us again."

Hiro let that one go.

Coop held up a hand. "If you're right—even partially—then we all have to take this more seriously."

Hiro studied him. Tried to read him. Was he finally coming around?

"Aw, come on, Coop," Gordy said. He turned to Lunk. "What do you think?"

"Overactive cop imagination," Lunk said.

Hiro ignored Lunk; she wanted to hear what Coop had to say.

"Look," Coop said. "You think there's a connection between the missing girl and Tommy Kryptoski, right?" He looked straight at her.

Hiro nodded.

"And if you're right—you let the wrong people know about your theory."

"I told you already," Hiro said. "I was baiting them."

Coop held up his hand again. "If you're wrong, no harm done. But if you're right about your theory ..." — Coop paused to look at Lunk and Gordy, then back at her — "then you'd *better* watch your back. We'll all have to."

Hiro suddenly felt really uncomfortable. Like maybe baiting Lynn *had* been a mistake. She could get any one of them hurt. Maybe that's what was bothering Coop. Maybe he was worried about her safety.

"Because if Hiro is right," Lunk said, "she's the only one who is challenging Kryptoski's story."

"So if the missing girl *was* the first one we saw in the boat ..." Gordy began.

Cooper looked at Hiro. "You could end up missing too."

CHAPTER 51

Two hours later Cooper was back on the boat. Dad headed for home after dinner. And Hiro convinced her mom to let her stay on board *The Getaway* until later that evening. To celebrate Cooper's progress in the water that afternoon, Gordy bought each of them a pint of ice cream from Scoops, which he didn't let them open until they were back on the boat.

They sat on the swim platform with their feet dangling in the warm water and ate their ice cream in silence. "Thanks for the ice cream, Gordy," Hiro said.

Gordy grinned. "I didn't mow lawns all summer for nothing."

Lunk took a bite of vanilla. "But nothing is what you'll have if you keep spending your money like this."

Gordy waved him off. "I'm on vacation."

Cooper stared toward the beach. Lake Shore Drive was quiet. And the weather was pretty typical for late August in the Midwest: hot days and cold nights. Steam rose off the lake and drifted over the still surface.

"Okay." Gordy broke the silence. "Who's got a spooky story? But it has to be about a lake—at night."

Classic Gordy. Cooper just couldn't go there. Not tonight. Their vacation already had more creep factors than he wanted.

He needed courage just to let his feet dangle in the black water—especially with the mist clinging to the lake. The last thing he wanted to think about was what was hiding below the surface.

Hiro lifted one leg out of the water but put it back just as quickly. "The water is much warmer than the air." She snuggled inside her sweatshirt. "I'm freezing."

"You're holding a pint of ice cream," Lunk said. "Of course you're cold."

No, it was more than that. Cooper set down his pint on the teakwood platform and rubbed his hands together. The chill went right through him, but not from the temperature. It was the thought of Hiro being in danger. What if she was right? What if Fat Elvis saw her as just another one of Kryptoski's messes that needed to be cleaned up? No matter what they felt about her theories, they'd have to somehow stay even more on guard. What if she was right about everything?

"Kinda creepy out," Gordy said. "I love it."

The moon shone bright and full, but the fog kept the light from reflecting off the lake. There was a time when Cooper would have enjoyed a night like this. But right now, his mind kept drifting back to Sunday night. What if the girl on the beach *wasn't* the same girl who picked up a pizza with Kryptoski? What if the girl holding the pizza box was Wendy Besecker—the missing girl?

Krypto Night sat at anchor. The line from the buoy to the boat hung slack, and the boat's silhouette turned slowly toward them. Moved by some invisible current, no doubt. It almost seemed alive, like it was watching them and turning to get a better view.

Hiro raised her chin toward the moon and closed her eyes. Her face practically glowed.

Gordy whacked at a mosquito. "Think there could be alligators in the lake?"

"Ridiculous," Hiro said. "This far north?"

"It's possible," Gordy said. "See, sometimes people buy cute little alligators and keep them in their bathtubs."

"Why would they do that?" Hiro said.

"To keep it as a pet. A novelty." Gordy waved her off. "Why do people buy boa constrictors?"

"Because the cheese slipped off their cracker," Hiro said.

Gordy laughed. "That may be true, but lots of people keep strange and really dangerous pets. Like alligators. And when the gators outgrow the tub—their owners need to find a new place for them to live."

Hiro shook her head. "So you're saying people dump alligators into lakes?"

"*I'm* not saying it. My dad told me that."

Cooper smiled. He could just hear Uncle Jim spinning a story like that. He was good at telling scary stories, which is probably where Gordy picked it up.

"Truth is"—Gordy paused, his eyes growing wide—"one could be down there right now." He leaned forward and looked down into the black water. "Close. Circling."

Hiro screamed and jerked her legs out of the water. "You just bumped my leg with your foot, Gordon Digby!"

"Me?" Gordy pasted on an innocent face. "Maybe it was —"

Hiro slugged him in the arm. "It was you. Well, good luck getting anybody to go for a night swim anytime soon."

Gordy and Lunk laughed.

Hiro was right about one thing: There was no way Cooper was taking a night swim. He'd made that decision long before Gordy started spinning his alligator story. It was dark. Dad was gone. The idea of swimming at night didn't sound good at all. He knew there were no alligators in the lake. But there was *something*. It couldn't all be in his head, could it? Casually, he pulled his feet out of the water, hoping the others wouldn't notice. He scooted backward, and leaned against the transom.

"Did the alligator bump your leg too?" Gordy grinned.

So much for not being noticed. The best way to handle Gordy's teasing was to give him a taste of his own medicine. "Not an alligator," Cooper whispered, "but something ... I could feel it. Something awful. And close enough to grab my ankles and pull me to the bottom of the lake."

The grin melted right off Gordy's face. "Seriously?" He yanked his feet out of the water.

Lunk and Hiro laughed.

"Ever thought about going into acting?" Lunk said. "You looked dead serious."

Cooper smiled, but that was the best he could do. The thing was, he wasn't acting. That was exactly what he believed. He couldn't explain it. He didn't want to try.

Hiro stood up. "Okay, let's cut the talk about creepy things in the lake."

"Why don't we sit on the bow?" Cooper said. "We can finish our ice cream there."

Hiro started climbing over the transom rail. "I love that idea."

Cooper followed her, glad to be off the swim deck. He felt better inside the boat. Higher. Safer.

"All right." Gordy sat cross-legged next to Cooper. "No more talk about creepy things *in* the lake. How about just a creepy story then? Who's going to start?"

Lunk leaned forward. "Ever hear the story about the Lady of the Lake?"

Cooper pictured the big excursion boat parked by the Riviera docks.

Gordy took a bite of ice cream. "You mean the steamboat with the paddle wheel on the back?"

Lunk shook his head. "An old lady who loved to go fishing in the lake. She knew the lake better than anybody, and she fished all year round, no matter the weather. In the summer she'd be out in her bass boat. In the winter she'd drive out on the frozen lake in her pickup and use one of those big augers to drill through the ice. They called her the Lady of the Lake."

He paused.

Cooper wasn't sure if the pause was for dramatic effect, or if he was making sure everyone was still listening.

"Well," Lunk said, "It was late winter—just last year. Southern Wisconsin went through a ten-day warm spell. Ice still covered the lake, but it was patchy. The old lady ate her dinner and headed out in her pickup to go fishing—just like usual. They say people warned her that the ice was getting thin, but she just laughed."

Lunk pointed toward the beach. "She drove her old Ford pickup right off Lake Shore Drive and onto the ice. She dropped it into four-wheel drive and headed to her favorite fishing haunt." He pointed to a spot about halfway between Maytag Point and one of the old Wrigley estates.

Cooper was picturing the scene. The ice. The lady driving her pickup.

"There was a guy out walking his dog along the north shore. He spotted her truck roaring across the lake. 'Is she insane?' the guy mumbled to himself. He knew the ice on his side of the lake wouldn't support the weight of that truck. He ran to the shoreline and waved his arms in the air, motioning her to turn back. And she must have seen him, because she skidded to a stop."

"This isn't a true story," Hiro said.

"Isn't it?" Lunk let the question hang there for a moment. "What the man saw next still gives me goose bumps. He heard a series of sharp cracks—like the sound of a huge limb snapping off a tree after an ice storm."

"Gunshots?" Gordy dug his spoon deep into his pint of ice cream.

Lunk shook his head. "A section of ice directly below and in front of the truck—it was the size of your average Taco Bell—yawned open like a giant trapdoor." He used both hands to simulate the ice giving way.

Cooper looked out over the black water and imagined what it would look like if it were covered with ice—and cracking.

Gordy seemed to be eating in slow motion now. He lifted the

spoon of ice cream from the pint, but then stopped, his eyes riveted on Lunk.

"As the pickup's front bumper disappeared under the black, icy waters, the old lady slammed the truck into reverse and tried to race up the incline and back onto solid ice. The man on the shore watched helplessly. Her off-road tires threw water eight feet into the air as she tried to back up. But she was trying to go uphill on wet ice. The engine was screaming as though it knew the danger it was in. The man could barely make out the lady's face, but he saw her sheer terror. She knew."

"Knew what?" Gordy whispered.

"That she was going down," Lunk said.

Cooper swallowed hard. He felt the woman's fear. It was just a story. He knew that. But it felt so real.

"And suddenly"—Lunk leaned in closer—"it was over."

"This is when you say that man woke up and it was all a bad dream," Hiro said. "Am I right?"

"Not this time, Hiro." Lunk wore a dead-serious expression. "With a giant *whoosh*, the ice gave way, and the truck vanished beneath the water. The sound of the engine cut off instantly—and the silence afterward was so creepy—so eerie—that the man stood there on the shore, and his whole body shook uncontrollably."

A tremor rippled through Cooper's body.

Gordy sat there frozen with his spoon in mid-air. The ice cream glossed over and dripped onto the deck as it melted. "The truck was just gone? It didn't bob on the surface for a minute so she could climb out?"

Lunk shook his head. "Gone. There was nothing on the surface but chunks of ice floating on black water."

"Ridiculous," Hiro said.

Gordy motioned her to be quiet. Yippee Skippee dripped onto his shirt. "So what happened?"

Lunk shrugged. "Rescue divers went down. They found the truck seventy feet below the surface. It was resting on all four tires at the bottom of the lake—up to its bumpers in muck. It looked like she'd driven the pickup there and gotten stuck."

Gordy dropped the spoon into his empty cup. "And the woman?"

"They never found her body. The window was rolled down—and she was gone."

Hiro crossed her arms. "Maybe she was abducted by aliens."

"It's the currents," Lunk said. "This is a spring-fed lake. They figure the currents keep moving her around."

Gordy stared at Lunk. "You're saying she's still in the lake?"

"Absolutely." Lunk swept his arm from one end of the lake to the other. "She could be anywhere. Fishermen claim to have seen her drifting under their boats. More than one has snagged her with a fishing line. But when they reeled their catch to the surface and saw they'd caught a dead woman's body, they cut the line and headed for shore. The body obviously drifted back to the bottom."

And Cooper's dad wanted to take him down to the bottom again this weekend? Great. Now he'd have this spooky story rolling around in his head too.

Gordy's eyes were wide.

"The Lady of the Lake doesn't eat fish anymore," Lunk said. "But you can bet they feed on *her*."

"Okay, that was disgusting." Hiro shook her head. "Impressive story, though, Lunk. Nicely done."

Lunk grinned.

"So, Gordy," Hiro said. "You up for a night swim?"

Gordy looked at the water like he wasn't sure whether Lunk's story was true. "It seems a little late to go swimming tonight."

Hiro and Lunk laughed. Cooper probably would have laughed too, but an uneasy feeling was growing inside of him.

He stared out over the deathly still lake. The steaming vapors danced and swirled as if to some mournful tune undetected by human ears.

A boat, maybe fifty yards away, caught his attention. Some

kind of a high-powered searchlight was lashed to a pole, and the beam was pointing straight down into the water. The boat crept along at barely more than an idle, following the south shoreline at just about the no-wake buoy point.

"That's weird." Cooper nodded in the direction of the boat.

Lunk followed his gaze. "Are they fishing?"

"Yeah, but for what?" Cooper could make out the silhouettes of two men on board. One was driving the boat and looking over the side, while the other one stood near the stern, peering down into the water.

"Where's his fishing pole?" Gordy whispered.

"They're searching for something," Hiro said.

Lunk nudged Gordy. "See? They're still looking for the Lady of the Lake."

Nobody said anything. The searchlight gave the mist an unearthly glow. The swirls swept around the mysterious boat. Ghostly. Mesmerizing. It was like the fog was trying to get inside the boat. Like it was reaching for something.

"I don't think we're supposed to be seeing this," Hiro whispered.

"Why are we whispering?" Lunk said.

Instinct. The word popped into Cooper's head. Something inside all of them was sounding a warning.

"Coop," Hiro said, "where are your binoculars?"

Cooper crept back to the cabin and returned in less than a minute. He focused in on the boat. The driver was too shadowed to make out his features. But the guy standing in the stern? Cooper sucked in his breath. "It's Fat Elvis. And he's holding something. Maybe a spear gun?"

"Let me see," Hiro said.

Cooper handed her the binoculars. The boat continued to snake its way around some of the moored sailboats.

"That's him," Hiro said.

"Spearfishing is illegal here." Gordy reached for the binoculars.

"I'll bet he goes out at night like this all the time. Probably snags some big ones."

Hiro removed the binoculars from around her neck. "Katie said he cleans up Kryptoski's messes, right? So what if he's cleaning up a mess right now?"

Cooper was way ahead of her.

Gordy squinted through the eyepieces. "He's looking for the camera? At night? That doesn't make sense."

"Not the camera, Gordy," Hiro whispered. "A body."

Gordy looked at Lunk. "The Lady of the Lake."

Lunk nodded. "Except this one is real."

CHAPTER 52

They're getting closer," Cooper said. "Let's get off the bow and into the cabin."

No one said a word until they were inside. Nobody turned on a light. They all seemed to understand that if Hiro's theory was true, then getting caught spying on Fat Elvis could be dangerous — or fatal.

"Calm water," Hiro said. "And a bright light. It would reflect off her white shirt — and her skin."

"You shouldn't have baited Lynn like you did," Cooper said, but then stopped. He'd covered this ground with Hiro already. If there had been a murder, Hiro already knew she could be a target.

"But nothing's happened," Gordy said. "No more warnings. No threats. Maybe there's another explanation for all this — like illegal spearfishing."

Hiro shrugged. "Sometimes the obvious answer *is* the answer. What if Pom-Pom is Wendy Besecker, not Lynn Tutek? What if Kryptoski *did* run over her with his boat in a fit of rage?" she said.

The cabin was absolutely silent.

"After Wendy is reported missing, as long as nobody can prove the two of them were ever together, Kryptoski is in the clear."

"That's why the police were so interested in your story," Gordy said.

"Exactly. If I could put the two of them together—they'd have something," Hiro said.

Cooper looked at her. "But when you couldn't identify the girl for sure, that ended that."

"Unless a body turns up in the lake," Hiro said. "That would change everything."

It definitely would—*if* the police ever found the body. Cooper couldn't quite wrap his head around that thought. Then the police would definitely want to question Hiro again. Unless Kryptoski or Fat Elvis got to her first.

Gordy peeked out a porthole. "If these two guys found a body ... what do you think they'd do with it?"

Hiro shrugged. "Make it disappear for good."

"How?" Gordy kept his eyes on the boat. "Drag the body to the deepest part of the lake—or haul it out of the lake and bury it?"

Hiro thought about that for a moment. "It would be dicey either way. Search and recovery teams could find it in the water eventually. But hauling a body into a boat and then transferring it to a car seems more risky."

Cooper agreed.

Gordy kept his eye on the boat as if he were afraid he'd miss something—like a body getting hauled into the boat. "He seems to be driving a grid pattern. So he's definitely looking for something. Should we call the police?"

"And tell them what?" Lunk said. "Some guys are shining a spotlight into the water? That isn't a crime. Without that camera—or a body—there's no proof of a crime at all."

"I hate to admit it," Hiro said, "but Lunk's right."

"We just need to lie low," Lunk said. "Mind our own business. If we come across as a threat to the wrong people ..." He drew his index finger across his throat.

Cooper had been thinking about that too. "If we call the police and they stop by *The Getaway*, Fat Elvis will know somebody was watching them."

"How hard will it be for them to figure out we're the ones who called it in?" Lunk said.

"And it's not like they're actually doing anything illegal," Hiro said. "They could toss the speargun over the side and just tell the police they were looking for a good fishing spot."

Lunk's story was creepy enough. But what if a body really was drifting somewhere below the surface of the lake? And if that were true, then it was somebody they'd seen just a few days earlier. Unreal.

The boat carefully weaved in and out of the sailboats moored in the bay, slowing down to take extra time at the buoys. It was as if they were making sure nothing was tangled in the chains anchoring the buoys to the cement blocks resting on the lake bottom. Were they really looking for a body?

"I still say they're spearfishing," Gordy said. "They've got a spear gun. Why would they need that if they were searching for a dead body? She's dead."

Hiro stared out the porthole. "Could they tie a rope to the spear? Maybe that's how they'd try to recover the body."

"They'd stick her and reel her in?" Gordy shook his head. "That is so sick, Hiro."

Hiro glanced at the time on her phone. "I hate to leave, but I have to get to shore. My mom will be waiting for me on the beach soon." She stared at the mysterious boat. "But I don't want them to see us."

Cooper couldn't agree more. And the thought of paddling through that fog unnerved him.

"He's stopping," Lunk said.

Hiro snatched the binoculars from Gordy and refocused them. "Fat Elvis is talking on the phone."

"You do realize," Cooper said, "that just two nights ago we were hiding in this boat, watching something strange going on."

He was hoping someone would come up with a logical explanation for the series of events. Something they hadn't thought of before. Something that would make the whole thing not seem as dark. Cooper couldn't come up with anything. Apparently none of the others could either.

Fat Elvis suddenly doused the searchlight. Cooper could barely make out the boat now, except for the green and red running lights on the bow. The boat did a one-eighty and cruised out of the mooring area. It picked up speed before it disappeared from view.

Hiro's phone chirped, and she checked the screen. "My mom's on her way." She looked at Cooper. "Can you take me to the beach?"

Gordy went to the bow with the binoculars. Lunk helped Cooper drop the inflatable into the water beside the swim platform. The steam on the lake twisted and swirled away as if it were alive. Startled. But it crept right back and surrounded the boat. Possessing it almost.

Hiro sat in the back. Cooper took his place in the bow, facing her. Lunk gave them a shove, and Cooper leaned back and paddled. He didn't want to think about alligators or the Lady of the Lake right now. Or the missing girl, either—the one who might be just below the surface. Silently drifting in the currents.

Cooper shook his head. He had to stop thinking about this stuff. He kept his strokes shallow. Every time he dipped his hands into the warm water, his stomach tightened—and not just because of the strain from paddling.

"That was soooo spooky," Hiro said.

"Since I'm the one with my arms in the water," Cooper said, "think we can change the topic?"

Hiro nodded. "I like the way your dad is going into the water with you. Think it will help?"

He wasn't sure this subject was much better. "I hope so," Cooper said. "I did okay. No panicky feelings." It sounded so lame. He'd never had a problem being underwater before. Never.

"That's good," Hiro said. "Really good."

Her tone had a "case closed" ring to it, as though she believed his panic attacks were behind him for good. Like he'd beaten it. If only it were that easy. Even now he felt something was stalking him in the black water. Carrying a chain with his name on it.

He kept his strokes quick. Short. And he didn't even want to think about paddling back to *The Getaway* alone.

"Looks like you'll be in for a night of more ghost stories with those two." Hiro jerked her thumb toward *The Getaway* behind her.

The waterline of his dad's boat disappeared in the fog. It actually looked like it was floating—but not on the water. On top of the fog.

He didn't believe in ghosts any more than Hiro did, or the stories he'd heard about them. But he believed in demons—which was a much scarier thought. He wondered if demons ever went underwater. Cooper pulled his hands inside the inflatable and let the boat drift for a moment.

They glided past *Krypto Night*, and Hiro stretched to look inside. But with the boat cover on tight, what could she hope to see?

She started paddling the inflatable herself. "Let's get away from this boat. Something about it makes my skin crawl."

Cooper reached back and pulled. Honestly? He didn't like being so close to the boat either. Maybe it was the fog. The black water. The boat with the searchlight. The spooky stories. Take your pick. But right now, Cooper wished his dad were still there. They'd be camping tonight instead of sleeping on *The Getaway*.

"That could be my mom now." Hiro pointed at a car driving down Lake Shore Drive. "The headlights, fog lights—yeah, definitely the right configuration for a Honda Civic."

The car pulled onto the shoulder and stopped. Cooper picked up the pace and headed for it. He passed the no-wake buoys, paddled into the protected swimming area, and ran the inflatable onto the beach.

Hiro swung a leg over the side and stood in ankle-deep water. "Be careful going back."

She looked dead serious. *Terrific.* The thought of going back alone was creeping him out as it was — and her comment certainly didn't help things. But he didn't want his true feelings to show.

"Is Gordy's alligator story getting to you?" Cooper tried giving her a convincing smile. "Or is it Lunk's Lady of the Lake?"

Hiro shook her head. "Neither. It's our own story." She looked toward the middle of the lake like she expected someone or something to rise up out of the water. "What's going on here is ..." Her voice trailed off.

She had that look in her eyes. She was seeing — or imagining — something. Whatever it was, it was spooking her good, which wasn't doing Cooper any favors.

"Just be careful, Coop." She touched his arm. "I mean it."

"You were saying something before," Cooper said. "Finish it."

She'd started walking toward her mom's car, but she glanced back at him for just a second. "Forget I said anything."

He stood there on the beach and watched as the car's taillights headed down Lake Shore Drive.

Right. Like that's *really going to happen.*

The car started up the hill — and moments later the taillights disappeared over the hill. A loneliness enveloped him that was just as real and thick as the fog shrouding the lake. He'd been resisting Hiro, hadn't he? So quick to discount her theories, when in reality they made a lot of sense. Maybe he'd been distracted with all his fears of the water. But it was more than that, wasn't it? He'd been in denial, not wanting to admit they really might be in danger. Because that reminded him of what happened to him in the basement too. But living in denial only increased the danger, didn't it? They were more likely to be off guard. Easy targets. And Hiro would be the most vulnerable of them all.

Maybe it was the way Fat Elvis was searching with the light that made Cooper turn the corner in his mind. Funny how it took a foggy night to help him see clearly. Now he wanted to talk to Hiro more than ever. To tell her he finally got it. To let her know he was all in. She was hurting, and he hadn't been helping her much.

Tomorrow he'd tell her. He'd talk to the guys too. But it wasn't like it would make a real difference. It's not like they were going to actually help with the investigation. Really ... what could they do?

A thought flashed through his mind—and a chill crept through like the fog had entered his very soul. No, they couldn't follow leads or help the police with the mystery. But there was one thing they could do. Had to do. Protect Hiro.

CHAPTER 53

Hiro stood on the balcony. Cooper and Gordy had already phoned to let their moms know they were safe aboard *The Getaway* for the night. That had been part of the arrangement. Their extra freedom came with the very small price of checking in regularly. Sometimes boys had it easier than girls did. This was definitely one of those times.

Lunk borrowed one of the boys' phones to talk to his mom, but the conversation had been different than the ones Coop and Gordy had. From what Hiro could tell, he didn't call to let his mom know that he was okay as much as he called to make sure *she* was doing all right. Interesting. That boy could get under her skin sometimes. But under *his* skin she'd discovered a softer heart than his tough façade suggested.

Had he always been like that—even back when she saw him as a bully? Or had he been changing? She was convinced he'd been changing. Little by little.

Coop was changing too. Mostly in good ways. He no longer took people's trust for granted. Since last October, he'd been working to earn back her trust. And he'd done that and more. Not that she was going to let him in on that little tidbit. She liked the new Coop and didn't want him coasting or going backward.

His panic attacks, if that was the right diagnosis, scared her. She couldn't imagine how Coop felt. At least his dad knew about them now, and it sounded like he'd help Coop work through them.

She touched her Chicago Police star necklace. Why did they refer to policemen who died in the line of duty as fallen? The word *fallen* was all wrong. It implied that her father messed up. But he didn't fall. He stood tall. He finished strong. And the days following his death had been the saddest time of her life.

"You'd like how Coop is turning out, Dad," she whispered. "He's good. He tries to do the right thing—even when he's scared. He watches out for me, but he tries not to let me see him doing it. All three of the guys do."

She'd lost her dad, but Coop, Lunk, and even Gordy had stepped up to serve as her protectors. Oh, sure, they gave her a hard time. But she knew they'd protect her—with their lives if they had to.

Was she really in danger? Maybe. But right now, standing here on the balcony and hearing the laughter coming from the other room, she felt safe. Everything looked different. Maybe she'd been taking her theory too far. Maybe the guys were right and she'd been connecting too many dots and trying to build a case where there wasn't one.

Could she be sure that Pom-Pom and Lynn weren't the same girl? No. Was somebody stalking her near the river? Maybe not. Did she know for a fact that Fat Elvis and his friend were searching the lake? Yes. But for a body? What if they *were* just doing some illegal spearfishing?

So what did she really have? Lunk's words popped into her head: an overactive cop imagination. Was that it? She had to be open to the possibility, as hard as it would be to admit it to the boys. And if she were wrong—if there had been no murder—it would be safer for all of them.

"God," she whispered. "I pray I'm wrong. Let there be some other logical explanation."

She rested her forearms on top of the balcony rail and looked out over the town. No black pickup. No bearded Fat Elvis creeping around. Even after all she'd said to Kryptoski's girlfriend at Scoops last night, nobody had come after her. Maybe she *was* making something out of nothing.

CHAPTER 54

Gordy tiptoed through the cabin and out into the cool night air. Coop and Lunk were totally out, which was a shame because Gordy wasn't a bit tired. Every time he closed his eyes, he saw that pickup falling through the ice—and the woman's body drifting in the current. Somehow he felt the cold of the water. The numbing, icy cold. It was just as real as if he'd been in the pickup with the lady. What was that all about? He was relieved that Coop hadn't wanted to take a night swim. Thanks to Lunk, the idea didn't sound like nearly as much fun as it had before.

It was kind of a problem. They were supposed to be having fun. But they were way behind in that department. Coop was taking everything too seriously. He needed to loosen up. Relax. And if he did, then his problems in the water would disappear.

Steam still rose off the surface of the water, making the lake look totally different at night. The scene was almost hypnotic as it drew him in—yet it was also spooky and made him wish he were standing on shore. The mix of fear and excitement ... he loved it.

What Coop really needed was a distraction. Stuff to sidetrack his mind from his fears. Uncle Carson's surprise visit had worked perfectly. Taking *The Getaway* out on the lake was the best day they'd had so far. Tomorrow was a whole new story, though. It was time to pull off the ultimate prank. And this would be way better than what they'd done on Kryptoski's boat.

Hiro wouldn't like the idea. But then again, when did she ever like one of their pranks? She'd never seen the sense in their "Spudzooka" potato gun, which only proved that Hiro didn't know much about having fun. She'd shoot down this new idea too, if she could. Which was why they were going to pull it off tomorrow morning before she arrived.

The thought of it made Gordy smile. They'd start the day with the perfect prank—and he'd get Coop to feeling better pronto.

CHAPTER 55

He clicked the remote and Black Beauty's lights signaled in response. Kryptoski was nuts. Tonight's little fishing expedition was proof of that. He was really tired of cleaning up after this kid. Somehow Kryptoski was going down — but he wouldn't go down alone. He'd suck in anybody who was associated with him. Kryptoski's old man may run a casino, but the punk was bad luck. Or was it the kids? They'd started this whole thing rolling. They were the ones who'd messed everything up.

It was time to cut and run. Just fire up Black Beauty and hightail it out of there. He opened the driver's side door and climbed inside his pickup. He could hit the road tonight. But to slip away in the dark didn't seem right. There were still some things he wanted to do here. Lessons he needed to teach. Fate was handing him an opportunity that he couldn't walk away from.

He started the pickup. Felt the soothing rumble of the seats. He could stay on for a few more days to tie up some loose ends. To finish this. He'd just need to step up his plans and cover all the bases. He'd make his exit, for sure. But why go out quietly when you can go out with a bang?

CHAPTER 56

Wednesday morning, Lunk stood at the wheel of *The Getaway* and ran through the steps that Coop's dad had taught him. Run the blower several minutes before you start the motor—just to clear out any gas fumes that could kaboom the boat. Good idea. Turn the key—after making sure both engines are in neutral. Goose the gas a bit to get both the engines running strong—and then ease the gearshift forward. Throttle up to cruising speed and hold a steady course.

He wanted to drive *The Getaway* again. He hoped Coop's dad would let him. Lunk still wasn't a big fan of the water, but driving the boat was something else again.

Coop stepped out of the cabin, squinted, and stretched. "Morning, Lunk."

Lunk let go of the wheel. "Sleep good?"

"Like a log." He leaned against the rail.

"Gordy will be jealous."

"What happened?"

Lunk shrugged. "He said he hardly slept. And when he did, he had bad dreams."

Coop laughed. "It was your story that did it."

"The Lady of the Lake?"

Cooper nodded. "Her body drifting around in the currents—are you kidding me? I'm surprised he slept at all."

"He's the one who wanted us to swap creepy stories."

"True," Coop said. "He asked for it. Great story, though."

"Thanks. But who says it was a story?"

Coop laughed. "Got any more like that?"

"I could keep Gordy awake all week," Lunk said.

Coop laughed, but then his face got serious. "Where is he now?"

Lunk jerked his thumb toward shore. "Collecting dead fish for the mailboat prank."

"He'll be doing it alone." Coop watched Gordy, like he was trying to figure something out.

"What is it?"

Coop shrugged. "Gordy and I were both in that basement. He was alone for days. It's gotta be affecting him somehow."

Coop didn't have to say more. Lunk had wondered the same thing. How did Coop get stuck with that water-panic thing, yet Gordy somehow got through the kidnapping without any aftershocks? "You think he's covering it up?"

Coop nodded slowly. "Yeah, sometimes I do."

"How?"

"The pranks. The constant push to have fun."

Lunk could see that. "Like he's running from it?"

Coop shrugged. "Something like that. I mean, he always liked a good prank. We both did. But it's getting worse. The mailboat idea is way over the top."

"You think the nightmares could be part of it?"

"Maybe." Coop thought a moment. "Your story triggered the fear, I'm sure. But I'd be interested to know what he was actually dreaming about."

Maybe everybody had their fears. Some people were just better at hiding fear than others. Lunk looked down at his lifejacket. Then again, some fears weren't quite so easy to hide. "So what are we going to do about it?"

"We have to talk to him. Before we go home."

Lunk nodded. They'd have plenty of chances. "But what about the mailboat prank? He thinks we're doing it this morning."

"There's no way. Somebody could get hurt. We could get arrested. It's just a bad idea all the way around," Coop said. "And if it has anything to do with being locked in that basement . . ."

Lunk waited to see if Coop would finish his statement. But he didn't have to. Lunk had a pretty good idea where Coop was going. What kind of a friend would Coop be if he helped Gordy run from his fears instead of facing them? Lunk left Coop to his thoughts and studied the instrument gauges.

"You handled the boat like a pro yesterday," Coop said. "Itching to drive again?"

Lunk grinned. "Definitely." Then again, was it really the driving that he hungered for, or was it something else? He relived the drive in his mind—like he'd done before he fell asleep last night. No, it wasn't just the driving. It was Coop's dad and the way he'd taught Lunk what to do. The way he'd encouraged him, trusted him with the boat. It was the way he'd put his hand on Lunk's shoulder and called him "Skipper."

The only thing Lunk's dad had taught him was how to hit. And truthfully, it had come in pretty handy. Especially when Lunk got big enough to force his dad to leave the house—for good. Somehow he knew he'd saved his mom's life in the process. Gave her back her life, anyway.

"Here he comes." Coop pointed toward Gordy pushing the inflatable off the beach. "You ready to help me talk him out of it?"

Lunk shielded his eyes against the sun. "It isn't going to be fun."

"Got that right," Coop said. "How about you, Lunk? Having fun? On the vacation, I mean."

Lunk glanced at him. He didn't need to pull pranks or go water-skiing or *do anything* to have fun. Just being with friends was enough. It was something he'd never had before. "I'm having the time of my life."

Coop laughed as though Lunk were joking. *If he only knew.* Lunk just hoped his three friends were as happy to have him around as he felt when he was with them.

CHAPTER 57

Hiro stood on the pier and leaned on the wooden rail just outside the Riviera building as the *Walworth II* approached the docks. She was a little early to meet the boys, but that was okay. She liked it here. Liked watching the people.

Hopefully the guys had as good a morning as she had. The time spent with her mom had been perfect. And needed.

Tourists stood in line at the Gage Marine ticket booth, looking up at the list of excursion boat options and pricing. They all looked good: *Louise*, *Grand Belle of Geneva*, *Walworth II*, and *Lady of the Lake*. Okay, maybe the *Lady of the Lake* wouldn't be her first choice right now—at least not after hearing Lunk's story last night.

It was ironic that his story included a woman drifting silently in the currents of the lake. Which is where Wendy Besecker might be right now. She shuddered. Or maybe Wendy swam to shore and went into hiding, afraid to report Kryptoski's actions to the police. The jerk came from money—and that bought him some clout. He seemed to be one of those guys who had no shortage of cash. He definitely had a shortage of character, though.

If Wendy had swum to shore, then it was likely that she had the camera. That would explain why nobody had found it yet. But if Wendy never made it to shore ... Hiro didn't want to go there.

Still, the cop in her wanted to know. She wanted to figure it out and put it all together like a puzzle. No, that wasn't it. It was more than that. It was about justice. It was about helping others. If Kryptoski was half the creep she thought he was, then she had a moral duty to protect others from him.

Which brought her back to what she could do about it. Nothing. Not unless she could find that camera. She'd talk to Coop. Maybe they could do a little snorkeling out where they'd seen *Krypto Night* making its loops in the water. If the camera housing was damaged—took in water and sank—the camera card could be salvaged. That was all she'd need.

Two sharp blasts of the steam whistle on *Lady of the Lake* brought her back to the moment. Now filled with a new group of passengers, the old-fashioned riverboat backed away from its berth at the pier. Did they have any idea about what might be drifting just below the surface of the lake?

CHAPTER 58

Cooper skidded to a stop in the grassy area in front of the Riviera. Gordy and Lunk pulled up alongside him. "Anybody see Hiro?" Cooper leaned his bike against a tree. There were plenty of tourists around, but no Hiro. He checked the time. They'd gotten to town quicker than he'd figured.

"Maybe she's in Scoops," Lunk said.

Gordy grinned. "Maybe you want to go check."

Lunk gave Gordy a look that shut him up—but didn't stop him from laughing.

At least he was doing okay. At first Gordy seemed crushed when Cooper told him they weren't pranking the mailboat. But once they got his mind on going to town for food he brightened right up. They still didn't talk to him about the fear thing. But that talk would come.

A black-and-white Ford Crown Victoria turned off Main and onto Broad Street. The squad car pulled up to the curb not more than fifty feet away. The cop got out and headed right for them.

"It's Officer Tarpy," Coop said. "I don't know about you guys, but I am *really* glad we didn't prank the mailboat."

Tarpy had his cop face on. No emotion. No telling what was going on inside his head.

Gordy turned dead serious. "You don't think he wants to ask us about the fish we planted inside Kryptoski's boat, do you?"

"Hello, gentlemen." Tarpy stopped and put his hands on his hips. "You're just the guys I wanted to see." He squatted down and unfolded a full sheet of paper and laid it face down on the ground.

"It won't happen again," Gordy blurted.

Tarpy looked at him with a slight smile. "*What* won't happen again?"

Gordy looked at Cooper—his eyes pleading.

"Tell us what you wanted to see us about," Cooper said. He wasn't about to lie, but there was no sense in confessing before they even knew what the issue was.

Officer Tarpy hesitated. He clearly wanted to follow up on Gordy's comment, but instead he turned the sheet of paper over. It was the same flier that Hiro had picked up at Culver's. The smiling face of Wendy Besecker looked up at them. Okay, this wasn't about the dead fish. Gordy looked as relieved as Cooper felt.

Tarpy tapped the picture. "Your friend Hiroko thought she may have seen this woman getting into Tommy Kryptoski's boat on Sunday afternoon. Then she wasn't so sure." Tarpy paused, choosing his words carefully. "She told me the rest of you weren't in the boat at the time—and you didn't get a good look at her. Is that right?"

Lunk raised his hand. "I wasn't in town yet."

"Okay." Tarpy turned to Gordy.

"I saw her," Gordy said. "But I didn't really pay much attention."

"A pretty girl like this sails past and you didn't pay attention?"

Gordy's face turned red. "I was kinda far away—and busy."

Tarpy turned to Cooper. "How about you?"

What was he supposed to say? *Gee, Officer, I was having some kind of panic attack at the time.* "Hiro was the only one of us who got a good look at her."

"When you were on the beach and Lynn walked up, did you

wonder—even for an instant—if she was the same girl that you saw on the boat?"

Cooper shook his head. "It never crossed my mind."

Tarpy nodded like that was all he needed to hear.

"Do you think she could have been kidnapped?" Gordy's voice sounded weak.

"Unlikely," Tarpy said. "Most missing-person cases turn out to be runaways."

Cooper believed it. "You think she ran away?"

"We got an anonymous phone call early Monday morning from a guy who claimed to be her boyfriend. He said the two of them were together, and he didn't want her family to worry. Young love and all that." Tarpy folded up the picture. "We traced the call to a cheap motel in Milwaukee. The night manager saw a couple go in late Sunday night. The girl matched the description."

Cooper wished Hiro was around to hear this.

"Then we got *another* anonymous phone call on Monday night," Tarpy said. "One of Wendy's girlfriends had seen the fliers posted around town, and she claimed Wendy took off with a guy early on Sunday afternoon. She didn't want Wendy's parents to worry—but she didn't want to snitch on her friend either."

Sunday afternoon? That would have been hours before the incident with Tommy Kryptoski. "So why are you talking to us?" Cooper regretted the question the moment he asked it. "I mean, it sounds like you have your answer."

Tarpy smiled. "I just need to be sure."

"It's because of Hiro," Gordy said. "She's paranoid."

Tarpy eyed Gordy."Paranoid?"

"Yeah," Gordy shrugged. "She wants to be a cop, right? And she's always getting these feelings about things. Hunches. She even felt like she was being stalked on Monday afternoon."

The cop raised his eyebrows. "Stalked?"

Gordy nodded. "But we looked around the area and didn't see anyone. Didn't hear anyone."

Cooper didn't like where this was going. This made Hiro sound ... bad. "Paranoid is way too strong a word here, Officer Tarpy. Actually, I think Hiro may be right—about a lot of this stuff." Cooper didn't know what to say next. He didn't have any more proof to back up Hiro's theories than she did.

"What about you?" Tarpy focused on Gordy. "You think she imagined the stalker?"

"Absolutely. She reads something into every little thing," Gordy said. "She thought that drunk driver on Sunday night was out to kill Coop—like on purpose."

Tarpy nodded. He folded the piece of paper and pocketed it. "Thanks, guys. I appreciate your help."

Gordy looked relieved. "Happy to help."

"So, you had something you wanted to confess when I walked up," Tarpy said. "Something that wasn't going to happen again?"

Gordy's eyes got wide. "I, uh ... well, I, um—"

Officer Tarpy laughed and stood. "On second thought, I don't want to know." He stretched, walked to his patrol car, and ducked inside.

Gordy blew out a loud breath of air. "I think that went well."

Cooper didn't agree. "If Hiro is right, the police will never take her seriously. Not after what you just said."

Gordy stared at Cooper. "I can't believe I'm hearing this. There's no way she's right. You heard what the cop said. The missing girl took off with her boyfriend."

Cooper raked his hands through his hair. "Honestly, right now I'm so confused I don't know *what* to think. Last night I was sure Hiro was right."

Lunk studied him. "And now?"

Cooper thought for a moment. "I think we need to lighten up on her a little. Back off."

Lunk whistled softly. "You *do* believe her."

Just hearing Lunk say it made him all the more sure. "I'll admit that everything Officer Tarpy just said made sense. And I hope he's right. But I trust Hiro's gut—don't you?"

Gordy looked out over the bay and shrugged. "Yeah. I guess."

Lunk clenched his jaw and nodded. "So what do we do?"

"What we've always done before," Cooper said. "Stick together."

CHAPTER 59

Lunk sat in the bow of *The Getaway* and thought about Coop. He totally understood Coop wanting to support Hiro, and Lunk would definitely go through the motions. He was a team player. But after what the cop said, he wasn't quite ready to buy into Hiro's theories completely. And the more he thought about it, the more he saw the flaws in Hiro's theory. Funny how the whole situation looked different now that a few more facts had come to light. The girl had run off. It made sense. These things happened all the time.

He remembered Hiro's expression when Coop told her everything the cop had said. She'd looked shocked. Maybe that was the wrong word. *Embarrassed* might be more like it. She'd never considered that the girl on the missing-person fliers that were plastered all over town could have run off with a boyfriend.

"So does that mean we're not looking for the camera?"

Lunk couldn't believe she'd even asked that. She didn't get it. But still, he felt kind of bad for her. She'd gone out on a limb with all her theories, and the branch had snapped off underneath her. Maybe that's why she was so quiet before they'd left her at The Cove.

She probably felt really stupid. But she wasn't. Hiro was the smartest girl he'd ever known—although he'd never tell her that. She just had it wrong this time.

If she had any hopes of them looking for the camera, they were shot down when Coop's mom announced they were going to the Walworth County Fair in Elkhorn the next day.

Coop and Gordy were revved up about the fair. Lunk had never been to one, so he couldn't relate. Actually there were a lot of things about those two that he couldn't relate to. They were different from him—but mostly in good ways.

A lot of it had to do with Coop's faith. It seemed more important to him than ever. But Lunk just wasn't there yet.

And that wasn't the only area where Lunk was different from Coop. So what did he have in common with these guys? Definitely not their love of the lake. The boat was good—better than he'd expected. And especially when Coop's dad let him drive it. But the water itself? Thanks, but no thanks.

Coop and Gordy loved the water—except for whatever was going on with Coop right now. But it was just one more way that Lunk was different from them. Why did they even let him into their circle? What did he contribute to the group? It was a real mystery. Yet he needed to figure it out because whatever it was, he had to keep doing it. Without his friends, Lunk knew he'd be right back where he'd been his whole life. Alone.

CHAPTER 60

Cooper hiked his backpack onto one shoulder and checked the sky. It still looked like rain, but there was no breeze. The gray sky stretched endlessly in all directions. He tossed his empty shake cup into the fifty-five-gallon drum used as a trash can at the Walworth County Fair. "I'm stuffed."

Lunk looked like he felt the same way.

Hiro shook her head and smiled. "And now you boys want to hit the rides? Am I the only one with some common sense?"

"Sense?" Gordy said. "Is that what you call it? We offered you roasted sweet corn on the cobb dripping in melted butter, and you passed. A corn dog? You turned up your nose. Bratwurst? You weren't interested. And you didn't want a shake either. Or elephant ears smothered with cinnamon sugar, ècream puffs, or anything in between. Which tells me *you're* a little malnourished in the common sense department."

"I'm quite content," Hiro said. "Which is more than you boys will be after you go on a few of these rides."

Gordy slapped his stomach. "This thing is like cast iron."

"Let the food settle first," Hiro said. "Maybe we should hit the games again." She pointed at the stuffed monkey hanging out of Cooper's backpack. "Maybe we can win Chimpy's girlfriend."

"Sorry," Gordy said. "It's time to hit the rides."

"Aren't you worried about the effects of centrifugal force — or is it centripetal?" Hiro said.

Gordy smiled. "I have no idea what you're talking about."

Hiro sighed. "The spinning force on some of these rides could bring everything up."

"Poor Hiro," Gordy said. "You are so sheltered. So uninformed. So — "

"So ready to deck you if you keep talking like that," Hiro said.

Cooper laughed. "Explain your theory to Hiro, Gordy."

Gordy bowed slightly. "Gladly. The way to do the fair is to eat all you can until you're stuffed."

Hiro pointed at his stomach. "Obviously, you've accomplished your goal."

"That's only part of it," Gordy said. "Now we hit a ride or two so the "'spinning force",' as you call it, packs the food down tighter."

Lunk nodded. "Then we can go back and eat some more."

"You three are seriously demented," Hiro said. "And I'm not buying that cast-iron stomach bit either."

"Pick the ride," Gordy said. He swept his hand across a section of the fairgrounds. "Typhoon. Pharaoh's Fury. The Zipper. Freak Out. Or the Matterhorn. Choose the wildest one you can — and we'll walk off of it with smiles on our faces."

"Right," Hiro said. "More like you'll crawl off the ride and upchuck your ècream puffs and bratwurst and elephant ears and who-knows-what-all that you just ate."

"Only amateurs hurl." Gordy patted his abs again. "I'm telling you, I have an iron stomach."

Hiro folded her arms across her chest and scanned the rides, most of which were in full swing. "We'll see, Mr. Iron Gut." She stepped over bundles of electric cables that were snaked across the midway. "You want me to pick a ride?"

Gordy snickered and bowed slightly. "What'll it be?"

Hiro closed her eyes and tilted her head to one side.

"What's she doing?" Lunk looked at Cooper.

"Listening." Cooper was sure of it. "She's going to make her decision based on which ride gets the most people screaming."

Hiro raised her eyebrows and gave a single nod—but kept her eyes shut.

"Better hurry," Gordy said, "or I'll have to grab more food."

Hiro opened her eyes and smiled like she really believed she could win this bet. "This way." She pointed toward Typhoon.

"Excellent choice," Gordy said. "I'm impressed."

Cooper and the guys followed her. Lunk and Gordy grinned like Hiro's choice had just made their day. She marched past the midway games without slowing down to watch. Cooper had to jog a few steps to catch up.

"Typhoon is just like the Orbitor," Gordy said, as though Hiro had asked him for a rundown on the ride. "Six spiderlike hydraulic arms hold clusters of two-man cars." Gordy hustled alongside her. "The center axis spins each arm in a circle, and the arms are already spinning their clusters of cars." He demonstrated with his hands, motioning wildly. "And then each spider arm—or leg or whatever—lifts its cluster of cars up to something like a ninety-degree angle."

"Sounds insane," Hiro said. "It's perfect for you."

"The ride is genius," Gordy said. "An engineering marvel."

Hiro stopped to face him. "Puh-lease. Do you have any idea how unsafe these rides are?"

Gordy waved off her comment.

"I'm serious," Hiro said. "This whole place is dangerous. If the food doesn't kill you, the rides certainly can."

"Oh, nice." Gordy nodded. "You're not riding, is that it?"

Hiro planted her hands on her hips. "Have you seen the rocket scientists who put these rides together?"

Cooper knew she had a point.

"What if the carnival workers didn't tighten the bolts down hard? Or what if they left out a bolt? They have to disassemble these rides in another week. Why would they want to make their next job tougher?"

Gordy shook his head. "The carnival workers aren't going to take any chances. Are you riding, or are you going to keep stalling?"

Hiro raised her chin and headed for Typhoon.

The ride was swirling at full speed as they approached. Cooper stepped up next to a row of metal fencing set up to keep spectators from getting too close. The hydraulic arms raised and lowered the spinning clusters of cars as the whole thing turned on its axis. The thing was out of control. Possessed.

Cooper hooked his backpack over the fence. Chimpy's smiling face poked out of the top of the pack. He looked like he wanted to ride Typhoon too—or at least watch the fun. Coop fished his phone from his pocket and slipped it inside the backpack. "Hiro. Gordy. Want to put your phones in here too?"

Gordy shook his head.

Hiro pushed her phone deeper into her jeans pocket but kept her eyes on the ride. "I'm okay."

She didn't look okay.

"You know," Cooper said, "you don't have to ride with us. Why not sit this one out?" He pointed at the stuffed monkey. "You can keep Chimpy company."

She raised her chin slightly. "I can do anything you boys can do. And do it better."

Gordy grinned. "We'll see."

She patted her pocket. "I'm keeping my phone handy so I can catch a video of you guys emptying your stomachs."

Gordy laughed and shook his head.

The ride slowed and the hydraulic arms yawned back into place. Those who were truly into the ride were easy to spot. Eyes bright, like they wanted to ride again. Others, with fake smiles frozen on their faces, clearly couldn't wait to get off. Typhoon finally came to a stop, and the riders staggered off.

A smile creased the weathered face of the Typhoon operator as he watched his latest victims exit the ride.

Gordy bounced on the balls of his feet—like he couldn't wait to get moving. "You want to back out, Hiro?"

She shook her head. "And miss my front row seat to see you lose it?" She marched toward the entrance. "C'mon, Mr. Iron Gut."

Hiro climbed into the closest available car. Cooper followed, taking the outside seat so he wouldn't smash her when centrifugal force took over. Lunk and Gordy grabbed a car on the same hydraulic arm. If Gordy got sick, Hiro definitely wouldn't miss it.

Cooper lowered the lap bar.

"Are you kidding me?" Hiro gripped the bar. "This is it? No shoulder harness? Nothing?"

"All part of the effect," Cooper said. "You gotta be like a cowboy on a bronc. Climb on and hang on."

Hiro shook her head. "It's old. I can't believe this passes safety regulations."

"Probably doesn't."

"Oh, that's comforting. Thanks, Coop."

A few people were climbing aboard the other cars. "You don't have to prove anything to Gordy, Hiro. You can still hop off—if you do it now."

She looked liked she was weighing that option.

"C'mon, Hiro. It's okay. I'll get off too."

She tightened her grip on the lap bar.

Cooper laughed as the operator revved the diesel motors.

Lunk looked grim—like he suddenly wasn't so sure about this ride either.

Gordy wasn't even holding the safety bar yet. He held both thumbs up. "Ready, Hiro?"

As if on cue, the Typhoon started turning. Slowly at first, like it was just waking from a power nap.

"Coop?"

Hiro's voice sounded as small as she looked.

"I don't like this," she said. "I mean, I *really* don't like this."

He wished she'd taken him up on his offer to get off the ride. "It will all be over in two minutes."

She nodded. Her knuckles were already white—and the color of her face was moving in that same direction.

Typhoon picked up speed and swept them around the inside of the makeshift fence again and again. Cooper spotted his backpack. The monkey watched them with a grin.

"I have a bad feeling," Hiro said.

"The ride?"

She shifted closer until there was no longer a gap between them. "I don't know."

The hydraulic arm raised them up and gave them a freaky-angled view of the fairgrounds. "Hang on!" Cooper said.

Maybe it was Hiro's comments about loose bolts or something, but Cooper felt like the entire car could fly off the hydraulic arm at any moment. They'd be dead. The lap bar seemed too small. The latch looked worn. Weak.

Gordy whooped from somewhere off to Cooper's right. At least Gordy was having a good time.

Typhoon had whipped itself into a frenzy. Turning. Spinning. Like it was berserk—or maybe the operator was. The force pushed Cooper into the corner of the car. Hiro pressed up against him. Out of sheer instinct, he clamped sweat-slick hands around the metal bar across their laps. Even this would be useless if anything went wrong with the ride. Like loose bolts. They'd be thrown half-way across the fairgrounds.

"I hate this!" Hiro said. "And if you tell Gordy what I said, I'll kill you."

He caught glimpses of Gordy and Lunk as they spun past them. Gordy was laughing hysterically. Lunk looked like he'd been hypnotized. Wide-eyed. Jaw clenched. Dead serious.

The diesels roared on with no signs of slowing. The ride had to be longer than a minute already. Maybe two. What was the guy waiting for? Maybe the riders didn't look sick enough yet. He obviously hadn't seen Lunk.

"Please, God!"

Was Hiro praying? No doubt—and with all her heart. He wished she'd climbed off the ride when she had the chance. He hated knowing she was scared, and that he couldn't do anything to help her. They flew past the Typhoon sign again and again. The thing seemed to mock them every time they went by. Cooper closed his eyes for a moment. That made the spinning worse.

"Bad. Feeling." Hiro pressed up against him. She seemed to be struggling to get the words out.

She was riding on an empty stomach. Always a bad idea. He glanced at her and instantly knew the look on her face. She wasn't feeling sick. She wasn't afraid of the ride either. It was something else—her woman's intuition. And whenever she got that feeling, it was never good.

CHAPTER 61

Hiro tried to pinpoint the feeling, but it was hard to do with all the spinning.

"Almost over, Hiro."

Coop tried to make her feel better. But the ride showed no sign of slowing. He put his hand over hers and gripped the bar tighter. Like he wanted her to know she wasn't going to fly out of the car. He wouldn't let her.

Their hydraulic arm lowered, spinning them parallel to the ground. "I feel like . . ."—Hiro scanned the crowd behind the fence—"we're being watched."

Coop hesitated. "Everybody's watching. Just like we did."

That wasn't it. "Someone is watching *us* specifically. You. Me. Lunk. Gordy."

Coop didn't answer. Did he think it was her imagination? She couldn't see his eyes to be sure. She watched the crowd instead. That's when she saw him standing at the fence—just for a split second before Typhoon swung her out of that line of vision. He was wearing the same baseball cap. Beard. It was definitely him.

"Coop!" She tried to turn so she could get a visual of Coop's backpack—the spot where she'd seen him. "It's Fat Elvis. I just saw him."

"You sure?"

Oh yeah. "Positive." And there was something more. That feeling was back. Like she knew him. "There!" She pointed—then grabbed the bar. Fat Elvis was there—pressed up against Coop's backpack hanging on the fence. For an instant their eyes connected—and a missing puzzle piece dropped into place.

"Where?" Coop said.

"Oh, God!" Her mind whirled faster than the ride ever had. Her vision blurred. She blinked back tears so she could get another clear view of him, but she didn't dare let go of the grab bar again.

"I don't see anybody," Coop said.

The operator backed off the diesels, and Typhoon slowed. They swung past Coop's backpack again—but Fat Elvis was gone.

"Where is he?" Coop squeezed her hand harder.

She searched the faces in the crowd along the fence. "He disappeared," she said. But he couldn't be far. She sensed that much. "It's him. It's *him*. He saw us. He was looking at me."

Typhoon tucked in its arms and came to a merciful stop. Gordy whooped in the car beside them. Obviously his stomach was truly made of cast iron. Hiro wished hers was the same. She felt like she was going to throw up, but it wasn't because of the ride.

"Fat Elvis?" Coop said. "You saw Fat Elvis watching us?"

Hiro nodded. "Only it wasn't him." She watched the crowd. She was afraid she'd see him again—and afraid she *wouldn't*.

Even though the ride had stopped, Hiro's stomach didn't. She fumbled with the latch. She had to get off this ride. She was going to lose it.

"I got it," Coop said. He raised the safety bar.

Hiro stumbled past him and jumped to the ground—which seemed to be moving. She felt dizzy. Knees rubbery. A wave of weakness washed over her, and she dropped to her hands and knees.

"Hiro?"

Coop's voice came from beside her. Everything was still spinning somehow. She gagged once. Her stomach contracted and tried to squeeze out what wasn't there.

"You're okay," Coop said. He put his hand on her back. Rubbed gently. "It's all in your head. It'll pass."

She coughed and cleared her throat. Her arms were shaking.

"Deep breaths," Coop said. "That's it."

The ground stopped moving. Her breathing evened out. The dizziness passed. Her stomach settled. But the weakness was still there. And a heaviness—like she'd gained a hundred pounds since the ride started.

"Clear the area. The ride's going to start." A carnival worker strode right past them and never even stopped to ask how she was. *Jerk.*

Cooper held out his hand and helped her to her feet. Lunk stepped up and grabbed her other arm. He looked about as good as she felt.

But Gordy was practically bouncing with energy. "How 'bout hitting this ride one more time? Then we'll swing over to the food aisle, eh, Hiro?"

She wanted to clench her fist and shake it at him—but all she could muster was a glare.

Gordy laughed. "You are a real piece of work, Hiro. Riding Typhoon on an empty stomach is really dumb."

The ride operator revved the diesels—like he was going to start while they were still in the danger zone.

"Let's get her on the other side of the fence," Coop said.

Coop and Lunk bent down so she could drape her arms over their shoulders. They stood, lifting her off the ground, and walked her over to where Cooper's backpack was hanging.

"She said she saw Fat Elvis watching us," Coop said.

Hiro didn't like the way Cooper had said that. *She said* she saw. Didn't he believe her?

"The way she looks right now," Gordy said, "I'm surprised she didn't see little pink elephants."

"Don't push it, Gordy." Hiro's strength surged once she got on the other side of the fence. "I saw him. He was standing right here." She pointed to Coop's backpack. "Watching." She shrugged free from Coop and Lunk. Tried to look stronger than she felt. By the looks on their faces, Hiro knew she was the only one who'd spotted him.

"We were spinning pretty fast," Lunk said. "How—"

"How could I see anybody? Is that what you want to know?" She scanned the crowd. "I *felt* him before I saw him."

"Let's find a place to sit down," Lunk said. "Tell us all about it."

Something in his tone irked her. He sounded patronizing. Lunk thought she'd imagined it. "I don't need to sit down," she said. "We need to find him."

"Why would we want to find Fat Elvis?" Gordy was still smiling.

"Because," she whispered, "I know who Fat Elvis really is. It all clicked in place while I was on the ride."

She glanced over her shoulder, afraid he was watching her now. Somehow she knew he was.

"Who he *really* is?" Gordy looked confused. "You mean—like his real name?"

Hiro nodded. She saw the doubt in Gordy's eyes, so she focused on Coop instead. "Fat Elvis is Joseph Stein."

CHAPTER 62

Cooper's stomach lurched "*What?*"

Hiro nodded. "It's him. I know it."

"But how could you possibly ..." Coop paused. "We were moving so fast."

She rubbed the necklace at her throat.

Cooper looked her in the eyes. "You actually recognized him?"

"Yes." She shrugged. "No."

"Which is it?" Gordy said.

"I only saw him for an instant."

"Fat Elvis," Cooper said.

She nodded. "And it was like I suddenly knew. It was *him*."

Cooper didn't take his eyes off hers. "Joseph Stein?"

Hiro nodded. Who she really saw, Cooper couldn't be sure. But she seemed convinced that it was Stein.

"Impossible," Gordy said. "He's been missing for almost a year. Why would he be here—watching us?"

Gordy had a point. Why would Stein take a chance that he'd be recognized? After the robbery at Frank 'n Stein's, he'd become a wanted man charged with robbery and multiple counts of attempted murder. The guy would probably spend the rest of his life in jail if he were caught.

"It was him," Hiro said. "I feel it in here." She pointed at her heart.

"Okay," Cooper said. "Let's say it's him. Maybe we should call the police."

Lunk held out his hands. "No offense, Coop, but what are you going to tell them? Hiro had a *feeling* that she saw a wanted criminal hanging around the fair?"

Cooper saw the conflict on her face. "Hiro?"

"What *do* I tell them?" Her eyes looked haunted. "So none of you saw him?"

Nobody answered. They didn't need to.

"He was standing right here. By Coop's backpack. His hands were right on it. I saw him." She looked back at the ride — now swinging at full speed again. "And he saw me." She rubbed down the goose bumps on her arms.

Gordy shrugged. "I never looked at the crowd. I kept trying to watch you to see if you'd get sick all over Coop."

Cooper tried to picture Fat Elvis the way he'd seen the guy outside Scoops. "Even when we saw him in town, I never got a close look at him." And neither did Hiro.

She looked at him and her shoulders slumped. "You're right." She turned and scanned the crowd. "Maybe if you saw him again, you could get close enough to recognize him."

Maybe. And maybe if Cooper got a good look at the guy, he wouldn't see any resemblance to Stein. Still, Cooper wanted to give Hiro the benefit of the doubt. He wanted to be there for her. Be a good friend.

"Okay, so you saw him and now he's gone. Think he's still here at the fairgrounds?"

She nodded. "I'm sure of it."

Cooper scanned the crowd now too. "Then let's find him and get a closer look."

"Wait a second," Gordy held up both hands. "You want to go searching — for *him*?"

"Unless we know it's Stein, we can't really go to the police," Cooper said. "And we'll always be looking over our shoulders."

Lunk nodded. "We could spread out."

Cooper wasn't about to leave Hiro alone now. "I'll go with Hiro. You and Gordy stick together." He slung the backpack over his shoulder. Chimpy grinned at him like this was all a big game. "Got your phone, Gordy?"

Gordy nodded.

Hiro pulled her phone out of her pocket. "Call me if you see him. And switch to vibrate. We'll never hear it ringing over this noise."

Cooper looked down the double aisle of rides. "We'll go along one aisle. You two go down the other. Same with the game aisles."

Gordy turned and started around the other side of Typhoon.

Lunk hesitated, then looked directly at Cooper. "No heroics." He didn't wait for an answer but turned to Hiro. "Call us."

She nodded.

Lunk hustled to catch up to Gordy.

Cooper went to the other side. "Did you notice what he was wearing?"

Hiro kept pace. "Black T-shirt with writing and a logo on it. Maybe it's the casino where he works."

Great. Half the men at the fair were wearing black T-shirts. Harley-Davidson logos. Bands. But at least it was something. He fought the urge to move fast—to cover more ground. If Stein was here and watching them, he'd be close by. Trying to blend in somehow. "Was he wearing a hat?"

Hiro nodded. "A baseball hat. Camo pattern."

If Stein knew he'd been spotted, he might have ditched the hat. But the T-shirt was another story.

Hiro's fingers flew over the screen of her phone. "I'm calling Gordy about the T-shirt."

Cooper nodded. He walked slower than he wanted to—but it

was the only way he could check out every person wearing a black shirt.

The whole fair had taken on a different feel now. The diesel motors roared louder. The people walking the aisle seemed more obnoxious. The ride operator at Pharaoh's Fury leered at Hiro. Checked her out — head to toe — without hiding it.

"This place is creeping me out," Hiro said.

Cooper picked up the pace. "Stay close." It had to be his imagination, but he felt like they were being watched too. He walked backward for a few moments. Except for the ride operator still eyeballing Hiro, nobody seemed to notice them.

Lunk and Gordy stood at the end of the ride aisles next to a ticket booth. They had a perfect view of anyone entering or leaving the ride section of the fairgrounds. Lunk shrugged and shook his head.

Cooper motioned back to him and then turned to Hiro. "Let's check out the games area."

Hiro walked beside him, but she didn't say a word. People crammed the aisles. Some walked in tight clusters. Others wandered aimlessly, caught up in the human flow.

Cooper stopped at the crossbow booth. Dozens of monkeys like the one in his backpack stared back at him, silently asking if he was going to play again.

Apparently Hiro's phone vibrated. She swung it up to her ear. "Gordy? Talk to me." Cooper leaned close, but with all the noise it was impossible to catch a word Gordy was saying.

Hiro hung up. "They've canvassed the game aisles. They're heading for the food aisles. They'll meet us at the big elephant."

Cooper nodded.

"They covered that pretty quick," Hiro said.

The way she said it made him wonder if she thought they were only going through the motions. Humoring her. Cooper wanted her to know he was taking her seriously. "I think we should stay put for a few minutes. Blend in. See if he passes."

Hiro agreed. They stood to the side of the crossbow booth and watched. Cooper looked down the aisle one way, and Hiro watched the other way.

The whole thing was unreal. And seemed impossible. But Cooper wanted to stick with the search long enough for Hiro to know he had tried. He wanted to tell her how he'd turned a corner. How he really believed there was a murder. But this was hardly the time or place. And now her theory had a whole new twist.

Could Fat Elvis really be Joseph Stein?

"Coop?"

Hiro's voice sounded weak. Small.

"What happens if we don't find him?"

Which was looking more and more likely. But the question that really bothered Cooper was just the opposite. What would happen if they *did*?

CHAPTER 63

Lunk hated to admit defeat, but they'd been up and down the food aisle twice. The search was pretty much over. Fat Elvis was gone — if he'd ever been there in the first place. And as for Hiro's theory about Fat Elvis being Joseph Stein? He wasn't ready to buy into that just yet.

"You thinking what I'm thinking?" Gordy said.

"I hope not."

Gordy laughed. "We're here at the elephant ear booth." He rubbed his stomach. "It's time to top off our tanks. We've burned off a lot of fuel with this whole manhunt."

"Manhunt?" Lunk checked over his shoulder to be sure Hiro and Coop hadn't walked up behind them. "More like a ghost hunt."

Gordy pulled a wad of singles from his pocket. "You don't believe in ghosts."

"Exactly."

Gordy snickered. He said something to the guy manning the deep fryer, paid him, and turned to Lunk. "You going to order one or not?"

Lunk shook his head. It wasn't just the cost. He wanted to keep his hands free, to be ready — just in case Hiro called. Even though it seemed like a long shot.

"The way I see it," Gordy said, "Hiro is singlehandedly ruining our vacation."

Lunk eyed him. "How do you figure?"

"She's got us looking over our shoulders all the time. First in town. Now here. At the *fair*."

He said it like the fairgrounds were sacred somehow.

"We should be taking in more rides—or spending more time packing in this amazing food. Not running around on some wild goose chase."

The guy passed Gordy's elephant ear through the sliding window. It was smothered with some sort of strawberry sauce and cinnamon sugar. It smelled good. Really good. Lunk's stomach growled. Maybe there was something to Gordy's theory about the force of the rides compressing the food.

"Tear off a hunk," Gordy said.

Lunk ripped a piece of warm dough off Gordy's plate. "Do you figure Fat Elvis is already gone"—Lunk hesitated—"or was he never here to begin with?"

Gordy worked his mouthful to one cheek. "Here's my theory. Hiro was totally freaked about riding Typhoon. She's been super-paranoid about all of this Fat Elvis stuff. And let's face it—she never got over the fact that Joseph Stein got away clean."

He set down his plate and used his hands to demonstrate. "So on the ride, these three super-fears of hers sort of collided—blame it on the 'spinning force.' Next thing you know, she's hanging on for dear life, seeing Fat Elvis, and thinking he's Joseph Stein."

Lunk couldn't help but smile at the way Gordy's logic worked. "So you think the whole thing was in her head?"

"Totally." Gordy took another bite. "And so do you. It's all a pigment of her imagination."

Lunk laughed. "A *figment* of her imagination."

Gordy nodded. "Probably that too." He used the back of his hand to wipe cinnamon sugar off his mouth. "And if we don't stop her, she'll ruin our time at the fair."

Lunk turned that one around in his head. He was having a great time, really. He didn't need food or rides or games. Just hanging with his friends was enough.

"Look," Gordy said, "I'm no psychologist—but yeah, I think this whole thing is in her head." He circled his ear with his forefinger and grinned. "The Typhoon just scrambled it up a little more."

Lunk snickered. Gordy had a way of scrambling things himself.

Suddenly, Gordy's grin disappeared as his eyes focused on something—or someone—behind Lunk.

"You're right about one thing, Gordy."

It was Hiro's voice. Lunk cringed.

"You're definitely no psychologist."

CHAPTER 64

Gordy wanted to hide behind the giant elephant. And Hiro looked like she'd just been trampled by one.

He forced a smile. "You aren't buying my stupid theory, are you?"

"Part of it," Hiro said.

Gordy relaxed just a bit. "Really? Which part?"

"About it being stupid."

Okay. She was giving him a bit of his own medicine. He could live with that. It was when she got quiet and stopped fighting that he worried. "Sorry, Hiro." Like a peace offering, he held out the paper plate with what remained of his elephant ear. "How about a bite?"

She glared at him. "I'd like to take a bite out of *your* ear."

"Okay," Coop said, stepping between them. "Before Hiro gets all Mike Tyson on us, tell us what you two saw. Anything?"

Gordy knew exactly what Coop was doing. He'd remember to thank him later.

"You're changing the subject, Coop," Hiro said. "Does anybody here believe that I saw Fat Elvis watching us?"

Gordy wasn't about to answer that. Lunk stared at his feet.

"Really?" Hiro jammed her hands in her pockets. She looked

kind of embarrassed. Hurt. "Really." Maybe reality was finally sinking in. And she seemed to be sinking with it.

"He could have been there," Coop said. "I believe that."

"You're a little slow on the draw there, cowboy," Hiro said. "The correct answer was something like, 'If you say you saw him—he's here. We should keep looking.'"

"You're upset—" Coop said. "I'm with you on this. Really. Most of it anyway."

"No. I'm alone," Hiro said. "And don't deny it. So I guess I don't need to ask the next question."

Gordy wondered what it was. But not enough to ask.

Hiro took a step back. "If you don't think I saw Fat Elvis, then there's no sense asking you if he could be Joseph Stein."

Gordy looked at Coop's face. Then Lunk's. Oh yeah. Hiro was all alone with her theories.

"You gotta admit," Gordy said, "that whole Stein thing is so random."

Hiro took another step back. Then two.

"Hiro—it's not like that," Coop said. "Not exactly."

She nodded and kept backing up. "I think I have a pretty good picture of how it is."

"Where are you going?" Gordy said.

"For a walk."

Gordy looked at Coop.

"Hiro," Coop said. "Hold on."

"Maybe I'll take another spin on the Typhoon." Hiro circled her ear with her forefinger. "See if it can unscramble my head."

"We'll go with you," Coop said.

She held up both hands but didn't stop walking. "I need to be alone."

Coop took a step toward her. "But what if he really *is* here? You could be in danger."

"You don't really believe that," she said. "None of you do."

She turned and bolted. Broke into a flat-out run and disappeared behind a group of geezers wearing straw cowboy hats.

Gordy shook his head. "She's *mad*."

"She's hurting," Coop said. "And we have to stop treating her like she's crazy. What kind of friends do that?"

"Agreed," Lunk said. "What now?"

Coop looked dead serious. "We find her. And we follow her. Make sure she stays safe."

"She won't like it," Gordy said.

"We tail her without her seeing us." Coop started running in the direction where Hiro had disappeared. "She won't know we're there."

Lunk took off after Coop.

Gordy dropped his plate in a trash barrel and hustled to catch up. Playing cat and mouse with Hiro. This was shaping up to be a great day at the fair after all.

CHAPTER 65

Cooper slowed after thirty yards. Where did she go?

"Do you see her?" Lunk fell in step alongside him.

Cooper shook his head. "She had to know we'd try to follow."

Lunk nodded. "And she wouldn't want to make this easy."

Got that right. Cooper hiked his backpack onto his shoulder and kept looking while he walked. Her height wouldn't help matters any. She could duck behind almost anyone and not be seen.

Gordy hustled ahead, then circled back. "If we're going to find her, we gotta think like her."

"Good luck with that," Lunk said.

At the end of the food aisle, they turned toward the games and rides. "Let's spread out," Cooper said.

They walked past the goldfish game, the basketball game with the bogus rims, and the BB machine guns. No Hiro. By the time they reached the end of the games, a new thought popped into Cooper's mind. He motioned the others over.

"The Typhoon. She said she was going there, right?"

Gordy didn't look convinced. "She was joking. She hated that ride."

"If you lose somebody in a mall or at a theme park … where do you look?"

Gordy smiled. "The last place you saw him."

"And she's looking for Fat Elvis."

"Let's go," Lunk said.

They fanned out, approaching the ride from three directions.

There. She stood with her back to the fence—almost exactly where Cooper's backpack had been hanging. She was surveying the crowd. Did she really think Fat Elvis would still be hanging around? One thing was clear—*she* believed that she saw him.

Cooper got a visual on Lunk. He'd spotted her too. Lunk leaned against a ticket booth and watched.

Hiro stayed put while the Typhoon thrilled and sickened two more loads of riders. Then she moved. Fast.

Past the Typhoon. Past Pharaoh's Fury. Did she see Fat Elvis? Sense him?

Cooper jogged to cut the distance between them. His backpack thumped against him like Chimpy wanted him to go faster.

"Coop!" Lunk's voice called out behind him. "Wait up."

Cooper kept his eyes on Hiro. She looked back over her shoulder.

"She thinks she's being followed," Lunk said.

Cooper nodded. "She is."

Lunk laughed.

Hiro cut between the Tilt-a-Whirl and the Himalayan.

"She's moving out of the ride area," Lunk said. "Where's Gordy?"

Cooper shook his head. "I'm sure he's around." It was hard enough keeping track of Hiro.

Hiro crossed the food aisle and ducked behind the Brat Pit.

Cooper and Lunk started running the moment she was out of sight. When they got to the back of the food booth, they barely got a glimpse of her disappearing behind SuWing's.

"She's sneaky," Lunk said.

Cooper picked up the pace. "Think she's onto us?"

"I don't see how. She's never made eye contact with me. You?"

Cooper shook his head. But she was definitely running from someone.

On the other side of SuWing's, Hiro zigzagged her way through the crowd until she got to the giant elephant.

"Right where she started," Lunk said. "Think she's looking for us?"

Cooper had no idea.

Hiro crouched alongside the elephant ear booth like she was watching for someone. Cooper sat at a table at SuWing's, where he could watch her without being obvious.

Lunk sat down beside him. "Now what?"

"We wait. See what she's up to," Cooper said. "Make sure she stays safe." He glanced down the aisle. "You keep an eye on her," Cooper said. "I'll keep a lookout for ..." He let the thought hang there.

Hiro stayed perched in her spot. Cooper could barely make out something in her palm. She shifted it from hand to hand. Her phone. In one of those indestructible cases. She started to text, then stopped and looked around.

"She looks jumpy," Lunk said.

Or fragile. Scared. Cooper figured any one of those words fit.

"She doesn't even know we're here," Lunk said. "Hiro better learn how to spot a tail if she plans to make it as a cop."

Hiro hadn't moved from her hiding spot. She looked so small crouching there. "I'm thinking we should just walk up to her," Cooper said. "If she's scared ..."

She fiddled with the phone again, as if debating whether or not to use it.

Cooper stood. "Let's go."

Lunk walked beside him. Casually. They acted like they didn't know she was there so she wouldn't think they'd been spying on her. They were nearly to the elephant when Hiro looked their way. Relief flooded her face.

"Coop! Lunk!" She stood and waved them over.

She took a half step toward them, but then a hand reached out from behind her and grabbed her shoulder. Hiro whirled around and struck at somebody with her phone.

"Hiro!" Cooper bolted toward her.

Free from the man's grip, she ran straight for Cooper and slammed into him.

"You're okay," Cooper said. "Nobody's going to hurt you now."

Lunk passed them both, his fists clenched, and disappeared around the side of the elephant. A moment later he was back. "You'd better get over here," he said. "She decked Gordy, and he's bleeding pretty good."

CHAPTER 66

Cooper sat on the bow of *The Getaway* and watched the green and red navigation lights of a boat heading toward them. "Seven stitches. You're never going to live this down, Gordy."

"Felt like she hit me with a brick."

Lunk laughed. "You sure went down like one."

Gordy nodded. "She's dangerous when she gets scared."

"She's always dangerous," Lunk said.

"Well, if it makes you feel any better," Cooper said, "she felt really bad about it."

"So she says," Gordy said. "But she laughed when I came out of the ER with stitches."

"We all did," Lunk said. "Even your mom."

Gordy smiled—then instantly winced. "I guess I did it to myself. I was running with scissors"—he pointed to his cheek—"and I got cut."

Cooper slapped his cousin on the back. "Your pranks have been backfiring this week. Have you noticed?"

"Coop whacks me in the nose. Hiro gets me on the cheek," Gordy said. "Lunk, if you take a swing at me, I'm going home."

Cooper and Lunk burst out laughing. Gordy bit his lip and tried not to join in.

Gordy shrugged. "The nurse says I have to keep it dry for a few days. Infection and all that stuff. How am I supposed to swim?"

Lunk tapped his lifejacket. "Like me. Wear one of these babies."

Gordy moaned. "Our vacation is ruined."

"Not ruined," Cooper said. "Just a little different than we expected."

They got quiet and sat looking out over the black water. Cooper's thoughts split in two directions. There was the dread of putting his head below the surface — especially if the water was deep or dark. And there was the whole issue of Joseph Stein. Hiro seemed so sure ... what if she was right?

"Coop?" Lunk said. "You still thinking there was a murder?"

It didn't sound like he really needed to ask. "Yeah. I do."

"Even after processing what the cop said about the anonymous calls?"

Cooper nodded. "I do. And I wanted to tell Hiro that today. Wanted to tell her I was sorry for going back and forth on it so much. I guess I bombed that one."

Gordy's eyes got wide. "What about the overactive cop imagination?"

Cooper shrugged. "Maybe I didn't want to believe what was happening. Maybe I was in denial or something. But we *know* Hiro. She's not always right ... but she's never all wrong."

"Agreed," Lunk said.

"What about you, Lunk?" Cooper looked right at him. "How do you weigh in on all this?"

"Definitely leaning toward Hiro's way of thinking. Even with the pickup trying to run you down." He got quiet, as if he was debating whether to say more. "You think she saw Fat Elvis at the fair?"

Cooper thought for a moment. "I really do."

Lunk whistled softly. "Now the big question. You think Fat Elvis is really Stein?"

"I've asked myself that a hundred times since the fair," Cooper said.

Gordy stared at him. "What did you come up with?"

Cooper shook his head. "I honestly don't know. It seems like a stretch—but what if?"

"So," Lunk said, "you're not ruling it out."

"I don't dare—no matter how much I want to believe she's wrong this time," Cooper said. "If she's right ..." He couldn't finish. Not out loud. If Stein was in the area, watching her, then she was in danger.

Lunk nodded slowly like he understood. "What should we do?"

Cooper thought for a moment. "We throw ourselves into the investigation," Cooper said. "If she wants to check something out—we do it. No questions asked."

Gordy touched his stitches. "I can't swim for a couple of days anyway."

"Exactly," Cooper said. "It's time we show her complete support."

Gordy sighed. "Okay. I'm in. But how do we help with the investigation?"

Cooper had been thinking about that. "We look for the camera. All of us. We'll check every inch of the shoreline."

"We should look out in deeper water too," Lunk said. "Where the girl jumped off *Krypto Night*—just in case the camera sank."

Cooper nodded. He'd forgotten about that angle.

Lunk and Gordy were quiet for a minute.

"Then it's settled," Lunk said. "Tomorrow, we look for the camera."

Cooper reached into his pocket for his phone. Then he checked his other pockets. "I don't know what I did with my phone." He looked at Gordy. "Let's send her a text so she doesn't go to bed feeling like we've all ganged up on her. Again."

Gordy whipped out his phone. His thumbs flew over the screen, saying the message out loud like he was dictating it to himself. "Let's-look-for-the-missing-camera-again-tomorrow. Send." He put his phone back in his pocket. "There. Now Hiro will have sweet dreams." He looked at Cooper. "Too bad that's not what you're gonna have tonight."

"What?"

"Lunk can't go underwater wearing a lifejacket. I can't go down because of my stitches. So that just leaves you to do the salvage operation, amigo."

CHAPTER 67

Hiro sat on the balcony and read the text again. Why the sudden interest in the camera? And why did Gordy send the text and not Coop?

Because if it came directly from Coop, it would be too obvious. Coop had probably talked the guys into playing along with her. Make her think they actually believed something very bad had happened on *Krypto Night*. That's why he had Gordy send the text. It would appear more innocent. "I know you better than you think, Cooper MacKinnon."

The fact was, *none* of them believed that anything bad had happened to the girl on that boat—other than a short argument and a long swim to shore. They didn't believe the pickup deliberately tried to force Coop into that wall. They didn't believe someone had been watching them. They didn't believe she'd heard someone stalking her by the river or that she'd seen Fat Elvis at the fair. And they certainly didn't believe Fat Elvis was Joseph Stein.

It all boiled down to one thing: They didn't believe *her*. She rubbed her necklace. They didn't trust her *judgment*. Her cop sense. Her intuition. And if they stopped trusting it, how long before *she* started questioning it?

She was already second-guessing herself. How many times had

she waffled on this thing? She'd been a pendulum. Back and forth. Back and forth.

And it wasn't just that the guys didn't trust her judgment. It was worse than that. They made a joke of it, laughed about it. Two days ago, she'd have said that what she really wanted from this trip was to find out the truth. To fight for justice. And that was still part of it. But what she really needed was to know that her best friends trusted her judgment — trusted her.

So now they wanted to look for the missing camera? Right. Coop didn't care about the camera because he didn't believe there had been a crime. Looking for the camera was all about Coop trying to make her feel better.

Thanks, Coop, but no thanks. She didn't want him to make her *feel* better. She wanted Coop to *believe* her. And that definitely wasn't going to happen if she kept waffling on these issues. So what did she believe? She grabbed a pen and paper to make a list:

- The girl on the beach (Lynn) was not the girl in the boat (Pom-Pom).
- The girl in the boat (Pom-Pom) was Wendy Besecker, the missing girl.
- Wendy Besecker is missing — but not because she ran off with some guy. On Sunday night she went on a date with Tommy Kryptoski on the *Krypto Night*. Wendy hadn't turned up because she is dead, drifting in the currents of Geneva Lake — just below the surface.
- Tommy Kryptoski isn't just an egomaniac with a nice boat. He is a charming sociopath — and worse. He is a murderer. A monster.
- Fat Elvis is Kryptoski's handler — or babysitter or bodyguard. We know him by another name: Joseph Stein. And that makes him a wanted man. And dangerous.
- Kryptoski isn't the only guy that Fat Elvis is watching. He's

also watching me. And Coop. Gordy. Lunk. He's watching all of us for some reason that only God knows.

Hiro set down the pen. She folded her hands to keep them from shaking and reread the list. This is what she believed. She just needed someone else to believe too. Coop? She wished. But how could she make him believe?

If Dad were alive, he'd believe her, wouldn't he? They'd work the case together and figure it out.

A name popped into her head. Someone she could talk to. She weighed the idea. Did she dare? Hiro tried to force the name out of her thoughts and think of someone else. But the more she tried to avoid it, the more that one name kept nudging its way back into her head.

She slipped her phone from her pocket, opened her contacts list, and scrolled down. She hesitated. If she made this call, she had to be sure. Really sure.

Hiro looked at her list again. Did she really believe? Back and forth. Back and forth.

C'mon, Hiro. Make up your mind. If you believe it, make the call. And if you can't make the call, then don't expect anyone else to believe you any time soon.

She could see the Riviera from the condo's balcony. The docks. Part of the lake. She just couldn't see a clear answer. "God, please. Guide me. Please."

"Hiro?" It was her mom's voice.

Hiro stood. "I'm out here."

"Can't sleep, honey?" Hiro's mom stepped onto the balcony, a sleepy smile on her face. "Give me a hug."

Hiro held her mom tight and inhaled—just drawing in the fresh scent of fabric softener on her mom's pj's. It was the smell of home. And good things. Safety. "Dad was a good cop, wasn't he." It was more of a statement than a question.

Mom put her hands on Hiro's shoulders and eased her back. "He was the best." Her eyes searched Hiro's.

"He had that cop intuition, didn't he?"

She nodded. "That was his gift."

"Was he ever wrong? His hunches, I mean."

Mom smiled. "Often. But he was right a lot of the time too. Does this have anything to do with that missing girl?"

Hiro nodded.

Her mom hugged her again. "Follow your gut, honey. That's what I always told your dad."

That was exactly what Hiro knew all along—deep down. But it was nice to hear it.

"We're going to hang around town tomorrow morning. Hit some shops. It might do you some good to take a little break from all this."

Hiro nodded. Her mom was probably right.

"Come to bed soon."

Hiro smiled and nodded. She looked back toward the lake again and bounced her phone in her hand. *Follow your gut, Hiro.*

She scrolled further down the contacts list on her phone until she came to the name. Hiro took a deep breath and let it out slowly. She touched the screen to make the call—and held her breath.

No turning back now.

He picked it up on the second ring. "Hammer."

CHAPTER 68

Cooper lay on his berth and stared at the ceiling long after Gordy and Lunk had grown quiet. He wished they were still awake. Then maybe he wouldn't feel so alone. The thought of looking for that camera was eating at him. Checking the shoreline? Not a problem. But going underwater? Not a chance.

It took everything he had to go under with Dad the other day. But without Dad? Forget it. He couldn't do this alone. Part of him was still chained in that flooding basement—and he didn't know how to get free.

Gordy stirred. Cried out. Settled down again. *Bad dream.* The abduction was haunting Gordy. Cooper was sure of it. He could try to fill his days with fun to bury his fears, but when he slept, the nightmares crept in. Cooper would talk to him about it. Maybe this weekend when Dad was here. Cooper could barely make out Lunk in the darkness. He was still wearing his lifejacket. They all had fears.

Sometimes fear was good. It was sort of like a bodyguard. It kept them from doing stupid things like walking down a dark alley at night. It kept them from taking dangerous risks that could hurt them.

Other times, fear was a prison guard. It kept people from being free. Dad didn't let fear paralyze him. And that's part of what made him a man, wasn't it? He did the right thing—even if it scared him half to death.

How did Dad do it? How did he check the dark basement when he heard a noise in the middle of the night? How did he walk onto a jobsite without knowing how to do the job? How did he become a man? Did it come with age?

It was more than that. A lot more. And Cooper knew the answer. At least part of it. Dad was never alone—even when no one else was there.

Cooper propped himself up on one elbow and peered out the porthole. Random waves lifted *The Getaway* and rocked it. He never actually saw them coming, and he didn't see where they went after they passed by. But they were there. And they were real.

Deep down, Cooper knew he wasn't alone either—even though it seemed that way sometimes. The same God who helped Dad become a man was with Cooper too—even if Cooper never actually saw him. He'd helped Cooper countless times, hadn't he? And some of those times were just as scary as going underwater. Some were a lot scarier. Like being locked inside the walk-in freezer at Frank 'n Stein's. Or trapped in the flooding basement. Cooper had never been alone. He could see that now.

He needed to grasp the truth of that thought. Tattoo it on his brain. He was not alone. *Not alone.* He wished he could stop time and roadblock tomorrow from coming. Cooper had a feeling—a sense—that Friday would be a test of some sort. Of manhood, maybe. Diving for the camera. Yes. But he had a growing feeling that there was something more.

What? Was he getting intuitions like Hiro now? Ridiculous. But he couldn't shake the feeling that something was going to happen. Something bad.

He sat up, shaking. This was insane. His imagination was taking him for a ride. But what if it wasn't his imagination? What if it was some kind of internal warning system that he didn't fully understand? He wanted to talk to Hiro. Needed to see if she felt it too. But it was way too late for that.

He stretched out on his berth again and tried to calm down. Tried to think about totally unrelated things. But like a storm on shifting winds, his mind kept circling back.

You are not alone. That was truth. And deep down, he knew that hanging onto that truth was critical. Maybe it was the only thing that would get him through whatever was to come tomorrow.

CHAPTER 69

Hiro had no idea how long she'd been spilling her guts. Detective Hammer had listened with hardly a comment.

Hiro paused. "Do you think I've gone off the deep end here?"

Detective Hammer chuckled. "No more than most women I know."

"Oh, thanks. I'm serious."

The detective sighed. "Actually, your theory makes sense." He paused for a moment. "How about I take a little drive up to Lake Geneva tomorrow?"

"And do what?"

"Keep an eye on you."

"Are you serious?"

"As serious as you are about your theory."

He *was* serious. "How can you do that—I mean, won't you be outside of your jurisdiction?"

"I'll check in with the LGPD first. I'll talk to that officer you mentioned, Ryan Tarpy."

"As a professional courtesy?"

Hammer laughed. "Something like that."

Hiro tried to picture Hammer showing up in town. "So, what—you'd be like my bodyguard or something?"

"Is that what you want?"

Hiro looked out over the lake. "Definitely not. I don't want the boys to know I called you. They already think I'm paranoid. If you show up, I'll never hear the end of it."

"Okay," Hammer said. "Then you'll never see me."

Hiro laughed. "I wouldn't be too sure about that."

"Do you know what kind of car I drive?"

Hiro had never seen him drive anything other than the police cruiser. She couldn't picture him driving anything else. "No, I guess I don't."

"Good. You'll never know I'm there."

"And what about the boys?"

"If you don't see me, then I guarantee they won't see me either. You get some sleep now, Hiro," Hammer said.

She wanted to sleep. Needed to. She'd hoped to get some advice from Detective Hammer. Encouragement. But the idea of him coming up here to help was more than she'd dared to wish for. She hesitated. "So, you're really going to do it? I mean, I'm really going to see you tomorrow?"

Detective Hammer laughed. "No. Remember? You *won't* see me. And neither will the guys. But I'll see you."

CHAPTER 70

He was up and about late for a Thursday night. But it was safer this way. He'd parked Black Beauty in the pizza joint's parking lot and thought about his day. He'd almost messed things up at the fair. He'd wanted the kids to see him, true. But something had changed. The way they'd reacted was an unexpected twist. Fear should have driven them away from him. Made them stay in a tight little cluster, looking over their shoulders every ten seconds. But instead they'd started searching for him. Why?

Whatever the reason, he was still glad he'd gone to the fair. The little bonus he'd picked up was well worth the risk he'd taken. It would make an absolutely delicious addition to his plan. A little good luck. A little bad. It all evened out.

The whole incident was a sign. Fate was warning him that it was time to take this to the next level. The last level.

He'd worked hard on his plan over the last couple of days—and it was a beaut. He grabbed the bolt cutters from the pickup bed and walked down to Big Foot Beach. Standing on the shoreline, he strained to see *The Getaway* floating in the darkness. The old cabin cruiser was anchored in the perfect spot too. When it was time to put the details in motion, nobody would even notice him swimming out to the boat.

And that time was nearly here. According to the weather report, the wind would be out of the southeast tomorrow night. It would blow the boat away from shore—which, of course, was absolutely ideal. It was an opportunity he couldn't pass up. So that was it. Decision made. Friday was the big day.

It would mean the end of his job, though. No big loss. He'd been an errand boy and babysitter for too long. Let the boss clean up his son's messes from now on.

He'd planned for everything. Plan A. Plan B. And a rock-solid exit plan for each one. Tomorrow he'd decide which plan to follow, depending on which way the wind blew. Then again, he knew which way the wind would be blowing. Out of the southeast. He chuckled quietly.

Hefting the bolt cutters onto his shoulder, he turned away from the water. It was time to get to work and send those boys one last message—just to be sure he kept a little fear burning in their guts.

"Sleep tight, fellas. I'll be back tomorrow night."

CHAPTER 71

Lunk was the first to notice that their bikes were gone. The three of them nearly sunk the inflatable paddling to shore.

Sprinting across the road, they ran to the tree where they'd locked up their bikes. Lunk had some choice names for whoever had done this, but he didn't want to say any of them out loud. Not while the other guys were within earshot.

Cooper held up the cable. "It's a clean cut."

"Are we going to call the police or what?" Gordy put his hands on his hips. "Who steals three bikes?"

"Somebody with a pickup," Coop said.

Lunk inspected the cable. "Fat Elvis?"

Coop shrugged. "It's like Gordy said. Who steals three bikes at a time?"

"I'd like to get my hands on him," Gordy said. "How are we supposed to get to Scoops?"

Lunk would like to take one swing at the guy with his concrete-filled bat. But his bat was gone too. There was no way he'd be able to buy *another* bike.

"I'm calling the police," Gordy said. He tapped out the numbers on his phone. "Somebody stole our wheels. In my book, that's grand theft auto."

Only Gordy would say something like that. He swung the phone up to his ear and started pacing. Lunk checked the ground around the base of the tree to look for tracks. That's probably what Hiro would have done.

"The police said we should come to the station to make a report," Gordy said. "It'll take us forty-five minutes to walk there."

Lunk picked up a stone and chucked it as far out into the lake as he could throw it. "What are they going to do, anyway?" He watched the stone hit the water with a splash. "The bikes are gone."

Coop nodded. "I think you're right."

Gordy pointed toward the state park guardhouse. "Maybe it was the ranger. Maybe he didn't like how we cabled the bikes to his tree."

Coop shrugged. "Might be worth a try. But something tells me this is all related."

"Another warning?"

"Something like that," Coop said. "We'll check with the ranger. Then we'll do what we should have done a couple of days ago."

Gordy looked at him. "What?"

"Look for that camera. Hard."

Lunk hardly looked up for the next three hours. They walked the entire beach. Slowly. And they sifted through every clump of seaweed. They picked their way along the rocky shoreline and searched under every dock all the way to The Geneva Inn. If the camera were there—they would have found it.

Lunk pressed his hands against the small of his back and arched backward.

Coop leaned against the Geneva Inn's pier. "Okay, now I'm sure the camera isn't here."

"Which means ... ?" Gordy let the question hang there.

Coop pointed out to deeper water. "It's out there. Sitting on the bottom of the lake."

Gordy nodded. He didn't say anything. None of them did. They all knew what it meant: it was up to Cooper now.

Gordy took the inflatable back to *The Getaway* to grab his phone and call Hiro. Lunk and Coop walked to the end of the dock and sat on the edge to wait.

Coop stared toward the spot where Kryptoski had gone berserk with *Krytpo Night*. "We need that camera."

Lunk was still thinking about the bikes. The warning. Hiro really had been right all along, hadn't she? Too many weird things had happened to chalk them all up to coincidence.

Coop didn't take his eyes off the spot. "I don't know if I can do it."

Lunk eyed him. Was he talking to himself? "You'll beat it, you know."

Coop shot him a questioning look.

"The water thing. Whatever is going on in there." He tapped Coop's head.

Coop didn't look so sure.

"Frank 'n Stein's walk-in freezer," Lunk said. "Both of us were trapped in there—with no hope. But you beat the odds."

Coop didn't answer but kept staring at the water.

"Last May—in the basement. There was no way you should have survived that." Lunk hesitated. "It's like you're immortal or something. I know you'll beat this too."

Coop smiled and shook his head. "Immortal? Really?"

At least he seemed to be lightening up a little. "All I'm saying is, somebody must be looking out for you."

Coop gave him a sideways glance and pointed to the sky. "I *know* somebody's looking out for me. I can't believe I just heard you admit it."

Lunk shrugged. "Totally out of character for me. But I'm a realist." He didn't believe in luck. And if God wasn't behind it, then what other explanation made any sense? "That's how I know you'll beat this."

"Hey." Gordy paddled up to them. "Hiro ordered a pizza for us from Olympic Restaurant. They're going to deliver it to the beach."

"Did she check to see if her bike got stolen too?"

"It was still locked up at The Cove, right where she left it last night. She's on her way here now."

Coop nodded. "What did she say about *our* bikes?"

"It really shook her up," Gordy said. "It rattled my cage too, as a matter of fact. I feel like we were robbed or something."

Lunk stared at him. "We were."

"Exactly," Gordy said.

Lunk just shook his head. The three of them wedged themselves in the inflatable and started for the beach.

"If we want to get to Scoops later, we're going to have to walk," Gordy said. "Everybody else is going back to that outlet mall in Kenosha. Hiro said they're going to a late movie too. Probably won't be back until way after midnight."

Lunk hoped the news about his bike wouldn't spoil his mom's good time. She needed this vacation.

"Is Hiro going with them?" Cooper asked.

Gordy shook his head. "I told her all about us looking for the camera. She wants to hang out with us."

"Back to the bikes," Cooper said. "Does she think this is related to all the other stuff?"

Gordy nodded. "She connected the dots immediately."

Lunk was connecting some dots of his own. His mind flew back to the other night when Coop got clipped by the pickup. Lunk needed to stay close now. Stay on guard. If something happened, he would do a better job of protecting his friend this time. He had to.

CHAPTER 72

Cooper treaded water and clung to the side of the inflatable two hundred yards off the beach. This was the spot—as best as he could figure—where Kryptoski had gone on the rampage with *Krypto Night.*

Four o'clock. Cooper wished he hadn't waited so long. The sun was getting lower—and without it shining directly overhead, the water would be shadowy at best. Storm clouds were moving in too. More than a front. It looked like a mountain range stretching as far as he could see.

Looking for the camera out here was a really bad idea. Stupid.

"We're in the zone," Gordy said. He stretched one arm toward the south shore and the other toward *The Getaway* moored at its buoy a hundred yards closer to the beach. "Oh yeah." He sighted down his arm like it was a surveyor's scope. "This should be about right."

Coop looked back toward *The Getaway*. Lunk stood at the bow with his lifejacket on, watching them. Beyond him, Tommy Kryptoski sat behind the wheel of *Krypto Night*, revving the engine. It was the first time Coop had seen him in days.

They'd picked a really lousy time to do this.

Hiro sat across from Gordy in the inflatable, hugging her knees to her chest. "It could be anywhere within a square block. There's no way Coop can search this whole area."

Cooper wasn't sure he'd be able to search even one square foot. "How deep is it here?"

Gordy peered over the side as though he could see the bottom. "Twelve, fifteen feet. Twenty feet max."

Twelve feet or twenty. It didn't matter. Either way, it was out of reach. But he had to try. He had to. This wasn't just about finding the camera. It was a way of showing Hiro how much he believed her—and how sorry he was that he hadn't done it earlier. He rinsed his mask and slid it into place. Dipped his face into the water. Looking parallel to the surface was okay—but looking toward the bottom? It was dark. So dark.

Gordy stared into the water. "You know, if Hiro is right, you could find a whole lot more than a camera down there."

"Gordy!" Hiro stopped him. "You're not helping."

But it wasn't like Coop hadn't already thought of that.

"Coop?" Hiro leaned over the edge. "I love what you're trying to do. But you don't have to do this."

He knew she meant well. But her offer didn't make him feel any better. "Thanks, *Mom*."

Even with the mask on, he saw the sadness in her eyes. Apparently he didn't make her feel that great either. "Sorry. I just—" How could he explain himself? This whole thing was maddening. He loved the water. Loved snorkeling. Twenty feet was nothing. He'd done it plenty of times. And now it had become some kind of a test of manhood. Terrific.

He pushed away from the inflatable, gave two strong kicks, and gulped in a deep breath of air. *Do this. Do this. Let's just do this.*

He emptied his lungs and took in one last big breath. Holding it, he bobbed below the surface, feet first. He piked his body, closed his eyes, and dove—forcing himself to go deeper. Into the dark. He opened his eyes. No bottom—there was no bottom. Only blackness—and an icy terror. Something was down here—waiting for him. *God, help me!* He spun and clawed for daylight. He broke the surface—still clawing. Was he shouting too?

"Help him, Gordy!" Hiro's voice.

He felt the inflatable. Clutched it. Tried to climb inside.

"Coop—you're going to capsize us!" Gordy's voice.

Somebody grabbed his arms and held them in place.

"God, help me. God, help me." Did he just say that out loud? Or was it only in his mind? His vision started to clear. He was halfway in the inflatable—like a beached whale. "God ... help." He lay there, panting.

"He probably should have prayed that *before* he went down," Gordy said.

He said it like Cooper wasn't there. And he wasn't. He was still in that basement—wasn't he? He closed his eyes. *You're at Lake Geneva. You're on vacation.*

Cooper's breathing evened out a little. His mask hung cockeyed around his neck. He didn't remember it coming off.

Hiro held his arm with both hands in a firm grip to keep him from slipping back into the water.

He looked up at her.

Tears formed in her eyes. "I'm so sorry, Coop."

He shook his head. "It's not your fault. It's me." It was true.

"Ahoy, there."

Coop recognized that voice. *Krypto Night* had crept up to them. Kryptoski leaned over the side. "Trouble?"

Cooper shook his head.

"Looks like you saw a ghost," Kryptoski said.

Gordy waved him off. "He's got a problem with water."

Thanks, Gordy. "I'm okay." Cooper's voice cracked—sounding as small and weak as he felt.

"If you're so afraid of the water," Kryptoski said, "what are you doing out here?"

"Great question," Coop said. And one he wasn't about to answer. He felt too drained. Embarrassed.

Kryptoski eyed him, like he was trying to figure Cooper out. Did he guess what they were really doing? Impossible. Still, Cooper held his gaze.

"Little raft like that ..." Kryptoski pointed at the inflatable. "Way out here. And a nasty storm is moving in." He checked the sky as if to make his point. "Some boater could clip you without even realizing it."

"Seems to me," Hiro said, "that you're an expert in that department."

Kryptoski flashed his teeth—but his eyes weren't smiling. "All I'm saying is you should get back to shallow water." He looked directly at Cooper. "You're in way over your head out here."

CHAPTER 73

Cooper watched Kryptoski ease his boat toward deeper water. He hadn't gone more than ten yards before he gunned the engine and took off like a shot. His wake jerked the inflatable around, making Cooper clutch the raft even tighter to keep from slipping under the water again.

Kryptoski was right; Cooper was in over his head. Drowning in his own fear. He shook it off. Tried to, anyway. He was better at burying it. But it was always there. Just below the surface.

Cooper watched *Krypto Night* run through a quick series of turns and switchbacks. Stops and starts. Almost like what he'd been doing on Sunday night.

"I feel it," Hiro said. "I get a really bad vibe from this guy."

"Yeah," Gordy said. "Because he's an idiot."

"More than that," Hiro said. "He's a murderer."

Gordy didn't argue that point. "We gotta get to the boat. Fast."

Hiro nodded. "Before he comes back."

Cooper totally agreed. Every natural instinct was signaling a warning.

"Can you climb in?" Hiro scrunched her legs to make room in the middle.

He'd totally weigh them down—if they didn't capsize first. "No, we'll get back faster if I swim."

Gordy grabbed his arm. "Keep your head above water."

Great advice. So helpful. So obvious. Cooper pulled his mask off and dropped it at Hiro's feet. "Don't worry. I'm okay now."

Gordy leaned back and paddled.

Cooper kept to a fast breaststroke, careful to follow Gordy's advice. *Keep your head above water.* That's what he'd been trying to do, hadn't he? Don't look at the thing that's scaring you half to death. Avoid it. Bury it. Pretend it isn't there.

He'd buried his fear. But that didn't mean it was dead. It kept coming back to life. Resurrecting itself. Like a zombie. If he didn't beat this—if he didn't kill this fear and bury it for good—it would bury *him*.

Gordy pulled ahead. Hiro paddled too, although it didn't look like she was doing much good. She kept watching Cooper.

Cooper rolled over into a backstroke. He could go faster this way—and he wanted to keep an eye on Kryptoski. *Krypto Night* sat dead still, two hundred yards out. The double hatch over the engine was open like giant fins, and Kryptoski was looking inside. Maybe he had motor trouble. Good. Whatever it was, Cooper hoped it kept him busy—at least until they reached *The Getaway*.

The storm clouds were advancing like an invading army bent on conquering. Destroying. The wind picked up, still blowing out of the northwest. Fortunately, the waves were pushing them toward *The Getaway*.

Lunk was reaching for them when they made it to the swim platform. He helped Hiro out of the boat, then held the inflatable as Gordy climbed out. Cooper picked up his mask and looked out over the lake.

Krypto Night was still drifting—engine hatch up. Kryptoski was standing midship, hand to his ear. Calling somebody. Maybe he wanted Fat Elvis to bail him out of another mess.

Lunk climbed over the transom rail, following Gordy and Hiro.

"So what happened out there?" Lunk let the question hang in the air for anyone to scoop up.

"We were out there just minding our own business," Gordy said, "when Kryptoski pulled up next to us."

Cooper tuned him out. At least Gordy didn't start the story with his panic attack—or whatever it was. He sat on the edge of the swim platform, letting his legs dangle in the darkening waters. Would he ever be right again?

He looked at his mask and thought about Dad going under with him. Promising he'd work with him this weekend. *What fun.*

He *had* done it with his dad, hadn't he? He'd gone under. He was scared but not out of control. But then, Cooper hadn't been alone. That had made all the difference, hadn't it?

"Coop—you coming?" Hiro leaned over the transom rail. She smiled kind of a sad smile.

"Just need to think through some things," he said.

She nodded.

"Sorry I didn't find the camera," he said.

She shook her head. "I never believed we'd find it."

Honestly? Cooper never did either. He'd been going through the motions out there. He did it for Hiro, really. But *she* didn't think he'd find it either? Terrific. She had no more confidence in him than he had in himself. Sometimes he pushed himself to try to be the person she thought he could be.

It was bad enough that this panic thing had robbed him of his confidence. But now it was stealing her confidence in him as well.

"You tried—and I know you did it for me. That means a lot."

This fear was all in his mind, wasn't it? He wished he could find the panic switch inside his head and just turn it off. Permanently.

"Coop!" Gordy's face showed up at the rail. "Kryptoski is on his way back. He's heading right for us."

CHAPTER 74

Now what? Hiro watched Tommy Kryptoski pull his boat alongside *The Getaway*. Coop stood on the swim deck, his mask still in hand. Gordy and Lunk moved to the side of the boat closest to *Krypto Night*. She wasn't sure if the guys wanted to keep the boats from bumping or provide a human barrier between her and the cold-blooded murderer. Lunk grabbed the pike pole lying on the deck and pushed it against *Krypto Night*.

"Hey, I've got a problem," Kryptoski said. "There's something wrong with the engine."

Hiro stepped up between Gordy and Lunk. *What was he up to?* None of them said anything.

"I called Gage Marine." He waved his phone. "But they suggested I check for seaweed around the prop before I have them tow the boat in for a look-see."

So why are you telling us this? Hiro wanted to ask the question, but she didn't really want to engage him in conversation. If he was a murderer, then she wanted nothing to do with him.

If he was a murderer? *If?* She knew he was. It made her sick. And he was getting away with it. She wanted to vomit all over his pretty boat. For an instant, she was glad Coop and Gordy had planted the fish there. She'd like to put a hole in the hull and send it straight to the bottom of the lake.

Kryptoski pointed at Coop. "I was wondering if you'd take a look at it for me."

No. No. Don't ask Coop to do that.

Coop swallowed. "I, uh ..."

"You've got a mask," Kryptoski said. "It's just a quick look." A slight smile. Like he was challenging Coop. A bully tactic.

You know Coop is afraid. You animal. You monster. Hiro wished she'd gone with her mom to Kenosha. Then Coop wouldn't have tried looking for the camera to please her. And Coop wouldn't be in this spot right now.

"Sure," Coop said. "Why not?"

Hiro could hear the strain in his voice. She wanted to tell him not to do it. He didn't have to prove anything. Not to her—and definitely not to Kryptoski. But she would hurt him if she said it. She'd be the mom again, treating Coop like a little kid. Hiro couldn't do that to him.

Coop dipped his mask in the water, rinsed it, and seated it on his face. "You going to turn off the engine?"

Kryptoski banged his forehead with the heel of his hand. "What an idiot."

Got that right.

Kryptoski turned off the ignition and walked to the side of the boat to watch.

Coop eased himself into the water slowly enough that his head didn't dip below the surface. He swam to the side of Kryptoski's boat.

"Still enough light," Kryptoski said. "You should be able to see without going under the boat."

Lunk held up the pike pole like a giant staff. He leaned in close and whispered, "If he makes a move toward that ignition switch, I'll skewer him."

Hiro nodded. She felt better already.

Gordy hopped over the transom rail and down onto the swim platform to wait. Maybe he wanted to be close if Coop had any trouble.

Coop lowered his face in the water for an instant—then raised his chin high like he'd changed his mind. He took a couple of deep breaths. His lips moved—but no words came out.

He's praying. Good. Hiro breathed a silent prayer for him too.

Kryptoski leaned over the side. "Want me to hold your hand or something?" There was no mistaking the jab in his tone.

Coop shook his head.

Lunk aimed the pike pole directly at Kryptoski. His jaw muscles were working hard.

"Easy, Lunk," Hiro whispered. "Coop's okay."

Coop placed his hands on the side of Kryptoski's boat and ducked under it.

Hiro held her breath as if she were underwater with him.

His hands dropped lower on the side of the boat. Clenched. Unclenched—and disappeared below the waterline.

"I should have gone under," Hiro whispered. "Why didn't I go under?" No, Coop had to do it. It was part of being a guy. And being Coop.

Coop broke the surface, gasping. He thrashed at the water. Even through the mask, Hiro could see that he had a wild look in his eyes. "Oh, God, help!"

Lunk was right there with the pike pole. He held it in front of Coop. "Grab it—I'll pull you in!"

Coop clung to the pole like he would have climbed it if he could. Lunk steered him to the swim platform, and Gordy reached out to help him onto it.

"Whoa." Kryptoski snickered. "I guess he really is afraid of water. Him and the Wicked Witch of the West, eh?"

Hiro sucked in her breath. She couldn't speak. She wished a horde of flying monkeys would carry Kryptoski off.

Coop sat on the platform and ripped off his mask. His chest was heaving. "I'm okay," he said. "I'm okay."

"Oh yeah." Kryptoski sneered. "I can see that."

Coop stood and squared his shoulders like nothing was wrong. "I checked the prop and rudder," Coop said. "There's not even a s-strand of seaweed."

"Thanks," Kryptoski said. "That's what I thought." He dialed his phone and talked with someone on the other end.

Lunk used the pole to push *Krypto Night* farther away from *The Getaway*. The wind caught it and sent it adrift.

Coop's knees were shaking. He leaned against the transom and rubbed them into submission. He looked up at Hiro.

"They'll be here to tow her in thirty minutes," Kryptoski shouted. "Just ahead of the storm, if I'm lucky." He fired up the engine. "Thanks for your help."

Coop didn't answer.

Kryptoski looked right at Coop. "And the way you are around the water, you might want to copy the big guy." He pointed two fingers at Lunk. "Keep your lifejacket on."

Hiro glared at Kryptoski. She wanted him to feel the fury rising inside her.

He grinned, spun the wheel, and headed for his mooring. She hoped Gage Marine towed him away with the boat—if the flying monkeys didn't show up first.

Lunk stowed the pike pole. "I don't mind if I never see that moron again."

"I wouldn't mind seeing him," Hiro said, "behind bars."

"Maybe you'll get your chance," Coop said.

He practically vaulted over the transom rail. Gordy looked a little surprised, but quickly followed. Coop knelt low on the teak deck and frantically motioned them closer.

Gordy stood over him. "You okay?"

Hiro sat down. "Coop?"

His eyes were blazing. "I found it. I *found* it."

Lunk squatted down in front of them. "Found what?"

Coop looked at Hiro and smiled. "The camera."

CHAPTER 75

Cooper couldn't have asked for a better reaction from Hiro. Her eyes went wide. "What?" She reached over and hugged him so hard that he couldn't breathe. He pried her arms off him. "Tell me you're not teasing me," she said.

"Where is it?" Gordy looked behind Cooper as though it might be tucked in the back of his swim shorts.

"The lanyard is wrapped around *Krypto Night*'s prop and shaft."

Hiro's smile faded. She popped her head above the transom rail. "He's in the boat. And he's going to stay there until Gage Marine tows it away."

She didn't have to say any more. If Gage Marine pulled the boat out of the water, they'd find the camera and Kryptoski would get it back. Or maybe it would break loose while the boat was being towed to the other end of the lake. It would drop to the bottom for sure. Either way, the evidence would disappear forever if they didn't do something before Gage Marine arrived.

Lunk whistled. "And the idiot did it to himself by asking you to check for seaweed."

Cooper nodded. "Beautiful, isn't it?"

Hiro already had her phone out. "I'm calling Officer Tarpy.

Once he hears about the camera, he'll come roaring down that hill." She put the phone to her ear and paced.

"Is it all busted up?" Gordy said. "The camera."

Cooper shook his head. "It looked perfect. But the lanyard was wrapped around the shaft so tight that I couldn't budge it."

Lunk stood and faced *Krypto Night*. "I'd love to see his face when he sees that camera. And it was under his boat the whole time."

Hiro pocketed her phone. She looked worried. "Officer Tarpy is working an accident scene. I talked to a dispatcher on the phone, and he said they'll send the next available officer."

"So what's the problem?" Lunk said.

"Nobody is available *now*," she said. "It could be forty-five minutes—maybe an hour before someone gets here."

"Which means," Cooper said, "we'll have to go after that camera ourselves. Now."

Gordy stared at him. "How are we going to do that?"

Cooper joined Lunk at the transom rail. *Krypto Night* bobbed at the buoy. Kryptoski was talking on his phone again.

Lunk glanced Cooper's way. "Got a plan?"

"Maybe." Cooper's stomach twisted. "Give me a minute." He stared out over the water, letting the details of the plan fall into place with amazing ease. *Executing* the plan would be the real challenge. It meant going underwater. Facing his fears.

God help me. God help me. He didn't know what else to say. He'd been fighting his fear with a shovel. Burying it. What he really needed was a sword. Something to attack it with. And in that instant, he knew it had something to do with what his dad had said. *You're not alone.*

"Coop?" Hiro studied his face.

"Let's get my dad's dive gear."

Gordy didn't look all that confident. "The tank?"

Cooper nodded. "Weights. Fins. Compass. All of it."

"You can't be serious." Gordy looked back toward *Krypto Night*.

"His boat is anchored fifty yards away. How are you going to do that?"

Gordy didn't say any more. He didn't need to. Cooper knew exactly what he wasn't saying. How was he supposed to go fifty yards when he could hardly put his head underwater?

"I will do it. I *have to* do it," Cooper said. If wanting it bad enough was all he needed, then he'd be fine. But he needed more than that—and he knew it.

He couldn't do it alone. But he wouldn't *be* alone. God was real—and powerful—and loving. He believed that, didn't he? Yes, Cooper would never be alone. God was with him—and God was big enough to handle whatever lay below the surface.

"Help me get the gear." He ducked inside the cabin and lifted the seat off the storage compartment. Lunk joined him and hauled gear to the teak deck as fast as Cooper pulled it out.

When Cooper put his head under Kryptoski's boat, he'd been okay. No panic attack. Just total shock at seeing the camera—but that was it. And he was going to do it again. He had to.

Gordy was trying to put a dive mask on when Coop stepped back on deck. Hiro stood with her hands on her hips, looking worried. Gordy winced. The seal of the mask crossed over the stitches.

Cooper stepped in front of Gordy. "What are you doing?"

"I'm going for the camera," Gordy said.

"If you seal that mask to your face, you'll bust your stitches wide open."

"Then I won't seal it."

"And it will fill with water, and you won't be able to see a thing." Cooper waited for Gordy to grasp the reality of what he was saying. "I can do this."

Hiro shook her head. "We'll wait for the police."

Thunder rumbled overhead. The clouds were darker now—and directly above them. They tumbled over one another like some kind of atmospheric tag-team wrestling match. And it appeared to be a fight to the death. *The Getaway* swung in a slow arc with the stern facing away from the beach.

"Wind shift," Lunk said.

The wind circled out of the southeast. "This is good. Maybe things are shifting in our favor all around," Cooper said. "Now Kryptoski won't see me gearing up on the swim platform."

Cooper climbed over the transom rail. The bow of the boat shielded *Krypto Night* from view. "Hand over that gear, would you?"

"We're not letting you do it, Coop." Hiro's jaw was set. Gordy stood by her.

Apparently they'd been talking while he was in the cabin.

Cooper gripped the rail. "You've been right all along, Hiro. Kryptoski ran over that girl. Are you going to let him get away with murder?"

"You're in no condition to be doing this, Cooper MacKinnon," Hiro said, "and you know it."

"No," Cooper said. "I don't know it. I don't even totally understand what's wrong with me. But I can do this. I won't be alone." He believed it.

Hiro tilted her head and studied him. She knew exactly what he was talking about. But probably her practical side—or maybe it was her fear—told her he couldn't do it.

He turned to Lunk. "Hand me the gear."

Lunk grabbed the tank and hefted it to the top of the rail. Cooper reached for it, but Lunk held it firm. "One condition." He looked Cooper in the eyes. "I'm going with you."

"What?"

"This tank has two mouthpieces. You and I go together—just like you did with your dad."

Cooper's own words came back to him. He couldn't beat this alone. But Lunk? He shook his head. "I don't know, I mean ..." What would he do if Lunk panicked? They would be clawing at each other, trying to get to the surface.

"No offense, Lunk," Gordy said, "but you're not exactly the water type."

Lunk raised both hands. "Agreed. Water scares me half to death. Seems to me it scares Coop half to death too." He shrugged. "Two halves make a whole, right?"

Hiro put her hands over her ears. "What kind of logic is that? This is insane."

Lunk looked at Coop. "We can do it. Together. We won't be alone — right?"

Cooper nodded, hoping he looked more confident than he felt. "Let's do it."

Lunk grinned and heaved the tank over the rail.

Hiro climbed over the rail and stood on the swim platform. "You expect Gordy and me to just sit here and watch?"

"No," Cooper said. "If we're going to pull this off, it will take all four of us. Stop fighting us and start helping." He screwed the regulator to the tank valve, cranked on the air, and tested the purge valve on each mouthpiece. The whoosh of air was a dose of reality. He really was going to do this. His knees started shaking.

Hiro reached over to steady the tank. "What can I do to help?"

"Take a couple weights off the weight belt. And get the duct tape."

Hiro scampered over the rail and disappeared. Lunk grabbed the fins and masks and joined Cooper on the swim platform. "What's next?"

"Light sticks. All we can get our hands on. In the toolbox. A dock line. And two ski ropes."

"I'm on it," Gordy said.

By the time Cooper had his fins on and the tank strapped to his back, Gordy and Hiro were there with the supplies.

"Now what?" Gordy said.

Cooper took a deep breath and let it out slowly. "Okay. We've got a compass here, but I've never done any kind of underwater navigation. If I rely on it, I may miss the boat and end up on the beach somewhere." He glanced out toward deeper water. "It will be even more dangerous if we miss *The Getaway* on our way back."

Gordy's eyes opened wide.

"Once we go under, we can't exactly pop to the surface to get our bearings."

"We might get spotted," Lunk said.

"Definitely," Cooper said. "So, Gordy, you're going to go out in the inflatable. Drag a dock line with a weight tied to the end of it. But first, duct tape some light sticks to the weight."

Gordy nodded.

"Paddle toward *Krypto Night* like you're on your way to the beach."

"Only I'll stay and chat with Kryptoski for a while."

"Right. We'll follow your glowing rope right to the boat."

"And while I'm talking to him," Gordy said, "you'll cut the camera free."

"The knife," Cooper said.

Gordy disappeared and was back seconds later with the dive knife. Cooper strapped it to his leg.

"Okay," Gordy said, "how will I know when to head back?"

"I'll tug on the rope," Cooper said. "And just in case we get separated, we'll tie the ski ropes together and to the back of *The Getaway*."

"You'll have one end," Gordy said, "and the rope will lead you right back to the boat."

Cooper nodded. Their plans were shaky. Having some kind of backup plan was critical.

"We should tape some glow sticks to the handles," Hiro said.

Cooper nodded. "Do it." He grabbed extras and tucked them into the waistline of his suit.

Hiro started to work on the ski ropes. Gordy attached a weight to the dock line and taped on the glow sticks.

"How long will that tank last?" Hiro said.

Cooper checked the pressure gauge. "The tank is nearly full.

My dad can get forty-five minutes on a full one at a shallow depth." But that was relaxed breathing. And with one person drawing on it.

"So you're talking twenty minutes for two people. Max," Hiro said.

Cooper nodded. He studied the distance between the two boats. It would be just enough oxygen to do the job and get back. It had to be. If he went alone, he'd have plenty of air, but could he even do it? Cooper needed Lunk. They'd just have to work fast.

Cooper went over some last-minute instructions with Lunk. "Okay, the mouthpiece goes in like this." Cooper went through the motions. "Clamp down on these bite tabs with your teeth so you don't lose it."

"What am I supposed to do?" Hiro said.

Cooper slid off the swim platform and into the water. "You stay on the boat. Move around. Pretend like you're talking to someone in the cabin. If he looks at our boat, we can't have him getting suspicious. And you've got the most important job of all."

She tilted her head to the side.

"Pray."

Her eyes were already teary. She swiped at them and nodded. "Already started."

Cooper set the compass, but he hoped he wouldn't need to use it. He wasn't so sure he could.

"Lunk," Hiro said. "I'll be praying for you too."

Lunk nodded. He slid his dive mask in place over the palest face Cooper had ever seen.

"And Lunk." Hiro smiled and pointed. "I think you'll need to leave that behind."

Lunk looked down at his lifejacket. "Right." His hands shook, but he managed to get the first strap unbuckled.

Hiro stepped over and helped with the next two.

Lunk shrugged out of the life vest and handed it to Hiro.

She gave it a pat. "I'll have this ready for you when you get back."

Gordy dropped the inflatable onto the water and jumped in. He played out the dock line with several glow sticks taped to a lead weight at the end.

Lunk slid into the water, his eyes wide. He slid the mouthpiece into his mouth. His jaw muscles tensed. He was breathing hard and fast. He held on to the swim platform and kicked hard, obviously feeling the weight of the belt around his waist.

"You sound like Darth Vader with that thing," Gordy said.

Lunk didn't react. But Gordy was right. The metallic sound of his breathing did sound like Vader. He'd need a lot more than the Force to pull this off.

"Breathing underwater will go against your instincts," Cooper said. "Your brain wants you to hold your breath—but keep breathing."

Lunk nodded.

"We've both got a lot of weight on these belts," Cooper said, "and this tank doesn't have a BC vest with it."

Lunk gave him a blank look.

"Buoyancy compensating vest. There's no way to add a little air to neutralize our weight. We'll go straight down." He hesitated. If Lunk was going to back out, now was the time. "Once we're on the bottom, we'll look for Gordy's line and follow it. Nice and easy."

Lunk nodded.

There wasn't time to teach him how to equalize the pressure in his ears. They weren't going very deep. Hopefully it wouldn't be an issue. He had no time to think about disaster scenarios.

"And, Lunk." Cooper hesitated. But he had to say it. Had to get it out. "If I ... panic down there and start thrashing around ..."

Lunk's eyes grew wider.

"You hold me down. Don't let me surface. Give me a chance to calm down. Got it?"

Lunk swallowed. Nodded.

Hiro handed Cooper the ski ropes with the light sticks and a weight taped to the handles. She was wiping back tears again. "Two tow ropes tied together—just like you said."

Cooper nodded. "That's one hundred and fifty feet."

"Is it enough?"

"Should be." He hoped so.

"Do not let go of this rope, Cooper MacKinnon," Hiro said, her eyes pleading. "I tied my end to the swim platform. I need to know you're holding the other end."

Cooper nodded. "Don't worry. This is our ticket back."

"Okay." Cooper looked at Lunk. "Ready?" He popped his mouthpiece in place and grabbed Lunk's wrist.

"Coop," Hiro said. "Look!" She pointed toward the middle of the lake.

The Gage Marine boat was just a dot—but it was coming fast. "We have to do this. Now!"

Lunk reached over and squeezed Cooper's arm. "Yuuuurrnnotalooone."

Whatever Lunk had tried to say, Coop missed it.

Lunk let go of the swim platform and pulled the mouthpiece out. "You're not alone!" He slapped the mouthpiece back in place.

Cooper nodded. *Neither are you, my friend.* He stopped kicking and let the weight pull him below the surface.

CHAPTER 76

You are not alone. You are not alone. The words replayed again and again on a seemingly endless loop inside Cooper's head. His breathing was jerky. Uneven. It was totally unnatural to be breathing underwater. But the panic didn't come. He kept his eyes on Lunk. And Lunk was doing the same back to him.

The visibility was better than he'd hoped, but that wasn't saying much. Still no panic. *Thank you, God.* Their fins touched the sandy muck bottom at the same time. Like astronauts touching down on the moon, disturbing places that had never been touched by humans. Coop still held Lunk's wrist. He gave Lunk an okay sign.

Lunk nodded and signaled with a thumbs-up. So far, so good.

The seaweed rose above their waists and swirled around their legs like creatures from an alien world, ready to coil themselves around the boys if they didn't keep moving.

The rope attached to the inflatable dangled no more than six feet away from them. Cooper pointed at it, then pushed off the lake bottom to get closer to it. He gave the rope a tug. *C'mon, Gordy. Let's do this.*

Almost immediately, the line started moving. Cooper gave the compass a quick check, and they were on their way.

Immediately, he knew he'd strapped on too much weight. The two of them had to use their hands to pull themselves along the bottom — and the weeds gathered so thick around their shoulders and arms that they had to constantly tear themselves free. But they were making progress.

Cooper thought about dumping some weight so they could swim above the weeds. But would there be time? And what if he took off too much and floated to the surface? He kept an eye on the light sticks ahead and pressed on. Reach and pull. Reach and pull.

The bubbles mushroomed out of Lunk's mouthpiece in an almost constant stream. He was sucking hard on the air — not the even, steady breathing that would make a tank last. Cooper tried to calm his own breathing, but the metallic hiss from the regulator and the bubbles flying past his own mask proved he wasn't doing much better than when he'd first gone under.

Cooper gripped the ski rope handle and imagined Hiro at the other end of the rope. It wasn't just a couple of ski ropes tied together anymore. It was their lifeline. How far had they gone? They had to be halfway to Kryptoski's boat by now.

Get to Krypto Night. *Cut the camera free. Get back to* The Getaway. A mess-up on any one of those parts would be disastrous.

Lunk tapped Cooper's arm and pointed up to the surface — then to his ear.

Pressure? Cooper tried to read his face. No pain — just fear.

Lunk pointed to his ear again.

Listen. Cooper held his breath. It was the unmistakable sound of an engine. But here underwater, it was impossible to tell which direction it was coming from. Was it the service boat from Gage Marine? He took a breath and listened again. By the growing intensity of the sound, one thing was certain. The boat was getting closer — fast.

CHAPTER 77

Hiro stood on the bow and tried to track their bubbles. They'd been easy to follow at first. Now she couldn't see them at all. What if they lost sight of Gordy's rope? She tugged at her braid. She should never have let Coop do this. But he wasn't listening to her about a lot of things. *God, please protect them.* Was God listening? She was absolutely convinced he was.

Gordy had nearly reached *Krypto Night* now. Tommy Kryptoski stood in the center of the boat, gripping the tower bar like he was thinking about doing some chin-ups. He probably would have if he thought she was watching.

The sky looked worse. Absolutely green. For a moment Hiro imagined Kryptoski's chin-up tower was actually a lightning rod. She looked at the clouds. "Now would be a perfect time, God," She shook off the ridiculous thoughts of judgment and refocused. If they did this right, Kryptoski would be facing a judge and jury.

Gordy must have said something to Kryptoski, because the monster moved to the other side of the boat and tossed him a dock line. Gordy grabbed it and held on.

"Okay, Coop. I hope you're there." She searched for more bubbles—any telltale sign. "You've got to be there."

By the way Gordy moved his hands, he obviously had some

kind of conversation going with Kryptoski. Good. *Keep him distracted, Gordy.* What if Coop or Lunk thumped the bottom of his boat while they were trying to get the camera free? Or what if he noticed their air bubbles breaking the surface?

She didn't feel good about this. Not at all. And the feeling was getting worse. What if they were in some kind of trouble? That was a ridiculous thought. They were in trouble the moment they disappeared below the surface of the lake. And there was absolutely nothing she could do to help them. They were on their own. She desperately wanted to see the guys surface. To know they were okay.

The sound of an engine approaching drew her attention. The Gage Marine boat slowed as it plowed by. Kryptoski waved it over, and the driver pulled up alongside him. Now the idea of the guys surfacing terrified her.

"Keep your heads low, guys. Forget the camera. Just get out of there."

CHAPTER 78

Cooper dug his fingers into the muck and hugged the bottom. The boat sounded like it was right on top of him. But it wasn't—he was positive of that. The boat directly overhead was *Krypto Night*. But the sounds of the engine of the Gage Marine boat kept him paralyzed.

Part of him wanted to stay here. Wait it out. And what, run out of air? It was too dim to see the pressure gauge—and he wasn't sure he wanted to. But Hiro was depending on him. Gordy was sticking his neck out. And Lunk had probably taken the greatest risk of all.

You are not alone. Lunk was here. His friends were on the surface.

You are not alone. But it wasn't just his friends, was it? Fear was here. His unseen enemy. It lurked in the darkness, below the surface. It had a grip on him, a stranglehold. Every fear he'd ever buried—some deep, and others in shallow graves—*this* is where they waited for him. Here. Now. He felt the presence of evil, like the zombies Gordy had talked about. But they were real. Nearby. And closing in fast.

I am not alone.

Cooper forced himself to his knees. He reached for a light stick in the waistband of his swim shorts and bent it until he broke the glass vial inside. He gave it a quick shake, and the stick came to life with an eerie green glow. Weeds danced in a hypnotic rhythm in front of his mask. He stared at the tank gauge. Tapped it once. *God help us.* They'd already used well over half the tank.

Unless they moved faster — and sucked less air — they weren't going to make it back to *The Getaway* underwater. They'd run out of air before they got close.

He was still holding on to the ski rope that tethered him to *The Getaway*. At least they could pull themselves back to the boat when this was over.

C'mon, Cooper. You gotta do this. If they tow Krypto Night *away, it's over. You lose.* It wasn't some game at the Walworth County Fair. There was no prize for second place here. If Cooper missed this opportunity ... they all lost. Hiro. Gordy. And Lunk too.

Cooper handed Lunk the glowing light stick, then cracked another one for himself. He carefully laid the weighted handle of the ski rope on the lake bottom. With the glow stick taped to it, he could find it after they got the camera. He'd need both hands free for what came next. He slid the dive knife out of its sheath and stood. He raised the light stick high and saw the camera.

Lunk nodded. He saw it too.

Cooper pushed off the bottom, kicked hard, and grabbed the propeller shaft. The lanyard was wrapped around it tight. The camera itself was wedged between two blades of the prop. No wonder Kryptoski felt like his boat wasn't running right. The camera would have thrown everything off.

The sound of the engine from the Gage Marine boat was deafening. What if the guy asked Kryptoski to start *Krypto Night's* motor while Cooper was cutting the camera free? Immediate amputation at the wrists. Cooper poked his knife between the prop blades. *Just get this done fast and get out.*

Lunk joined him, holding himself up by the rudder. He held his light stick close to the camera so Cooper could see better.

The boat bucked with the waves. Coop let go of the shaft,

grabbed the camera, and pulled hard. It didn't budge. *Cut it free—cut it free.* His angle was bad. One blade from the prop blocked his view. Cooper couldn't see the spot on the lanyard where he needed to cut. He sawed anyway—fighting every instinct that told him to just get out of there.

Lunk tapped Cooper's arm, pointed at the knife and then back at himself. Cooper handed it to him. Lunk attacked the lanyard with the knife from his angle.

The boat lurched forward—slamming Cooper and Lunk against the bottom of the boat. *We're being towed!*

Cooper gripped the camera tighter. The boat was going slowly now—but once they got clear of the other moorings, he'd open it up. Cooper twisted and turned in the current. He bit the mouthpiece harder and prayed his mask wouldn't get ripped off. He slammed into Lunk, who was struggling as hard as he was. They were like two human torpedoes.

Hang on! Just a few more seconds. We have to get that camera!

Lunk grabbed onto the camera too and hacked away at the lanyard again—and the camera suddenly broke free!

Krypto Night's rudder sliced by, and the weight belts dragged Cooper and Lunk down. Both of them held onto the camera—and to each other. They hit the lake bottom a few seconds later, landing on their sides in the soft muck. Cooper still had his glow stick. Lunk had obviously lost his. But they had the camera!

They got on their knees and checked the camera. It looked perfect. No cracks in the housing. For a moment Cooper felt total elation. They'd done it!

Billows of silt surrounded them like cream pouring into coffee. Only this was black cream. Cooper looked for the glow stick at the end of the towrope. Nothing. How far had they been dragged? The water was so ... dark.

Reality must have hit Lunk too. He was doing a slow three-sixty—obviously looking for the rope hanging from Gordy's inflatable. But the only glow stick around was the one in Cooper's hand.

CHAPTER 79

Hiro watched the Gage Marine boat tow *Krypto Night* right past her. Kryptoski stood in the cockpit with the driver and stared at Hiro as they passed. She hugged herself and stared back like she wasn't one bit afraid. Like the sight of him didn't make her want to hang her head over the railing and heave.

Once past the no-wake bouys, the boat picked up speed and cut a straight course toward William's Bay and the marina.

Good. They were out of earshot. Hiro felt like if she had to wait even a second longer, she'd explode. "Gordy!" she shouted. "Where are they?"

Gordy raised both hands. "He never pulled on the rope. I—I don't know."

"But they made it to the boat, right?"

Gordy was on his knees now, peering into the water. "I have no idea. Kryptoski was right there watching me. I was just trying to keep him busy so he wouldn't get suspicious."

Hiro climbed over the rail to the swim platform and pulled on the ski rope lifeline. There was some resistance—but was it enough? If he was swimming with it—definitely. Hand over hand she pulled in the rope, faster and faster. "C'mon, Coop. Hang on." Loose coils spilled around her feet and back into the water.

"Is he there?" Gordy shouted.

The rope was getting heavier. It bit into her palms, but she kept pulling. A mass of seaweed surfaced with the weighted handle. "No!" she wailed. "No!"

Hiro fought back panic. She dropped the rope and motioned Gordy over. "Pick me up. I'll help you search."

Gordy hesitated as if he was afraid to leave the area in case Coop was close by.

"Hurry!" she shouted. She had to do something. She had to help.

Gordy dug in with both arms and paddled hard.

Hiro hopped into the inflatable the moment he swung it around the back of the boat.

"Go, go, go!" Hiro said. She leaned over and paddled with him and didn't stop until they neared the empty buoy where *Krypto Night* had been moored. Both of them kneeled and searched the surface of the water.

"C'mon, Coop!" Hiro looked for bubbles or a disturbance in the water. Anything, really. But the water was getting too rough for that. Foam trailed the waves. Their bubbles could be breaking within ten feet of them, and she'd never spot them. "Could they be caught in the weeds? Trapped somehow?"

Gordy shook his head. "Tangled, sure. But they should be able to break free, right?"

"That's what I'm asking you."

Gordy pulled in the line like a fisherman checking his bait. The light sticks were still attached and glowing. "How long have they been under?"

Hiro bit her lip. "Twenty minutes. Twenty-five." It was too long. Too long.

"They're lost," Gordy said.

Hiro eyed him. Did he think they were *gone*, gone?

"He's lost his bearings," Gordy said. "That can happen underwater." He peered over the edge.

"He's got a compass, right?"

Gordy stared into the water. "It's dark. I'm not sure he could see it. And navigating underwater isn't like doing it on land." He hesitated. "It's . . . tricky."

Which was Gordy's way of saying it was nearly impossible unless you really knew what you were doing.

"What can we do?"

Gordy leaned over the edge and dunked his head underwater. He screamed. At least that's how it sounded to Hiro. Giant bubbles broke the surface around his head.

His actions totally unnerved Hiro. Gordy was losing it, which wasn't helping her one bit.

He raised his head—water streamed from his hair—and took two quick breaths before he did it again. Longer this time. He lifted his head and gulped in some air.

"What are you *doing*?"

Gordy shook his head like a dog. "Trying to signal them. Sound travels a really long way underwater."

That actually made sense, no matter how strange it looked. "I'll help." She leaned over the side, dunked her face in the water, and screamed. Not that she really believed it was going to help Coop find them. But screaming made her feel better—because she'd wanted to do exactly that from the moment Coop announced his wild plan.

She raised her head just enough to get some air, then plunged back underwater. She screamed until her vocal chords felt like they were going to rip right out of her throat.

Gordy was doing the same thing on the other side of the inflatable.

Hiro did it again. And again. She opened her eyes underwater—staring into the inky blackness. Coop was down there somewhere. She went back up for air.

"Hiro." Gordy put a hand on her shoulder. "Take a break."

She nodded, panting, her face dripping. "See anything?"

Gordy shook his head. "Their air must be really low."

Or gone already. "Why don't they just surface?"

Gordy kept scanning the water. "Maybe they're just waiting until they think it's safe."

He didn't sound like he believed it. "Do you think the boat clipped them?"

Gordy shook his head. "One of them? Maybe. Both of them? No."

Hiro wiped the water from her eyes. "Surface, Coop. Surface!"

The look on Gordy's face said it all. They didn't surface because they couldn't.

Hiro rolled onto her stomach and hung her head over the side, inches from the water. She drew in several deep breaths.

"What are you going to do?" Gordy said.

Hiro didn't answer. She closed her eyes, stuck her head in the water ... and screamed.

CHAPTER 80

Cooper heard it again. An unearthly scream warbling from the depths. The Lady of the Lake. Lunk's story popped into his mind. He knew it was just a *story*—one that Lunk had told to scare Gordy. It was doing a pretty good job of scaring Cooper now too. He had to keep from panicking. There was no body floating around in the currents of the lake. Or was there?

The images on the camera's memory card would likely tell a story a whole lot scarier than Lunk's. And if Cooper didn't keep his head, they could get clipped by a boat before they got to safety themselves. Then there really *would* be bodies drifting in the underwater currents of the lake.

Cooper shook off the dark thoughts. He had to stay focused. They tried swimming in a large circle, hoping to catch sight of the ski rope or Gordy's line. Nothing. They must have been dragged farther than he thought.

Cooper felt the waistline of his shorts. Two more light sticks. He grabbed both of them and cracked them. As soon as they started glowing, he let one go. It rose to the surface with the bubbles. He let the second one go. Maybe Gordy would see it and come find them.

Lunk flashed him a thumbs-up.

The idea of making another circle, another sweep for their lost line, didn't seem like a good idea. What if they ran out of air and had to surface—and they were far from shore? They'd be sitting ducks for somebody out joyriding in a boat or on a jet ski. And the thought of running into a dead woman's body on the lake bottom haunted him no matter how much he tried to tell himself it wouldn't happen.

No sign of Gordy. The idea of waiting in this spot for Gordy to find them didn't give Cooper a good feeling at all. He had no idea where they were. They could be outside the no-wake buoys.

He checked his compass. There was no way he could navigate his way back to *The Getaway*, but the beach would be straight east. Why didn't he think of it before?

Cooper signaled to Lunk, and together they followed the compass. His stomach twisted, forcing the bitter taste of bile in his mouth. Were they going in the right direction? The water was so dark. He'd have to trust the compass to guide them, although by the looks of the lake bottom, they could be heading toward the middle of the lake. They kicked and pulled their way along the bottom with everything they had.

It was definitely getting harder to breathe now. It took more effort. Was it because they were moving faster? No. Without even looking at the pressure gauge, Cooper knew they were almost out of air.

He glanced at Lunk. His friend's eyes were wide. Scared. Cooper pointed east again. They'd go as far as they could before surfacing—just to be safe.

Reach and pull. Reach and pull. The weeds wrapped around his head and shoulders; they caught on the tank and snagged the air hose between Cooper and Lunk. Together they ripped free and the routine started all over again. It seemed like the weeds had their own plans. They wanted the boys to stay.

Cooper was sucking hard on the mouthpiece now. Draining the tank.

Lunk grabbed his arm and clutched at his throat.

Cooper stopped. This was it. He pointed up. Lunk nodded.

Cooper reached for Lunk's weight belt, released it, and let it drop. Lunk's feet lifted off the bottom, and Lunk grabbed Cooper.

Cooper didn't release his own belt. He didn't want them going up too quick. And if a boat were to head their way, they'd need to duck down fast.

Cooper raised the light stick and camera over his head. He looked up and listened for the sound of an engine. Certain it was clear above him, he pushed off from the bottom. He kicked hard, and Lunk was right there beside him.

Seconds later, they broke the surface. Immediately, Cooper ditched his weight belt and spit out the mouthpiece.

It was brighter outside than Cooper would have guessed, even though rain fell steadily. And they weren't more than twenty yards from the beach!

"We did it!" Lunk said. "We *did* it!"

"Thank you, God!" Cooper slapped the water with both hands. Together they struck out for shore. When his feet touched the bottom, Cooper scanned the horizon for Gordy and Hiro. He saw them bobbing in the inflatable out near the no-wake buoys.

Cooper whistled and waved.

Both of them jerked around and looked his way. Gordy waved both arms over his head and whistled back like his baseball team had just scored a home run. Cooper gripped the camera tighter in his hands. They'd done better than a grand slam.

His foot hooked on something. He peered underwater. A bike. With a Wiffle ball bat strapped to the frame. "Hey, Lunk—take a look at what's down here by my feet."

Lunk bobbed underwater and came up laughing. "Do you think yours and Gordy's are here too?"

"Probably within ten feet of me." Cooper glanced underwater again and saw the shadowy frame of another bike. "After we ditch our gear, we'll come back and fish 'em out."

Lunk nodded.

Gordy was on his stomach now, paddling for shore like a madman. Hiro knelt in the back of the inflatable, doing the same.

When Cooper got to waist-deep water, he shrugged out of the tank harness, pulled off his fins, and dragged his gear to the beach.

For a moment, Cooper and Lunk just looked at each other—then Cooper grabbed his friend and gave him a bear hug. "I could *not* have done that without you."

Lunk hugged him back. "I wasn't going to let you go down there alone."

Cooper couldn't describe what he was feeling, and he didn't even want to try. It was like he and Lunk were war buddies now. They'd stuck together and survived a battle. Somehow, Cooper knew he'd never feel alone again.

Cooper stepped back.

Lunk grinned at him. "And if you ever get a bozo idea like that again—"

"Talk me out of it," Cooper said.

They both laughed hysterically as the relief swept over them.

Cooper set the camera down next to the tank, and the two of them waded into the water to meet Gordy and Hiro. At this moment, Cooper felt like he could do anything. He could swim across the whole lake even in this storm. He'd faced his fears with a sword instead of a shovel. And it felt good. This wouldn't be the last time he tangled with fear, but now he knew how to fight it.

Hiro's hair was soaked. She looked like she'd been crying. Cooper grabbed one side of the inflatable, Lunk grabbed the other, and the two of them pulled it to shore.

Hiro was on the beach instantly. She threw her arms around Cooper's neck and squeezed him hard. He pried her arms loose and gasped for air.

"You scared me!" she said. "I was afraid I'd lost you."

"*You* were scared," Gordy said. "I think I peed in my swim shorts."

Hiro punched him in the arm. "That's disgusting."

Gordy rubbed his arm. "It's true." He pointed at the inflatable. "That wasn't just lake water sloshing around in there."

Hiro's eyes narrowed to a glare, and she rushed into the water and started rinsing furiously.

Gordy, Lunk, and Cooper started laughing. Cooper felt giddy.

Hiro got out of the water and tried to put on a mad face. But she was a lousy actress. She stepped over to Lunk and gave him a hug. "How can one girl have three such courageous friends?"

A police car raced down the hill and reality hit. The camera.

"We have something for you, Hiro." Cooper grabbed the camera and held it out to her.

She took it in her hands like a lost treasure. "You got it!" There was a sense of wonder in her voice. She touched the frayed edge of the green lanyard where they'd cut it free.

Gordy crowded in. "Think there's any juice left in the batteries?"

Hiro hesitated. She wanted to turn it on to check out the pictures. It was all over her face. "This is evidence," she said. "I'm not sure I should." She turned the camera over, examining it. "It's in perfect condition."

The police car screeched to a stop on the shoulder of Lake Shore Drive, and Officer Tarpy jumped out. He left the motor running. His wipers slapped out a rhythm that matched his excited mood. "I got here as quickly as I could. The dispatcher made it sound urgent. What's up?"

Hiro held up the camera.

Tarpy stopped in his tracks. "Is that what I think it is?"

Hiro nodded and quickly filled him in. Cooper stood there watching her, listening to her. It was like she really was a cop. A good one.

"The housing looks fine," she said. Her finger hovered over the power button. "May I?"

Tarpy hesitated, then gave a single nod.

Hiro pressed the button, and the camera came to life. Everyone pressed in closer to see. Hiro pressed the display button and held the camera up so Officer Tarpy could see too.

"You'd better let me have a look first," he said.

Hiro looked disappointed but handed him the camera. Tarpy held the camera so none of them could see as he scrolled through the pictures.

Cooper watched Tarpy's face. He stopped on one of the pictures and stared at the screen. He swallowed hard. Tarpy studied the screen again as if to be sure.

"How long ago did Gage Marine pick up Tommy Kryptoski's boat?"

Gordy looked at Hiro and shrugged. "Fifteen minutes ago? Maybe twenty."

"And Kryptoski was with him?"

Gordy nodded.

Hiro pointed at the camera. "What did you see?"

Tarpy's jaw muscles tightened. "Enough."

He hustled over to his car, talking into the shoulder mic as he ran. "I need a car at Gage Marine. Now. Call WBPD too. And tell the chief to phone me directly. We're going to need a warrant for Tommy Kryptoski." Tarpy paused and looked back at them like he'd just realized everyone was listening. He cupped his hand over the mic, but not well enough to keep from being heard. "We got him," Tarpy said. "First degree."

The look on Hiro's face confirmed she'd heard everything Tarpy said.

The cop slammed the driver's door and called out through the open passenger side window, "I'm going to need to get a statement from each of you tomorrow. But right now I have to fly." He touched the camera to his forehead in a salute. "Great work, kids." He shook his head and smiled slightly. "Amazing." He gunned the engine, sending gravel flying. Tarpy made a squealing U-turn and raced along the beach toward town, siren blaring.

Cooper stared after him until the car was out of sight.

"What do you think he saw that made him so sure?" Gordy asked.

Cooper knew what he was really asking. *Did the girl's murder get captured on the memory card?*

"I know what he saw," Hiro said. "At least the first few images." She gazed out toward *The Getaway* as though she was reliving the moment. "Kryptoski took a picture of Pom-Pom. Then Pom-Pom grabbed the camera from him and took a picture of the two of them together. Officer Tarpy saw that Lynn Tutek wasn't in the boat that night. It was the missing girl: Wendy Besecker."

"Proving that Lynn was lying the whole time," Gordy said.

"Exactly," Hiro said. "Then Kryptoski took a picture of me on *The Getaway*. That would help establish the timeline. After that . . . who knows *what* Officer Tarpy saw." She shuddered.

Hiro got a faraway look in her eyes. A sad look.

"But now we know that Kryptoski definitely phoned Lynn," Cooper said. "He told her what to wear. Told her to get soaking wet and walk down to the beach." And it had almost worked.

"She's toast," Lunk said. "Tarpy will pick her up next."

Hiro nodded. "She's an accessory."

"Gee, Hiro," Gordy said. "You were right all along." He looked over the water, shielding his eyes against the rain. "There really is a body out there. Somewhere. Under the surface."

Hiro dropped to her knees on the narrow strip of beach. She looked weak. Small. A siren wailed in the distance. "Poor Wendy. I wish I'd been wrong."

CHAPTER 81

The moment he turned onto Gage Marine property, he spotted a cop car. Make that three black and whites. No lights were flashing, though. Strange.

He pulled Black Beauty into a nearby parking space, killed the lights, and watched. The cops stood in a cluster looking at something. A phone? He recognized one of the men. Tarpy—and he seemed to be doing all the talking.

Another squad car peeled into the lot. *Okay, what was this all about?*

He dialed off the dome light so it wouldn't turn on when he opened the door, and slid out of the pickup. He inched closer to the cops, sticking to the shadows. He was good at that.

Minutes later, he'd learned everything he needed to know. Tommy Kryptoski wasn't going to need a ride from him tonight—or any night in the near future. The cops were here to pick up Kryptoski—and cuff him too.

Tommy's old man would *not* be happy about this. Not one bit. And Jerry Kryptoski would find a way to blame *him* for not handling things properly. He'd probably even send a couple of the enforcers over to deliver the message personally. There was no going back now. He glanced at Black Beauty. If he didn't get moving, he might find himself doing synchronized swimming routines with Tommy's girlfriend at the bottom of the lake.

The Gage Marine boat approached with Tommy's boat in tow. The cops hustled down to the dock to meet it. The police boat appeared from around the bend, its lights flashing and the motor throwing up spray.

Time to go. He carefully worked his way back to the pickup and climbed inside. He reviewed his options. Figured the odds. He'd have to leave town — that was a given. But he'd prepared for that. He'd known about the murder and helped cover Kryptoski's rear end afterward. That made him an accessory of some sort. The cops would want to question him at the very least — and then everything would change.

He needed to slip away, but there was some unfinished business to take care of first. His plan was all worked out, down to the last detail. First he'd initiate the little distraction at the casino. Actually, it was gonna be a big distraction. Big enough to ensure that Kryptoski's old man — and the police — would be too busy to look for him.

After that, he was gonna pay one last visit to the kids before hitting the road. And he was really, really looking forward to that visit. What kind of guy would he be if he didn't say a final good-bye?

CHAPTER 82

Hiro sat on the edge of the bed in the condo. She was still in a bit of a fog. She should have celebrated more with the guys. After they'd pulled all three bikes from the bottom of the lake, they'd gone to Olympic Restaurant for some pizza and then over to Scoops for dessert. They'd done their best to include her. Even after she'd received Officer Tarpy's phone call confirming that Tommy had been arrested and that they were picking up Lynn Tutek next, Hiro still didn't feel like doing cartwheels. Officer Tarpy had no idea where Fat Elvis was — and Hiro sensed he was the most dangerous of them all.

She rubbed her Chicago Police star necklace. Why couldn't she shake off her intuition or fear, or whatever it was, for just one night? The guys deserved better than that.

And sitting alone in the condo at The Cove wasn't helping things. Right now, Hiro wished her mom were here. She needed to talk to her. Maybe that would make Hiro feel better. Mom could lift her out of this mood.

But deep down, Hiro knew she wouldn't be able to rest easy and truly celebrate until Fat Elvis had been picked up. Then they'd know for sure if that man was actually Joseph Stein. She eyed the door for a moment. The security locks were set. Still, she walked over and pressed on the door—just to be sure.

She padded back to the couch, pulled out her phone, and scrolled through her list of contacts. Should she call Detective Hammer again? Maybe he'd found some info on Fat Elvis. But if he had, wouldn't he have called to put her mind at ease? Had he even come to Lake Geneva today? If so, then Detective Hammer was *really* good at shadowing. She'd never seen him—and she'd been looking.

No. She wasn't going to bother Detective Hammer with this. And she didn't want to call her mom, either. She and Coop's little sister and the other moms would all be sitting inside the movie theater by now anyway. Hiro was just tired. That had to be it. In the morning everything would look different.

CHAPTER 83

He felt like a spy on some covert mission. He'd been sneaking around undetected since watching Tommy get arrested. And it had been a busy night. He'd set the fires at the casino like a pro. The cops were going to be way too busy to come looking for him tonight. And by the time they did, he'd be long gone.

The water was chilly, but wearing Tommy's wetsuit helped. It gave him all the buoyancy he needed too for the swim from the Geneva Inn's pier. The black neoprene made him blend in perfectly with the water, and the waves and wind would mask any noise he might make once he got to *The Getaway*. He wasn't just an ordinary spy. He was a regular Jason Bourne. Smart. Efficient. Deadly.

No lights shone from the portholes, but that didn't mean the kids were asleep. He climbed onto the swim deck, hesitated for just a moment, then carefully climbed over the transom rail.

The way the wind was howling, he probably didn't have to worry about being quiet, but he didn't get to where he was by leaving things to chance.

He tiptoed over to the cabin door, listened for a moment, then pulled a padlock and cable out from were he'd stuffed it inside his wetsuit. Less than a minute later, the job was done. There was no way anybody was getting out of that cabin tonight.

Within seconds he climbed over the transom rail and was back in the water. He couldn't help but smile. This was going exactly as he'd planned. Now came the tricky part. He bobbed under the swim platform and felt along the boat's transom until he found the threaded brass plug—just like he'd seen in the drawings. Even with the help of the wrench he'd brought with him, it took a little effort to break the plug loose. But once he did, he was able to finish unscrewing the plug by hand.

He thought about dropping the plug to the bottom of the lake but decided he'd keep it as a little souvenir. He tucked it inside his wetsuit and dropped the wrench instead. He held his hand in front of the hole to make sure the water was going in and was surprised at the powerful suction. It was like the boat was thirsty. He smiled again. The boat would fill quickly and silently. And with the wind and rain and waves, there was no chance they'd hear it. By the time water seeped above the floorboards and the boys noticed it—there'd be too much water for them to bail out.

One last detail. He swam to the front of the boat. The old cruiser was bucking and pulling at the anchor. Holding the line that connected the boat to the buoy in one hand, he slid the knife out of its sheath and started sawing away at the rope. The instant the rope broke, *The Getaway* started drifting toward the middle of the lake. He treaded water for a minute, watching the boat rock and pitch in the waves.

Oh yeah, he was a spy just like Jason Bourne. And Bourne was more than just an ordinary spy. He was an assassin. How perfect was that? He saluted the boat. "See ya, fellas."

By the time he made it back to the Geneva Inn pier, it was hard to pick out the boat as it moved like a silent shadow farther and farther away from the shore. He climbed onto the dock feeling totally energized. Which was good. There was one more stop he needed to make before he left town. He couldn't wait to see the look of surprise—and terror—on her face when she saw him.

CHAPTER 84

Cooper laid in his berth with his hands beneath his head, listening to the storm still blowing out of the southeast. Every time a lightning flash lit up the sky, he got a glimpse of those clouds through the rain-streaked porthole. Dark. Angry. And a greenish color that reminded him of the seaweed he'd been tangled in just hours ago.

At least they'd made it back to *The Getaway* before the storm kicked in again. Every lightning flash blinded him for a moment. Then his eyes readjusted to the shadowy darkness of the cabin. He could make out Lunk and Gordy just fine. Lunk still wasn't wearing his lifejacket—even with the storm raging outside. What was up with that?

And Cooper still hadn't found his phone. It was probably buried in the growing piles of stuff that littered the cabin floor. "We'll have to do a little picking up before my dad gets here in the morning."

"No problemo," Gordy said. "Right after breakfast."

Lunk shifted in his berth until he was facing Cooper. "Looking forward to him getting here?"

"Yeah. I really am."

Lunk was quiet for a moment. "Me too."

Cooper swallowed the lump in his throat.

"Bet he was really proud of you when you told him about the camera," Lunk said.

It had been a great phone call with his dad. One that Cooper would never forget. "He said he was proud of *all* of us."

Lunk leaned up on one elbow. "Really?"

"Yep. He wanted me to tell you guys to be ready for a lot more celebrating. He's stopping by the Donut Shop in Hebron on the way here."

"Best donuts in the world," Gordy said. "We'll have to save a couple of them for Hiro. Maybe that will help."

Cooper figured it would take a lot more than donuts. "She's not going to rest easy until Fat Elvis has been picked up."

"That weasel?" Lunk snorted. "He's probably in Minnesota by now."

The cabin got quiet. The truth was, Cooper wouldn't feel totally at ease until he knew that creep was gone for good.

"Listen to the wind howling," Gordy said. "I'm surprised the waves aren't a mile high."

"The trees from the state park shield us here," Cooper said. "And we're too close to the beach." It was a good thing too. If they were moored on the other side of the lake, the boat would be bucking them out of their berths.

Frantic pinging came from every sailboat anchored around them. The sound of metal clips banging against the aluminum masts.

"Sounds like Morse code," Lunk said. "The sailboats are tapping out a warning."

"Oh, there's a comforting thought," Gordy said. "Anybody up for a scary story? The weather is perfect for it."

Cooper wasn't in the mood. Their underwater salvage operation was too recent and way too intense. What he really wanted was more laughter. But something still bothered him.

"When Lunk and I were underwater ..." Cooper began. Did he really want to go there?

"Yeah?" Gordy said. "Keep going."

"I heard . . . something."

"What was it?" Gordy propped himself up on one elbow. "What did you hear?"

Now Cooper wished he hadn't said anything. It was bad enough he'd had those panic attacks underwater. Would they think he was losing it?

"The screams?" Lunk said.

Cooper's stomach twisted. "I was afraid it was just me."

"Creepiest thing I've ever heard," Lunk said. "All I could think about was that missing girl. I actually wondered if it was her."

Gordy slapped his mattress and laughed. "That was me and Hiro. We stuck our heads underwater and screamed. We were trying to signal you two so you'd get your bearings."

Cooper stared at his cousin. "Seriously?"

"Honest!" Gordy said. "Remember that old TV show, *Flipper*—the one about the dolphin? Whenever they wanted Flipper to come, they signaled him with this horn thing—underwater. Sound travels super-well underwater."

"You're an idiot, Gordy," Lunk said.

"With all that talk about bodies in the lake," Cooper said, "did you really think a scream was going to make us swim *toward* you?"

They laughed until they couldn't laugh anymore. Lunk was wheezing.

Cooper finally stopped and tried to catch his breath. His side ached, but if felt good. The cabin got quiet. He listened to the storm. Was it just his imagination, or was the storm gaining intensity? Maybe the other guys sensed it too. Lunk gripped the side of his berth. Gordy used his legs to brace himself so he wouldn't roll off the mattress.

"I know Hiro was doing her best to celebrate tonight," Lunk said, "but she's still wondering about Fat Elvis, isn't she." He said it like it was a statement. A fact, not a question. "She still thinks he's Joseph Stein."

That was *exactly* what was bothering her. No . . . bothering wasn't the right word. *Scaring* her. "Honestly?" Coop hesitated. "I think she's right."

Lunk whistled softly. "The truth comes out."

"And you don't think she is?"

"Actually, I think I do," Lunk said. "She had Kryptoski figured. And she was dead on about the missing girl."

"*Dead* on?" Gordy said. "I get it."

"What about you, Gordy?" Cooper said. "What do you think?"

He didn't say a word.

"Gordy?"

"I've tried *not* to think about it," he said. "At the fair, I didn't really give her Stein theory a chance, you know? I mean, if I don't admit there's a problem, maybe there isn't one, right?"

Cooper wasn't so sure about the logic of that. But there was something more going on here, and Gordy had just cracked open the door so they could see inside. Gordy had been stuffing his fears too.

"But when the bikes were missing this morning, my first thought was Stein. I remembered how his hired muscle almost caught you last October ... a couple days after the diner had been robbed. How you scrambled over the fence, and the guys took your bike."

Cooper shuddered. "And later dropped the bike by the bell tower—all twisted up."

"They were sending you a message, Coop," Gordy said. "Just like they were sending all of us a message this morning. Both times they used bikes."

Cooper hadn't thought of that—the similarity.

"That is a *creepy* connection," Lunk said. "You love scary stories. Why didn't you say something about it this morning?"

"I like scary *stories*," Gordy said. "But this is real life."

"So," Lunk said, "you keep your brain busy planning pranks or having fun or making up scary stories—so you don't have to face what's really scaring you deep down inside."

Gordy was silent for a moment. "Something like that. Yeah.

I guess so. I like life with a lot of noise. When things get quiet, sometimes I think too much."

Maybe Gordy's abduction did have more of an effect on him than Cooper thought. "Anything else you want to talk about? Other deep-down fears?"

"Maybe," Gordy said. "But not tonight. Next week ... when my dad is here."

Fair enough. But he'd opened the door, and that's all Cooper would need.

"Do *not* tell Hiro I said all this," Gordy said. "She'll make it her personal mission to get inside my head and figure out what's going on in there."

"And she could do it." Lunk laughed. "She's done a pretty amazing job of figuring out things these last few days. And do not tell her I said *that*."

All three of them laughed.

"I can say this only because Hiro isn't here right now—'cause I don't want her to get a big head or anything," Gordy said. "But I think she's going to make a really good cop someday." He rolled onto his stomach in his berth. "I'm going to cheer her up right now." He whipped out his phone, typed out a text, and sent it. "There."

"What did you say?"

Gordy held up the phone. "Coop has a surprise for you. Guaranteed to make you feel better."

Cooper wasn't sure what he was referring to. "Surprise?"

"Yeah," Gordy said. "Donuts. The ones your dad is bringing in the morning."

Lightning lit up the tiny cabin for an instant. The boat rolled and pitched. Rain drummed steadily on the deck overhead.

"If Fat Elvis is Stein, it's kind of freaky that he ended up here," Lunk said.

Cooper propped himself up on his elbows. "Maybe not as freaky as you think. Stein has a gambling problem. He borrows money from the wrong guy—somebody involved in organized crime.

They demand payment. So to save his own skin, Stein set up the robbery of his own diner. Right?"

"That pretty well sums up the events of last fall," Lunk said.

"But a week later his secret gets out. And somehow, in all of the confusion and gunfire, he slips away. There's a warrant out for his arrest in Illinois. He can't go home. He can't access a bank account. He can't get a legitimate job."

"So he goes into hiding," Gordy said.

"Exactly. But without money, he's limited to park benches."

Lunk thumped his head with his open palm. "So he went to the man who loaned him the money. The guy already had all that money from the robbery, so Stein's debt was probably erased."

"Why would he hire a guy like Stein?" Gordy said.

Lunk sat cross-legged in his berth. "Why not? He'd *own* Stein. He could make Stein do anything he wanted."

"In other words," Cooper said, "what if the guy who gave Stein the loan, masterminded the robbery of the diner, and then hired Stein as a bodyguard is Kryptoski's dad?"

"That's a lot of what-ifs," Gordy said.

"But it's possible," Lunk said. "His casino isn't much more than an hour's drive from Rolling Meadows. Why couldn't that be the place where Stein liked to gamble?"

Nobody said a word.

"But even if Fat Elvis *isn't* Stein," Lunk said, "there could still be trouble."

"Right." Cooper said. "Maybe Fat Elvis was supposed to scare Hiro—and us—so we wouldn't keep asking questions about the missing girl. Maybe he was supposed to find that camera—or keep us from finding it. If he was supposed to keep junior out of trouble and he messed up on every count ... what do you think happens to him? Do you think a boss who's involved in organized crime will just fire the guy who totally blew it?"

"He's dead meat," Gordy said.

"He wouldn't dare report back to the boss now," Cooper said.

"He'd run," Gordy said. "As far away and as quickly as he could."

Nobody said a word. Cooper's mind raced as fast as the wind whipping the waves outside. "If we're lucky, he'd run. Fat Elvis has to be really angry right now. And if he *is* Stein, then this would be the second time we've messed up his twisted plans." They were all in just as much danger as they had been before Kryptoski got arrested. And if this guy *was* Joseph Stein, then they could multiply that danger times ten.

"What time is it?" Cooper had a sick feeling. "Maybe we should go talk to Hiro tonight."

"In this storm?" Gordy said. "There's no way. We'd be soaked before we got to the beach. And it's already ten thirty. We wouldn't get back here until after midnight."

"And nothing good happens after midnight," Lunk said.

Cooper rummaged around in the berth for his phone. "Scoops is closed, and Katie was going to walk her to the condo, right?"

"That was the plan," Lunk said. "You don't think he'd try something tonight—do you?"

Lunk's question fueled the fear smoldering deep inside Cooper. What if Fat Elvis—or Stein—wanted a little payback before he left town? Cooper wanted to push the thought back down. Bury it deep. But he was done burying his fears. The only way to keep the fear from paralyzing him was to face it. And facing it meant that he had to find out if Hiro was okay.

He wanted to talk to her. Just hearing her voice would be enough. It seemed ridiculous. Of course she was safe. Still, he wished they'd been the ones to walk her back to The Cove.

"Guys," Gordy said, "we're spooking ourselves here."

"Where *is* my phone?" Cooper said. He checked his pockets again.

"When's the last time you remember using it?" Gordy said.

Cooper thought. "It's been missing all day. So I guess I used it sometime yesterday." Cooper checked under his pillow.

"The fair," Lunk said. "You had it at the county fair."

Now Cooper remembered. "I put it in my backpack before we

rode Typhoon." He reached for his backpack hanging from a hook on the wall. He dug through the front pocket. "I *know* I put it in here."

Gordy's phone chirped. "It's Hiro … answering my text." Gordy's face glowed in the light from the screen.

"What did she say?"

"She texted, 'This better not be a prank. Remember what I did to you guys the last time? I'm warning you.'" Gordy snickered. "I'll just send a quick reply." He tapped away on his phone. "How's this sound … 'No tricks. No pranks. This is legit and you'll love it.'" He looked up. "Send."

"She's a firecracker," Lunk said. "Sounds like she's okay."

Cooper needed his phone. He wanted to call Hiro and talk to her himself. Even if it was late. He mentally retraced his steps. He'd definitely stuffed his phone into his backpack at the fair. After the Typhoon ride, he hadn't put it back into his pocket because there wasn't time. They'd started looking for Fat Elvis immediately—and then tailed Hiro when she broke away from them.

The boat suddenly pitched and slammed Cooper against the hull. Had the wind shifted again? The waves were really rocking the boat now. The wind was still howling, but with more rage than before. And something else was different. He couldn't hear any pinging on the masts. Which was strange. Could the sound of the rain be drowning it out? He held his breath and strained to hear. Not a single ping. Strange.

Cooper's mind switched back to the missing phone. After they left the fair, he'd never made any calls. And the backpack had been hanging on the wall hook ever since they'd returned to the boat last night.

Cooper rummaged through the backpack again. Except for Chimpy the stuffed monkey, it was definitely empty.

So if Cooper never took his phone out of the backpack—who did? *The Getaway* rolled heavily, and a puzzle piece dropped into place. His stomach twisted—and he sat up straight. "Fat Elvis took my phone."

CHAPTER 85

Hiro looked at the text from Cooper again. "*Meet us at LeatherLips—by the spillway. We have something important to show you.*" She scrolled down to reread her response. "*Now? Seriously? It's 10:30. And it's raining.*"

Coop's response was immediate. "*You'll dry. 5 minutes. That's all we need.*"

That's when she'd sent the text to Gordy. If this was another prank, she definitely wasn't in the mood.

Her phone chirped and she opened the message. *No tricks. No pranks. This is legit and you'll love it.*

Okay. They were still out celebrating. She got that. She really didn't think Coop would have tried pulling something stupid. Not now. But getting that little bit of assurance from Gordy eased her mind. Knowing Gordy, the big surprise was probably food. Maybe they'd ordered another pizza since she didn't eat much at dinner. She still wasn't hungry. And why didn't they just meet her in the foyer of the condo? Why make her go out in the rain? But then again, why did she expect the guys to start doing things that made sense?

Hiro sighed. "This had better be good." She slipped on her sweatshirt, tucked an umbrella under her arm, and grabbed the room key. She thought about leaving a note for her mom, but she was still at the movies somewhere in Kenosha with the others. They wouldn't be back for at least another two hours. Hiro would be back in twenty minutes.

CHAPTER 86

He crouched in the shadows of the little cove and waited. Keeping the wetsuit on had been a great idea. It felt like he was wearing some kind of body armor. He was invincible.

He bounced the kid's cell phone in his palm. Did the girl suspect anything? If she did, the cops would already be here, wouldn't they? The real question was, would she take the bait?

A small figure holding an umbrella hurried toward the lake. He stared. By the time she crossed the street and started walking his way, he was absolutely sure it was her.

He took a deep breath and let it out slowly. *Relax. Don't rush this. Everything is going according to plan.*

He kept the gun in the plastic bag. No sense getting it wet. And he really had no intention of using it. Not unless he had to. But she wouldn't know that. Just the sight of it would be enough to force her into the tunnel. He'd say good-bye to her there.

CHAPTER 87

The wind was blowing offshore, whipping the rain under Hiro's umbrella. The streets were strangely empty, but then why would *sane* people go out in this storm? She looked out over the water. Sailboats bucked and pulled at their buoys as though something far out in the lake was drawing them closer to it. Wisps of steam rose off the lake—like rising spirits of the dead. Hiro thought about Wendy. Was she still in that lake?

Hiro heard sirens in the distance. Lots of sirens. Fire trucks. Police cars. Even ambulances. Each had their own sound. She turned her head to hear better. Whatever was going on, it was big. She stopped on the bridge that overlooked the tiny bay and waited at the railing. Everything at LeatherLips—the docked boats and the spillway—looked quiet. Absolutely still—except for the rain. Either the boys were hiding or they were never here. Maybe they'd just sent her on a wild goose chase. *Thanks, guys.*

Something inside of her burned. Maybe it was frustration. Actually, it *was* frustration. She was ready to deck Gordy again. She whipped out her phone and fired off a message to him.

What was the plan here? Were they going to jump out and scare her? If this was some little joke they were playing on her, she definitely wasn't going to make it easy for them. She trekked down the incline and stood on one of the docks. Out in the open. Right where they could see her—and more importantly, where she could see them sneaking up on her.

CHAPTER 88

Cooper tossed his backpack to the side.

"Hiro said she saw Fat Elvis with his hands on my backpack. Remember? He must have taken my phone."

"But why?" Lunk leaned on one elbow. "What could he possibly want with your phone?"

Gordy's phone chirped. "It's Hiro ... she says, *'If this is a joke— I'm really not in the mood. And if this is another dead fish prank— you're all dead meat.'* " Gordy laughed and whipped back a response.

"What did you say?"

"I told her she'll find out when we see her tomorrow." He grinned. "I'm not telling her it's only donuts. Let her sweat a little."

The Getaway rolled and bucked.

Gordy's phone chirped again. "She's not letting this go, is she?" Gordy opened the text and his smile faded. "This makes no sense."

"What?" Cooper said. "Read it."

Gordy cleared his throat. "Okay, she says, *'Tomorrow? Coop's text said to meet you now. Tonight. I'm at LeatherLips—where are you?'* "

Cooper's heart started racing. "I didn't send that text." He swung his legs over the side of the berth. "Tell her to run, Gordy.

Tell her I lost my phone at the fair—Fat Elvis has it. He's using it to bait her."

Gordy hunkered over the phone, his thumbs flying over the screen.

"We've got to get to town. Now." Cooper stood—and landed in water past his ankles. "What?" A wave caused the boat to lurch, throwing Coop back onto the berth. He scrambled to his feet. "Water!"

Lunk jumped off his berth. "Waves washing over the bow?"

"Impossible." Coop raced for the hatch. It wouldn't budge. Not even when he threw his good shoulder into it.

"Let me try that," Lunk said. He pushed at it, then stood and kicked it. The hatch held.

"Guys," Gordy said. "Look out the window—our anchor line must have snapped."

Lunk kept kicking the hatch.

Cooper cupped his hands against the window. They had to be a mile from shore.

"This isn't jammed," Lunk said. "It's locked. From the outside."

The boat was adrift, taking in water, and they were locked inside. "What are the odds of all this going wrong at the same time?" Cooper's mind raced. More pieces started flying into place.

"We've been set up," Lunk said. "Somebody wants us dead."

CHAPTER 89

Lunk kicked at the hatch again — but he wasn't getting anywhere with his bare feet. "Where's a concrete-filled Wiffle ball bat when you need it?"

Cooper laced up his shoes. "Let me try."

Lunk didn't wait to see if his friend broke through. He dug out his own shoes. A moment later he took over for Coop. They had to get out of here. Lunk fought back the panic. The image of *The Getaway* sinking with all three of them trapped inside seared his mind. He wanted to strap on his lifejacket. A lot of good it would do him inside a flooding cabin. If the boat went to the bottom, they were going with it — lifejacket or no lifejacket. He threw his whole body against the solid oak hatch.

"The air tank," Coop said. He tore the seat off the storage compartment and tossed gear to one side. "We'll use it as a battering ram," he said, pulling the air tank free.

Lunk grabbed one side with both hands; Coop grabbed the other. Together they swung the tank and slammed the flat bottom into the hatch again and again. The force of each impact sent shock waves through his hands and shoulders.

"Harder!" Coop shouted.

The hatch cracked.

"Again!" Lunk said. They swept the tank high and rammed it so hard that Lunk was afraid the tank would explode. If it had been full, maybe it would have. "One more time." Wood split and broke out in sections.

They dropped the tank and kicked free the remaining splinters. The three of them squeezed through and piled onto the deck. They were definitely drifting with the monster swells. Rain beat down on them, smacking them in the face. The idea of being trapped inside the cabin was bad — but this wasn't much better. Lunk wanted to find a lifejacket and strap it on so tight that it would never come off.

Lightning split the sky. They were in the middle of the lake. As far from the north shore as they were from the south. Vicious, dark waves rolled past with white-capped heads. Foam trailed each one as though the waves were alive — and rabid.

Gordy pointed toward the north shore. "The waves will smash us onto the rocks."

Lunk glanced at the waves and the distance from shore, then looked back into the flooding cabin. *We may sink before we get there.* Lunk didn't want to think about it. His friends needed his help.

"Hiro's in trouble," Coop said. "I feel it."

Lunk's stomach lurched. Whoever did this wanted them out of the way. Hiro was his next target.

Gordy stuffed his phone into his pocket. "What do we do?"

Cooper looked toward town. "Did she answer your text?"

Gordy shook his head.

"Oh, God, help her," Cooper said.

For a moment he looked lost. Scared. "Get the spare key — give it to Lunk. — Let's get the bilge pump going."

Gordy whipped out the toolbox and dug through it.

"Grab the flare gun too."

Gordy found the key and handed it to Lunk.

Lunk missed the slot twice. He grabbed the wheel to steady

himself and tried again. This time the key slid home, and he turned on the ignition—stopping just short of cranking the engines. The dials came to life. Good. At least they had battery power. He toggled on the bilge and heard the pump motor hum. "Bilge on."

Lunk glanced inside the cabin. The water was rising—and no wave had crashed over the top since he'd been on deck. Yet the lower they sank in the water, the greater the risk that waves would start coming over the side. Then it would all be over. "Where's the water coming from?"

Cooper heaved open the engine hatch. Lunk gave him a hand. Oil and gas fumes rose to meet him. He peered into the dark compartment. Water sloshed around the twin engines. "We've got a couple feet of water in there," Cooper said. "We're going down!"

Lunk glanced over the transom. The swim platform was under water.

Gordy loaded a round in the flare gun, held it over his head with both hands, and squeezed the trigger. A red tracer arced high overhead—lighting up the raindrops like they were laser beams streaking down on them.

Who would be stupid enough to be out in this storm? Who would even see the flare? Lunk kneeled on the wet deck next to Cooper and stared into the flooding compartment. "How's the water getting in?"

Cooper shook his head. "Don't know. There must be a hole."

Whoever wanted them out of the way had done something to the hull. Probably while they were talking inside the cabin. But wouldn't they have heard some kind of drill?

Lunk looked inside the engine hatch. "Can we fill the hole with something? Plug the leak?"

Cooper grabbed the side rail and looked into the water. "We don't even know where it is."

Gordy shot off another flare. "We gotta abandon ship."

Lunk rushed to the transom rail—but the inflatable wasn't

there. They'd tied it to the buoy. The only way off *The Getaway* was to swim. Whoever did this wasn't leaving much to chance.

"If this thing goes under, and we're still on it . . ." Gordy pointed the flare gun at the waves.

It would suck them down with it. Lunk knew it. And they'd be as dead as the girl floating in the underwater currents of the lake.

CHAPTER 90

Hiro's phone chirped. She ignored it and kept her eyes open. The moment she looked at her phone, they'd jump out of hiding. She wasn't going to give them the satisfaction of catching her off guard. The rain eased up, but the wind didn't. She walked carefully along the boat slips in the tiny lagoon. Even though the water was shielded from the brunt of the storm, tiny ripples trembled across the black water.

If this was their idea of a joke, they had a demented sense of humor. It was a creepy spot to meet up. Why would Coop do it?

Lightning washed the entire scene in raw, electric light. *What was she doing here? Why did she leave the condo?* She touched her queasy stomach. It wasn't the typical butterflies inside. They were bats. Diving and dodging—and frantic to get out.

Okay, this whole thing was ridiculous. It was time to go. "I'm not playing your games, guys!" she said. Loudly. Did her voice betray her fear? She hoped not. The whole idea was to come across as unafraid. Casual. But right now she wanted to run.

Ruby Slipper tugged at its dock line as if an invisible hand were pulling it from under the water. Hiro wished she were wearing a pair of ruby slippers right now. She'd click those heels together and go home. And she'd go back in time if she could. To when her dad was still alive. She'd run right into his arms and be safe.

Hiro slowly backed down the dock. A small stretch of water separated her from the concrete dam and the spillway that emptied into the demon tunnel. She shuddered at the thought of that place. Her waiting text signaled again. She had no intention of opening it. Maybe when she got back to the room. A strong sense knifed through her that she shouldn't be here. She'd played their game too long. She needed to leave. Now. "Do you hear me?" She moved faster. "Adios, boys! I'm leaving!"

"Sorry, Hiroko." A man's voice. Behind her. "You're staying with me."

She knew that voice. Hiro whirled around. *Oh, dear God, no.* It was Fat Elvis—otherwise known as Joseph Stein.

CHAPTER 91

"We should have listened to Hiro," Cooper said.

Gordy's eyes were wide. "We gonna abandon ship?"

Lightning ripped across the sky in a jagged line. For an instant, every detail around them was clear — and horrifying. The clouds were wicked. Tumbling over one another in confusion — or in their lust to punish the earth below.

"We can't stay here. We're the highest thing on the water for a mile around." They'd be a target for lightning — a magnet — right up until the moment *The Getaway* slipped under the dark waters forever. The rain seemed to lighten up, but the storm didn't look like it was through with them just yet. More like it was refueling for another assault.

"I'll get lifejackets," Lunk said. He disappeared inside the cabin.

"Hiro," Cooper whispered. They couldn't just sit here waiting to go under. They had to do something. Had to get to her. Cooper rushed back to the engine compartment. He stared at the water swirling around the twin motors. Would they even start?

"Lunk!" he shouted. "Fire 'em up!"

Lunk dropped the life vests on deck and stood behind the console. He toggled on the blower. Made sure both engines were in neutral, goosed the gas, and turned the key. The motors rumbled to life. Lunk revved the engines to keep them going.

Cooper pulled open a storage compartment. Dad kept a hand pump in here somewhere.

Lunk grabbed the wheel. "Head for the buoy?"

Cooper pointed toward town. "The beach. It's closer to Hiro. We'll run it aground—keep it from sinking."

Lunk shifted into gear and opened up both throttles. *The Getaway* lumbered forward. Fought to gain speed.

"Can you handle the helm?" Coop said. "You've got more driving time than I do."

Lunk nodded. Gripping the wheel with both hands, he cut it hard and leaned his body against it to hold the course toward town. *The Getaway* reeled and bucked like it was moving in slow motion.

"It's handling like an elephant!" Lunk said.

"We gotta make this elephant dance, skipper!" Cooper said. "Hiro's walking into a trap—she needs us!" He turned to Gordy. "Call 9–1–1! Tell them where Hiro is! Tell them she's in trouble!"

Gordy nodded and ducked inside the cabin to call.

As if on cue, the rain pounded down again with fresh fury.

Cooper dug out the emergency hand bilge pump and lowered himself into the engine compartment. The sound was deafening—and terrifying. *God, protect Hiro. God, please.* He dropped the hose into the oily, black water sloshing around in the hull and snaked the other end over the transom rail. He started pumping.

Gordy leaned his head in. "What are you *doing*?"

"Trying to help the bilge pumps catch up!" Cooper shouted. "Are the police on their way?"

"The police boat is on its way from Fontana!" Gordy shouted over the twin motors.

They'd be here too late to do them any good—or Hiro. "What about Hiro? Did you tell them?"

Gordy nodded. "But no guarantees! The dispatcher said all the cops are at the casino—a big fire broke out earlier! People are trapped!"

Fat Elvis. It had to be. "So nobody is coming?"

"A car is on the way—but the casino is ten miles from here!"

Hiro may not have that long. *God help us.* The hose over the rail flipped back onto the deck. Everything he'd just pumped would run back inside. "Hold that hose over the rail!" Cooper yelled.

The boat rocked to the port side, nearly slamming Cooper into the hot engine.

Gordy reached down a hand. "Get out of there, Coop! It's too dangerous!"

Gordy was right. This was insane. He couldn't pump the water out fast enough to do much good. And if the boat did go under, it would sink quickly—trapping him inside the compartment. Cooper grabbed Gordy's hand and climbed out. They dropped the hatch in place. No sense letting the rain get in there and help finish them off.

Lunk was still muscling the wheel. His arms shook from the strain. He had the engines at full power. He was soaked. They were all soaked. "I'm making this elephant dance!" he shouted.

Cooper nodded. But *The Getaway* moved like it was dragging a grand piano. The boat rode low. Really low. Or maybe the height of the waves made it seem that way. *The Getaway* hit the waves head-on—spray exploded off the bow in both directions and into their faces. Cooper staggered over to the wheel to help Lunk hold it steady.

They were past Maytag Point. If they'd headed for Big Foot Beach, they'd be nearly there by now. But the beach was so narrow, the bow would've come to rest on Lake Shore Drive. And then they'd still have to get all the way into town to help Hiro. They didn't have that kind of time. Cooper's gut told him that much. Or was it telling him that Hiro was already beyond help?

Cooper took a wide stance and gripped the wheel beside Lunk, helping hold *The Getaway* on a direct course for the town beach.

"We gonna make it?" Gordy grabbed the windshield and fought to stay on his feet.

"Have to!" Cooper said. Were they slowing—or was it his imagination? Both engines were still at full throttle.

Cooper shouted to his cousin. "Hear anything from Hiro?"

Gordy checked his phone and shook his head.

"Call my dad! Tell him what's happening!"

Gordy nodded and ducked inside the cabin again.

Cooper pushed the throttles forward even though he knew they couldn't go any further. He never should have left Hiro in town alone. They should have stayed together—at least until the rest of them got back from the late show. Until he knew she was locked in the condo. Safe. *God, please help her.* "Fat Elvis is Stein!" he shouted to Lunk. "I feel it!"

Lunk gave a quick nod. "This is definitely payback!"

Gordy stumbled out of the cabin and grabbed the back of the seat to steady himself. "I left a voicemail!"

Cooper made out Stone Manor on their right. They were heading smack down the middle of the bay—on a collision course for the beach beside the Riviera. He strained to see anything in the direction of LeatherLips. Rain stung his face and eyes. It was impossible to see. *God, keep her safe.*

The rain plastering the windshield made it practically useless. Gordy squinted and raised himself on his toes to look over it. "We're getting close. How are we going to play this?" Gordy said.

Cooper hadn't planned out that part yet. He still wasn't sure they'd make it to the beach. "There are two swim platforms by the beach—if we hit one of them, we're dead!"

Lunk rocked up on his toes and nodded. "I've got a visual! I'll bring us in closer to the Riviera pier!"

Closer to shore, the waves were definitely smaller. *The Getaway* built more speed.

"We're pushing twenty-five," Lunk said, looking at the speedometer. "We're gonna hit hard!"

Too hard. They'd rip the bottom off the hull—and maybe get so banged up in the process that they wouldn't be able to help Hiro. "How fast do you think we need to go to beach it?"

Lunk glanced at the dials. "Not this fast!"

Cooper agreed. They'd have to slow up—but not yet. Do it too soon and the boat was liable to sink. "Okay, as we pass the Riviera piers, I'll drop our speed! If we hit the beach at ten—that should be enough!" He hoped that was fast enough to get the boat onto the beach. But hitting with too much speed would be disastrous for sure.

Lunk took a fresh grip on the wheel to brace himself.

"Gordy!" Cooper said. "When we get close, I want you to bail out over the back—Navy Seal style. If I can't run after the boat hits—find Hiro!"

Gordy nodded and staggered to the back of the boat. He gripped the corner railing and watched the approaching shoreline.

Cooper flipped open the toolbox and strapped his dad's dive knife to his right calf. He grabbed the flare gun and tucked it into his waistline and pocketed the two remaining shells.

Lunk glanced at him. "Good idea! When you're outgunned or outnumbered—hit fast and hard! No hesitation!"

Cooper had no problem with that. Not now. He just hoped he wasn't too late.

CHAPTER 92

Hiro had to keep stalling. Keep Stein talking. Pray that someone would see them. The rain unleashed a fresh attack, but she dropped her umbrella on the dock. It wouldn't do her any good against a gun—and she needed to keep her hands free.

Stein kept the gun pointed at her. He held it waist high, like he didn't want to attract attention if someone happened by.

"What is it with you kids?" Stein said. "You're always getting in my way. Always messing up my plans. But not tonight." He held up a phone. "Recognize this?"

"Is that Cooper's?"

Stein nodded. "Backpack. County fair. I slipped it out while you were riding Typhoon."

Hiro sucked in her breath.

"Genius, right? And you took my bait."

His eyes were wild. Hypnotic. Was he on something? Possessed? And why was he wearing a wetsuit?

"I knew my luck was changing when I first saw you at the beach on Sunday night."

Keep him talking. "That was you—in the black pickup?"

Stein nodded. "I hated my job. Wiping that rich kid's nose. Actually, I'm glad he got what was coming to him."

It wasn't that Stein cared about the girl or getting justice for her. His hatred of Kryptoski governed his sense of right and wrong.

"You tried to run Coop down, didn't you?"

Stein snickered. "I couldn't help myself. Just having a little fun while waiting for the right moment to strike."

Another chill flashed through her. *The right moment.* What was he going to do to Coop?

"By the way"—Stein glanced over his shoulder—"leaving the condo at this time of night?" He tapped his forehead. "Not too smart, Hiroko. You've got to use your brains. It's a big, bad world out there, and a girl could get hurt if she's not careful."

The guy was sick. Deranged. "Just let me go," Hiro said. "I'll toss my phone in the water. I won't be able to call a soul. You can get away clean."

Stein laughed. "I'm not worried about a clean getaway. I'll roll the dice on that one."

"Hasn't gambling gotten you into enough trouble?"

"This one's a sure bet," Stein said. "There's a nasty fire blazing at the casino right now. The cops won't be here quick enough, even if you did call. I've got plenty of time."

The sirens. A fire. A diversion. Of course. "You decoyed them."

"I needed to keep the boss busy. After his boy got arrested, he was in a hellish mood."

No more than Stein seemed to be in now. "Somebody could get hurt."

Stein shrugged. "Just the boss, if I'm lucky."

He was a sociopath. No conscience. No remorse. "Coop knows where I am. I sensed it was you. I told the boys—and they'll be here soon to check on me. You have to leave. Now."

Stein shrugged. "I already took care of them. Right after I started the fire. Now I'll be free of all of you."

Hiro felt her knees go weak. What had he done? She'd just gotten a text from Gordy, hadn't she? Maybe Stein was bluffing.

He smiled. "A little boating accident. They're all swimming with Tommy's girlfriend now."

Wendy? She was dead. *Oh, God.* Could he be telling the truth? Tears blurred her vision. He was a creature of the dark now—one who dragged away innocent people and devoured them. "You're an animal."

He raised his head and howled.

It didn't sound human.

"Now you're coming with me—unless you've got your heart set on going out with a bang." He waggled the gun at her and grinned.

She had to run. The gun wasn't as much of a threat as it looked. Not here, anyway. Likely Stein intended to use the gun, but someplace where he wouldn't be spotted or heard. If she went with him, she'd die for sure. But if she ran and he fired, he might miss.

The tiny bay was to her right. She could jump in, but where could she go from there? It would be like that shooting gallery game at the fair. She'd be a sitting duck. Especially if she tried climbing out of the water on the other side.

The spillway was to her left. If she could jump to that wall and slide down the spillway...

Stein checked over his shoulder toward Wrigley Drive. "Let's go. Come with me." He took a step backward.

She took a step toward him as though she intended to follow his orders.

"That's it." He backed his way off the dock. "Nice and easy."

Nice would be seeing him behind bars. But that wouldn't be easy. She took another step. Then two. Did he really expect her to follow him without a fight?

"Get in the water." He motioned with his gun toward the spillway. "We're taking a little shortcut."

No—not down there. "Please," she said.

"Scared, aren't you, Hiroko?" Stein's eyes got wide. "And you should be. Now move."

She'd never get past him—he was blocking her way off the

narrow dock. All she could hope to do was go where he directed her and get ahead of him somehow. She judged the distance to the spillway — and jumped. But she fell short and landed in the shallow water. She got back on her feet.

Stein laughed. "Seriously?"

She heard a splash behind her.

Hiro grabbed the wall and pulled herself over it, sliding past the edge with the rushing water. Stein's hand raked her back, but she wriggled free and dropped onto the concrete spillway below. She rolled — over and over. Slipping and sliding on the mossy surface.

"Stop!" Stein growled.

He was close. She didn't dare look back but crawled, ran, and clawed her way down the incline. He could have fired his gun. She would have been an easy target.

Stein kept coming. Why didn't he shoot? She knew the answer. He intended to kill her — but he didn't want to do it here.

The spillway dropped lower and lower. Concrete walls on either side towered well over her head. There was no escaping. Like the shallow water rushing all around her, she had no choice but to go down the ramp.

"I'm not going to hurt you."

He was gaining on her.

Stein grunted behind her. Swore. "Actually," he said, "I *am* going to hurt you."

Please, God! The concrete chute led directly to the black hole. The demon tunnel. Like a gaping mouth — greedy, thirsty — it gulped down every gallon of water the spillway shot at it.

Stein laughed behind her. "I'm having fun. But I think Hiroko made another mistake. She got herself trapped."

Hiro was on her feet again, — but making her way across the moss-covered concrete was like running on ice. Backtracking would be impossible. There'd be no getting past Stein on the slippery spillway slope. There was only one way out. *God, help me!* She ducked inside the black tunnel.

CHAPTER 93

Get ready, Gordy!" Cooper shouted. *The Getaway* was on a collision course with the shore. It was insane. He wiped slick hands on his soaked jeans and grabbed the controls again.

Lunk maneuvered the boat directly between the closest swim platform and the Riviera docks. The *Lady of the Lake*. The *Walworth II*. All of the excursion boats sat there silently. They pulled at their ropes like they wanted to get out of the way—or get a better view of the guys hitting the beach.

Cooper kept both hands on the throttles. Eased them back. Braced himself. The empty beach loomed thirty yards dead ahead. Every instinct screamed for him to turn the wheel. But they'd never stop in time now.

He turned to his cousin. "Jump!"

Gordy disappeared over the transom. Cooper fought the urge to join him.

Lunk widened his stance. "We're coming in fast!"

Cooper pulled back on the throttles again. "Here we go!"

The instant Cooper felt the bow touch bottom, he threw the levers back to the neutral position and turned off the key. The bow rose sharply as the keel plowed into the sand and rode up onto the beach. Cooper slammed into the console so hard that he bounced back and rolled onto the deck.

The Getaway yawned over to the starboard side and stopped. *It stopped.*

Lunk was lying on the teak floor next to Cooper. "It worked!" He sounded surprised.

Cooper untangled himself and vaulted over the rail onto the soft sand. Lunk dropped down beside him. Huge waves from *The Getaway*'s run for the beach broke on the shore and rushed to meet them, dragging Gordy in with them.

Gordy coughed and spit. "We're alive!"

Alive. Cooper broke out in a flat-out sprint for LeatherLips—praying Hiro was alive too.

CHAPTER 94

Stein kept pace with Hiroko inside the tunnel. This couldn't have worked out any better if Stein had scripted it. She was going exactly where he wanted her to go. And the chase was good too. She was a scared rabbit. No, a mouse. And he was the cat.

He did *not* want to use the gun. Not unless he had to. It wasn't just the risk of it drawing unwanted attention. It was everything he'd miss. He didn't get to see the boys panic as their boat sank to the bottom with them locked inside. But he wasn't about to miss Hiroko's moment of terror. A bullet was too easy. Too quick. Too clean. He wanted to get his hands around her neck and feel her fear.

He'd toy with her inside the tunnel. Maybe he'd wait until she was almost to the end, and then the cat would pounce.

"Marco," he said. He chuckled to himself as he thought about the childhood water game. "Don't you want to play, Hiroko? You're supposed to say 'polo.' "

She was close enough to grab now. But he resisted the urge. He had no idea he'd enjoy the chase this much. He'd give her another fifty feet.

CHAPTER 95

The tunnel was as black as Stein's heart. And as cold. Hiro crouched low as she ran. She kept one hand touching the wall of the underground passage to give her a sense of direction. Stability. If that were even possible in a place like this. The rough surface of the concrete tunnel rose and fell under her fingertips. Like the sound of Stein's panting behind her. Water rushed by her feet.

"I like it in here." Stein's voice seemed amplified in the tunnel. "You've picked a perfect spot, Hiroko." His voice echoed past her. Sounded distorted. Or maybe his voice had become as twisted as Stein was on the inside.

Her foot hooked on something on the tunnel floor—and she went down. Instantly, she was on her feet again. But now her knee throbbed and felt like it would buckle. Webs stretched across her face. She swatted past them and kept going. It was like the tunnel was aware of her presence—and it didn't want her to leave.

She was in a place of death. She felt it. This tunnel was a concrete coffin. What if Stein had fished Wendy's body out of the lake and hidden it in here? An image of a tattoo—a pair of dice—flashed in her mind. Could there be a dead body in this tunnel? If she didn't keep moving, there definitely would be.

Something in the water at her feet wriggled and thrashed. Hiro screamed.

"I'm catching up to you." Stein laughed like he was enjoying the chase. "I can smell your fear."

He really *was* an animal. He could shoot her now—or lunge and take her down. Why didn't he? Because he was toying with her. Letting her grasp a thread of hope. He'd wait until she was within inches of freedom.

Hiro tried to go faster, but the tunnel slowed her down. Made her lose her footing.

She should have gone into the tunnel with the boys. Maybe she'd be less terrified now. *Gotta go faster.* She could hardly breathe. She expected Stein's hand to grab her shoulder at any second.

She saw a smudge of gray ahead. The end of the tunnel. It was too far away. Too far. And Stein was too close—and gaining on her.

CHAPTER 96

Rain pelted Cooper's face, but it didn't slow him down. He vaulted over an iron fence and picked up speed as soon as he got off the beach. He sprinted past the fountain. Lunk and Gordy were right behind him.

No traffic. Cooper bolted across the street. "Hiro!" He reached for the iron gate leading down to LeatherLips rentals and the docks in the bay below. Locked. "Hiro!"

The inlet was still. Lifeless. Covered boats were tied in the slips. They looked like funeral barges. Was she inside one of them? An open umbrella was lying on the dock at the far side of the little bay. *Please, God, no.*

Gordy and Lunk pulled up beside him. "Anything?"

Cooper pointed at the umbrella. "Hiro!" He looked in the black water for any sign of a disturbance. Nothing.

They crossed the bridge and hustled toward the docks. "Let's spread out."

Gordy passed him and headed down the narrow pier along the spillway. Lunk followed.

A shrill scream pierced the air. "Hiro!" Cooper wheeled around. "The tunnel."

Gordy leaped off the dock into the water, then climbed over the concrete dam. Lunk was right behind him.

"I'll go around," Cooper said. "Meet you where it dumps into the river."

Lunk waved a hand and ran past Gordy, but he never looked back. Together they raced down the concrete ramp.

Cooper darted around the spillway and headed toward the parking lot. *Hang on, Hiro. Hang on!* Out of the corner of his eye, he saw a figure running in the same direction, but on the other side of the tiny bay. Looked like he had a hand to his ear—was he on the phone? Did Fat Elvis have an accomplice?

Cooper pulled the flare gun from his waistline and loaded a cartridge in the chamber.

CHAPTER 97

Lunk ducked into the tunnel just ahead of Gordy—his head low, fists clenched. He couldn't see a thing, but he fought against every instinct that screamed for him to slow down.

Hiro needed him. Cooper needed him. And Lunk knew he would need some kind of miracle to get there in time.

"Right behind you," Gordy panted. "Slow up and I'll run you down."

Gordy obviously couldn't see a thing either. He was counting on Lunk to keep his speed up and stay ahead of him.

Lunk skittered for a second, regained his balance, and pressed on. He heard voices echoing ahead of them, getting louder. He was closing the distance between them.

Water poured in from overhead. Some kind of drainage pipe from the street? There hadn't been anything like that the other day—but it hadn't been raining then, either. He splashed through and kept running.

Whimpering. He was sure he heard whimpering, but he couldn't stop to listen and be sure. It was Hiro. Had to be. What was Stein doing to her?

CHAPTER 98

Hiro tripped again and her injured knee struck the tunnel floor. She struggled to get up, limping hard this time. Terror behind her. Terror ahead. But if she stopped — if she slowed down — he'd get her. This wasn't the boogeyman. It wasn't an overactive imagination. It was Stein. He was real. And he was going to hurt her. Holding one hand out in front of her, she ran.

"You run like hell, Hiroko," Stein said, laughing.

Not *like* hell. She was running *from* hell. And she could feel the heat.

The air felt heavy. Stagnant. Dead. Even the tunnel felt evil. Like it was alive. Grabbing at her. Wanting to pull her down. Hold her back for Stein.

The tunnel opening grew bigger. *Almost there. Almost there.* And then what? At least she'd be out of this demon tunnel.

But the demon would still be chasing her. Her phone was in her pocket. If she could get some distance on him, she could call — someone.

"You're mine!"

Stein grabbed her braid — slowed her — and slammed into her. She went down, and her head plunged underwater for an instant.

She squirmed and twisted to face him—then kicked with all her strength.

He grunted. Swore.

She kicked again. Connected.

Stein snickered. And took a swing at her.

The blow glanced off her cheek. She raised her arms to protect her face. "Please!"

He forced her head underwater—then jerked her out again. She gasped for breath.

"I am so sick of you and your friends!" His fists exploded against her jaw. Shoulders.

Hiro ducked. Screamed. It was impossible to fight back. "God, help me!"

Stein drove his knee into her stomach. She couldn't breathe. "Time to say good night, Hiroko." He leaned into her, ground his knee in harder—forcing her head under the black water.

She reached for his face. Felt his beard. Clawed at his eyes.

Stein roared and recoiled—and Hiro wriggled free. She crawled through the rushing water for a few seconds before getting back on her feet. But Stein's iron grip locked onto her ankle.

"Daddy!" Hiro screamed. "Help me!" Her dad couldn't come to her rescue, though, could he? Yet she was running to him—and in moments she would be safe in his arms.

CHAPTER 99

Cooper heard a police siren in the distance. He pounded across Center Street and headed for the other end of the tunnel. Hiro's scream was different this time. Not just terror. Pain.

She screamed again. She was close. Was she out of the tunnel?

He swung past the trees, down the embankment, and toward the river. Hiro was there at the mouth of the tunnel. Thrashing, trying to kick free from someone. She fell backward into the shallow river and slammed against a rock.

Cooper splashed into the river. Raised the flare gun.

A figure stood over her. "It's time to say good-bye, Hiroko."

Stein. Wearing a wetsuit? Cooper clambered over the rocks. Had to get to her. Now.

Stein raised his arm like he was pointing at her. Something glinted.

Strike first. Strike hard. Cooper aimed the flare gun at Stein's chest and pulled the trigger.

The flare hit Stein in the gut. Bright red sparks and flames shot in all directions, but the flare deflected off the wetsuit. Stein, momentarily blinded, dropped to his knees in the river. The cartridge lodged itself between the rocks on the shoreline—still alive and lighting the area with an eerie glow.

Hiro struggled to her feet. Cooper ran to her, loading the second cartridge on the fly. He grabbed Hiro's hand. "C'mon!"

Hiro clutched his hand with both of hers.

"Run!" He tore right down the middle of the stream—pulling Hiro along as his own feet stumbled on the rocky bottom. He had to put distance between them and Stein. *Too slow. Too slow.* He chanced a shoulder-check.

Stein was on his feet again. He looked at Cooper and smiled. His face glowed red from the nearby flare. With dark shadows shrouding his eyes, he only needed a pair of horns for the effect to be complete.

"Stop!" Stein raised his gun. "This is a Saturday Night Special. Untraceable 22-caliber. Six shots. Should be plenty to finish the job."

Cooper squeezed off his last cartridge. Stein ducked—and the flare whizzed past his head.

Lunk appeared in the tunnel opening and did a flying leap for Stein, tackling him hard.

Cooper tried to pull his hand free from Hiro's grip so she could get away and he could go back to help Lunk. "Run, Hiro!"

She didn't let go.

And everything went into slow motion. Stein was on his feet again somehow. Lunk was sitting in the river—dazed—blood trickled from a gash in his forehead. Gordy flew from the mouth of the tunnel, rushing toward Lunk.

Stein glared at Cooper. Raised the gun. Cooper turned, pushed Hiro behind him to shield her—heard the shot—felt himself falling.

CHAPTER 100

Cooper felt the water rush around him. Felt Hiro squirming. He was alive. She was alive. Had Stein missed?

He tensed, expecting a second shot to do the job where the first one had failed. Cooper looked behind him. Stein was lying on his back—half in the river, half on the bank. He was clutching his shoulder and moaning. Gordy was helping Lunk to his feet.

A figure climbed down the embankment on the other side of the narrow stream. He was holding a gun.

Cooper pointed. "Lunk—Gordy—look out!"

"Easy, Cooper," the man said as he stepped out of the shadows.

Detective Hammer? "How in the world . . . ?"

Hammer waded into the river and picked his way closer to them. "Ask Hiro."

Hiro let go of Cooper's hand and splashed over to the detective. She threw her arms around him. "I didn't think you'd come."

"I've been hanging around for nearly eighteen hours."

"I never saw you."

Hammer laughed. "You'll never see me. Didn't I mention that?"

Stein groaned louder and rocked from side to side. His pistol lay on the bank, a dozen feet away.

Hammer waded over to Stein and held up his gun. A red

laser dot danced in a tight circle on Stein's forehead. "This is a 9mm Beretta 92-FS semi-automatic. Luminescent and laser sights. Seventeen shots—plenty to finish the job."

A police car screeched to a halt on the roadway above them. Officer Tarpy bolted out of the car. "Everyone okay?"

"Everyone that matters," Hammer said.

Tarpy ran down the embankment and splashed into the river. He stopped next to Hammer and put a hand on his shoulder. "Thanks for the call. Got here as fast as I could."

"I need—" Stein gasped and gritted his teeth against the pain—"an ambulance."

"It could take a while," Tarpy said. "Some idiot set fire to the casino. Every ambulance within a twenty-mile radius is busy at the scene. We're calling in help from Kenosha."

Stein held up a bloody hand. "But I need help!" He clamped his hand around his shoulder again. "Can't you see that?"

"Oh yeah," Hammer said. "You need a lot of help. Life in prison isn't going to be much fun."

EPILOGUE

Cooper sat on the bow of *The Getaway*, taking it all in. Mom. Dad. Mattie. Gordy's folks. Lunk's mom. And Hiro's mom. Everyone was present and accounted for. Even Detective Hammer and Officer Tarpy were there. The adults stood on the teak deck on the other end of the boat and laughed. Hugged. Downed more pizza from Olympic Restaurant.

"We're like celebrities now," Hiro said. She sat cross-legged next to him. "Katie says they've renamed *The Getaway*."

Cooper exchanged glances with Lunk and Gordy. "Really?"

Hiro nodded. "The *S. S. Minnow*. She said it's a reference to an old TV show back in the sixties."

"*Gilligan's Island*," Gordy said.

She shook her head and smiled. "What? You know *all* the old TV shows?"

He looked at her like she was joking. "Only the important ones."

"Anyway, "Hiro said, "that would explain why they're calling you Gilligan."

Gordy grinned. "Gilligan. I like that. I should get a white sailor hat and a red shirt or something. Walk around town."

Lunk snickered. "Wasn't he, you know, like a bozo or something?"

Gordy shook his head. "He was the star of the show. Without Gilligan—no *Gilligan's Island*."

"Katie calls Lunk 'Skipper,'" Hiro said.

Lunk smiled at Cooper. "Your dad called me that too."

"The way you handled that boat—it sounds like you earned the title," Hiro said. "And Katie called Coop 'Professor.' She posted a bunch of pictures of the boat from when it was still on the beach."

Cooper pictured the scene the way he and his dad had seen it late on Friday night after it was all over. *The Getaway* did look like the *S. S. Minnow*, beached and tilted to one side on the sand. But they were hardly shipwrecked.

"And she posted *lots* of pictures of some guy named Matt Ripkey from Gage Marine when they came to tow it."

Cooper replayed the scene in his mind. Even though Dad had told him not to worry about *The Getaway*, Cooper was on the beach with him when Matt arrived in the *Alert* early Saturday morning. Cooper felt like a weight had been lifted when they found the source of the leak wasn't a hole in the hull. Stein had unscrewed the threaded brass drain plug on the transom below the waterline.

Matt screwed in a new plug, pumped out the water, and towed it off the beach. Besides a little scraped paint—and the smashed cabin door—no serious damage had been done.

And now, not even forty-eight hours after Lunk had beached *The Getaway*, the cabin cruiser was tied to the pier at the Riviera for their celebration.

"Think Kryptoski and Stein will end up in the same prison?" Gordy said.

Cooper thought for a second. "Wouldn't that be something?"

"It'd be perfect," Gordy said. "Stein could keep his babysitting job."

"Babysitting? I don't think so," Hiro said. "Stein didn't do such a great job the first time."

Cooper nodded. "I don't know why he started gambling. He's not very lucky—and he makes really bad choices."

"And sooner or later, poor decisions land you in some sort of prison," Lunk said.

Hiro smiled and shook her head. "Uh oh. Listen to Lunk. He's really getting to be the philosopher of the group." She stood up and waggled her phone at them. "You guys sit tight. I have a carryout order to pick up." She climbed over the rail and jumped onto the dock.

Minutes later she was back with a bag from Scoops. She handed each of the guys a spoon. "Just a little something for the men in my life."

She pulled a pint container from the bag. "For Gordy. Because you never change."

Gordy pulled off the lid. "Yippee Skippee! My favorite."

Hiro shrugged. "That's what I'm saying. You don't change."

She pulled out another pint. "This is for you, Lunk."

"Vanilla," Gordy said. "Am I right?"

Hiro shook her head. "Dead wrong."

Cooper moved in closer to see what she'd ordered.

Lunk pried off the cover, tilted his head, and gave her a questioning look. "Chocolate?"

"Zanzibar Chocolate." She said. "The deepest, darkest kind."

"That's a total switch," Gordy said.

Hiro nodded. "I chose that flavor for Lunk because nobody has changed more than he has in the last year."

Lunk laughed. "I don't know if that's good or bad."

"It's all good," Hiro said. "I even like the new haircut."

Gordy reached over and rubbed Lunk's head.

"There was a time when you wanted to be rid of me." Lunk glanced at her like he was joking. But there was something deeper there. Like he really wanted to be sure of their friendship.

"That's ancient history," Hiro said.

Lunk stared at the water.

She studied him for a moment. "You don't seem to realize how much you belong with us. How much we need you."

Lunk's face turned red.

"Let's put it this way. I'm like a tattoo," Hiro said, making a fist. "And if you try to get rid of a tattoo, it can get pretty painful."

Lunk laughed and shook his head.

"Welcome to the club, Lunk. Once Hiro gets in here"—Cooper tapped Lunk's head—"it's all over."

She tilted her head and smiled. "Consider yourself warned." Hiro reached inside the bag again. "And for Cooper." She handed him a pint packed with red, yellow, and blue swirled ice cream.

"Looks like Froot Loops cereal," Gordy said.

Cooper stared at it. He wasn't sure what flavor it was—or what it meant.

"It's called Superman," Hiro said. "And after all that the four of us have gone through this last year, it totally reminded me of you."

"Super Cooper," Gordy said. "I like that."

Lunk laughed and clapped.

Hiro just watched Cooper with the slightest smile on her lips.

"If Scoops had a flavor called Millionaire," Cooper said, "that's the one I'd pick for myself. 'Cause that's how rich I feel with three friends like you."

Lunk looked down and cleared his throat. Was he getting choked up? Hiro was right. None of them had changed more than Lunk had.

"So what did you pick for yourself, Hiro?" Lunk said.

Hiro raised her chin in the air. "Chocolate Raspberry Truffle, of course."

Coop smiled. "And is there a hidden meaning behind it?"

"Definitely," Hiro said. "It's sweet, addicting, and has deliciously zingy streaks running through it."

Gordy pointed at the scab below his eye. "I think I get the zingy part. Or is it zany?"

They all laughed.

The sun hovered above the horizon, like it wanted to hang there just a little longer and take in the beautiful sight before moving on to less picturesque views of the globe.

"And now," Hiro said, "I'm going to take a little siesta. You boys enjoy your ice cream."

Hiro stood, brushed off her jean shorts, and walked to the back of the boat. A minute later, she was paddling out in the inflatable. She laid on her back while the raft drifted just off the bow of *The Getaway*.

"We should prank her," Gordy said. "Where's a dead fish when you need one? I could just lob it right onto her lap."

Hiro was right. Gordy didn't change.

Cooper watched her floating out there in her dry clothes, totally unaware. "I think she looks lonely," he said. "All by herself out there."

"Yeah," Lunk said. "And she's expecting us to stick together."

Cooper moved closer to the rail. "Are you thinking what I'm thinking?"

"All three of us at once," Lunk whispered. He crouched by the rail.

"Oh yeah," Gordy said. "See, this is what I'm talking about. This is how to have a great vacation." He moved into position.

Cooper motioned to Gordy and Lunk and began a countdown. "Three ... two ... one!"

Hiro looked up—her eyes wide.

The boys jumped toward the inflatable as one unit. Hiro squealed and covered her head with her arms. They splashed down in a half-circle around the raft, and Cooper frog-kicked to the surface alongside Lunk and Gordy.

"Are you crazy? Now I'm soaked!" she wailed. "You boys will pay for this."

Gordy and Lunk laughed even louder than Cooper did. Gordy started scooping water into the inflatable.

"I see I'm going to have my hands full with you three." She reached over and tried to dunk Cooper, but he was holding on to the inflatable, and she couldn't get his head under. "I hate you, Cooper MacKinnon."

But her smile—and her eyes—said something very different. She tried pushing him under again.

Cooper smiled back. "I hate you more."

She stopped pushing on his head and tilted her own to one side like she was trying to read his expression.

He didn't look away. Her smile grew wider.

"You really do, don't you," she whispered.

It was a statement, not a question.

Cooper didn't answer. He didn't have to. Apparently she really *could* read his mind.

She looked at Cooper, Lunk, and Gordy. "With friends like you—I'm the luckiest girl in the world."

"We know," Gordy said. "Glad you finally noticed."

"And now," Lunk said, "the luckiest girl in the world is about to get tossed out of the boat." He ducked underwater and the inflatable flipped over.

Hiro surfaced instantly. She wiped the water from her eyes and beamed.

They treaded water for a long time while holding on to the inflatable. Talking. Laughing. Dreaming. Apparently, none of them were in any great rush to get out of the water. The sun finally disappeared. The water grew dark. But that didn't matter. All the light Cooper needed was inside of him—and he knew that was never going to change.

"Hey, Gordy," Lunk said. "It looks like you finally got your night swim."

Gordy looked across the inflatable at Cooper and smiled. "This is perfect. Now who wants to hear a scary story?"

Lunk reached over and dunked Gordy. Gordy resurfaced with a laugh.

"This one's mine," Hiro said. "Once there were four really good friends who went on a vacation together. To a lake. Just before they started high school. There were three guys and one girl. And the girl was *way* smarter than the boys realized. In fact, they were about to realize just how wrong they'd been about her."

"Oh, so this is fiction," Lunk said.

"Mr. Lunquist," Hiro said. "Are you going to let me finish my story?"

"Save your breath, Hiro," Gordy said. "I think we all know this story a little too well. The real question is what happens next."

That was a good question. They'd be starting Fremd High School in a matter of days. If any of them were scared, none would admit it. Besides, Cooper had learned a lot about fear in the last few days—or at least how to handle it. Fear had lost its teeth.

"So, Hiro," Lunk said. "This story. Does it end when the vacation is over—or does it just keep going?"

"Oh, it keeps going," she said. "They have more adventures in high school. And none of them ever feel alone again. The four friends stick together. Forever."

Cooper looked at her. She was right. Even when he was all by himself, he would never feel alone. He got that now. And one day Lunk would too.

"I think I'm going to like this story," Lunk said.

"Definitely," Hiro said. "But do you know how it ends?"

"Like all great stories should," Cooper said. "Happily ever after."

Hiro raised her eyebrows and smiled. "I guess you *do* know the story."

A WORD FROM THE AUTHOR

The heebie-jeebies. The willies. Creeped-out. Spooked. Jitters. Cold feet. There are lots of names for fear and different degrees of intensity. Fear can be something deep and shadowlike — something you can't quite put your finger on, but you sense its presence. Fear can be something you try to bury, something you dread. Or fear can be obvious, a pulse-pounding terror you can't avoid.

Sometimes people *like* getting scared. *Sometimes*. They love a scary story or movie. Some deliberately do risky things just to get their pulse pounding. Some people never feel more alive than when they're scared to death.

But usually fear makes us uncomfortable. People don't like to be scared — so they fight fear in one of four ways: run from it, bury it, face it, or get help.

I'd like to talk a little bit about handling our fears. But first let's talk about two basic kinds of fear: good fear and bad fear.

Good Fear

We were created with the gift of fear. Yes, sometimes fear is a gift. It's an internal warning when we're in some sort of danger — or headed that way. Near the end of the book, Hiro felt that sense of fear when she went out in the storm to meet Coop. But she pushed it down and tried to ignore her fear. As a result, she walked into a trap and almost got killed. Some fear is good — if you listen to it and react quickly. It could save your life too.

And sometimes good fear drives us to improve ourselves in some way. Fear of a bad grade pushes us to study. Fear of failure makes us practice some skill or sport or job. Fear of punishment or nasty consequences often keeps us in line. Fear of being rejected by others pushes us to act and talk in decent ways — and to watch our hygiene.

Good fear can be our friend and it can work *for* us.

Bad Fear

Sometimes fear works against us, and it can weaken us. Petrify us. This happens when there is something we dread—but we don't do anything about it or we try to ignore it. Fear can chip away at us and even make us feel physically sick if we don't deal with it properly. This kind of fear of something or someone can be our enemy. Sometimes we call this type of fear *worry*.

Fighting Fear

Let's look at the four ways that people tend to deal with their fear.

Run from it. When you feel fear—that internal warning of sorts—and sense you are in danger, often the smartest and bravest thing to do is run. Get out of that place or that situation—fast. Survivors of violent crimes tell how they saw a red flag—they sensed danger just before the attack. But they pushed the feeling down. They should have run away—and later on, they wished they had.

Sometimes we're *afraid* of looking weak or foolish, or looking like a coward or a baby—so we stay in a bad place or situation. In many ways fear is an internal mechanism designed to protect us from making huge mistakes.

Imagine walking out of some store. You're alone—it's nighttime—and you sense that someone is following you. You glance back and see a guy—but only for a moment. Sometimes that's all the information your brain needs. We tend to forget that the brain subconsciously functions so incredibly fast. It factors in what the person looks like, his body language, any similar experiences you've had and that you've heard about—and it processes all of that info instantly. If your brain concludes that this person could be dangerous or that the situation could turn out that way, fear taps out a warning.

Now you have a choice. You can push down your fear and keep walking alone—or you can hurry back to the store where there are more people, find a security guard, or whip out your phone and call a parent or the police for help.

Those who ignore fear's warnings end up in the hospital—or worse. Sometimes their pictures end up on milk cartons or the evening news. Listen to that internal alarm in your head. If you are afraid because you feel you're in danger, sometimes the most courageous thing you can do is run.

Bury it. This is almost always a bad move. Burying fear is not a brave thing to do. It's the opposite of brave. It is being too scared to do anything about whatever is making us feel afraid. People bury fear by refusing to think about the person or situation that scares them. They'll keep their minds distracted with music, entertainment, friends, homework, or maybe by working hard so they don't have to think about it. Bad move. Like Cooper learned, our fears can be buried, but that doesn't mean they're dead. And if the fear isn't truly dead, then like a zombie, it will rise up and attack you. Not good.

Face it. Rather than bury our fears, what we really need to do is face them. This is about looking at whatever or whoever is scaring you—and dealing with your fear. Sometimes that means fighting. Attacking it. Conquering it. Coop's dad helped him to start facing his fear of the water. Some fears will put you inside a type of prison, and the only way you'll ever truly be free is to face them.

Get help. Talk to somebody about your fears—a parent or maybe a teacher or youth worker. Many times just talking about it will be enough to keep the fear from haunting you. An adult may be able to help you in a way that provides some real relief.

Sometimes guys think that being brave or courageous or fearless is all part of being a real man. That's only partially true. Real men have fears—but they still do the right thing even though they're afraid. *That* is courage.

The biggest thing that has helped me when it comes to fighting my fear is remembering that I am not alone. I am a man of faith. I believe in God—that he is real and in control. And I put myself in his hands. I trust him. When I am afraid, I always turn to God. That's a pretty good place to be.

I always thought "the heebie-jeebies" was a funny name for fear. But fear isn't funny. It can paralyze you—but it can also protect you. Coop wrestled with his fear in *Below the Surface*. But we all have fears. So let's deal with them in the most effective way.

One last thing. I've loved this series—and I hate to say goodbye to Coop, Hiro, Gordy, and Lunk. I hope you've enjoyed them as much as I have, and I hope you'll continue to grow in character and integrity just like they've been doing. Maybe we'll come back at some point and see how they're doing in high school. In the meantime, I'm starting to work on another series!

—Tim

P.S. Contact me on my Facebook author page. I'd love to hear how you liked the series—or hear any questions or comments you may have. *www.facebook.com/AuthorTimShoemaker*

QUESTIONS FOR FURTHER DISCUSSION

1. Cooper talked about fighting fear with a shovel—or a sword. What does that mean?
2. How do some people try to bury their fears?
3. How is fear that is "buried but not dead" kind of like a zombie? How is it like a prison guard?
4. What fear was Lunk dealing with, deep down inside?
5. What fear have you buried? Whom would you trust enough to talk to about your fear?
6. Besides talking to someone, what might be a first step toward dealing with or facing buried fear?
7. Sometimes fear can be a lifesaver because it keeps people safe from danger. Can you think of some examples of how that might happen?
8. When Stein cornered Hiro and held her at gunpoint, how did she fight back? How do people hurt themselves when they let fear paralyze them into doing nothing?
9. How can you fight back when somebody pressures you to go someplace or do something that you feel is wrong or may hurt you?
10. List some specific situations where the best way to face your fear would be to run.
11. When she was afraid, Hiro screamed for her dad. She knew he would help her if he could. Is there some fear that you need to talk about with your mom or dad to get their help in some way?
12. Throughout the story, Lunk, Gordy, and even Coop discounted Hiro's fears. How was that a bad thing for them to do?

13. What are some of the signs that someone might be afraid (not just the obvious ones, but the more subtle ones too)?
14. Are you discounting the fears of a friend, a brother, a sister, or even a parent? How can you help them get over their fears?
15. Hiro was afraid they were all in danger, but the guys thought she was overreacting. Have your friends ever warned you about some danger? Are you taking them seriously or discounting them?
16. Lunk took off his lifejacket and got in the water to help Coop. How might you need to lay aside your fears to help someone else face theirs?
17. There were times when Lunk feared he might lose his friends. How can a fear of losing friends cause someone to make bad choices?
18. How do people make big mistakes when they make decisions that are based not on what's the right thing to do, but out of a fear of what others will say about them?
19. Coop thought about what made his dad a man, and part of it was that his dad did the right thing—even when he was afraid. Coop wanted to be like that. Is that what you want too? How can you do that?
20. When Coop's dad was about to take Coop underwater with the tank, he assured Coop that he wouldn't leave him. How would knowing you weren't alone help you face your fears? Who could fill that role in your life?
21. Coop realized that his dad was able to face his fears because "Dad was never alone—even when no one else was there." What do you think that's all about?
22. Cooper finally began to conquer his deepest fears when he realized he wasn't alone. How can you do that?

Telling the Truth Could Get Them Killed. Remaining Silent Could Be Worse.

A Code of Silence Novel

Code of Silence

Living a Lie Comes with a Price

Tim Shoemaker

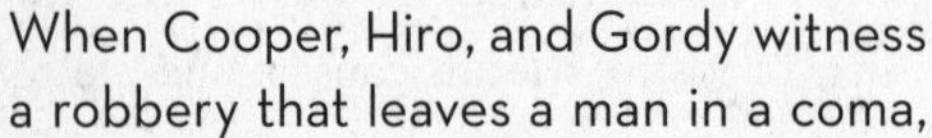

When Cooper, Hiro, and Gordy witness a robbery that leaves a man in a coma, they find themselves tangled in a web of mystery and deceit that threatens their lives. After being seen by the criminals—who may also be cops—Cooper makes everyone promise never to reveal what they have seen. Telling the truth could kill them. But remaining silent means an innocent man takes the fall, and a friend never receives justice.

Is there ever a time to lie? And what happens when the truth is dangerous?

The three friends, trapped in a code of silence, must face the consequences of choosing right or wrong when both options have their price.

ZONDERkidz

A Code of Silence Novel

Back Before Dark

Sometimes rescuing a friend from darkness ... means going in after them

Tim Shoemaker

Taken!

A detour through the park leads Cooper, Gordy, Hiro, and Lunk straight into a trap, and Gordy is abducted!

For the kidnapper, it's all a game, a way to settle an old score, with no one getting hurt. But evil has a way of escalating, and once his identity is discovered, the rules change.

Despite the best of police efforts, the hours tick by without a clue or a ransom call, leaving everyone to their own fears. Gordy is gone. Cooper descends deeper into a living nightmare, imagining the worst for his best friend and cousin. Hours stretch into days, and talks of a memorial service begin to surface. But Cooper still feels his cousin is alive and develops a reckless plan, changing all the rules. Now the one who set out to rescue his friend needs to be rescued himself. Sometimes rescuing a friend from darkness means going in after them.

"Deliberate, plausible, and gritty whodunit."
–*Booklist* Starred Review